THE AUSTRIAN BRIDE

HELEN PARUSEL

Boldwood

First published in Great Britain in 2023 by Boldwood Books Ltd.

Copyright © Helen Parusel, 2023

Cover Design by Becky Glibbery

Cover Photography: Shutterstock and iStock

A CIP catalogue record for this book is available from the British Library.

Paperback ISBN 978-1-83751-541-7

Large Print ISBN 978-1-83751-542-4

Hardback ISBN 978-1-83751-540-0

Ebook ISBN 978-1-83751-543-1

Kindle ISBN 978-1-83751-544-8

Audio CD ISBN 978-1-83751-535-6

MP3 CD ISBN 978-1-83751-536-3

Digital audio download ISBN 978-1-83751-538-7

Boldwood Books Ltd
23 Bowerdean Street
London SW6 3TN
www.boldwoodbooks.com

To Dad, who found his own Austrian bride.

1

ELLA

Linz, Austria, Saturday 12 March 1938

The tram trundled away from the platform, the wooden carriages mellow gold in the late-afternoon sunshine. Ella slowed from her sprint as she watched the tram disappear through the stone arch and down the steep hill. She let out an exasperated sigh. Now she would be late, and she only had herself to blame.

He was coming to Linz. The man himself. The town was buzzing with nervous energy. Everyone would be fighting for a good view when he arrived. And what had she been doing? She had been wandering amongst the swathes of snowdrops, dreaming of spring and picnics to come, up here on the Pöstling-berg. In summer, secretarial school would be over, and she would turn twenty-one. An adult. Her life was opening up like an alpine rose. She had stood in front of the brick house that was her former primary school, reminiscing. From there, she'd looked down on the majestic river Danube, glassy grey, flecked with silver, weaving its way through Linz.

The next tram wasn't for another hour. She crossed the track, and sped down the steep gravel path that wound down the mountainside. As a child, she'd never had money for the tram and had walked this route twice a day for five years.

She'd wanted to get a place near the front when he came, but as the bells from the grand church atop the Pöstlingberg chimed five o'clock, she knew the crowds would already be gathered below in the town square.

She descended past rustic chalets that clung to the hillside, their flowerboxes empty. Spring would soon be here; the flowerboxes filled with trailing red geraniums and ivy, and hanging baskets would burst with violet petunias. There were grand white stone villas too, boasting balconies with views over the mighty Danube, the life blood of Linz.

Thirty minutes later, she arrived home, her shoes covered in mud, and the hem of her long wool coat soaked through. Home was a small three-storey apartment block adorned with window shutters and flowerboxes.

The rich smell of goulash greeted her as she opened the front door, but she would have to eat later, for her parents stood waiting in the hallway wearing coats, hats and grim expressions.

'Where on earth have you been?' said her father. 'What will people think of us when we don't show our respect?'

'Sorry, Vati,' Ella said, grabbing her beret off the hook on the wall and linking her arm in her mother's. 'Let's go.'

It was already dark as they crossed the Donaubrücke over the Danube and approached the town centre. Ella's father strode ahead.

She turned to her mother. 'I don't know why Vati is so bothered to be here. He doesn't even like the man. It's all about appearances, I suppose.'

Before her mother could answer, a roar of voices rose into the cold air. She and her parents joined the back of the huge crowd that filled the Hauptplatz. Spotlights had been positioned to light up the crowds, their faces spectre-white under the harsh glow. She could feel the static of excitement all around, an energy that pulsed through her. The message was being passed back through the crowd: the motorcade was arriving. She could see the expectation and hope on the many tired faces. After years of unemployment and food shortages, the prospect of change was intoxicating.

She noticed others too, with dubious expressions, who hung back from the seething masses. But they were the minority. It was hard to tell how many Austrians, who opposed the Nazi party, had stayed at home. The Nazi supporters were highly visible with their red armbands displaying the black swastika. Officials were animating the crowd and photographers jostled for position.

'They're putting up a good show for the newspapers tomorrow,' said her father, his expression, grim.

Ella stood on the tips of her toes, straining to see.

A shout went up. 'He's here!'

The crowd pumped their right hands as one, and as one mighty voice, roared, 'Heil Hitler!'

Ella looked to her parents and followed their lead, keeping her right arm pressed against her side, their voices silent. But a part of her wished she could join the euphoria. Until this morning, when the Austrian chancellor had resigned, the Nazi Party had been banned. Everything was changing so rapidly, it was hard to keep up with what was going on.

In the centre of the square stood the imposing, baroque Trinity Column, its white marble shimmering bright under the spotlights. Atop, the round gold sculpture shone like a sun. People had clambered onto the base of the column, clinging to the saint statues, to get a better view. She recognised a face: Maximilian Giesler. Tall, athletic and handsome. Every girl's dream of a boyfriend. He could take his pick from his beautiful admirers, yet he had chosen her. Max was hers. She waved in his direction but of course he couldn't see her.

All faces were now turned to the curved town-hall balcony. A flag had been draped from the balcony railing. Not the Austrian flag, but the red Nazi flag with the black swastika. It rippled in the breeze.

'But it's not official, Vati, is it?' Ella said. 'We haven't yet voted to be part of Germany.'

Her father shook his head. 'There's no stopping them now.'

Conflicting emotions coursed through her in a tumult. Max had told her how everything would be better for the Austrians. No longer would they be the poor relations. There would be jobs, new homes and good schools, sport and social clubs, and a thriving culture. But whose culture? Would she be Austrian or German? Looking at the Nazi flag, she felt a flicker of uncertainty.

There was a flurry of movement on the town-hall balcony. Officials, their faces urgent, calling instructions to each other. A standing spotlight was adjusted. An SS officer in black uniform marched out. He checked around him and then raised his hand. The officials stepped aside.

And out he walked. Reichskanzler, Herr Adolf Hitler. There on the town-hall balcony. Ella gasped. The cheer that went up was deafening. It went on and on. She was transported up on a wave of elation and hope, and without realising what she was doing, she cheered and cheered.

Life would get better now. Everything would be fine.

* * *

Ella inhaled the deep, rich smell of coffee infused with the sweetness of freshly baked cake. Max had brought her to the prestigious Leopold Café on the Linzer Landstraße. They sat opposite each other at a round, polished wooden table. The waitress, in a black dress and white apron, arrived. She held a silver tray and served them Viennese coffee and Linzer torte. Ella had a swirl of whipped cream with her cake. Max had none.

Max took a sip of coffee and smiled at her. 'This will be an important summer for you, *Schatz*. You'll finish secretarial school, start work, officially become an adult. We shall celebrate your birthday in style. In fact, there is so much to celebrate right now. After the referendum in two weeks, the Anschluss will be official, and Austria will become part of the Third Reich.'

'What I don't understand is if we haven't voted yet, then why is the German Wehrmacht here? We also have a new mayor, and the German flags are everywhere.'

'You saw the jubilant reception Hitler received when he arrived in Linz. And in Vienna, the crowd went crazy. Women threw flowers. That's why Hitler declared the annexation; he knows what the Austrians want, and that the referendum is a foregone conclusion.'

'You're right. It does seem that way.' Ella sliced her fork into the golden, latticed pastry and popped a piece in her mouth, savouring the tang of redcurrant jam. 'Hopefully, it will be easier for me to find a job. And maybe there will be more work for Vati, for everyone. Things have been so dire.'

Max leaned forward and took her hand. She looked at him: his blue-grey eyes, blond hair and broad chin. He reminded her of a Greek god she saw in a film once.

'There will be changes in Linz. You know the Führer went to school here and has fond memories of his teenage years. He loves this town and plans to make it as great as Vienna.'

Ella laughed. 'Oh, Max. Don't exaggerate.'

But although she was laughing, she wanted him to be right. For years, she'd seen ragged children begging in the street, and men, wounded in the Great War, limbs missing, sitting on the ground with upturned caps, collecting coins. It was heartbreaking. Things had to change. She wanted her parents not to struggle over every *Groschen*. She wanted to have a job, earn money and really start her life. Thinking of the possibilities, her heart lifted. She savoured the last piece of her Linzer torte and beamed at Max.

Max picked up her coat and held it as she slipped it on. As they left the café, she allowed herself a moment of pride when heads turned, although she knew the glances were more at him than her.

It had turned cold again, and a flurry of snow fell from a white-grey sky. Outside stood a group of men holding up placards:

Freies Österreich!

Most people passed by averting their eyes, but a man and a woman had stopped to talk to the group quietly protesting for a free Austria.

Two police cars suddenly appeared, rumbling over the cobblestones, and screeched to a halt. The police jumped out, batons held high. They were from the new force that had recently taken over and was now under fascist command. An officer pointed his pistol at the group.

'You're all under arrest.' He nodded at his men. 'Handcuffs.'

A protester yelled, 'We live in a democracy. We have the right to protest peacefully.'

There were grunts of agreements from the bystanders.

Max tugged Ella's arm. 'Let's step back into the café.'

There was a scuffle and a shout, and suddenly, the police were clubbing the protesters to the ground, kicking them with their heavy boots. The man and woman who had stopped to talk tried to retreat, but they too were caught up in the scramble.

Ella heard the woman cry, 'But we weren't protesting.'

A policeman grabbed her arm and tried to handcuff her, but

she struggled. The man shouted, 'Leave her alone,' but he was soon silenced by a club that smashed into the side of his face. He crumpled onto the cobblestones.

Ella was rooted to the spot, horrified by what she saw, but too stunned to turn away.

The woman shrieked and managed to yank herself free. She bolted down the street, her heels clicking on the stones as she ran. Her hat flew off, freeing a wave of auburn hair that fell down the back of her camel coat.

'*Halt!*' an officer shouted.

The woman ran on.

A shot rang out.

She dropped face down onto the ground.

Ella screamed. Max pulled her towards the café.

As she followed him, she glanced back to see the woman's camel coat erupting in liquid, glistening red.

* * *

As Ella and her best friend Hedy crossed the iron Donaubrücke on their way home from town, the moody Danube was steel grey. A raw wind whipped off the water and the girls linked arms, huddling into each other for warmth as they strode along.

'I can't get the picture of that poor woman out of my head,' said Ella. 'At night, I can see her running in her heels and her hat flying off. And the blood...'

'It's terrible. Do you know who she was?' asked Hedy.

'That's the strange thing. Nobody knows anything. I scoured the local newspapers but there's nothing. I have no idea. Why did they shoot her?'

'What does Max say about it?'

'He says it's an unfortunate, isolated incident. He's sure the officer will be suspended and investigated. But he said we must distance ourselves from those against the Nazi Party.'

They reached the end of the bridge and made their way into the Urfahr district where they lived. Hedy lowered her voice as they passed three men in black overcoats.

'Neighbours in our block were arrested last night. They were supporters of the Communist Party. My father says it's dangerous to express any left-wing views right now.'

'I don't know what to think. Max keeps telling me everything will work out. We just have to wait till things settle down after the referendum.'

'How are things with you and Max?'

'He was so sweet after the shooting. I was still shaking an hour later. At home, he made me a hot water bottle and tucked me in with a blanket on the sofa.'

'I think you might be a little in love,' said Hedy, a smile in her voice.

'I think I might be. A little,' Ella replied, her heart beating fast.

2

MARLENE

Marlene flipped the feather quilt off her body and turned onto her back, taking deep breaths. It had been like this every night recently. The heat started in her pelvis, rising swiftly to her chest and spread to her face till her cheeks were burning. Drops of sweat prickled beneath her arms and breasts.

Franz lay snoring softly next to her. Marlene sighed. Her husband never had problems sleeping. This fact made her angry, then tearful. As the heat subsided, she got up and stomped out of the bedroom. But when she came to Ella's room, she tiptoed past. Her daughter needed her sleep. She had secretarial school tomorrow and was still recovering from that terrible scene she'd witnessed.

Marlene went to the small alcove off the kitchen which served as their bathroom. She filled the sink, stripped off her damp nightdress and, taking an old, stiff flannel, washed herself down. Why did she feel so low all the time? Of course, there were things to be miserable about. But weren't there always? That was life. She should pull herself together. Her days were too busy to mull around in the doldrums. And she had much to be thankful for.

Two wonderful children: Freddie studying in Vienna and Ella completing her training and becoming a young woman.

Marlene had asked advice from Rosa, an older lady who lived upstairs. Rosa had shrugged saying she'd been too busy raising a family to think about *those* problems but advised drinking sage tea for the night sweats. Marlene had started drinking copious amounts of the stuff, but the only effect was that she needed to go to the toilet so often that her sleep was disrupted further. In desperation, she had visited her doctor. He'd said her symptoms were all in the mind and she should start a new hobby.

She dried herself with a towel and slipped her nightdress back on. As she crept past Ella's bedroom, she heard whimpering. Ella was having a nightmare. No wonder after that awful shooting. Marlene climbed into the bed and wrapped her arms around her, soothing her until she quietened.

Marlene pictured herself at a similar age, a couple of years younger, sitting in the sun-filled *Biergarten* on a narrow bench squeezed between two boys. One of the boys put a hand on her knee and began to push it under her *Dirndl*. She felt his warm palm on her skin and giggled. After a moment, she shoved his hand away. She glanced at the boy on the other side of her. He was staring, his pale-blue eyes steel hard.

* * *

Marlene forced herself to slow her stride and relax her shoulders as she turned onto the sandy path, allowing herself one casual glance over her shoulder. Ahead, four wooden huts huddled on the outskirts of a forest where towering Austrian pines dropped three-inch-long cones. Her husband's hut was the largest, a good size for a cabinet maker's workshop. The hut next door was derelict so that was no problem. Another stored timber but the owner only came twice a week and always at dawn. The smallest hut was used as a workshop by a burly man who repaired ancient farm equipment. They would have to be wary of him.

She rapped on the door, calling softly. Franz appeared and beckoned her inside. Various items of furniture stood around: a sideboard, a coffee table, several kitchen cupboards and a drinks cabinet with intricately engraved double doors; the latter being a special commission from a wealthy family on the Brucknerstraße. It was the only work Franz had received in months.

Her husband leaned over his work bench. 'It's safe, Willie,' he said.

A thin, frightened man arose from behind the workbench where he'd been crouching.

Marlene hugged him. 'What happened?'

Willie shrugged his bony shoulders. 'What's happening everywhere. A friend becomes a collaborator and betrays you to the Nazis. The Gestapo are after me because of the socialist meetings I've held in the past. They're not tolerating any opposing politics.'

'We'll take care of everything.' Franz gripped his arm.

'I can't thank you enough.'

'It's my headstrong wife you have to thank,' he said, nodding at Marlene with affection. 'She's in charge.'

'Don't worry, Willie. We can get you into France,' she said, sounding more confident than she felt. She pulled a packet from her handbag and laid it on the work top. 'I brought you both something to eat.'

Franz kissed her cheek and took her hand.

'Let me show you something,' he said, leading her across to a large oak wardrobe against the back wall of the hut. He turned the small brass key in the lock and opened both doors. Marlene peered into the empty space, breathing in the earthy scent of the wood. She turned to him and frowned.

Franz removed a small chisel from his work overalls and wedged it between a spot where the floor met the wall. With a flick of his wrist, he prised the wooden floor up and open. Beneath was a shallow space large enough to hide an adult.

Marlene gasped. 'That's brilliant!'

'Only to be used in an emergency,' said Franz. 'I've drilled air holes in the corners.'

Marlene suppressed a shudder. A coffin. But one that could save your life.

3

ELLA

The manager of the Phoenix cinema stood in the foyer, saying goodbye to the guests and wishing everyone a good evening. Ella smiled at him but Max ignored him as they left. Once outside the building, Max said, 'That manager will soon lose his job. He's a Jew.' Ella thought that was a shame; she liked the man. But she said nothing.

They stopped on the Donaubrücke and looked through the iron latticework out over the Danube, a gentle swell of black velvet. It was a clear night and speckles of stars were reflected in the water below them. Max took her hand. Such a romantic moment. Maybe he would kiss her, right here in the middle of the bridge in front of the crowds returning from a night out in town.

'You're cold,' he said when she gave a slight shiver. 'Let's head home.'

'No, I'm not—'

But he was already leading her onwards. It was a stupid thought. That he would kiss her in public. Inappropriate. It wasn't in his nature to behave like that.

Ella felt the vibrations under her feet before the clang of the bell drove everyone from the tramlines to the sides of the bridge. The tram clattered past on its way to the Urfahr district. The crowds closed in again along the tracks. When they reached the river bank on the other side, Max stopped to light a cigarette.

After a few puffs, he said, 'The newsreel before the film was interesting, don't you think?'

'It was much longer than usual, wasn't it?' Ella gazed across the black water at the twinkle of town lights on the opposite bank. The Linz skyline was defined by an assortment of proud church towers and onion-shaped domes.

He looked sideways at her. 'That's because there's a lot of important information for us to understand before the vote next week. We must appreciate the incredible benefits of the unification. The vote will cement the Führer's decision to unite Austria with Germany.'

Ella's father had used different words to describe what Max spoke of – *invade* Austria – but Ella knew better than to say anything.

'Yes, it all sounds very good,' she said, fighting back the image of the woman in the camel coat face down on the street.

Max laughed. 'Just good? You're not very political, are you? But that's all right for a woman.'

His words were like little spikes.

'Are your parents interested in politics?' He threw his cigarette down on the pebbles and stubbed it out with his heel.

'Not really.' She made her voice sound dull, uninterested. She wanted to avoid discussing her parents' opposing views with Max.

'I'm boring you. Enough of such talk. Let's think about what we're going to do at the weekend...'

As usual, Max walked her to the entrance of her small apartment block where he would give her a chaste kiss on the mouth, lips closed. A lantern hung over the entrance, but today, for some reason, it wasn't lit. It felt different saying goodnight in the dark.

Exciting.

Her heart quickened as she lifted her face to his. They had been dating seven weeks and four days. She longed for a proper kiss. She was grateful for his gentlemanly behaviour but his lips were on her, pressing lightly on her mouth. She couldn't help herself. Her lips parted. She felt his brief hesitation. Then their tongues were touching. She leaned her head back allowing him to push further into her mouth. His hands were on her shoulders. Maybe he would lower a hand to her breast. Touch her through her coat.

He pulled back and straightened his hat. 'Sorry, Ella. I got carried away.'

'No, it's fine. Really,' she said, cringing at how breathless she sounded.

'I like you very much, Ella. More than like. But I don't want to take advantage. You'll be twenty-one soon. We should wait till then.'

Ella wished she could see his eyes but she could only just make out his features in the dark. And now he'd tipped his hat forwards so she could see even less.

'I'll call you.'

And with that, he turned and left.

Up in her room, Ella stood by her window. From here, she could see Linz's landmark, the Pöstlingberg. On top stood the twin-towered church, its white stone façade an ethereal glow beneath a startling clear sky.

She thought about what Max had meant by waiting till her birthday. Different scenarios tumbled through her head. As she looked at the church, she wondered what the nuns would think if they could read her mind. She had been brought up a good

Catholic girl. Just once she had strayed: a one-night stand in a car after a dance. The sex had been quite unspectacular, but at least she'd impressed Hedy when she'd said, 'I did *it*!' Then she thought about the kiss she had just shared with Max. No, she decided, she didn't care what the nuns thought.

* * *

It was a few days after the Germans had arrived that Ella passed the department store on the Landstraße and stopped in surprise at the entrance. The door was closed, the lights off. A poster was plastered across the door:

Juden raus. Geschlossen.

It had only been a couple of weeks since she had shopped there with Mutti.

Herr Pisinger had been standing in front of his department store window with a bucket and large sponge, scrubbing furiously at the glass.

'*Grüß Gott*,' said Ella and her mother in unison as they approached. Ella was surprised that his normally cheerful greeting was a mere mumble. As they passed him to enter the shop, Ella noticed the red painted letters scrawled across the glass.

Ella exchanged a look with her mother.

How could people be so hateful? Just because the Pisingers were Jewish. Their family had lived in Austria for generations.

Mutti gave the tiniest shake of her head. *Don't say anything, be careful*, it said.

At the front of the store, customers were greeted by polished wooden cabinets that displayed a fan of silk scarves and long white gloves behind the sparkling glass. A sales assistant greeted them and offered them to try the new scent from Chanel. They proffered their wrists and wafted away in a floral mist towards the dress department.

Ella gestured to a mannequin on a square wooden platform which displayed a dress for springtime: a fitted navy and cream spotted dress with a round collar and puffed sleeves.

'That's very smart, Mutti,' she said. 'It would suit you.'

'Maybe. But today, we are looking for you. A dress for your birthday. I've saved up for it. After all, twenty-one is a special occasion.'

They milled around the racks, exclaiming at each lovely dress they found and showing them to each other.

'Hello, ladies.' It was Jayden Pisinger, the eldest son of the family. He had just returned from studying at the business academy in Vienna and was being trained to take over the store one day. Ella had known him since childhood.

He asked how they were and if he could be of assistance.

'I'm looking for a dress for my twenty-first,' Ella said proudly.

'My goodness. When did that happen? Suddenly an adult.'

His black hair had grown longer and was starting to curl at the ends, she noticed. He'd lost weight since he'd been in Vienna, his face more angular.

'How's Ruth?' she asked. The name caught in her throat. Ella had envied Ruth in the past.

'She's well, thank you. She's visiting her mother in Salzburg. Actually...' He paused and gave a broad smile. 'We've just got engaged.'

Marlene exclaimed in joy and offered her congratulations.

Ella gave a false laugh. 'About time. You've been together for years.'

She had been sweet on Jayden when she was about twelve years old and used to browse around the store after school, hoping to see him. But when he did appear, she couldn't string a sentence together, and always berated herself afterwards for being the most boring girl on earth. At first, when Jayden and Ruth started dating, she was bereft. Ruth sparkled and chattered and bounced as she walked. Ella was both in awe and jealous of her.

Time went by and the two had remained inseparable, yet Jayden seemed to notice Ella's adoration and had flirted with her on occasion. Once, he had given her a swift, playful kiss on her cheek and Ella had never forgotten it. Nevertheless, she'd moved on and started to notice other boys.

And then came Max.

Ella tried on some dresses whilst her mother sat on an uphol-stered stool outside the changing room. One of the times she parted the velvet curtains to show her mother – a sky-blue dress with matching short-sleeved jacket – Jayden had passed by and had said, 'Beautiful.'

Had he meant her or the dress?

Now she stared at the closed door of the store, unable to believe this had happened to Jayden and his family. She was aware of course of the rise of anti-Jewish feeling, but that the Nazis would close businesses just days after the annexation was shock-ing. Where was Jayden now?

She started to bite her nails, feeling confused, and guilty. She had been excited when Hitler arrived. Max had said things would improve now. She needed to talk to him.

4

MARLENE

The sun was shining when Marlene joined the queue outside the town hall. It was the tenth of April, the day Austrians would decide: to be absorbed into the Deutsche Reich or not. Franz had stayed at home, refusing to vote, saying the whole thing was a farce and that the result would be manipulated.

Marlene looked up at the huge portrait of Adolf Hitler that already hung over the door of the town hall. The blaze of red and black swastikas assaulted her from every direction. Posters blared, declaring work for everyone, and banners hung from balconies were emblazoned with the words:

JA Dein Führer!

Citizens were bombarded with the message: yes to Hitler. On her way to the Hauptplatz, she had passed German trucks giving out baskets of food. 'No one shall go hungry under the Führer,' shouted the soldiers as they handed out their bribes to the public.

Could people be bought so easily? Marlene hoped not, but her stomach was in knots as she fought back a sense of hopelessness. The air began to thrum. People craned their necks as German planes, the Luftwaffe, swept over Linz, demonstrating their prowess, and headed east towards Vienna. Marlene wondered if this air display was meant to impress or intimidate. Both, she decided.

Everyone had turned out in their best clothes to vote. Marlene had chosen her charcoal-grey wool coat and black felt hat. She had powdered her face and applied rose-coloured lipstick.

Excited chatter surrounded her as the queue edged forward.

'...if they bring jobs and put food on the table, then that must be good, surely? I don't agree with everything they're doing, but politics is never perfect, is it?' A young, slim man spoke.

His older companion replied, 'The immigrants are the problem. All these Jews, taking our jobs and getting rich.'

An elderly woman turned round. 'Well, I for one am grateful for what Jewish families have brought this town: department stores and shops. And what about the leather glove factory? They all gave jobs to locals. And my doctor, a kind good man is a Jew who—'

She snapped her mouth shut as a German soldier and an SS officer appeared, surveying the queue.

That's the problem, thought Marlene. People might not agree with the NS party but they were too scared to speak out. At least they could protest with their cross on the ballot paper.

The queue moved out of the bright sunlight into the dim corridor of the town hall. Marlene was momentarily blinded until her eyes adjusted. The smell of stale cigars and sweet perfume hung in the air. Her stomach churned.

An official was directing people through a doorway to her right and when she passed through, she found herself in a crowded room, the walls plastered with Nazi slogans: *Ein Volk, Ein Reich, Ein Führer*. One people, one Reich, one leader. We support mothers

and children. We build homes. And placards all around the room
with the word *JA!* written boldly in red.

Marlene's head swam. She looked up at the photograph of
Hitler framed with flowers. His thin hair parted to the right. Stern
eyes and a small moustache over a small, tight mouth. He would
be nearly fifty now, she thought. Just one year older than her. And
as she stared at his face, she saw him, seventeen years old, looking
at her across the crowded Edelweiss café...

'He's an angry-looking man.'

Marlene recognised the voice in her ear and turned round. It
was Frau Eckl from the bakery.

'But what should we do?' The woman looked over her
shoulder and added quietly, 'They're already here now. We don't
want any fighting. We must think of our sons.'

An official ushered them along to a line of tables where
Marlene gave her name to a man in a three-piece suit. He gave her
a ballot paper and signalled to a low screen where an armed
German soldier stood on either side. An SS officer in black beckoned her forwards. The silver skull emblem pinned to his collar
glinted in a shaft of sunlight.

Her legs went weak, boneless. The room was too hot.

The SS officer frowned and motioned to her to hurry up.

She stumbled around the screen where a tall table stood with a
pen on a string. She stood, looking left and right at the profiles of
the soldiers. Hands shaking, she placed the ballot paper on the
table. There were few words.

Did she agree with the decree March 13 to the Unification of
Austria with the German Reich?

Marlene nearly laughed out loud. There were two circles
where you could place your cross: in the middle of the ballot was a
large circle labelled *Ja*, and to the right, a tiny circle labelled *Nein*.

She picked up her pen and hovered over the small circle.

We must think of our sons.

Freddie in Vienna. Just twenty-one years old. Always so hot-headed. Getting into arguments over injustices. Her husband, Franz – over fifty, not as fit as he used to be. She had put him in danger persuading him to help Willie. They had got him away, but there were others needing help now.

And she had to protect Ella too, who didn't know what they were up to.

To her right, the soldier turned and looked at her, his face expressionless. He couldn't see the ballot paper, but would he be able to judge where she placed her cross? She would then have to walk past him to the ballot box that stood in front of the screen.

And what about the SS officer? What if he shouted *Halt*! And demanded to see her vote?

No, she would not be intimidated. She was entitled to free speech.

Thankfully, the soldier looked away.

Her hand jittered. She tried to swallow but her mouth was too dry.

She saw those eyes of ice. The scorn in that pinched mouth. The anger within.

She placed her cross.

* * *

It was bad enough that she dreamt about that night on the bridge all those years ago, but now the memory occupied Marlene during the day. Images of her young self, distraught and soaking wet from the driving rain, battling the wind as she crossed the angry Danube...

The shrill whistle of the kettle jarred Marlene from her thoughts of the past and back into her kitchen. Her body felt heavy and cumbersome as she took the kettle from the stove and poured the boiling water over the sage leaves. She then shuffled in her worn-out slippers into the sitting room and sat in the armchair by the window. The net curtains needed washing she noticed vaguely as she placed the mug on the side table. She wouldn't drink the tea. She didn't like the taste, just the ritual of making it.

She had been angry with Franz for staying at home on the day of the referendum last week, for wasting his vote. He'd argued that by abstaining, he had made his views clear. She hadn't agreed and had marched out purposefully to the *Rathaus*. And what had she done? Weakened in the face of the Nazi uniforms, stern faces of the SS, the posters and banners screaming at her. She had crumpled at the sight of Linz turned blood red in swastikas. Overwhelmed with raw fear, she'd placed her cross in the box that went against her beliefs and principles.

She'd been too ashamed to tell Franz what she'd done. How ironic that she was brave enough to aid someone hunted by the Nazis, but not brave enough to vote against them.

On the armrest lay the sketchbook with her designs for printed scarves. She enjoyed working at the small textile factory. The people there were like her second family. An image popped into her mind and she started to sketch: clusters of edelweiss. So perfect for a neck scarf. She drew until the page was full of the tiny star-shaped mountain flowers, then she turned the page and started again. Page after page, she drew the national symbol of Austria until her fingers cramped. This scarf would never be printed, of course, but she could imagine one that would be: covered in giant birds. Black eagles. The emblem of the Third Reich.

Tears ran down her cheeks and dropped onto her drawings, smudging the lines and softening the paper.

5

ELLA

The place to meet was the Klosterhof Biergarten: a large, cobbled courtyard beneath a sprawling canopy of chestnut trees. Lanterns stood between the wooden tables enabling people to drink their *Weißbier* and eat *Brezeln* late into the evening. Teenagers met in large groups and drank homemade ginger beer and shared a *Bratwurst*.

Ella had been delighted and grateful when Vati had offered to book a celebration there for her birthday. She knew he had to watch his money; he was a self-employed cabinet maker, and his income was irregular. One month, he would receive a commission from a wealthy family on the Stockbauernstraße to build a complete library; another month, there would be nothing.

The middle of May was the perfect time to have a birthday. Spring was in full bloom and the weather was nearly always warm. Today was no exception.

Ella walked with her guests through the small stone archway on the Landstraße that opened into the courtyard which had been previously a cloister garden.

Max linked his arm in hers and smiled. 'I know I keep saying it, but you look beautiful.'

Ella smiled at him. She had chosen the sky-blue dress and jacket; the one Jayden had said was beautiful. That morning, she'd rinsed her hair with vinegar to make her brunette hair shine, which she wore in soft waves to her shoulders. She'd powdered her face and curled her eyelashes, framing her amber eyes. Deciding against lipstick, she'd glossed her lips with a dab of Vaseline.

The party was made up of twenty guests, a mixture of family and friends. Older relatives sat on wooden chairs at square tables whilst the younger ones squeezed side by side on narrow benches at the long trestle tables. The waiters, dressed in short *Lederhosen* and brown and white checked shirts, took their orders.

Ella felt blessed to be tucked in between her best friend, Hedy, and her handsome Max. Even more so that her brother Freddie had travelled from Vienna to celebrate this day with her. He grinned from across the table.

'So, my baby sister is an adult now. Are you still thinking of studying in Vienna, just to annoy me?'

She laughed. 'Don't worry. You wouldn't have to babysit me. Anyway, I haven't decided yet.'

She glanced at Max. When she had mentioned studying, Max had given a short laugh and said, 'Whatever for?' She'd told him she was interested in history and literature. 'Let's wait and see,' he'd said. Now, he gave a quick smile and squeezed her hand. She knew studying was unrealistic financially; her parents were stretched to the limit supporting Freddie.

The waiters arrived with the food, huge plates in each hand. The guests had been given the choice between *Sauerbraten* and *Knödel* or *Wienerschnitzel* and potato salad.

Ella laid her serviette carefully on her lap. She didn't want to get an oily stain on her new dress.

The afternoon sped by, the sound of laughter and clinking of glasses filling the air. As dusk seeped into the garden, the lanterns and fairy lights which had been draped through the trees lit up and the two musicians arrived with their accordions. Ella danced with her father, brother and male cousins, but mostly with Max. He was particularly attentive that evening and hardly left her side, his arm snug around her waist or his fingers entwined with hers. She loved the attention. It made her feel special.

After the musicians had packed away their instruments, people began to say goodbye and drift off, and when the last of the guests had gone, Ella's parents and Freddie went inside to have a *Schnapps* with the landlord.

Max drew Ella to an iron seat beneath a lantern. She thought how smart he looked in his three-piece suit. She tipped her face towards him for a kiss. He smiled, cupping her cheek with his hand, and pressed his mouth against hers. His cool lips and warm tongue sent a shiver through her.

He moved from her mouth to her cheek, and then to her ear before whispering, 'I have something for you, *Liebling*.'

He pulled back, slipped his hand inside his breast pocket and withdrew a tiny black velvet sack.

Her stomach flipped as he opened the palm of her hand and placed it there. He looked at her, his blue-grey eyes intense.

'What is it?' she said, her mouth dry.

'Your twenty-first-birthday present. Open it.'

She felt as though she was in a film. Her fingers were not a part of her as she pulled on the strings and with great care, tipped the bag over her palm.

She stared at the gold ring, the small diamond sparkling under the lamplight.

'Oh, Max... I—'

'Please wait. Before you say anything, hear me out.' His words tumbled after each other. 'I know this may seem unexpected. And I know we haven't been together long, but the thing is, I can't stop thinking about you. You have captured my heart. I'm simply besotted. And I need to know you are mine. Even if we don't get married for a while, I want everyone to see that you are my girl. Even if you go to Vienna, everyone will know your heart is taken. Maybe you'll decide to stay in Linz and find a job. My father has connections. Maybe I won't have to live through the despair of us being apart.'

'Max, my darling, I don't know what to say. I—'

'Here, just try it on.'

She trembled as she held out her finger. He slipped the ring on. It was too big, so she swivelled it in place.

'I'll get it made smaller,' he said.

Her heart hammered, her thoughts and emotions a tumult in her head. She loved Max. Didn't she? But marriage? So soon? She hadn't even met his family yet. They had only kissed once or twice...

'Max, I'm flattered. No, honoured. No, sorry, that sounds terribly trite. I love you...' She slowly removed the ring. 'But I need time to think about it.'

'Of course.' His voice was tight as he took back the ring.

'I would like to meet your parents,' she said.

Was it her imagination or did he flinch? He nodded and said, 'Of course.'

* * *

Modest and spotless. That's how her mother would've described the house, thought Ella as she entered the hallway. And Max's mother, Frau Giesler, resembled her house: modest and spotless. She wore a cream blouse buttoned to the neck, her hair wound into a tight bun, and in her ears were tiny pearl earrings. For the occasion, she had powdered her face and applied a trace of blush lipstick. Ella was relieved that she herself had decided on a demure look: no makeup over her tanned face, and a round-necked, mid-calf dress.

Herr Giesler stood at the window, looking out. He did not turn around when Ella, Max and his mother entered the sitting room.

Frau Giesler spoke in a thin voice. 'Fraülein Ella has arrived, dear.'

He turned. He was tall, straight-backed and good-looking for his years. She imagined Max would look the same at his age. Herr Giesler did not smile.

'At last, we get to meet the young woman who has been enticing our son. Maximilian has been very secretive about you.' He gestured to the set table. 'Please, take a seat.'

Ella's appetite disappeared as she took her place, nerves knotting her stomach. She had been invited to *Kaffee und Kuchen*. A lace tablecloth covered the round table and, in the centre, perched a *Topfentorte* on an elegant cake stand. As they sat down, Frau Giesler straightened a cake fork and adjusted the handle of a coffee cup.

The conversation was polite small talk, mostly initiated by Max's father. How was her training progressing, what sports interests did she have and what did her father do for a living? Even though the sponge cake filled with cream cheese was light and fluffy, Ella could hardly swallow it. Her throat had tightened from the moment she met Max's imposing father.

Max barely said a word, but when his father asked Ella for her plans after her training was complete, he shot her a look.

'I am looking for a secretarial position in Linz,' she answered.

Or to study in Vienna.

Herr Giesler nodded his approval. 'I may be able to help you there. I have connections here in Linz. As I'm sure you know, our vinegar factory is an important business for the town.' He nodded at Max. 'A business that Max will one day take over. If he proves himself.'

Max looked anything but excited at the prospect.

When they had finished their coffee, and the conversation dwindled, Max and his father withdrew to the armchairs and his mother started to clear the table. Ella jumped up to help and followed her into the kitchen, where the two women washed the dishes.

'Tell me, Ella, are you fond of children?'

'Yes, I am.'

'That's good. Children can be hard work, but there is no greater reward than providing one's husband with a family.'

'I'd like a family, one day.'

'One day? What do you mean by that?' Frau Giesler looked up from the soap suds, frowning.

'I'd like to wait a little while.'

'Wait? Whatever for? It's best to start as young as possible. Are you aware that women of the Reich who bear four children for the Führer receive a medal, the *Mutterkreuz?*'

Ella wasn't sure how to reply – four children sounded alarming – but Frau Giesler continued.

'As you know, Max has two younger brothers at university. Twins. It was a difficult birth with... with some complications. Unfortunately, I was not able to conceive again. Such a disappointment for my husband. And myself, of course. But we are grateful for our wonderful sons.'

Ella's cue to pay a compliment. 'You have a wonderful family.'

She placed the last of the dried plates on the counter.

'You're young enough to have six children, if God blesses you.'

She looked Ella up and down, like the farmers that eyed the cattle at the market. 'You are skinny, but you have good hips.'

Thank you?

Ella had a sudden desire to run home. Instead, she followed Frau Giesler back to the men in the sitting room for a further round of stilted and troubling conversation.

6

MARLENE

Marlene heard the shouts before she turned the corner. She hesitated. Loud, aggressive men's voices and a quieter voice pleading, 'No, no, please...'

She ought to turn on her heel and head straight back home and start preparing the *Knödel* for dinner; danger was around that corner.

Grunts and a thumping sound. A whimper and a moan.

She couldn't ignore someone in trouble and turned the corner, bracing herself. Two young men in brown shirts wielding sticks were leaning over an elderly man crouched on the ground.

'Dirty Jew,' spat the taller one and smashed his baton down on the old man's shoulder.

'Stop that!' Marlene called out, horrified.

The two looked up at her in surprise. They were no more than boys, maybe seventeen years old. But they were strong, their toned biceps protruding from their short-sleeved shirts.

The shorter, broader boy took a step towards her.

'What are you, a Jew lover?' he snarled.

Marlene forced herself not to take a step back.

'And what are you? A hooligan?'

The old man groaned and tried to get to his feet, but the taller boy kicked him back down.

'Stay in the gutter where you belong.'

'That's enough.' Marlene took a step towards the man lying in the street.

The shorter boy pressed his baton across her chest, perspiration on his smooth forehead, eyes lit with excitement.

Marlene fixed her gaze on him.

'I'm old enough to be your mother. I have a son who probably went to the same school as you. What are you going to do? Beat a middle-aged woman? How brave and noble of you.'

He sneered at her and pressed the baton harder against her. She swallowed and mustered up her most authoritative voice.

'Let me pass.'

He didn't move. The power of his arm across her chest did not ease.

She swallowed hard and spoke again, louder this time.

'Let me pass. Now.'

He glanced at his friend, who gave the slightest nod.

The boy lowered the baton and gave a false laugh. 'Go ahead. We'll find ourselves another rat to play with.'

The tall boy leaned down and snatched something from the old man's jacket pocket and the two of them sprinted off.

Marlene knelt next to the man. He had a cut on his cheek and blood trickled from his nose.

'Shall I call a doctor? Let me help you sit up.'

'I have no money for a doctor,' he groaned. 'They took my wallet. The money from the watch I just sold. What will I tell my wife? How shall we pay our rent?'

His tired eyes brimmed with tears.

'Let's go to the police,' Marlene said, but even as the words came out of her mouth, she knew they were meaningless. The police were all Nazis now. Those police who did not agree with the new regime were dismissed from the force or arrested or they disappeared. There was nothing she could do for this man right now other than help him home.

'God bless you,' he said, his hands trembling as he clasped Marlene's in his. 'You may have saved my life.'

After Marlene had returned the elderly man to the care of his wife, she hurried home, shaken by the events of the evening. Those youths had been Austrian boys: bullies with ugly fascist mouths spouting vile hatred. How had Austria become like this? Just a few years ago, the NS party was a minority, and the socialists were fighting for workers' rights. Somehow, the poison had set in, sending out its tendrils like cancer that spread and grew into an unrelenting monster.

She climbed the path alongside the meadow that led to their home, her dress damp from sweat. How wonderful was nature; it continued its cycle oblivious of the disaster gripping the country. The wildflowers still bloomed, the bees collected nectar, the grass grew long, hiding the crickets that chirped throughout the summer. Yesterday, she had planted geraniums in the window flowerboxes. Her yearly ritual. Such rituals made her feel secure. Safe. But that was an illusion.

How many Linz citizens were active Nazis? And how many opposed the regime but stayed silent and hidden like her and Franz? She wondered about Max. Till recently, he had been the perfect gentleman when collecting Ella for a date or joining them for Sunday lunch. He'd avoided conversations about politics, making polite small talk, complimenting the food and praising everything about Ella. Marlene had been quite taken with him. Of course, she still had reservations about his father, but that was all long ago now.

Outside the apartment block, two of the girls from downstairs were holding the ends of a skipping rope whilst their sister jumped in the middle. Their childish voices chanted out a rhyme. The main door was open and Marlene was relieved to pass into the cool hallway.

As she climbed the stairs, exhaustion swamped her. In the last few weeks, she had noticed changes in Max. He'd become more vocal in talking about the advantages of Austria being part of the Reich. Excited, even. He made angry comments about the communists or let a snide remark about the Jews slip from his lips. Franz remained stubbornly silent, avoiding confrontation in front of Ella, as had Marlene. But was that the right thing to do? To not speak up?

As she entered the apartment, she was welcomed by the smell of cooking. Ella had started dinner. In the kitchen, the *Knödel* bobbed in the hot water and pieces of bacon sizzled in a pan.

Ella looked up and smiled. 'There you are, Mutti. Go and join Vati and I'll bring the dinner in a moment. Then you can tell us all about your day.'

7

ELLA

The house stood in a smarter part of town but it was not as grand as the villas in Stockbauernstraße. Ella had stopped here several times recently but had seen no one. She gazed at the white stone façade and varnished wooden shutters with vague, fond memories. A couple of times, when she was young, she had been invited to a party here. She remembered dancing around the garden in a white, embroidered dress with a blue velvet belt tied into a large bow. Jayden, thin and tall, had handed her a yellow balloon on a piece of string. She had taken it home with her and kept it in her room until it shrivelled into nothing, after which Mutti had disposed of it.

As she stood there, Ella felt that same tightness in her chest she'd felt all those years ago when she had come back from school and discovered the balloon was gone.

In those days, she hadn't been aware the family was Jewish. It was only later that she began to hear the derogatory comments, and prejudice had certainly increased in recent years. She studied the windows upstairs and saw movement behind the laced net curtains.

Suddenly embarrassed at the idea of being caught snooping, she turned away and headed in the direction of the Danube.

Walking towards her was Jayden, head down, hands shoved deep in his trouser pockets. He didn't see her till the last moment. He seemed wary, as if he wasn't sure how much she knew and what she thought of recent events.

After an uncomfortable silence, she blurted out, 'The shop is closed. What's happening?'

He sighed and looked away. 'New rules from the authorities. Jews are not allowed to run businesses any more.'

'But why?' She felt stupid as soon as she said it.

'Oh, come on, Ella. Because we're undesirable. And good Austrians should not be buying from us and feeding our undesirable mouths.'

She startled at the bitterness in his tone.

'Sorry,' he said. 'I didn't mean to snap at you.'

'It's all right,' she said.

He was looking up the road, signalling he wanted to end the conversation.

'I'm really sorry, you know, Jayden.' She put her hand on his arm. He had rolled up the sleeves of his shirt and her fingers brushed his soft, dark hair. He glanced down in surprise and she let her arm drop. 'This isn't the Austria I wanted.'

In a quiet voice, he said, 'We're not called Austria any more. We're called Ostmark.'

They fell silent.

The summer sounds around her felt louder than usual: bees and birds and the call of an ice-cream seller.

'What will happen to the shop?' she asked.

'They are forcing my father to sell at a ridiculously low price. Every day that he doesn't agree, the price falls further. They've already taken the keys.'

Ella fought to find some words that didn't sound futile but she couldn't, so she just stood there feeling useless. As tears threatened, she too looked up the road, desperate suddenly to be gone. He spared her then and made some excuse about a pressing chore at home and said goodbye.

Ella crossed the bridge over the Danube as a cargo boat laden with logs eased down the river to the timber factory. Today the river shone blue and silver, gliding unhurriedly on a windless day. She saw people swimming further downstream where the current was gentler. She could imagine their shrieks as their bodies hit the cold water and the laughter of friends watching from grassy banks sprinkled with daisies. Everything was the same as every summer, and yet nothing was the same. It was the perfect June day that was anything but perfect.

They sat in the exact same spot as when he had proposed to her: on the iron seat under the branches of a chestnut tree. Then, it had been cool and dark. Tonight, it was a warm, light summer's evening. The Klosterhof Biergarten was crowded, and it was now a common sight to see young men in military uniform. Ella could hear the distinct difference in accents. The lilt of the Austrian soldiers mingled with the staccato of the Germans. She found it jarred her nerves.

Max touched her cheek. 'What's the matter, *Liebling*?'

Ella took a deep breath. She had been thinking about what to say all day. If she were even to consider marrying Max, she must speak her mind. Max was skilled in evading certain topics in such a way that she sometimes felt she didn't really know him at all.

'I bumped into Jayden Pisinger in town this morning.' She saw his jaw tighten. 'And he told me they've been ordered to close and sell their store. How can that be allowed to happen?'

Max sighed. 'They are Jews, sweetheart.'

He spoke in the tone of speaking to a child and she felt a flicker of anger.

'You know that Jews take jobs from Austrians,' Max continued. 'They grow rich at others' expense. They are different to us. Not of the Germanic race. We don't want them here.'

Her chest tightened. She had voted yes to the reunification; the day of the vote had been filled with excitement and optimism. Hand in hand, she and Max had entered the town hall and placed their cross. A cross for a better future. An end to poverty, to children hungry and begging in the streets. She'd simply blocked out any uneasiness about the new Reich and its Führer. Their Führer.

She shook her head. 'I don't agree with what's happening to the Jewish community.'

'You must understand that the Germanic race has to keep together as a community; it has to become strong, stay pure and reject those who try to poison our society.' Max flushed and looked around him in embarrassment. 'But I don't want to upset you talking about politics.'

'But I want to talk about politics, and I want to talk about people. Austrian people and their families who are being hounded. Just because I want a good job, doesn't mean I don't care about what happens to others in the process.'

Ella could hear the shrillness in her voice. She must calm down. A woman had turned to look at her.

Max frowned and lowered his voice. 'You are distressed, and this is not the best place to talk about these things. Let's continue this conversation later.'

Ella snapped her mouth shut and ground her jaw. She didn't want to argue in public. There would be time when Max walked her home. But later, walking across the Donaubrücke, he told her he wanted to take her for a boat trip along the Danube. They would admire the ancient monasteries and magnificent castles that lined the banks and afterwards have lunch in his favourite *Gasthaus* beside the water. The mood had lightened, and she had lost the energy for an argument. And when she stood at the entrance to her apartment, he pushed her against the heavy wooden door, kissing her with more passion than usual. She felt her body respond despite her anger at him.

After they'd said goodnight, Ella went up to her bedroom, stared at the Pöstlingberg, and imagined what it would be like to make love to Max. How was it possible to feel desire for him when she'd been so angry with him earlier?

She had a restless night and woke before dawn. She felt flat after her evening with Max. She tried to relive the magic of their goodbye kiss, but it hovered out of reach. Instead, his words from the previous evening echoed in her head. *They are different to us. We don't want them here.*

All was quiet in the apartment block: no clunk of water pipes, no heavy footsteps from upstairs. The chatty sisters from below were still asleep.

A low rumble outside broke the silence and an arc of light swept past her window.

Ella sprang from her bed and peered through her curtains. A car drew up and three men jumped out. She heard their fists on the front door, followed by the scuttle of feet downstairs. The Bauer family.

Voices and shouts from below.

She heard her parents stirring and she opened her bedroom door. Her mother stood in the hallway, her eyes wide.

'They've come, Franz.'

Her father came out of the bedroom and wrapped his arms around her mother, burying his head in her hair.

'Who are they?' Ella asked. 'What do they want?'

No answer came and she dashed back to the window, her stomach roiling.

Light spilled out from the downstairs apartment. Down below came the clatter and thump of things being thrown around. The three young sisters were screaming. Moments later, their father, still in pyjamas, was dragged out by the men. They wore dark suits and carried pistols.

Gestapo.

The men shoved Herr Bauer into the black car.

His wife ran after them. 'Please. He hasn't done anything!'

The car screeched away and Ella watched as the three sisters huddled around their mother, sobbing into her nightdress.

She turned to her parents. 'They've taken Herr Bauer.'

She could see the look her mother gave her father. Was it Ella's imagination, or was there a flicker of relief in her mother's eyes?

8

MARLENE

Marlene liked market day, not just for the fresh groceries she bought, but for the social interaction. It was a day when the Linz community came together, exchanging news whilst bustling around the stalls and carts laden with produce.

She crossed the bridge to the sound of chiming church bells emanating from the numerous churches across the town, and into the town square, cringing at the newly erected street sign: Adolf Hitler Platz. It had been a week since poor Herr Bauer had been taken and still no one knew why. No doubt he was being interrogated. She shuddered. It could have been her and Franz dragged from their beds; they had helped two further people since Willie.

The familiar bustle of the market enveloped her and she fell into her routine of visiting her favourite vendors. Some had brought their wares on horse-drawn wagons, whilst others used strong farm dogs to transport the smaller carts. She waited behind a customer at Frau Seidl's stall, noticing the display of vegetables was more meagre than usual. The customer was complaining at the lack of cucumbers and dill for the salad she'd intended to make.

Frau Seidl shrugged. 'What can I do? The Wehrmacht came to the farm yesterday and bought up nearly everything I had. They gave me a fair price too. There are thousands of German soldiers to be fed.'

The customer tutted and mumbled as she shuffled away.

Marlene stepped up. '*Grüß Gott*, Frau Seidl.'

She surveyed the produce whilst the woman chatted away about the weather, the soldiers and her arthritic knee. Then the woman looked left and right and lowered her voice. 'Terrible thing about Frau Ingrid Muller. The news is out now.'

Marlene felt her stomach clench. 'What news?'

'It was her who the police shot. In the back as well. Dead before she hit the ground. Heinous crime. They say the policeman who shot her was all jittery and lost his senses when he fired. I didn't really know her—'

Marlene's head spun. She swayed and grabbed the table, knocking against the potatoes. Two rolled away and fell to the ground. She heard Frau Seidl call her name: far off, muffled.

A wave of nausea. Blackness rushing in. Nothing.

When she opened her eyes, she was propped up against a barrel, a crowd around her.

Frau Seidl held a cup of water to her lips. 'Take a sip. Are you all right? Dropped like a stone, you did!'

Marlene nodded and drank the water, waiting for the dizziness to subside. 'I'm fine, really. It's just the heat.'

A man offered her his elbow and she clambered to her feet.

'Was it the news of Frau Muller? I'm sorry. Did you know her?'

'No, I didn't know her. Not really.' Marlene picked up her empty basket, steadied herself and stumbled off. She had to get away from the crowds and the noise. Away from the town centre, over the Danube, north to Urfahr.

She battled through the oncoming people on their way to market. Too many faces, too many stares.

Hot and breathless, she reached the other side of the Donaubrücke and collapsed onto a bench at the water's edge. She dropped her head to her knees. Why did the shot woman have to be Ingrid Muller? It was too terrible to comprehend. And what about *him*? Was he still in police custody?

Had they shot him too?

Her stomach heaved and she vomited onto a patch of dandelions.

* * *

Behind the small row of houses, the verdant hills rose steeply, crowned by the Pöstlingberg and church, magnificent against a brilliant blue sky. Marlene stood before the house, emotions and memories tearing her insides. Her body sagged and she turned away, but something within snapped her back round. She straightened her shoulders and strode to the front door.

A slim woman wearing an apron and holding a duster opened the door. Her eyes flickered from polite enquiry to surprised recognition.

Marlene, her mouth dry, said, 'Can I see him?'

His sister led her down a narrow hallway past a sideboard where a young bride smiled up at her from a silver photograph frame: Ingrid Muller. The sitting room looked out onto a garden where courgettes were flowering and carrot greens had sprouted.

He sat on the sofa. On his lap was a plate of uneaten strudel, soaked in a pool of melted ice cream. He turned at the sound of their footsteps, his face etched with sorrow and exhaustion.

'Marlene?'

'Hello, Otto.'

She sat beside him and took his hand. His shoulders started to shake. They murmured each other's names and together they cried.

9

ELLA

It was the perfect day to be rummaging around in Hedy's attic. The weather had broken after days of intense heat and rain poured down as thunder growled in the distance. Ella and Hedy waved aside cobwebs and knelt amongst the dust, burrowing into cardboard boxes that had grown soft and sagging with age.

'Here are some clothes,' said Ella as she pulled out a fringed woollen shawl.

'That could be the box with my grandmother's clothes,' said Hedy.

Earlier in the day, Ella and Hedy had been studying a faded sepia photograph of Hedy's grandmother in a long full-skirted dress. Ella had exclaimed how beautiful the clothes were at that time, and now, with the house to themselves, they were searching for the pieces to try on.

Ella delved back into the box and her hands touched a stiff fabric. She pulled out a shiny, voluminous skirt in burnt-orange taffeta.

'It's beautiful,' she breathed. 'I wonder if it's real silk?'

'I doubt it.' Hedy took the skirt and held it against her. 'I don't think my grandparents were very well off. It looks so old. It could even be my great-grandmother's.'

Ella found something wrapped in yellowed newspaper: a small object but quite heavy. As she tried to unwrap it, the newspaper disintegrated between her fingers.

The object was wrapped in purple velvet.

'What's this?' she said, unrolling the velvet cloth.

Hedy threw the skirt over her arm and knelt beside her.

'It's some sort of small candelabra,' said Ella.

The girls studied the curious, blackened candlestick. It had eight slim holders in a line with an additional raised holder in the middle.

Ella rubbed her finger over the metal. 'I'm sure it's silver.'

'I'll run downstairs and get polish and a duster,' Hedy said and disappeared through the trap door, down the ladder.

Ella stood the object on the floor, contemplating why it seemed vaguely familiar.

When Hedy returned, clutching a round tin and two cloths, the girls set to work, smearing cream from the tin onto the cloths and rubbing away the tarnish till the silver shone through.

'It's beautiful,' said Ella.

'I wonder where it came from.' Hedy ran her finger round the rim of the centre candle holder.

A voice called from below. 'I'm back. Anyone home?'

'We're up here, Mutti,' Hedy shouted back.

Hedy's mother, Hilde, popped her head up through the attic door. 'What are you two up to?'

'Treasure hunting,' Hedy replied. 'Look what we found.' She held up the candlestick proudly.

Her mother's face paled. She opened her mouth to speak, changed her mind, and clambered up into the attic. As she knelt beside them, she said nothing but took the candlestick from Hedy, gazing at it intently.

Ella exchanged glances with Hedy. Something was wrong.

'We must put this away immediately.' Hilde's voice shook. 'Hide it.'

'Why? What's the matter?' said Hedy.

Hilde looked at Ella, fear in her eyes. 'You must mention this to no one.'

Ella turned cold. 'No... no, I won't.'

'We need to talk, Hedy. Alone.'

'Mutti, you're scaring me. What have I done wrong? You can talk in front of Ella. I tell her everything anyway.'

The silence in the dusty air was stifling. Ella could hardly breathe.

Hilde's shoulders sagged. Then she sighed, straightened herself and in the calm, even voice of a storyteller, said, 'What the two of you have found is a menorah. It is used during the Jewish festival of Hanukkah, which means the festival of lights. The celebration lasts eight days and each evening, an additional candle is lit.' She tapped her finger on the raised holder. 'The candle here is used to light the others.'

She paused, a faraway look in her eyes.

It was then that Ella remembered why the menorah looked familiar. She had seen it once or twice in the shop window of Jayden's family's department store. And maybe she'd seen another through a house window, alight. But that was years ago. It seemed in recent times, Jewish families were more reticent about displaying their menorahs.

'But why do we have one?' Hedy frowned. 'We're Catholics.'

'It's true your father's family is Catholic. Your grandfather's too. And both you and I were brought up Catholic. But your grandma was Jewish. The menorah belonged to her.'

Again, that suffocating silence. The confusion Ella saw in Hedy's face reflected her own. Ella wished she wasn't there. This was such an intense and private moment between mother and daughter. She looked down at the floorboards and watched as a spider crawled in front of her and disappeared down a crack.

'Why have you never told me this before?' Hedy's voice was hoarse.

'I don't know. It didn't seem... necessary. Important, somehow.'

But it was important now. Ella knew they were all thinking the same.

Hilde started to wrap the menorah back up in the purple velvet, her touch delicate, her expression sad. She started to look around the attic, then went to the far end and jiggled a wooden board until it jutted from the wall. Behind was some straw for insulation which Hilde pulled out. Enough to make space for the menorah, which she tucked inside and then she shoved the board back in place.

She turned to Ella. 'You are like one of our family. I know I can trust you never to repeat what you have just heard and seen.'

Her heart hammering, Ella said, 'I would never betray you. Never.'

She looked at Hedy's pale and shocked face. Ella would rather die than betray her best friend.

* * *

The market stands were a burst of colour, with summer fruit and vegetables proudly on display. Ella had offered to go shopping as Mutti lay in bed with a migraine. She didn't understand her mother lately. She complained of headaches and was continuously tired and short tempered. Ella kept out of her way as much as possible, retiring to her room in the evenings where she lay on her bed, reading.

She ambled along, enjoying the early-morning sunshine, swinging her basket as she walked. First, she would get the basics: potatoes, carrots and onions. She was so relieved to have her secretarial exams behind her and the long summer days ahead. Picnics in the mountains and swimming in cold lakes. Lying in the long grass reading a book—

She stopped in surprise.

Jayden was unloading a cart of vegetables and arranging them on a stand. She had never seen him look like this. His hair was dishevelled, stubble covered his chin, and he was wearing some sort of working clothes.

'Hello, Jayden.'

He looked up, wiping his forehead with the back of his hand.

He smiled. 'Can I offer you the first strawberries of the season?' He lifted a basket of the deep-red berries, and checking the farmer wasn't looking, he picked one out, pulled out the stalk and held it to her mouth. 'Try one.'

Ella's mouth opened automatically, and Jayden's fingertips brushed her lips as he popped the fruit into her mouth. The combination of his touch and the sweetness of the strawberry made her stomach do a small flip. She flushed and took a step away from him. 'What are you doing here?' she asked.

'Earning some extra money. Odd jobs here and there. It's getting harder to find people willing to hire us. We're moving, by the way. My father has been ordered to sell our house to an SS officer.' His tone was flat, tired. 'At a price way below its value.'

'Oh, no, Jayden. Where will you go?'

'My uncle has a spare room in his apartment. I'll stay there with my parents until we figure out what to do next. Luckily, my brothers have lodgings in Vienna. I'm thinking of joining Ruth in Salzburg.'

Ella felt a pang in her chest. Her cheerful mood from a few moments earlier had disappeared.

Jayden checked over his shoulder and whispered, 'The problem is, we don't know what's really going on. Will the Nazis now leave us in peace or is there worse to come? What are their plans? We don't want to leave the country. Here is our home, but —'

'I'm paying you to work, not flirt with pretty young girls,' the farmer's gruff voice bellowed.

Jayden gave Ella a wink and turned away.

She watched him a moment working behind the stand, before walking on.

Instead of heading home with her basket of groceries, Ella hung around town, looking in shop windows and stopping at a stand to buy a *Brezel*.

At one o'clock, the market sellers started to pack up their wares. Ella stood on the corner of the Hauptplatz watching Jayden help the farmer load up his truck. Why was she watching him? Why hadn't she returned home?

When the farmer had driven off, Jayden ran his hand through his hair and straightened his shirt before setting off.

He headed in Ella's direction, but she stepped back into the doorway of a shoe shop, not wanting him to see her. She watched as a ragged young girl ran up to him and held out her palm. He dropped some coins into her hand. Probably most of what he'd just earned.

Ella was about to slink back home when she heard men's voices and the sound of boots stamping along the cobblestones. A gang of brownshirts yielding batons were marching towards the market square, their eyes darting around, eager for trouble. Mutti had told the story of her encounter with the youths and the elderly man and fearfully, Ella glanced back towards Jayden. He was heading directly towards the mob.

She sprang from the doorway and rushed at him. He looked at her in surprise as she grabbed his arm.

'There you are, *Schatz!*' she exclaimed as she pulled him into a narrow alleyway.

As the brownshirts marched past, she dropped her basket and flung her arms around his neck, shielding him from view. She watched his expression flicker from confusion to understanding, his hazel eyes flecked with green, locked on hers.

'Thank you.' He sighed after the group had passed, his breath hot on her cheek.

Ella's heart raced. Danger had been averted. She could lower her arms and step back. But she didn't.

'I didn't want you to get hurt,' she whispered, still pressed against him.

He leaned closer, his thick hair brushing her face. Lips hovering, parting. Her head swayed. Then she clasped her hands firmly behind his head and pulled him to her, pressing her mouth against his. She felt the heartbeat of his hesitation before he sighed and gave in to her.

Their kiss was passionate but brief.

Jayden pulled away. 'No, Ella. I can't do this. It's not fair to you.'

'Why? Because you're engaged?' Ella tried to catch her breath.

'That, of course. But even if I were single, I'd be bad news for you. Even as a friend. Any association with a Jew is dangerous for you.' He glanced up and down the alleyway, picked up her basket from the ground and held it out for her. 'Go home, Ella.' His tone had turned sharp.

'Don't speak to me as if I'm a child,' she said, grabbing the basket, anger and hurt tightening her chest.

'It's for the best.'

'I think so too.'

She turned and strode from the dimness of the alleyway into the blazing, white light, her eyes blinded by the sunshine and her tears.

* * *

Ella was becoming uneasy in the company of Max's friends. Since the referendum, the talk had turned increasingly to the benefits of the Nazi regime. Some had started to wear the armband with the swastika emblem and shout 'Heil Hitler' when they greeted each other. Ella always thought of her parents: how their arms had stayed firmly by their sides the day Hitler arrived in Linz, and how similarly, she'd chosen not to pump her hand in the air in the manic gesture the others were performing. But a few nights ago, Max had begun to join in, his face lit up in euphoria. He'd given Ella a pointed look. And yesterday, he had arrived in the *Biergarten* with two new German friends. Max was wearing the red Nazi armband. She couldn't keep her eyes off it the whole evening and had gone home early, claiming a headache.

* * *

The department store was open again. Only it had a different name. Ella peered through the window. There was no sign of Jayden or his family. What had she expected? *Aryanization* it was called: the removal of Jews from property and businesses. Well, she certainly wouldn't be shopping there in future.

She turned into Herrenstraße and paused in front of the Mariendom, grateful for the shade of the grand cathedral. Looking up at the ornate façade, she tried to recall the last time she'd prayed. She had been lax recently. Tonight, she would pray for the safety of her family, and for Hedy that the menorah stayed hidden, and that Jayden and his family would be left in peace.

The library books she'd ordered had arrived that morning and now having collected them, she would find a quiet spot in the park to read. She stepped out of the shadows into the glare of the midday sun. It was an incredibly hot summer that year and everyone was wilting in the heat.

She had reached the centre of the park when she heard a commotion ahead of her. A young couple were sitting on a bench. The man wore *Lederhosen* and the girl a white sundress. Three men in shorts and trekking boots were shouting and gesticulating at them. Ella stopped in her stride. The men were Max and his two new German friends.

'I'm not going to repeat myself,' said one of Max's friends. 'Get off that bench and clear off.'

'We have every right to sit here. Now, leave us in peace.' The young man placed a protective arm around the girl's shoulders.

Max leaned forward and poked the man in the chest. 'You think wearing *Lederhosen* makes you one of us?' he sneered.

Stunned, Ella crept behind a tree and peered out. What was wrong with Max?

The Germans laughed. 'A Jew in *Lederhosen*. That should be banned too!'

'We want to sit here.' Max put his hand on his hips. 'Get up you filthy Jew.'

'There is no sign on this bench that says we can't sit here.'

'Here is a sign.'

And with that, Max pumped his fist in the young man's face.

The girl screamed.

'Run, Sarah,' the young man shouted, his face in his hands, blood seeping through his fingers. 'Go!'

The girl hesitated, then jumped up and ran to a clump of bushes.

Ella felt sickened to her core. She trembled as she watched the scene unfold before her.

Max yanked the man onto the ground, stepped over him and sat on the bench.

Groaning, the man raised himself on all fours, but Max thumped his hiking boot down on his back, forcing him face down into the earth. Smirking, he laid his feet on the man's back, crossing his ankles, and said, 'Join me, my friends. I have a comfortable footstool here.'

Reality squeezed her heart. She had been blinded by his looks and charm. How foolish and shallow of her. Here was the real Max.

Her Max. His face, cruel.

Twisted. Ugly.

The Germans hooted with laughter and followed his lead, joining him on the bench, propping their feet on the prone young man, watching him squirm under their heavy hiking boots.

Ella heard the sobs of the girl crouched in the bush.

'To be honest, I'm bored of sitting here.' Max slapped his hands on his thighs and rose, followed by his friends. 'Let's get ourselves a nice cold Pils.'

They stepped over the young man and swaggered away in high spirits.

Ella leaned against the tree, tears running down her cheeks. She watched the girl run from the bushes and kneel beside her love, lifting his head onto her lap, cradling him, her white sundress pooling crimson.

* * *

They had arranged to meet at the top of the Freinberg. Max was already sitting in the long grass enjoying the view of the river below. As Ella approached, he started to whistle Strauss's waltz, 'The Blue Danube'. Ella cringed. At one time, she would have found that charming.

A million different speeches had played out in her head since she'd witnessed the horrific scene in the park two days ago. Everything from how she'd seen his vile actions in the park to how she vehemently opposed his politics to deciding to study in Vienna. Whatever reason she gave would end in them breaking up. She had been repelled by his behaviour and no longer wanted to have anything to do with him. With a Nazi. With each week that passed, it became clearer that her vote for the Anschluss had been a terrible mistake. Her stomach knotted with a blend of anger and fear as she approached him.

Max grinned, looking excited as she sat beside him. She winced as he gave her a peck on the cheek.

'*Liebling*, I can't wait to tell you some fantastic... Jesus, Ella, what's the matter? You look grim.'

Her mind went blank. There were so many reasons to break off their relationship that she didn't know where to start.

'You first. What were you going to say?'

Play for time. Get your thoughts together.

She tore at a handful of grass, hardly registering his words.

'...through a contact of my father who's organising the school. It's normally only available to fiancées of SS officers. Imagine. You'd be mixing with the elite, making friends with the inner circle. No doubt you'd hear all the latest gossip.'

She held another handful of grass, ready to rip out. Releasing her fingers, she studied him.

'What type of school, did you say?'

'Really, Ella. You're not listening. A Bride School, modelled on the German format.'

'You've found me a place at a Bride School?'

'A Reich Bride School. It's the first one in Linz and is being organised by some important SS figures in the Party. It's an incredible opportunity for us to get in with the top brass.'

'What would I have to do at this school?' she asked thoughtfully.

'I don't know.' He sounded agitated. 'How to run a household, I expect. I thought you'd be a bit more enthusiastic. You'd be socialising with SS officers' brides-to-be. We'd be invited into the social world of the NS elite.'

Max had her attention now. A spark of an idea began to form in her mind.

'The school starts in September,' he continued. 'It's only twelve weeks and then you would be a certified Reich bride!' He spoke with awe, his eyes alight.

She looked away from him and down on the Danube, trying to collect her thoughts. Jayden's words from the day she'd met him at the market came to mind. *The problem is we don't really know what's going on. Will the Nazis leave us in peace now or is there worse to come? What are their plans?* His family needed information.

'Don't I need some sort of qualifications for this Bride School?'

'You need to be engaged to a Party member.' He puffed out his chest. 'My application to join the NS has been accepted.' He reached for her hand. 'All we need to do now is announce our engagement.' He gave her hand a firm squeeze.

She looked into those blue-grey eyes that she had once found so attractive. Now all she saw was coldness. Jayden's soft hazel eyes sprang into her mind.

It was the perfect moment to tell Max it was over, and yet...

'I need some time to take this all in, Max. Let me think about it.'

He dropped her hand abruptly and ran his hand through his

hair.

'We need to let the Bride School know soon, or you'll lose your place.' His tone had turned impatient.

'I'll let you know after the weekend.' Her mind whirled.

* * *

When it came to saying goodnight, Ella proffered him a cheek, faked a yawn and flitted up the stairs to her home. Adrenaline flared through her as she got undressed. Maybe there was a way she could fight back against the regime. A regime she had voted for. She couldn't take back her vote but she didn't have to stand by helplessly either. Her best friend Hedy could be in danger. Would the Nazis search family trees for non-Aryan blood? And Jayden and his family had already lost their business and home. What would come next? If she went to this Bride School and associated with the Nazis, she was bound to find out information that could be helpful for Hedy's and Jayden's families.

She gazed out of the window at the Pöstlingberg. The sun was setting and the twin towers of the church were etched black against a copper sky. The desire to help burned within her. She had glimpsed a chance to do something meaningful. She wasn't sure exactly how yet, but the first step to find out was to become Max's fiancée and attend Bride School. That's why she'd changed her mind about breaking off with him. She wouldn't marry him, of course. Just delay the break-up till Bride School was over.

She imagined befriending loose-tongued Nazi fiancées, and feigning her love for Max.

Could she pull it off?

She only knew one thing. She had to try.

On Sunday evening, she accepted Max's proposal and he slipped the ring on her finger.

10

MARLENE

It was cooler outside as Marlene left the stifling factory, her yellow blouse soaked with sweat; the heat was killing her. Both from the weather and her own body that had turned wild on her. Her naked feet slid around inside her sandals as she made her way home.

The path wound past a meadow, the grass turning yellow from lack of rain. Three boys were playing with a dilapidated football that was so soft, it made a plump sound when it hit the ground. She had just walked by when she heard running footsteps behind her and a child's voice calling for her to stop.

A boy with grass-stained knees and bare feet ran up to her and held out his hand. 'You dropped your shopping list, miss.'

Marlene frowned. 'I didn't have—'

He widened his eyes and tried to shove a folded piece of paper into her hand.

She took it from him and he grinned, revealing a variety of missing milk teeth before running off. After a quick glance at the note, she shoved it in her skirt pocket and hurried home, her heart racing.

Franz was sitting on the lawn with the neighbours outside

their apartment block, all of them trying to escape the oppressive air inside.

She would wash herself down, she told him, and then they could eat.

After she'd splashed herself all over with cold water that had now turned tepid in the pipes, she joined Franz in the kitchen. He'd come in, taken yesterday's potato salad out of the fridge and was now warming the *Wiener Würstchen* in a pan of water.

Marlene flopped onto the chair.

Franz poured her a large glass of the local pear cider and placed a plate of food in front of her. She was quiet as they ate, distracted by the note the boy had given her. Franz finished his food and studied her.

'You look exhausted, *Schatz*,' he said. 'You should rest after dinner.'

She took the last gulps of her cider and put the glass down shaking her head.

'I have to go out, I'm afraid.'

'Out? Where?'

She looked at him; he was wearing a white sleeveless vest that had grown grey. Stubble darkened the lower half of his face, and his brown eyes looked tired. She loved this man. She didn't want to lie to him.

'I'm going to visit my aunt.'

'You don't have an aunt.'

'Exactly.' She smiled.

He jumped up, scraping the chair along the linoleum.

'No, Marlene! We agreed we wouldn't do this any more. That it's too dangerous.'

'I'm just going to hear what they want. I won't agree to anything until I've spoken to you.'

He leaned forward, his palms flat on the table, his eyes fixed on her.

'I'm coming with you.'

'No. I'm going alone. I'm the contact. Don't worry. I know what I'm doing.'

She pushed her half-eaten dinner to the side, her appetite gone, and got up to leave.

* * *

The port was bustling as Marlene approached the river. The blue Danube was turning navy in the oncoming dusk; the mountains framed purple against the darkening sky. Men were unloading cargo from boats lined up on the quay, working stripped to the waist, their muscular, tanned backs glistening with sweat. Their grunts of exertion mingled with the noise of the port: the putt, putt of boat engines, the grind of the cranes, the cries of the port workers. The Danube had been an important trade route for centuries, traversing Europe and linking a myriad of cultures.

Marlene strolled along, trying to look casual. Just a woman out for a wander on a warm summer's evening, enjoying the view of the Danube. A swift glance at the black painted numbers on the warehouses then back to admiring the river.

She stopped when she reached 47a. Her stomach tightened. The warehouse was closed. A padlock hung on its door. There was no one around.

She checked her watch. She was five minutes early. Rather than stand there awkwardly, she perched on a low brick wall, facing the water, taking deep breaths. Would her contact show? Would she know him?

Footsteps on cobbles. A swish. A flash of apple green out the corner of her eye. Two tanned legs under a pleated skirt. Her contact was a woman. That surprised her, but then she breathed a sigh of relief; it looked more natural. Two friends watching the water.

'No wonder Beethoven was inspired by the Danube.' The voice was gravelly.

Marlene looked up. The woman was about her age with thick, black hair threaded with silver that fell in soft waves to her shoulders. She smiled with red lips. Marlene had never seen her before.

'And Franz Schubert too,' answered Marlene, completing the coded greeting.

'Hello, Marlene. I've heard you've helped before. We need your help again.'

'I'm sorry. I don't do that any more. It's too big a risk. I have family.'

The woman sighed and was silent for a moment.

'Everyone has family.' There was sadness in her voice. 'Why are you here, Marlene?'

Why was she here? Curiosity? Or did her desire to contribute, be relevant, be worthy, force her? Maybe her reasons were selfish, not benevolent at all.

'How can I help?' she said.

Dusk was falling as Marlene walked along the river towards home. The air was still heavy with the day's heat. She resisted the urge to hurry and measured her pace to match other revellers enjoying the warm evening. Guilt lay like cement in her stomach. She'd promised Franz she wouldn't agree to anything without his consent, yet she'd done the opposite. But mixed with the guilt was something else. Excitement. She was transported from being just another tired, middle-aged woman to someone with purpose. She could help save someone's life. She mattered.

Her feet were swollen, and she stopped to adjust the ankle straps on her sandals. Kneeling on the dry grass, she felt a strange sensation: it was as if she was being watched.

Still on one knee, she glanced back the way she'd come. An elderly couple ambled past, holding hands. Two young women eating ice cream that dripped down the sides of softening cones sauntered along.

A man standing by an empty bench caught her eye. He was reading a newspaper folded into precise quarters. Why was he standing to read a newspaper? He was smartly dressed: white shirt tucked into dark trousers. His sleeves were not rolled up on this hot evening.

Marlene rose and continued walking. He was following her. She was sure of it. He was an official. Probably secret police.

Gestapo.

A picture of a building popped into her mind: the Kolping-haus, the Gestapo headquarters. It was an innocuous-looking building, but what went on inside was anything but. People were being denounced in droves and all of them had disappeared. Just like Herr Bauer from downstairs. His distraught wife had still heard nothing.

Marlene checked her stride. She was walking too fast. Her throat was parched, and her left temple throbbed. She couldn't help herself. She must look. She halted, unclasped her handbag and retrieved a cotton handkerchief, making a show of blowing her nose. She gave a half turn and sneaked a glance.

He was marching straight towards her. Grim faced. Eyes narrowed. She looked around her wildly. There were people about to help. But would they? He didn't appear to have a pistol, but he was a big man.

She bolted.

People looked in surprise as she rushed past. Away from the river, into Urfahr, past the post office and towards home. She was panting. It was a long time since she had run anywhere. Her body resisted as she pushed herself on. Her legs were weakening, her knees giving way. She lumbered into the old high street and slowed, her breaths painful and ragged. It was over. She'd put her whole family in danger through her carelessness. It had been a mistake to run; it made her look guilty and now she had no strength left to fight. Trembling, she turned to face her pursuer.

A small boy stood in the dusty, unpaved street, his head to one side. He was holding a paper plane, looking at her with a puzzled expression.

'Have you seen a man?' she panted.

'What man?'

She turned her head from left to right. Some people sat in front of their houses: a woman was knitting, a man smoking a pipe. But the newspaper man was nowhere to be seen.

She collapsed onto a small stone garden wall, relief making her limbs slack. The small boy stared at her for a while, then turned away, kicking a stone down the road.

Franz was pacing in front of the apartment building when she arrived home, dishevelled and drenched in sweat. Her heels were raw with blisters.

He let out a cry and ran to her, pulling her into his arms. 'I've been out of my mind with worry.'

'I'm sorry,' she said, pressing her face against his shoulder.

'What happened?'

'I'm sorry,' she said again. 'I broke a promise and made a promise.'

He put his hands on her shoulders and searched her face.

'I agreed to help. We're going to have guests.'

Dawn was a long way off. There was no birdsong yet. Marlene had dreamt again of that night so long ago. The wind buffeting down the river, the black water churning. And the bridge. Always the bridge. And of course, him and the way he'd looked at her with the coldest eyes she'd ever seen. Shaking her head to free her thoughts, she took a book from beside her bed and limped into the sitting room. She had twisted her knee fleeing from the Gestapo. She was still convinced that the man had been following her and that he was from the secret police.

She fumbled with the cord of the table lamp, found the switch and flicked it on, before settling down in her armchair to read her book.

This was one of the few advantages of the 'change'. The sleep-less nights meant she had time to read again; her days were filled with work, grocery shopping and the household. At night, she collapsed into bed, too exhausted. Even now, she read the same sentence four times.

Her contacts were not an organised resistance group; just a few local people doing what they could. Franz was uneasy that she had again agreed to help, but as was his nature, he'd let himself be reassured by her.

* * *

It was one week later, nearly ten o'clock, when Marlene left Franz smoking his pipe and listening to the new German music station on the wireless: all marching bands and euphoric songs about the *Vaterland*.

She kissed his cheek. His eyes welled up. 'Be careful. I couldn't bear it if—'

'I'll be fine. I'm getting quite skilled in all of this.'

She sped off, hating the fear in his eyes.

Dusk was creeping over the lilac Alps on the horizon. It would soon be dark. She must hurry; she didn't want to have to use the torch in her pocket.

The forest loomed ahead, shrouding the huts in darkness as she approached. She saw the flash of a red fox dart between the pines. She moved to the shutters on the windows each side of the door. With swift movements, she bolted the shutters, entered the hut and lit a small oil lamp. Sitting in a rocking chair that Franz had carved years ago, she waited. Back and forth she rocked, attempting to soothe her nerves.

Her contact had told her to expect a girl, only nineteen years old. Younger than her own daughter. The girl's father was a staunch communist and had been arrested. A hunt was launched for the daughter who was suspected of distributing anti-Nazi pamphlets. So brave and passionate. So dangerous. Marlene didn't ever want Ella to be at risk like that. She wanted her kept safe. That's why, with conflicting emotions, she'd accepted Ella's engagement to Max. Ella was on the side that now held the power, although a part of her hoped that Ella's experience at the Bride School would open her eyes to the evil of the fascist regime. It had taken some effort to persuade Franz not to oppose Ella, to let her find her own way. But finally, he agreed when Marlene had said she would keep a close eye on Ella, there to help and guide when needed. Franz had always let Marlene have the final word where Ella was concerned.

A soft rap at the door startled Marlene back to her present task.

Marlene rose, hoping she wouldn't have to lift the wardrobe floor and lower the girl into the black hole in the ground.

11

ELLA

'A Bride School?' Hedy jolted to a stop and stared at her. The two friends were climbing the sandy path up the Pöstlingberg. Hedy's voice rose an octave. 'A Nazi Bride School? You must be joking!'

'It's not what you think.' Ella had known it would be difficult to explain to her best friend, but seeing the alarm in her wide, brown eyes, she realised she'd underestimated the task. 'I don't want to say too much, but I'm doing research for my writing.'

She had said it. Her planned excuse.

They came to a stop beneath the trees, the dappled sunlight fluttering across Hedy's flushed cheeks.

'You haven't written anything since your second-grade fairy stories.'

'I thought I'd start again.'

Although it was an excuse, Ella quite liked the idea of writing again.

'Under this regime, you want to start writing about Nazi secrets?'

'Just for myself. Not to publish, of course.' Even to Ella, her explanation sounded lame.

Hedy gaped at her.

Ella stared down at the frenetic ants in the dry earth. She didn't want to involve Hedy – to endanger her. But she didn't want to lose her friendship either. Hedy was already sceptical of her engagement to Max.

A group of excited children approached on their way to the fair ride at the top of the hill. The two girls stood to one side to let them pass, and Ella waited until they were out of earshot before continuing.

'Please, Hedy. Trust me. I'm trying to help: to gather information about what's going on. About what *will* be going on.'

Hedy's expression softened.

'Please, don't press me,' Ella continued. 'I can't explain at the moment. But I will when I know more.'

'You're the best friend I ever had, Ella. I trust you with my life.' Her face solemn, Hedy turned and carried on up the path. Ella followed, the weight of her friend's words heavy on her shoulders.

At the top of the Pöstlingberg, they paused for breath and took in the view of Linz, its church spires and domes shimmering in the sun's glare.

Hedy leaned against the stone wall and said in a low voice, 'My father talked to me about his school days yesterday evening. Hitler was in his class for a short time.'

'Did your father have much to do with him?'

'Not really. Hitler was a moody boy. Other children gossiped that his father was an authoritarian who beat him. He didn't see him much after he changed schools, but when my father was around nineteen or so, he'd sometimes see Hitler around Linz's social scene; said he seemed melancholy at times, awkward around women and never had a girlfriend.'

Ella was surprised. 'And now women idolise him, throw flowers at his feet and want to bear his children.'

A crowd of sightseers ambled up beside them and the girls ended their conversation. They walked past the huge twin-towered church and joined a queue outside an old citadel tower, once part of the fortification wall that encircled the Pöstlingberg.

Inside, they bypassed the families and children waiting for the dragon ride through the fairy-tale grotto, and instead headed down the spiral stone steps to the circular cavern below. It was cool and dark inside the old tower. They wandered into the new underground exhibit: a replica of the Linz Hauptplatz from the year 1900, recreated on floor-to-ceiling canvases. It was a night scene: a black sky above sprinkled with hundreds of tiny lights that flickered like stars. The artist, Ludwig, was a friend of Ella's parents.

'Such wonderful detail,' she said as she studied the façades of the buildings: bakeries, apothecaries, chocolatiers and haberdashers. Above the shops rose Linz's stately town houses in pastel colours: mint green, peach and pink. The miniature town ran the full circle inside the tower. There were hand-painted figures of the townsfolk: a chestnut seller, an organ grinder and a ragged girl selling boxes of matches.

'Look here,' called Hedy from where she'd disappeared down a narrow alley. As she spoke, two small girls exited, squealing.

In the dim light, stuffed bears, wolves and foxes peered at them with dead eyes, their fur dull and brittle. Figures of witches, gnomes and frightened children stalked amongst the gingerbread houses and gloomy castles.

'The Brothers Grimm have come to town,' Hedy said. 'I must bring Trudy here.'

'She'll love it,' said Ella, who was very fond of Hedy's ten-year-old sister.

Ella studied the claws of a huge stuffed bear rearing up on its hind legs, brandishing teeth like daggers.

'I'd hate to be locked in here at night.' A shiver ran down her spine.

* * *

The Nivea suntan oil was nearly empty. Ella shook the last few drops onto the palm of her hand and smeared it across Max's shoulders. She followed the contours of his muscles with her fingers. It was strange that here on the beach, in full public view, she could run her hands over his half-naked body. Yet in private, she had only ever seen him fully dressed.

She had worried that after their engagement, he would make further physical demands on her, but he seemed satisfied with a kiss goodnight. Once, he whispered what he would do to her after they were married, sending a shudder through her body. But when she went up to her bedroom, it wasn't Max she fantasised about.

Now they sat on the beach alongside the Danube. After a scorching day, a few clouds drifted across, and a merciful breeze ruffled the surface of the grey-blue water. The skin on Ella's shoulders felt tight.

'I'd like to leave soon. I'm getting sunburnt.'

'Just another quarter of an hour. You just covered me in oil.' He gave her his *I'm so handsome* smile. 'Did you enjoy touching me?'

She laughed. Even to her, it sounded fake. She took a swig of warm cider and jumped to her feet.

'I'm going for a last swim.' She adjusted her black bathing suit and began to tiptoe across the hot sand.

The water, cool and clear, lapped around her ankles, and tiny fish darted through the ripples she made. She waded in, feeling her way, mindful of sharp stones. When the water was up to her thighs, she did a shallow dive and swam with assured front-crawl strokes out into the river. The cold water was a balm for her sun-reddened skin. Mutti had taught her to swim in the Danube but had always emphasised the dangers of the current. Ella was a good swimmer, but she had respect for the river's power. Now, sensing a change in the undertow, she turned back and headed for the shore.

As she waded out of the water, she saw Max gesticulating at two young men clutching towels under their arms.

Her heart jumped. Jayden. And a friend.

The men were arguing. She heard Max's harsh tones and as she neared, Jayden's response.

'...a public beach and I have every right.' Jayden stood just inches from Max. He was smaller, more compact than Max, but his legs were strong from years of football. He was lithe and agile, carrying his muscle with ease, whilst Max was as rigid as a wooden oar.

They looked at her as she approached: Jayden surprised. Max annoyed.

Jayden was wearing khaki shorts and a white shirt that framed his dark waves of hair stroking the collar. In turn, she noticed Jayden looking over her wet bathing suit. She adjusted a strap that had slipped down her shoulder and said hello, her eyes meeting Jayden's for only a second before she looked away. This was the first time she had seen him since their kiss in the alleyway.

'You know each other?' Max frowned at her.

'Of course we know each other,' Jayden snapped. 'My family ran a store in town for years. That is before it was stolen from us. We know nearly everyone in Linz.'

'Is there a problem?' asked Ella.

'I was just advising these young men to go elsewhere.' Max glowered at Jayden.

Ella swallowed. She wanted to retort that that was absurd. Unjust. But she had to be careful not to make Max suspicious of her anti-Nazi views. Otherwise, her plans for Bride School would be ruined. She clenched her teeth and said nothing.

Jayden's friend nudged him. 'Come on, let's swim somewhere else.'

'No,' Jayden said, setting his jaw.

Max flexed the muscles of his right arm. Ella reached out, placing her hand on his forearm, and said, 'We were just about to leave anyway. I need to get out of the sun.'

Jayden glanced at her hand. Her engagement ring gleamed in the sunlight.

'I see congratulations are in order,' he said, his words clipped.

'What business is that of yours?' said Max, looking from her to Jayden.

Jayden flashed her a look. A flicker of hurt mixed with anger.

'Let's go,' she said, giving herself a quick dry and then stuffing the towel into her canvas holdall.

Jayden stepped back and nodded to his friend. 'We'll sit further down the beach.'

Ella sighed with relief as they walked away. The picture of Max beating the young man on the park bench still haunted her. Max was bristling with aggression, and she knew a full-scale fight had been narrowly averted. If she hadn't been there, Max would have attacked Jayden.

As Max pulled on his shorts, he muttered to himself. '... dirtying the beach like that. It's disgusting.'

'That's a bit extreme,' she said, keeping her voice even as she pulled on her dress over her swimsuit, avoiding his gaze. She needed to hide the revulsion she felt at his words. He was getting worse.

'Extreme? Necessary, I'd say. Did you see how he looked at you? The intent in his eyes? Disgusting.'

'Nonsense.' She slipped on her sandals and pulled on his arm. 'Time for a cold beer, sweetheart.' She flashed her brightest smile.

As they left the beach, she forced herself not to look back. Not to see Jayden slip off his khaki shorts. Not to see the dark hair on his chest when he undid his shirt. *The intent in his eyes.* Her skin turned to goosebumps despite the heat. But she had seen something else in his eyes the moment he saw the ring on her finger. Disappointment. How she longed to see him and explain. That was impossible, of course. If Max ever caught them together, there was no telling what he might do.

12

MARLENE

Wild poppies had found their way into the garden, peppering patches of red amongst the dry grass. There had been no rain for weeks and the air was thick with heat and the incessant buzz of insects.

Marlene and Otto sat on a splintered wooden bench under the shade of an oak tree.

'You must do something with the courgettes,' she said, gazing at the bulging vegetables that had taken over the vegetable patch: a clutch of limp parsley and a bunch of wilting dill.

'I don't know what.'

She laughed. 'Let's pick them first and we'll think of something.'

'It's too hot now. Later. Anyway, I don't like courgettes.'

Marlene looked up at the searing, merciless sky.

'This is the hottest summer for years. The last one I remember like this was when we met.' The wistful memory expanded in her chest and she gave an involuntary sigh, immediately regretting she'd mentioned it.

Her words hung between them.

A charged silence.

'You were wearing a long green dress.' His voice was hoarse. 'And a straw hat.'

She had kept that dress: grass-green, dotted with small yellow flowers, tiny covered buttons on the bodice and voluminous sleeves that finished at the elbow. The hat had a matching yellow ribbon. She'd been nineteen years old.

'You looked so serene. Alone. Like a painting,' he said, not looking at her, his eyes fixed ahead on the forests hugging the mountain slopes.

That afternoon, around thirty years ago, Marlene had sought solitude on the river bank, a quiet spot where the current was strong, dissuading swimmers from the area. Sitting on the folds of her dress, she'd watched the Danube sweep past: a shimmer of blue, streaked with green reflections of forest, a few barges and a pleasure boat passing by in the distance. A bright blue kingfisher had darted from a riverside perch and dipped its long bill beneath the surface of the water.

She'd felt too hot, and the water was inviting. Checking first that no one was in sight, she pulled off the garters from her thighs and rolled down each white stocking, before laying them on the grass beside her. The relief as the air swept over her skin was bliss. She lifted her dress and petticoat to her knees, stretched out her legs and wiggled her toes. She heard the slap of waves against the rocks and the rhythm of the river became a life that pulsed through her. Within a few steps, she was down the narrow shingle slope that led to the water's edge; her toes had grazed the slippery stones of the riverbed and cool water had swirled and tugged at her ankles.

'I watched you hitch up your dress,' Otto said. 'Underneath, you wore a white petticoat with a frill. You lifted that too. I hid behind a tree and watched you. Watched you roll down your stockings, baring one leg after another.'

His words were a whisper.

'And then you called out to me to be careful of the current.' She turned to look at his profile.

'I longed to observe you unnoticed, but I was worried about you.'

'A lifetime ago. We had a Kaiser then and Austria was part of an empire. Those were good years back then, before The Great War.'

'They could have been better, if I hadn't been so foolish.'

There was regret in his voice.

Pain clawed at the hidden wound deep inside her, prising it apart, squeezing out fresh blood. She fought to staunch the flow, take control again like she always had.

'Why do you come here?' he asked softly. 'After what I did?' He turned to her, his eyes moist. 'You've come once a week since I lost Ingrid. Why?'

His hand moved a fraction along the bench. His little finger touched hers. The heat was unbearable, from within her as well as from outside.

Another dizzy spell. The ground would rush up towards her. Struggling to stand up, she said, 'I'll fetch lemonade.'

Later, she left, with a basket of courgettes in her hand and a head spinning with memories.

13

ELLA

The once-grand villa was now faded, its pink paint peeling. Perched on the side of the Pöstlingberg, it commanded a spectacular view of the Danube. Ella knew it had been empty for a while. The depression had taken its toll and the owners, unable to pay for the upkeep, had moved to a small house in the countryside. The Reich had recently purchased the old villa, no doubt at a bargain price, and had appointed it the first Reich Bride School in Linz.

Ella took a deep breath and approached the entrance, as nervous as on her first day of secondary school. A group of young women stood on the stone porch chatting. They were all modestly dressed, as requested in their welcome letter: muted colours, skirts to mid-calf and high necklines. Their hair was either cut short or tied back. Makeup was kept to a minimum.

As Ella had few clothes and little makeup, she was quite happy about the regulations. She smiled at the girls and stood to one side on her own, her small suitcase clutched firmly at her side.

The front door opened and a short, thin woman in a navy suit appeared. She blinked at the young women.

'My goodness, you're here already. Come on in and follow me please.' She spoke in a high, breathless voice.

The future brides passed under the faded inscription above the door:

Villa Rosa

The first thing Ella noticed was the chill. It was a mild September day, but the air in the villa was heavy and damp. The intense smell of disinfectant made her eyes smart: German hygiene. The women were led across a hallway, the floorboards as bare as the walls, stripped of their paintings, leaving discoloured, empty patches where they once hung.

Ella followed the group into a large front room with a herringbone parquet floor, a bay window and an empty fireplace. There were no curtains, rugs, tables or ornaments. Just two rows of stiff-back chairs. Twelve of them. Everyone found themselves a seat, placing their small suitcases on the floor beside them. The woman stood in front of the naked fireplace clasping her hands as they settled, and when a quiet descended on the room, she introduced herself as Frau Fink, the headmistress.

'We are delighted to welcome you to one of the first Reich Bride Schools in Austria,' she said, blinking more than was necessary as she spoke. 'Our wonderful Villa Rosa. Before we show you to your rooms, it is with great privilege I introduce you to our guest speaker, the leader of the NS Women's League, Frau Gertrud Scholtz-Klink. She has travelled from Berlin to greet you on our school's opening day.'

All heads turned as a trim, straight-backed woman entered. She was dressed in a crisp white blouse and a grey mid-calf skirt, and her fair hair was styled in one tight plait wound across the top of her head. She wore a navy scarf at her throat clasped with the bronze *Mutterkreuz,* the brooch that honoured her service of providing four children for the Reich.

Ella had read about Frau Scholtz-Klink in the newspapers; she was the woman with the highest-ranking position in the Reich and was often seen in the company of Hitler. After greeting her audience, she launched into a passionate speech.

'...women are the bedrock of our society. Our duty is to support our husbands, yield the Reich with numerous healthy children and provide for our community. It is our Christian duty to obey our husbands and nurture our family. *Kinder, Kirche, Küche.* Children, Church, Kitchen.' Frau Scholtz-Klink paused and looked around the room, her freshly scrubbed face solemn. The women shuffled in their seats and sat up straighter. 'Feminism has no place in our society. A woman belongs in the home. This is a duty, but also an honour. We serve our Führer.'

She gave the Hitler salute which was returned with enthusiasm. Ella gave a reluctant 'Heil Hitler' and raised her arm.

A picture of her kissing Jayden in the alleyway popped into her head.

* * *

'What an inspiration that Frau Scholtz-Klink is!' said a well-built young woman who had just introduced herself as Tanja.

Ella gave a weak smile and looked around the small bedroom: three steel beds, grey-white walls and a metal cupboard. Some yellow curtains had been hung at the window at an attempt at cheerfulness. Ella was relieved that the brides, as everyone here was referred to, were allowed home at the weekends.

Ella and Tanja had begun to unpack their few possessions when another roommate appeared, a thin, young girl with a sallow complexion. Her name was Lisl, she told them as she took in her surroundings.

'They certainly don't want to spoil us here,' she said.

'We're not here for frills,' snapped Tanja, her strong arms flinging her empty suitcase on top of the wardrobe. 'We're here to learn how to be efficient SS wives.'

'Of course.' Lisl's face tightened and she busied herself with her suitcase.

When in the afternoon, the brides received their timetables, it was clear that learning to run a household was hard work. The day started at six-thirty with the preparation of breakfast and ended at nine in the evening after the NS wireless broadcast. The brides would cook their own food, attend classes and wash every surface with disinfectant.

The Reich liked disinfectant.

In classes that afternoon, they learned they should buy German products only, and how to improvise when things such as butter were in short supply. One of the most important skills was thrift, their household management teacher told them. Ella wanted to say her family had been practising that since she was born, but when she saw the puzzled look on some of the girls' faces, she kept quiet. It was obvious most of them came from wealthy families.

During dinner, Tanja leaned across the table to Ella, her round, brown eyes shining.

'My fiancé will be visiting soon,' she said in a low voice. 'He's been asked to oversee the Bride School project here.'

Ella stopped eating. This could be interesting.

'He's German,' Tanja continued, jutting out her chin.

'Aren't we all? Now.' Ella couldn't help her ironic response.

'Well, yes. You know what I mean. He's from Munich.'

'What exactly is this project we're in all about?' asked Ella.

'We're being groomed. The success of this school depends on how we perform. Someone very high up in the hierarchy is keeping an eye on us. But I can't say any more.'

Ella tried to look casual. It was better not to press. Tanja was someone Ella wanted to get to know better.

After dinner, the girls were knitting in the sitting room when Tanja's fiancé appeared in the doorway, his uniform pristine, his boots shining.

Tanja jumped up. 'There you are, Hein—'

But her smile dropped when his ice-blue eyes glowered at her. She plumped back down.

His name was SS Officer Heinrich Steiner, he said, and that he was responsible for overseeing the new Bride School.

'You are all extremely fortunate to be here,' he said, looking around the sparse room and empty fireplace. 'This school has been chosen for a special purpose. I am not at liberty to explain further, but all will be revealed in due course. Enjoy your evening.'

He gave a slight bow and turned sharply on his heel without a second glance at Tanja.

Ella sat down beside Tanja, who looked as if she was about to burst into tears.

'Don't be upset. Officers have to remain professional when in uniform.'

'I'm not upset. I'm tired, that's all. I'm off to bed.' She lifted her chin and marched out.

Lisl moved over to Ella. 'What do you think he meant by "a special purpose"?'

'No idea. Must be something exciting.'

But if that was the case, then why did she feel so uneasy?

* * *

The dark. The cold. And the sound of the jangling alarm clock. These were the three things that Ella awoke to; followed by the groans of her roommates. It was their first full day.

She stumbled into the bathroom, where she shared the sink with two other bleary-eyed girls as they splashed their faces with cold water. Hot water would only be available in the evenings, Frau Fink had warned, and then not every day.

The girls gathered in the kitchen where they met their cookery teacher. Ella had expected her to be round and jolly, the comforting sort she'd read about in books. Frau Hahn was none of these things; she wielded her potato peeler with ferocity, and lined up carrots in neat rows before she beheaded them with a huge gleaming knife. Whilst Ella and Lisl helped prepare vegetables for the *Eintopf* that would be served for lunch later, others prepared breakfast.

'I'm starving,' whispered Tanja, nibbling a piece of raw carrot behind Frau Hahn's back.

Ella's stomach rumbled in agreement. 'According to the timetable, we have to wait a while.'

Outside the window, dawn was beginning to break. The girls completed the food preparations and sped upstairs to change clothes for the next class: gymnastics.

Their legs shivering and their skin as white as their plimsoles, the girls stood in a semi-circle, pulling at the hems of their black shorts in an effort to cover more of their thighs. Their instructor, standing in the middle, wore a bright smile and a whistle hung around her neck. She blew it sharply three times before she spoke.

'Good morning, my sleepy-eyed brides. Who can tell me what a healthy body means?'

'A healthy mind,' said Ella, noticing the admiration from a few girls that she'd spoken out.

'Ahh, that old adage. Important of course, but we must

consider our wider purpose: to serve the Reich. A healthy body means healthy children.'

At this, she gave a shrill blow of her whistle and began to shout instructions. They jogged around the garden, knees held high. Ella enjoyed the early-morning air, cool and damp against her skin. She glanced at the view below, the town barely visible beneath the mist.

The instructor led them through a range of exercises including star jumps and several rounds of leapfrog. Ella was fit and had no problem with the class but she noticed Lisl struggled to leapfrog over the taller girls. The instructor, not satisfied with her performance, ordered Lisl to perform an extra round, and when she tumbled to the ground, there was a chorus of sniggers. Lisl looked crestfallen as she picked herself up, but the instructor just smiled. 'Practice, practice. We'll have you leapfrogging over the Pöstlingberg by Christmas.'

Half an hour later, Ella was wide awake and ready to get into warm clothes for breakfast; she was ravenous. The girls were now running on the spot, any early enthusiasm having dissipated with the mist. A watery sun climbed the sky. Ella's plimsoles were now damp from the dew on the grass and her heel was rubbing. Her pace slowed.

'Knees up, girls. Nearly finished.'

All the girls were panting heavily, their knees dropping.

'And, stop.'

Audible sighs of relief followed. The girls had survived the class and would now finally be allowed the porridge that they'd prepared earlier. The instructor beckoned impatiently to the old gardener who was wheeling a coiled hosepipe across the lawn. He stood it beside her and walked away. Did the instructor intend to water the garden? Ella wondered.

A maid appeared and left a basket laden with towels on a bench on the terrace.

'Leave your clothes on the bench and line up, please.'

The girls gave each other confused looks.

'Which clothes, exactly?' said Tanja, frowning.

'The ones you are wearing.' The instructor smiled, her voice light, as if it was obvious. 'I'm sure you have all heard of Dr Kneipp's advice on a cold shower and its positive effect on circulation.' She reached for the hosepipe. 'Snap to it. Strip off. A quick cold burst. Then fetch a towel from the basket and give yourself a brisk rub down.'

Tanja was the first to rip off her top and step out of her shorts. She stood without shame, her shoulders back, emphasising her large bosom. The other girls reluctantly followed her lead.

The naked girls stood in a line, their warm skin from the exertion cooling quickly. Any satisfaction Ella had felt about completing the class disappeared as the instructor turned on the hose and moved along the row of girls towards her.

One girl after another shrieked as the spray hit them. The instructor held the hose steady for a few moments then nodded, indicating the ordeal was finished. The girls ran for their towels. Ella held her arms across her chest and pressed her thighs against each other to stop herself from shaking; she was freezing now. Not afraid, though. After all, it was just a quick spray of cold water to toughen them up. Worse things were endured in the army.

She looked down the line of girls who were standing there, submitting themselves, vulnerable in their nakedness.

The instructor maintained a neutral expression. But as she neared, Ella saw a flicker of light in her eyes. Pleasure.

Ella braced herself as the woman stepped in front of her and aimed the hose. She gasped as the jet hit her stomach; her skin puckered under the stream of water shooting across her shoulders then back down her body, over her pelvis and down her legs. She waited for the dismissive nod.

It didn't come. The instructor twiddled with the ring around the hose opening. The water gushed out with more power.

Ella took an involuntary step back.

'Not so fast,' the instructor said. 'I repeat my earlier question. What does a healthy body mean?'

Ella hesitated and then sighed. 'Healthy children.'

The gleam of satisfaction lit up the woman's eyes.

The nod came. Ella sprinted for her towel, angry at the humiliation. Angry at herself for giving in to the awful woman.

She rubbed herself briskly with the rough towel, wrapped it around her and then snatched her clothes and plimsoles from the bench. She cast back a look. Lisl was last in line and was cowering under the water stream before being given permission to bolt towards the basket of towels. Ella watched her blue-white limbs speeding across the grass, wet hair plastered to her face. A moment later, her legs crumpled beneath her and she dropped like a rag doll.

Ella cried out Lisl's name and reached her at the same time as the instructor.

'The silly girl has fainted,' the woman said as she knelt down and hoisted Lisl to a sitting position.

Lisl stirred. Her whole body trembled. Ella ran to fetch towels and draped them over her shoulders whilst the instructor held Lisl's head between her knees.

When Lisl had recovered slightly, the instructor told Ella to take her inside and ensure she ate her bowl of oats as quickly as possible. Her tone was dismissive.

As Ella helped Lisl inside, the girl mumbled, 'I'm so embarrassed. I don't want my fiancé to hear about this.'

Before Ella could say anything, the instructor's voice drifted behind them.

'Your circulation just needs practice. We'll have you swimming across the Danube by Christmas.'

It wasn't even time for breakfast yet on this, her first morning at the Bride School, and she already could sense a toxic undertow that pervaded the place.

Two weeks later, on Friday at four o'clock, the brides were dismissed for the weekend. Some of the girls had come from outside Linz and had longer journeys home. One girl had to travel to a village near Salzburg which was a two-hour train ride. Ella's journey was a thirty-minute walk down the Pöstlingberg.

She had never been so grateful to get back home. It had been a strain playing her role as the enthusiastic Nazi bride for the last two weeks. She had avoided mentioning the fact that Max was not an officer; it was vital she cultivate friends first and make connections. Hopefully, when people found out eventually, it would seem less important.

The tang of cooked apple and the scent of sweet pastry filled her nostrils before she even got her key in the door: Apfelstrudel. Mutti. Home.

Mutti rushed to greet her and threw her arms around her. Ella hugged her close, pressing herself against her mother's soft belly. Mutti had put on weight recently, although the portions she ate were always small. Her mother sometimes shook her head and mumbled about the 'change', but when Ella asked her about it, she just waved her hand, saying she just had to get on with it.

Ella peeled potatoes whilst Mutti fried the onions. Ella enjoyed these moments of bonding with her mother; they made her feel secure.

'How is it at Bride School?' her mother asked.

Ella felt her mother studying her. 'The place is very austere, but that's not important. The girls are friendly.'

This wasn't quite true, but she thought it was what her mother wanted to hear. She had the urge to tell her mother the truth, the real reason why she was there, but that would only worry her. She'd tried to soften the news to her parents about her engagement to Max. Her reason for attending the school, she'd told them, was to find out if becoming Max's wife was the right decision. It had saddened her to see the initial shock in her parents' faces, and worse, the disappointment in her father's eyes. That evening, as Ella had tried to fall asleep, she'd heard her parents' hushed voices late into the night. The following day, however, they'd been more composed, obviously having talked it all through.

She now looked at her mother: at the thin, dry skin around her eyes, her dark, swept-back hair flecked with dull, grey strands. A lump formed in her throat; her mother had aged.

'How are you, Mutti?'

Her mother glanced up from stirring the onions, surprised at the rare question.

'Oh, I'm fine. Just a bit tired. I'm not sleeping so well at the moment.' She turned the gas down. 'Frau Bauer came by for coffee this afternoon.'

As always, she deflected conversation away from herself.

'How is she? Any news?'

'Not good, I'm afraid. She's been informed by the authorities that Herr Bauer has been sentenced to some sort of camp: Dachau, near Munich. It's where political opponents are sent, apparently.'

'That's terrible.'

'Obviously, the children are distraught. They're falling behind with their schoolwork and Frau Bauer is too overwhelmed to help them.'

Ella put the pot of potatoes on the stove.

'I'll pop downstairs at the weekend and see if I can help.'

'She'd appreciate that. Are you seeing Max later?'

Ella explained that Max had an engagement that evening, but she would see him on Saturday. Instead, she would meet some of her new friends from the Bride School. In reality, Ella would have much preferred to see Hedy, but Tanja had suggested the idea and Ella had to take the opportunity. Tanja liked to talk a lot about her SS fiancé and Ella hoped to find out some useful information.

* * *

The streetlamps threw a sallow light on the wet pavement. The rain became heavier as Ella and two other girls hurried after Tanja, who led the way. They had met at a coffee house where Tanja had chattered excitedly.

'Heinrich has been provided with a house. It's not grand, but it's large and he has the whole place to himself.' She had given a coy smile. 'It's nice we can be alone.'

'You'll be able to host parties,' Lisl had said.

'Absolutely. Actually, Heinrich is at home this evening, busy with paperwork. He said I could invite you ladies back for a night-cap. I'd love to show you the house.'

Now, as they rushed towards Tanja's fiancé's new home, they huddled together, eager to get inside out of the wet. Ella was curious; she recognised the area.

Tanja halted and threw out her arm. 'Here we are.'

Confusion assaulted her senses. Ella held her breath for a few heartbeats before reality crashed down on her.

Jayden's house.

She stood stock still.

'Come on, Ella,' called Tanja as she rang the doorbell.

Ella climbed the two front steps in disbelief.

The door opened. Herr Heinrich Steiner in SS uniform gave a formal smile.

'Welcome, ladies. Please come in.'

The coffee from earlier rose bitter in Ella's throat as she entered, feeling like a traitor. They were shown into the sitting room, where Tanja indicated they should sit down. Tanja took the armchair, leaving the others to squeeze next to each other on the settee.

'Please excuse the old-fashioned furniture,' she said with a derogatory laugh. 'We'll be throwing it out as soon as possible. I would like to refurnish before we're married.'

Tanja threw a smile in Heinrich's direction, but he stood with his back to her, studying the gilt drinks trolley. Ella thought the room looked homely: somewhere where a family had lived and grown together. But there were no personal effects. No photographs, paintings, ornaments or cushions. These had all been removed. Ella's throat ached with sadness.

'What can I offer you fine ladies?' said Heinrich, turning to face them. 'Whisky, brandy or an excellent plum *Schnapps*?'

Ella rarely drank hard alcohol but, hoping to calm herself, she took the *Schnapps*. It was sweet and strong. They raised their glasses and said, '*Prost!*' Ella emptied the small squat glass and jolted when the fiery liquid hit her stomach. The rush to her head felt good. Heinrich refilled her glass, watching her as she drank. The telephone rang from the hallway and Heinrich left to answer the call. When he returned, he raised his voice and addressed the group of women.

'I'm afraid I have to leave you for a short while. Something has come up auf der Gugl.'

'Headquarters again?' Tanja pouted. 'Oh, no, Heinrich.'

'Duty calls,' he said, smoothing down his thinning hair.

After he left, Tanja was subdued for a while. 'He's always work-ing,' she mumbled. 'He's brought a whole load of paperwork home for the weekend too.' To lift her spirits, Ella asked about the plans for her wedding, after which she rattled on about bridal gowns, the hotel venue, food and the brass band. The girls chatted and drank, and two hours passed seemingly quickly.

Ella got up to use the downstairs cloakroom. She was giddy from the *Schnapps* and had to concentrate hard to walk in a straight line. As she walked down the hallway, her mind was in turmoil. How sad to be in what was once Jayden's home. His father had been finally forced to sell at an unfair price, no doubt. What would Jayden think now if he could see her here in his childhood home, socialising with Nazis? He would hate her.

The thought made her feel sick.

When she left the cloakroom, she glanced to the end of the hallway. A memory flashed. She, in her white party dress, running along, heart thumping with excitement. Jayden's voice: '...forty-nine, fifty. I'm co-ming.' Pushing open the heavy door. A room full of books, thick curtains that fell to the floor. They had been playing hide and seek.

Now Ella was drawn to the room, the alcohol making her bold. The door to the library was ajar and she slipped inside. The same heavy curtains where she had hidden herself within their folds still hung at the window – where Jayden had found her and tickled her mercilessly till she cried for him to stop, tears rolling down her cheeks. His expression had turned serious, and he'd planted a kiss on her cheek before running away, shouting that he'd found her.

The same imposing desk and high-back leather chair remained. The room was dimly lit by the glass-based lamp on the desk. Files lay scattered across the surface. A fountain pen without its cap lay on the black leather blotter. Heinrich had obviously been in the middle of working before being called away to head-quarters.

Ella felt outside of herself, her head muffled as she reached for a file and peeked inside. It contained what appeared to be invoices: electricity, telephone and such like. She snapped it shut and reached for another. After briefly scanning carbon copies of internal memorandum that proved of no interest, she picked up a further file. It contained a typed list with the heading:

Linz Citizens of Non-Aryan Heritage

Ella's breath caught in her throat. Some of the names had been circled with an ink pen; she glanced at Heinrich's fountain pen lying on the blotter. The image of her and Hedy polishing the silver menorah flashed in her mind. She ran her eyes down the list. Thank goodness Hedy's name was not there. But what about the other people on the list? And what did the ink circles mean?

The names swam before her. She shook her head; if only she hadn't drunk so much. Panic gripped her. What should she do? She fought the urge to snatch the list and put it in her pocket. That would be madness. She needed to think things through with a clear head: have a plan. After glancing again at a couple of the circled names and committing them to memory, she replaced the files to their original position. Standing back, she surveyed the desk, satisfied everything was in order.

'Can I help you?'

She jumped and turned around.

Heinrich stood in the doorway, insect-like, his long, lean body backlit by the hallway light.

'No, sorry. I was just admiring the library.' To her dismay, her lips had turned numb, and her words were slurred.

'Do you always wander uninvited around people's homes?'

He walked towards her.

'I apologise. I was just curious.'

'I don't find curiosity becoming in a woman.'

She said nothing. He glanced at his desk and then back at her.

'Curiosity is not a suitable trait for a future bride of the Reich. Curiosity is in fact dangerous. It was the reason that I was called out tonight: to show someone the error of their ways. A woman. She *had* been beautiful. No man will be beguiled by her looks ever again.'

He studied his immaculate fingernails and gave a snide smile.

Then, leaning down, he locked his flint eyes on hers. She shuddered. The smell of whisky and cigarette smoke filled her nostrils.

'I'm sorry. It won't happen again.' Her voice shook.

'That's good to hear. Because if it did...' He ran a finger along her cheek. 'Such soft, young skin. It would be a shame...'

She nodded, swallowing back her terror.

Then stepping back, his tone light, he said, 'I would very much like to meet your future husband. No doubt you know I am acquainted with his father. It was me he approached to arrange a place for you at the Reich Bride School.'

Ella tried to mumble a reply, but her mouth was frozen. Heinrich knew Max's father?

'We are having a party here at the end of the month,' he said. 'Please come and join us.'

She managed to nod.

'I'm pleased that's sorted. Let's join the others, shall we?'

He held out his arm, inviting her to walk first, and as Ella stumbled down the hallway, she sensed him staring at every inch of her, from the crown of her head to the backs of her stockinged heels.

14

MARLENE

There was no way to avoid the Donaubrücke. If Marlene wanted to go into the centre of Linz, she had to cross the bridge, either by tram or on foot. Usually, she walked to save the fare. Again today, as she peered at the swollen, grey water surging beneath her, the memories leaped at her: the roar of the river that night, crashing against the pillars of the bridge, the rain pinging off the ironwork.

Recently, those events had begun to haunt her daily. She was consumed with 'what ifs' and 'if onlys'. She dragged her gaze from the hypnotic water and hurried along the bridge towards Urfahr. She'd spent too long in town and was now running late.

A boy and a girl in tattered clothes stood at the end of the bridge. The girl wore a dirty summer dress, not warm enough for autumn. The boy in short trousers had scabs on both of his skinny legs.

He held out his cap. 'Can you spare a pfennig, *liebe* Frau?'

Marlene gave the children a soft smile and dug some coins from her purse. She popped them in the cap where they clinked against the other collected coins. The girl had goosebumps on her arms. Marlene's heart wrenched. Didn't the girl even have a cardigan?

She walked on, heaving out a sigh; there was still so much poverty in Linz despite the new regime's promises. But at least there were more soup kitchens and trucks handing out bread. Probably those children's parents were grateful for Hitler and his policy to build housing and create jobs. She understood why so many people had voted yes to the annexation, including herself. But had the citizens realised the consequences? The price to be paid? Did they even care? People had their own pressing concern: their family's survival.

Once home, she pulled off her skirt and blouse and reached for her smartest dress: calf-length, burgundy crepe with short, puffed sleeves. She let out a cry of frustration as she struggled with the zipper. It had been a while since she'd worn it. Blast, it was tight, but it was her favourite dress and she was determined to get into it. She was gaining weight and eating less; it was so frustrating. She lifted the hem and pulled off her pants, before exchanging them for a firm girdle. Breathing in, she eased the zipper shut. Smoothing down her stomach, she surveyed herself in the mirror. She would have to do.

When Franz arrived home, he changed his clothes and then they set off to the party of their good friend, Ludwig. The sun was setting and the leaves of the trees flamed orange and yellow in the golden light. Only the fir trees remained unimpressed by the onset of autumn, sporting their deep evergreen needles.

When they arrived at the two-storey gabled house, Ludwig was greeting guests at the door. On seeing Franz and Marlene, he gave a cheerful wave. Ludwig Haase was an artist whose father, also an artist, had been friends with Marlene's mother. Today, Ludwig was celebrating his birthday. They all shook hands, and Franz clapped Ludwig on the shoulder, wishing him all the best.

Inside, guests were drinking *Sekt*. Ludwig proffered them a glass. Marlene sipped the sparkling wine and looked around the room. Landscape paintings hung on the walls: azure lakes reflecting snow-dusted mountains, huts on the *Alm* where the fresh grass was lime green.

Turning to Ludwig, she said, 'Your painting of Linz in the Pöstlingberg grotto has been a wonderful success. It must've been an incredible amount of work painting such huge canvases.'

'It was but I enjoyed the challenge. The idea of recreating the town in an underground cavern appealed to me.'

A heavyset man in a traditional *Tracht* waistcoat approached them. It was Ingolf, a mutual friend. He embraced Franz with a bear hug and kissed Marlene three times on her cheeks.

'How's life up on the Pöstlingberg, Ingo?' asked Franz.

'I've had easier jobs as a janitor. It's busy; maintenance on the Grottenbahn and taking care of Ludwig's little Linz. The children can be tiny devils climbing into the fairy-tale alcoves.'

Franz laughed. 'Be careful one is not locked in for the night!'

Marlene felt a familiar throb at the base of her neck. She shouldn't drink any more. The last thing she wanted was a migraine; she had been looking forward to this evening.

She mingled with the guests, but the whole time, black lines darted before her eyes. Why did she keep getting these headaches? She was annoyed with herself; a shame she hadn't thought to pop some aspirin in her bag. Her dress was uncomfortably tight. It was making her sweat. Were damp circles appearing under her arms?

She exchanged her *Sekt* for a glass of water but the pain spread up from her neck and over her forehead. Her right temple began to throb. It was no good; she would have to leave.

'I'm sorry, I have to go home,' she said to Franz, quietly in his ear. 'I have a terrible headache, but you stay here.'

'You're not walking home alone. We'll leave together.'

Marlene tried to talk him into staying but he wouldn't hear of it. So they said goodbye to their hosts, fetched their coats in the hallway and opened the door. A man stood outside, his finger poised over the doorbell.

It was Otto.

'Hello, Marlene,' he said, startled.

'Hello, Otto,' she said, a hot flush erupting to her face.

Now? Of all moments?

Franz glanced from Otto back to her, a question in his eyes. Marlene took a deep breath and steadied her voice as she gave a brief introduction. Then, after excusing herself for being unwell, she continued down the front steps.

As they walked, Franz said, 'Who's Otto?'

Thousands of tiny hammers beat in her head. 'He was just one of the crowd when I was young,' she said. 'You wouldn't know him.'

Should she mention he was the widow of the shot woman outside the café? For some reason, she thought better of it.

'You've never mentioned an Otto before.'

She gave a nonchalant shrug. She had no reason to keep Otto a secret.

Or did she?

15

ELLA

The blacksmith looked up from his work as Ella stood in the open doorway of his workshop, blocking the weak winter sunlight. He lowered the horseshoe he was forging and with surprise in his voice, he said, 'Can I help you, miss?'

'Herr Gunther Krauss?' she enquired.

He nodded and looked at her expectantly. Ella stepped forwards, took a breath, nervous how her prepared words would come across. She had to give as little information as required but enough to be of help to Herr Krauss. It was also a delicate matter that she had to treat with tact; the last thing she wanted to do was come across as some prying busybody.

'My name is Ella, and although you don't know me, I have come across some information that I think you should know.'

He raised his eyebrows, took a handkerchief from the pocket of his overalls and wiped the sweat from his forehead. She chose her next words carefully.

'I have come into contact with some NS party members and have reason to believe that there will be an imminent threat for citizens of mixed heritage.'

The blacksmith flinched, then his face turned wary. 'Why on earth would you think that is of concern to me?'

She pictured the ink circle around his name on the list in Heinrich's study. 'Your name was highlighted and—' She paused, trying to suppress the tears that threatened, and suddenly overwhelmed by the task, words tumbled out. 'I understand you have no idea who I am and if you can trust me. All I know is that a high-ranking SS officer has reported that you have Jewish roots, which is none of my business, and may or may not be true, which may or may not put you in imminent danger. I don't have the faintest idea what you can do about it...'

Breaking down in tears, she felt utterly useless. What good did her information do? Looking around the shed, crammed with this man's work, his life, what did she expect him to do? Believe her emotional ramblings, run away and leave everything behind?

He was silent for a while, a conflict of emotions passing over his face. Then he nodded, sorrow in his eyes. 'Thank you for this information. What I do with it is for me to fathom out. I think it's best for you if you leave now.'

Before she turned to go, she said, 'Was I right to tell you?'

'Absolutely. I'm grateful and I am sure others would feel the same.'

As Ella walked home, she tried to quash the feeling that she had just ruined Herr Krauss's life.

* * *

Ella and Lisl sat in front of the gaping, cold fireplace embroidering napkins they had starched and ironed earlier. It was only October, but the room was like ice. Both girls had shawls over their shoulders which they'd knitted earlier in the handicraft class. Lisl looked up from her stitching. 'Can you imagine how cold it will be in here by the time our training finishes at Christmas?'

Ella gave Lisl a sympathetic smile. 'They think it's character building for us. Only soft women need warm rooms, apparently.'

Ella didn't really mind the austere surroundings, the cookery classes and the sewing circle. What bothered her was the way the women were so proud to become Nazi wives; to embrace the NS ideology for women; the emphasis on obedience. Especially to one's husband. The thought of obeying Max made her squirm. She had seen his violent side in the vicious attack on the young man in the park. If she were to marry him, she had no doubt he would raise his hand against her eventually. But she wouldn't marry him; that wasn't her plan. How she would get out of her betrothal, she wasn't yet sure.

She stopped sewing and gazed at her work. The initial M was nearly complete. The perfect NS Frau embroidered her husband's initials on napkins. It was absurd. To distract her thoughts from plunging into a downward spiral, she asked Lisl about her fiancé. Lisl had spoken little about Erwin; merely that he was older and had been married before.

Lisl paused before answering, her head to one side. 'He's a clever man. Very cultured.'

'Then you have some catching up to do!' Tanja had risen from her seat by the window. Lisl started at the remark, her mouth falling open. 'Just kidding,' said Tanja, her smile too bright. But Lisl's expression showed her hurt.

Ella bristled. Were they careless words, or intended barbs?

'I feel I need a bit more culture in my life,' said Ella, smiling in Lisl's direction. 'Books, art, theatre. How about we see a play together? Or visit the new art gallery?'

Lisl nodded gratefully.

Tanja held up her napkin as if she expected a drum roll,

displaying the initials HS neatly embroidered in the bottom left-hand corner.

'Wonderful, Tanja. I'm sure Heinrich will be very proud of you.' Ella clapped her hands.

Tanja pursed her lips at the sarcasm.

The moment of tension between the girls was relieved when Frau Fink fluttered into the room, her movements true to the meaning of her name: finch. Today, she seemed more nervous than usual, almost in tears.

'Ladies, please line up the chairs whilst I get everyone together. Herr SS Officer Steiner is here to make an announcement.'

Ella saw the surprise in Tanja's eyes; she hadn't been expecting her fiancé.

The twelve brides gathered in the chilled room, whispering to each other. They fell silent when Steiner marched in, his knee-high boots gleaming. Ella imagined what Tanja would be like in the future, the perfect wife, furiously polishing his boots and ironing his uniform, shining the SS skull pinned to his collar. He would stand stern and rigid as she adjusted his tie. There would be no hug or soft kiss goodbye as he left for the SS *Zentrale*.

Following Steiner was Frau Fink and a statuesque woman dressed in black, her fair hair in a tight bun at the nape of her neck. The three faced the expectant brides and Steiner stepped forward.

'I would like to introduce to you Frau Gruber who will be overseeing the school, reporting directly to me. She will be here daily to guide and assist Frau Fink in her important role here.'

Ella looked for a smile on Frau Gruber's pale, long face as she studied the girls. There was none. The woman towered above Frau Fink: an eagle and its prey. Wary looks passed between the girls as they assessed the new situation; it appeared Frau Fink had been demoted in favour of a more formidable character.

Frau Gruber announced that new classes would be added to the timetable which she would take personally. The first would be the next day: *Rassenkunde*. Racial science. A new schedule would be pinned to the notice board in the hallway. Also, there was to be a new regulation: the Führer's prayer would be compulsory at the evening meal. Ella's chest tightened. Whatever happened to saying grace to the Lord at mealtimes?

They all filed out in silence, Frau Gruber eyeing each girl as she passed. As Ella stepped by, Steiner leaned towards Frau Gruber and murmured something. She gave a nod and a grim stare. Ella hurried into the hall, eager to get away. She felt suddenly enclosed, trapped.

The front door was straight ahead of her and there was nothing to stop her running through it and speeding down the Pöstlingberg towards home. Except fear at what consequences such an action would cause. She had a clear objective now: to remain so-called friends with Tanja and get into Heinrich's office, to find the list again and warn others of the danger. She had passed the blacksmith's workshop a few days later to find it boarded up. She'd kept thinking about where he might have gone, what his future might be and if she had been right to intervene. Eventually, she'd decided it had been right to act. Unfortunately, she had been unable to locate the other person whose name she'd memorised.

Now she stared at the front door of the Bride School. It was not locked. Nor was there a bolted gate outside. And yet there might as well have been; she could not leave. Even now, people were watching her as she stared at the entrance, desperate for fresh air.

Lisl looked at her, concerned. And behind Lisl stood Heinrich Steiner and Frau Gruber, watching.

* * *

Shimmers of satin and blushes of lipstick. Signs that the strict protocol for the German housewife had been relaxed for the party. Ella had chosen a modest high-neck dress and now felt dowdy in comparison to the other wives. She looked round the sitting room in which Jayden had once played, read and chatted with his family. Their three-piece suite had been replaced with two new stylish sofas. What had happened to the old furniture? A swell of sadness engulfed her.

She and Max stood with his parents; his mother looked tense, her mouth pursed, her eyes darting from one guest to another. She was not used to socialising with the SS. Max's father took a glass of sparkling wine from a waitress and stood erect, chest puffed out, his gaze always flitting back to Steiner in his official black Nazi uniform. Both Max and his father stood out in their civilian clothes.

Herr Steiner tapped the side of his glass with a spoon and called for attention. Everyone fell silent. He welcomed his guests and talked about the success of the Anschluss and the bright future ahead.

'...and finally, I would like to announce our newest member of the National Socialist Party, Herr Max Giesler.'

Max stepped forward, his eyes alight.

Steiner raised his glass, and everyone did likewise. '*Prost!*'

'I'm delighted you have joined us,' Steiner said turning to Max. 'And of course, I have already met your charming fiancée.' He gave a snide smile.

Her stomach clenched at the memory of him catching her in the library: the waft of whisky on his breath. Now, he watched her as if considering whether to say more, but at that moment, Tanja, in a fitted green satin dress that emphasised her curves, glided up to them in practised, elegant steps and put a hand up to the pearl necklace at her throat.

'What a wonderful evening,' she said, laying a hand on his arm.

'Indeed. If you will excuse me? I must mingle.' He gave a curt nod to everyone and strode away.

Tanja made a small O with her mouth then, collecting herself, leaned towards Ella. 'What do you think of Lisl's fiancé? He's quite old, isn't he?'

Ella looked across the room. Lisl had shrunk back against the wall, her small frame contrasted by the broad, stocky frame of her fiancé; the receding hairline and sag of his jawline highlighted the years between them. He moved away and left her standing, awkward and alone.

'I'll join her,' said Ella, relieved for a reason to get away from Tanja.

Canapés and wine were served, and Tanja put records on the gramophone player: German singers only. No American music and definitely no swing, which was now banned.

Ella chatted with the brides and made polite conversation with the SS officers. Occasionally, she caught Max throwing a glance in her direction. Her social interactions were important to his standing.

She caught snippets of conversation as she circulated around the room.

'...and there will be more jobs now that Göring is building a giant steel works in Linz.'

'Then our Führer's deputy will be honouring our town more frequently. What will Göring be building in this new steel works?'

'An intriguing question...' For this conversation, voices were lowered and Ella heard no more.

She moved on.

A woman she did not know was gazing doe-eyed at an attractive officer. The woman's voice quivered. '...but what are we going to do about them. They're a plague!' Her face contorted with distaste.

The officer's jaw tightened. 'Do not fear. We will drive them out of our land. They have no place in our society, poisoning our blood. Rest assured, action will be taking place. Soon.'

The woman caught sight of Ella hovering. She could try to join the conversation, she thought, but her mouth was dry, and she found herself looking around for the waitress with her silver drinks tray. She took another glass of *Sekt*. The drink prickled her tongue as she took several sips to calm herself.

That woman's words had been spoken with such hate. The word *plague* was bandied around often now to describe the Jewish population. But what had the officer been referring to when he'd spoken of upcoming action? Hadn't the Jews suffered enough at the hands of the Third Reich? She thought of Jayden and his parents driven from this very house, now sharing a room in his uncle's apartment.

Glass in hand, she wandered back over to Max. Maybe he would learn about the planned upcoming action, whatever it was, this evening; she would sound him out over the weekend.

Yet on Sunday evening, when she was packing a few things ready for Bride School, she was none the wiser.

November blustered in with driving sleet and an icy wind that whipped across the leaden Danube. The girls shivered in the Villa Rosa, reaching for their warmest pullovers and wrapping themselves in thick woollen shawls. Every morning, they prepared their *Haferbrei*, stirring water into the oats and topping it with a teaspoon of the elderberry jam they'd made in autumn, after which, they reluctantly left the warm kitchen and filed into the chill of the austere sitting room for their lessons, their Führer's cold eyes on them from his portrait over the empty fireplace.

It was Monday morning, two weeks after the party, that their lesson in household economy was interrupted by Frau Gruber, her long body stooped over a trolley that she'd wheeled into the room. The bulky wireless sat on top.

'Excuse the interruption,' she said to the teacher. 'Something momentous has happened.'

Her eyes glinted with excitement, although her tone was grave. She plugged in the wireless and fiddled with the dials. Static and hiss spat into the room.

The brides shot each other looks, expectation on their faces.

Ella felt uneasy. This was not going to be good.

An announcer's voice burst at them.

'Good morning, ladies and gentlemen. This is the midday news on Monday, 7 November. A German diplomat, Herr Ernst vom Rath, has been shot at the embassy in Paris and is fighting for his life. The culprit is Jewish, seventeen-year-old Herschel Grynzpan who was arrested immediately. This heinous act has been condemned...'

There were gasps of shock and the shaking of heads.

'The Jews again,' said Tanja.

Nods of agreement followed.

'Something must be done,' said another girl.

When the broadcast was finished, Frau Gruber, her face solemn, her body rigid, faced the class.

'We will keep you informed of developments. Herr Ernst vom Rath comes from a noble family and is an eminent Party member. Let's pray he makes a swift recovery.'

But by the evening, the victim's condition had worsened and the radio broadcasts raged about the attack and the Jewish threat against the nation. Tension crackled in the dining room that night.

'What will happen now?' asked Lisl.

'There will be trouble for the Jews,' said Tanja as she stabbed her fork at her *Sauerkraut*.

'But this was one man. A boy, really,' Ella said. 'Why would he do such a thing?'

The evening news offered an explanation. The boy's parents, Germans of Polish descent, had like thousands of others been thrown out of their homes, and deported.

'An act of vicious revenge,' Frau Gruber had said.

An act of desperation and anger, thought Ella now as she ate the last of her *Bratkartoffeln*.

The thought was wrong, of course, but why did she feel more sympathy for the culprit than the victim?

That night, Ella could not fall asleep. The wind hurled rain against the windows; the glass rattled in the old frames. The Villa Rosa creaked and shifted in the storm; cold draughts seeping through every crack. When Ella finally fell into a fitful sleep, she dreamt about the shot diplomat; he contorted into the shot woman outside the café. A shadow ran down an alleyway, past a couple kissing, and stopped under a streetlamp, panting. His face was clear in the sallow glow. Jayden. He lifted the gun and pressed it to the side of his head. Ella screamed and emerged from her shallow sleep, her breath coming in short gasps. But when she saw her roommates still sleeping, she knew her scream had been silent.

The next morning, newspapers lay scattered throughout the house, headlines blazing about the Jew's attack on Germany: a monstrous act that the German people would not tolerate. Frau Gruber announced that the Führer had sent two of his personal doctors to attend to the wounded vom Rath in Paris. Heated discussions, angry accusations and talk about 'The Jewish Problem' continued amongst the brides all day. The fear in some of the girls' eyes made Ella want to weep. They were scared of Jews; the malicious propaganda had worked its poison.

By now, Ella no longer felt sympathy for the attacker, but anger at him for putting innocent Jews at further risk.

Ella passed another sleepless night and woke up with a knot of dread in the pit of her stomach. At breakfast, they were told that vom Rath was struggling heroically for his life. By five thirty, he was dead. A hush fell on the brides gathered in the cold, dimly lit sitting room.

Frau Gruber, pale and trembling, said, 'They will be made to pay.'

That evening, there was no babble of chatter as the brides worked on their embroidery, listening to the ranting of speakers on the wireless. Ella wanted to scream at the girls that they were blind to the truth; she wanted to fling her embroidery to the floor and rush from the room. But she bowed her head and continued to sew whilst the hateful words against Jews bellowed through the room, squeezing her heart.

Frau Fink entered and told Tanja that Herr Steiner was on the telephone. Tanja sprang up and left to take the call in the office. It was unusual for her to receive calls from her fiancé.

It was a short conversation, and Tanja returned with a slight frown.

'Is everything all right?' asked Ella.

'Yes. Heinrich just wanted to check that none of us had asked permission to go into town this evening; he said that it was safer to remain at the villa.'

'Safer?' asked Lisl.

Tanja shrugged. 'He said something about a special operation. I assured him we were all staying here, ears glued to the wireless.'

Ella's right temple throbbed; her mind whirred.

'I think I'll go up now. I have a headache.'

As she crossed the hallway, she saw Frau Gruber lock the front door and put the large brass key in her cardigan pocket. It was only seven o'clock. The door wasn't normally locked till late evening. She slipped into the downstairs cloakroom and waited until Frau Gruber's footsteps had passed by.

Something was definitely going on. Something bad. What had Steiner meant by a special operation?

When the coast was clear, she slipped out of the cloakroom, grabbed her coat from the row of hooks in the hallway and tiptoed into the empty dining room at the side of the house, praying no one would see her. She hurried to the large sash window and pushed against the old lock. It didn't budge. Using the palm of her hand, she put her whole weight behind her. Still nothing.

She held her breath. If she got caught now, there would be no way to explain herself.

Fighting the grip of panic, she clenched her teeth and exerted every ounce of strength she possessed. A satisfying click. She exhaled and jiggled the frame up and open, climbed over the sill and sped away through the garden.

Adrenaline spurred her on down the Pöstlingberg path. Tanja and Lisl would discover her empty bed and inform Frau Gruber. Ella had no idea how she would explain her absence, but that was unimportant right now. All she knew was that something bad would be happening in town that night. At Tanja's recent party, there had been talk of *upcoming action* regarding the Jewish community. And since the shooting of the German diplomat in Paris, everyone was expecting trouble for Jews. Frau Gruber's words, *they will be made to pay*, echoed in her head. Her stomach churned with fear for Jayden and his family. She had to warn them.

As she stumbled along in the near darkness, between the tramlines and houses, she was grateful for occasional pools of light that spilled out from windows facing her. The tramlines began to tremble beside her. The harsh clang of metal on metal signalled the oncoming tram. Ella stepped into the shadows and waited for it to screech past. There were few faces at the window; most people were already home for the evening.

She continued to race on down.

There was frost in the air and her breaths came as short puffs of white mist that danced in front of her. Breathing heavily, she made it to the bottom of the Pöstlingberg and from here, she ran towards the Donaubrücke, where the familiar silhouette of church spires and baroque buildings stared back at her.

She heard the first shouts as she ran off the bridge and headed towards the Hauptplatz.

A woman hurrying in her direction glanced at her and stopped. 'I'd turn around if I were you. There are gangs milling around, causing trouble, shouting abuse about Jews.'

The woman scuttled away and Ella, deciding to avoid the centre of town, slipped down a side street.

Ahead of her, a group of men, some older, some teenagers, had gathered. They carried sticks, bats and bricks. A young man hurled a brick at the window of a dilapidated cobbler's shop and the men cheered as the glass shattered across the street, their faces contorted in a mixture of rage and delight.

A window opened above the shop and a woman cried out. They looked up and raised the weapons in their hands, shouting abuse about Jews. Ella watched in horror as they started to smash against the entrance next to the shop. They were going to barge their way into the cobbler's home. The woman at the window screamed and disappeared from sight.

Terrified, Ella backed down the way she'd come and took another turning. She was dazed but her feet knew where she must go: to Jayden's uncle's house. She must warn them.

Shouts and cries rose in the air. Footsteps echoed down the cobbled streets. People rushed past: a woman clutching a baby, a man with a child bouncing on his back. Gangs of youths wielding weapons and yelling raced through the streets, smashing windows and battering doors. Glass and splintered wood flew. People screamed.

And then came the smell. Smoke. Ahead, a crowd was gathering. Some people stepped back, afraid. Others pointed, their voices excited.

Ella knew then. The dread that had lurked inside her since that morning sprang up, clutching her throat. She pushed her way through.

The synagogue was on fire. Fingers of orange flame grasping and ravaging. A man cradling books rushed out of the building, but he was thrown to the ground by waiting youths, his books knocked from his hands. Another man emerged, clutching something covered in embroidered cloth. He too was attacked, his possessions yanked away. The man lay on the ground, his arm outstretched, his cry a wounded, feral sound as a youth tore the cloth off to reveal rolls of sacred parchment.

'No! Not the Torah!' he pleaded. But the holy rolls were thrown on top of the books and set alight.

There was a cheer from the crowd.

Ella was sick to her core. Anger flared as hot as the blaze around her, and she rushed up to the fire brigade that just stood beside their fire wagon, watching the flames leap higher, their water hoses turned off.

'Why don't you do something?' she screamed. They ignored her. She ran up to an older fireman and shouted, 'There could be people trapped inside. Why don't you do something?' Her voice was hoarse.

'Orders,' he said. 'We act only if German property is threatened.'

Disbelief and confusion paralysed her.

Wisps of ash floated down on her hair; her throat was raw with smoke. The crowd turned away as the heat intensified. The fire crackled and the fall of masonry shook the ground. An orange glow filled the sky and black soot rained down.

Ella turned, and ran on, her shoes crunching over shards of glass.

The street where Jayden's uncle lived was away from the centre of town and when she reached the area, the streets were quiet, but she knew it wouldn't be long before the mobs were on their way. Would they break down the entrance door to the apartment like they had done to the cobbler's home? Jayden's family were well known in Linz.

The thought spurred her on despite her breath coming in short, painful rasps, her lungs choking from smoke.

Jayden had said the apartment was above the *Apotheke* on Fichtenweg. As she arrived, she saw the first-floor window was open and Jayden was leaning out. He spotted her below.

'Ella? What are you doing here? What's going on? We can smell smoke.'

'The synagogue is on fire! Hordes are on the rampage. You must get out of here!'

Jayden stared at her, transfixed, as if her words made no sense.

'Jayden!' she called. 'Let me in. Hurry!'

His head snapped back, and he disappeared inside.

* * *

Ella and Jayden led the family – his parents, uncle and aunt – down the back streets. They wore their hats tilted low over their faces to prevent recognition. The problem was they had to get back over the Donaubrücke into Urfahr without being stopped. When they first came into sight of the burning synagogue, Jayden halted on a corner and stared at the orange fireball above the town, but Ella tugged on his arm and they moved on.

When they neared the bridge, chaos greeted them. Marauding men shoved passers-by. Townsfolk, their arms full of shop goods, hurried home with their loot: shoes, clothes, pots, cutlery. People hurried over the bridge, away from the swirls of smoke and ash. Heads down, Ella, and Jayden's family sought to mingle with the crowds.

'Halt!' A broad-shouldered man in a shabby coat stood in their path; he gripped a shovel in both hands. 'What are you lot up to?' His voice was slurred as if he'd been drinking.

'We're on our way home to Urfahr,' said Ella.

'All of you?' The man cocked his head sideways and fixed narrow eyes on Jayden. 'I know you, don't I?' He lifted the shovel an inch.

'We just want to get to safety.' Jayden's mother spoke, pale and frail in her large coat. In a thin voice, she added, 'We're scared of the troublesome Jews. Thank goodness we have the likes of you.'

The man frowned, considering her words. Then he turned slowly from Jayden to his mother and grinned. 'We'll sort them out. Get on home.'

They sped past him and onto the bridge.

'God forgive me,' said Jayden's mother.

'He already has,' replied her husband. 'You just saved us all.'

On the other side of the river, Ella steered them towards the forest at the foot of the Pöstlingberg.

'You brought the torch, Jayden? We'll need it soon.'

He pulled the torch out of his coat pocket and held it ready. Darkness enveloped them as they took the narrow, sandy path, and when Jayden flicked the torch on, he kept the dim circle close to the ground.

Ella's father's workshop came into view and they all huddled in front of the door.

'I'll run home and get the key,' Ella said. 'Stay here.'

The dense blackness of the forest pressed in on them. The unseen trees moaned in the wind.

'I'll be quick,' she added as she began to run back in the direction they'd come.

Her leg muscles screaming, her breaths ragged, she raced home as quick as she could. How would she explain to her parents that she needed the key to the workshop? Possible answers swam around her head, out of grasp.

When she arrived home, her eyes and nose were running as she bent over, hands on her knees, gasping for breath. Her parents' alarmed faces greeted her.

'What on earth—' her mother started.

'The synagogue is on fire...'

In a rush, she told them everything. It was the simplest thing to do. She had no strength left for lies. To her surprise, there were no reprimands or cries of horror. Within moments, her father had the keys in his hand.

He reached for his hat behind the door.

'No,' said Marlene. 'You can't run as fast as me.' She placed a hand on the left side of his chest. 'You have to be careful.'

'I'll go,' panted Ella.

Marlene took her by the shoulders. 'You can hardly stand up. I don't want you in any more danger. I'm fresh, alert and on my way.'

She grabbed the keys, her coat and was soon out the door.

Ella fell into her father's waiting arms and as he stroked her head, she sobbed.

16

MARLENE

Marlene could hear the cries and the smash of glass. The mobs had now come out in Urfahr. She avoided the small high street and surrounding houses, slipping through shadows and out towards the forest. Only once did she turn to look across the Danube at the arch of flames that lit up the town. She couldn't believe the horror that was unfolding before her, and she couldn't forget the image of her daughter's face smeared in soot and tears.

As she arrived at the workshop, a light flashed in her eyes.

She called out in a hoarse whisper, 'It's me, Marlene, Ella's mother.'

The torch light was lowered. The group were huddled together, their pallid, terrified faces staring at her. She fought back the sadness that threatened to overwhelm her and tried to focus on the task ahead.

Once inside the hut, she lit the oil lamp, stoked the wood burner, set a pot of water on top and prepared coffee. The family gathered around the stove, holding their hands out to the heat.

'You can all stay here tonight till things calm down,' she said, looking around for things to make them more comfortable. She found a pile of dust sheets that Franz used to cover furniture with and a large picnic blanket that he used in the summer to take his lunch break outside. She laid these out on the floor for everyone to sit on and then began to serve steaming mugs of coffee.

Her heart ached at their forlorn faces, and she was uncertain what to do: stay with them overnight or venture home and return in the morning with food? If she didn't come back home, Franz and Ella would be beside themselves with worry.

In the end, she stayed; she simply could not leave them alone. She prayed there would be no thumps on the door. The hiding place under the wardrobe could hold only one person. Maybe Franz would have to create more hiding places in future.

No one could sleep. They sat in silence and at times, talked in hushed voices, drained from exhaustion and fear. Marlene studied Jayden as he comforted his mother, reassuring her that everything would be all right. It made her think of Freddie in Vienna and what might be happening there. There was a large Jewish population in the capital, many of whom studied with her son and were friends of his. She asked herself for the thousandth time how this could be happening. In a civilised country. Her country.

Dawn crawled in, heavy with a cold, steel-grey mist. They shuffled out of the hut, backs aching and legs stiff. They crossed the Donaubrücke and approached the town centre with hesitant footsteps. Marlene gasped and held her hand to her mouth. Fragments of glass, lumps of stone and broken bricks littered the streets. Shop windows gaped like open wounds, their belongings dangling and strewn. And everything was shrouded in a charcoal ash that mingled with the moist air, smearing the façades of the buildings.

A tired-looking woman in a coat and slippers was sweeping outside her front door, whilst a small boy kicked at the rubble. She shouted at him to go indoors. Two men were shovelling debris into a cart. They glanced up as Marlene, and Jayden's family passed but said nothing and returned to their task. Wary faces peered out of windows and doors and a few people were venturing out with brooms and shovels.

'I want to see,' said Jayden's father, gesturing to his left. He trudged ahead, his face grim.

They all followed him up Bethlehemstraße towards where the synagogue had stood. The stately white stone building was gone. A mass of twisted, blackened, smouldering ruins was all that remained. There was a huge, racking sob, and Jayden's father sank to his knees, his body shaking.

A short while later, they turned into the street where the family lived. Marlene held her breath, afraid of what they would find. The first thing they saw outside the apartment was a mattress on the ground, ripped open, its stuffing gouged out. A torn pillow lay on the pavement, its feathers strewn along the cobbled street.

Jayden pushed back what remained of the front door and they climbed the stairs, passing a slashed portrait on the wall.

The attack on the sitting room was savage: chairs, table, a grandfather clock, rugs, all slashed or smashed. Shards of the family's china lay embedded in the wooden floor. Drawers yanked opened, their contents of letters and photographs shredded and scattered around the room.

In the kitchen, the pillaged cupboards were empty. Packets of flour and sugar had been opened, the contents tipped on the floor, congealed from some kind of wetness. Marlene smelt it at once. Stale urine.

There wasn't a chair intact so they sat on the floor amongst the devastation, Jayden with tears in his eyes, his mother sobbing into her drawn-up knees.

When his father spoke, his voice cracked.

'Our home. Our refuge. This is the ultimate violation.'

* * *

Ravaged by everything she'd witnessed, Marlene returned home. Ella, in the hallway, her coat on and about to leave for Bride School, cried tears of relief when she saw her. Franz, dressed for work, rushed up and embraced her. 'Thank God, you're safe!'

'Thank you both for helping,' Ella said. 'Mutti, you were so brave.'

Marlene had the urge to confess about her role in the resistance. The intensity of the moment made her want to unite with her daughter, bond together in the fight against evil. But Franz gave her a warning look, and she bit her lip. She must keep Ella away from danger.

'What will you do about Bride School?' she asked instead. 'You'll be in terrible trouble for leaving last night. You may be expelled.'

'I'm going there now, and I'll think of something.' She looked from Marlene to Franz and sighed. 'I want you to know, I don't agree with what the Nazis are doing. I don't agree with Max's vision of the future.'

She paused, uncertain. She opened her mouth to say something but closed it again.

Marlene noticed the hesitation. What had her daughter wanted to say? What was she up to? What was the real reason Ella was at Bride School?

Silence.

'Ella, it's your life,' she said. 'But you must think carefully about marrying a man whose views you oppose. On the other hand, being a Nazi wife is probably the safest thing for you right now.'

Marlene hated her own words, although they were true. She wanted the best for her daughter: for her to be safe. And at the moment, that was to be on the side of Nazi supporters. But she also wished for her daughter to find her own moral compass and in her heart, she hoped that her time at the school would make her reject the NS ideology. After Ella's experiences last night, she felt her daughter was already on that path.

Ella gave her a reassuring hug. 'Now I must leave and face the fearsome Frau Gruber.'

The tick of the carriage clock was loud in the silence. Hostility pulsed from Frau Gruber in waves.

'I'm waiting.'

Ella sat across the desk from the grim-faced woman. Like all the rooms in the villa, her office was stark, the only adornment being the obligatory portrait of Adolf Hitler. And there was a lit fire in the fireplace.

Ella took a deep breath and sat up straight. 'I offer my upmost apologies for leaving the school yesterday evening without permission. You have every right to be angry, but please let me explain what led to my actions.'

A picture came into her head: Mutti putting her hand on Vati's chest and her quiet words: *you must be careful.*

'My father has been unwell lately; he has heart problems. Before I left home early on Monday, he had stabbing pains in his chest. My mother promised she would use a neighbour's phone to call me here on Wednesday to let me know how he is. We don't have our own phone.'

'Get to the point, please.'

'Yes, sorry. I didn't receive a message from you or Frau Fink that she'd called. I panicked, imagining all terrible scenarios: that he was ill, in hospital, or worse.'

'Surely, your mother would have telephoned us in such circumstances.'

'But she'd promised to call here, and she didn't. Mutti always keeps her word. I had an awful feeling something was wrong. I needed to see Vati for myself.'

'And you didn't consider asking me permission to visit home?'

'I heard that Herr Steiner had advised us not to go to town last night, and I thought you'd refuse my request. I was mad with worry, so I climbed out of the dining room window. I intended to come back here later in the evening, but there was all that trouble in town...'

Frau Gruber steepled her fingers and leaned her chin on them.

'And how is your father?' Her voice was devoid of emotion.

'He's well, thank you. My mother was unable to use the neighbour's telephone. It was out of order.'

The weight of the lie sat between them. Frau Gruber studied Ella for a long time, her expression pinched, hard.

The clock ticked loudly.

'I shall consult Herr Officer Steiner as to what is to be done with you. In the meantime, you may attend your lessons.'

Ella waited nervously all day to hear the verdict on her behaviour. It would be a shame to be expelled now when she'd just been able to act on some information she'd gleaned at the school. If she hadn't been able to lead Jayden's family to safety, would they have been attacked? The horrors of yesterday evening made her even more determined to find out more about Nazi plans and her contacts at the school were invaluable in achieving this.

Eventually, after dinner, she was called to Frau Gruber's office.

She would have extra cleaning duties and house arrest during the week for a month. The incident would be added to her report card. But she could stay. As she scrubbed the bathtub that night, she was already scheming about what form of resistance she could do next.

* * *

Cold, crisp and dry. The perfect November evening: as perfect as November could be. It was Ella's least favourite month. The colours of autumn had long faded, and the candlelight and warmth of a family Christmas a long way off.

It was the Friday evening after the horrific riots and attacks, and Ella dreaded what she would find when she ventured into town over the weekend.

As she reached the bottom of the Pöstlingberg, hurrying towards home, a figure emerged out of the shadows of the trees and hovered for a moment on the path in front of her. She glimpsed a dark, bulky coat and the shape of a fedora before the figure retreated back out of sight. Ella slowed her step. Was she being followed? She fought back her alarm. There were people around on both sides of the street. But then that didn't always help; she had witnessed that herself only a few nights ago: the way people turned away from trouble, not wanting to get involved.

She heard the crunch of feet over dead, brittle leaves in the trees beside her. The figure had doubled back. As she stepped away to cross to the other side of the road, she heard her name whispered urgently.

She turned to see who'd called her.

The figure tipped back his fedora. It was Jayden, half hidden in the woods that ran parallel to the pavement.

'Ella, please, I need to talk to you. But it's better for you if we're not seen together.'

She joined him and they slipped further into the darkness between the fir trees. Hardly able to see his face, she put a gloved hand on his thick coat sleeve.

'Are you and your family all right?'

Her words sounded stupid to her ears. Of course they were not all right. But he understood.

'Yes, thanks to you. That's why I'm here: to thank you. It was brave of you to cross town to warn us. I can't bear to think what would have happened if the mob had found us at home. There have been some brutal attacks, I'm afraid.'

'It's terrifying what people can do. I can't understand how the people of Linz can behave like this. The hate in their faces...' She trailed off, lost for words.

'I know. And the irony is that the propaganda minister, Göbbels, is blaming the Jewish community for starting the trouble and has issued us with a huge fine to pay for repairs. That night was a turning point. Thousands of Jewish men across Austria have been arrested and sent to Dachau concentration camp. Many of our friends realise they must get out of Austria somehow. Even my father is talking about applying for exit visas.'

'Is that possible?'

'At a price. I'm not sure we can pay the exorbitant amount that is being demanded.'

Ella fought back her tears and pressed closer to him.

'I'm so sorry,' she said.

'No need.' He shook his head. 'That's twice you saved me and I don't know why you did it.'

His words squeezed her heart and she reached for his lips. He stopped her, his hands clutching her shoulders.

'No, Ella. We're both engaged to be married.' He took a step back from her and shook his head. 'I can't understand you. You're together with a Nazi sympathiser and yet you help me. Why?'

She could hear the pain in his voice.

'It's not what you think,' she said.

Voices drifted from the street. A rustle of footsteps neared them. They stood rooted to the spot. They could just make out a man in front of a tree. Ella held her breath as the man fumbled with his coat and relieved himself against the tree trunk.

A voice yelled from the street, 'Get a move on, Reiner!'

Eventually, the man adjusted his clothing and sauntered away.

'It's not safe here,' Jayden said. 'We must part.'

'Wait. How did you know I was here?'

'On the night we stayed at your father's workshop, your mother told me about the Bride School and that you come back from the Pöstlingberg this time on a Friday. I had a long talk with your mother. She's a remarkable woman.'

'I know. I wish I was like her.'

'You are.' He gave her a soft push. 'Now, go.'

He turned and sped away, vanishing into the cold darkness.

Ella had the urge to run after him, to explain why she was mixing with the Nazi elite. For some reason, it was important what he thought of her.

All the way home, she relived their few moments hidden amongst the trees. And she imagined that he'd kissed her instead of pushing her away. Then she instantly reprimanded herself for such thoughts. He was engaged; what was she thinking? And so was she, but not for long. After she had completed Bride School, she would break it off.

As she climbed the stairs to their apartment, Ella could smell her mother's *Schmorbraten*. She sighed, the tension in her shoulders easing; just the smell of Mutti's cooking evoked a feeling of love, safety, home. Always when Ella returned home, Mutti would stop what she was doing, give her hands a quick wipe on her apron and hurry to greet her with a smile.

Today, the smile was weaker than usual. The events from the other night and its aftershocks had taken their toll.

Ella sat at the kitchen table and watched her mother slice fat carrots and chop parsley. She saw her in a different light now: not just a mother, or a housewife or a part-time factory worker. There was much more. A defiant, courageous woman who'd risked her life to get Jayden's family to safety without a moment of hesitation.

'We had no time to talk on Thursday morning,' said Ella. 'What happened after you left for Vati's workshop?'

Her mother checked the roast inside the oven before pulling up a chair.

Ella listened to how Mutti had made everyone as comfortable as possible and how they had talked and dozed through the night.

'I spoke a lot with Jayden,' she said. 'He's a good young man. He asked about you.'

A flush crept up Ella's throat. 'Oh?'

'It was awkward talking about Max. Jayden knows he's a Nazi supporter.' Ella couldn't meet her mother's eyes. She wanted more than anything to explain her motives, to gain her mother's respect and admiration. To be worthy, especially after Mutti's bravery the other night. But Mutti would be consumed with worry about Ella's safety, so she remained silent.

'What was it like in town the next day?' Ella asked.

When her mother told her of the devastation in Linz and the destruction of the homes, she was overcome with despair. There had been no time during her brief meeting with Jayden for him to describe the wreckage of his uncle's home.

She put her head in her hands and mumbled, 'Why are Austrians behaving like this?'

'Half the population are Nazis; the other half are afraid,' Mutti said, her voice strained. 'We don't always do what our conscience tells us we should when we fear the consequences.' Ella looked up and saw her mother gaze into the air, her expression troubled. They fell silent for a few moments before Mutti asked, 'Are you in trouble at the school?'

'I'm definitely in Frau Gruber's bad books,' said Ella with a wry smile. 'I thought I'd be expelled. But for some reason, Herr Steiner has given me a second chance.'

'I think we both need a drink,' said Mutti as she hoisted herself up from the table. She opened a cupboard and retrieved two small glasses and a bottle of apple *Schnapps*. She poured them both a good measure and they clinked glasses.

'*Prost*,' they said in unison.

The phone rang.

'I'll go,' said Ella, remembering the lie to Frau Gruber that they didn't have a phone.

It was Freddie.

He told her about the violence and destruction in Vienna, and how the city's streets were a sea of shattered glass.

'It seems the same thing happened all across Austria,' said Ella. 'I was here that night—'

She stopped herself, distracted by her mother, who was waving her hand and putting a finger to her lips. She cupped an ear and pointed to the phone. Ella gave a nod.

'...we were all at home playing cards.'

Ella yearned to talk about what she and Mutti had experienced but who knew if the operator was listening in, eager to report what she had heard? Collaborators were increasingly betraying their fellow citizens for favours from the Nazis.

'Many of my fellow students have been arrested.' Freddie spoke in a sombre voice. 'The whole of Vienna is in turmoil. I'm looking forward to being home for Christmas.'

Later at dinner, Mutti complained about the meat. 'It's tough. Food is expensive enough and when I treat us all to a roast, the butcher sells me this! I'm sorry.' She sounded close to tears.

Ella watched her father reach across the table and put his hand on hers. 'It's delicious, Marlene. You're a wonderful cook.'

He gave her a soft smile. A loving smile. Marlene's eyes brimmed with tears; her mother used to rarely cry, but recently, she'd become more emotional.

They spoke little as they ate, chewing on the meat and giving appreciative nods. Ella served dessert: baked apples with vanilla sauce. When conversation finally started up again, inevitably, it was about Hitler.

'He'll take our country into war,' said Vati.

'I thought Hitler was offering the people peace and prosperity. He was going to make Germany great again,' said Ella, aware she was reciting what they were taught at Bride School. But she wanted to hear Vati's point of view.

'Exactly. His vision of making Germany great again is invading other countries. He's got Sudetenland back from Czechoslovakia now but that won't appease him. He's bound to have his eyes on Poland too. How long will the world just sit and watch?'

'If there is war, will our men be called to fight for the Wehrmacht? Will Freddie be forced to join the army?'

The question hung in the air. Her mother let out a sob and tears ran down her cheeks.

* * *

On Saturday evening, Ella and Max were invited for drinks at Steiner's house, which Ella still thought of as Jayden's home. When Steiner proffered her a plum *Schnapps*, she declined. This time, she would keep a clear head.

'How is your father now? I heard from Frau Gruber that he was so unwell that you absconded from the school to see him,' Steiner asked, his expression one of fake concern.

'Better now, thanks, Herr Steiner.'

'Please. Call me Heinrich. I understand your father is a cabinet maker.' At this, he gestured to the gilt drinks trolley on the side of the room, tightly packed with decanters and bottles of liqueur. 'Not only is the thing an inadequate size; it's ugly too. I thought I might commission him to make a cabinet for me: fine wood, glass doors. That sort of thing.'

Ella quelled a flash of anger at his assessment of Jayden's family's belongings, calling the drinks trolley ugly.

'I can ask him for you, Heinrich.'

His name caught in her throat and she recalled how he'd loomed over her in the library.

'You must tell me where his workshop is. I could come by and have a look at his work.'

A flutter of panic. Images of Jayden's terrified family shivering outside the hut. Why this sudden interest in her father's furniture making?

Careful, Ella.

'I shall ask my father to contact you.'

'What are you two conspiring?' Tanja sidled up and linked her arm into Heinrich's.

'Nothing, my dear.' He patted her arm.

Tanja's outfit this evening was markedly different to what she'd worn at the last party. Today, she wore a traditional Tyrolean wool jacket and full, long skirt. Her face bore a trace of powder, but no lipstick, no rouge. Her hair was plaited around her head. A true Reich wife.

When Heinrich excused himself, Tanja leaned towards Ella.

'He's very busy at the moment. There's so much to do after the riots in Linz. The Jews started it, you know?'

'Really? I thought they were the victims.'

'They only got what they deserved. Anyway, Heinrich explained it all to me. The uprising wasn't organised by the authorities. It was caused by ordinary civilians standing up against the Jewish threat.'

Ella had recognised faces of the SA and the Hitler Youth dressed in civilian clothes.

'I'm not sure we should believe everything we hear, Tanja.'

Tanja narrowed her eyes. 'Are you saying that Heinrich is a liar?'

'Of course not. I'm just saying there are always two sides of the story.'

'Not where Jews are concerned.' She waved a dismissive hand as if suddenly bored with the conversation. 'What do you think of my outfit this evening?' she said, brushing some non-existent fluff from her jacket. 'Makes me look dowdy, don't you think?'

'Not dowdy, but not your usual style.'

'Our Führer has instructed women to wear traditional clothes of the Reich. Designs from foreign designers are now *verboten*. Modest, wholesome and made in Germany is the fashion of the future.' Glancing over at Heinrich, she whispered, 'He doesn't want me to wear lipstick in public any more. But in private it is a different matter.'

She gave Ella a wink.

Ella did not possess designer clothes and seldom wore lipstick so was not directly affected by these regulations, but she found the increasing number of rules being imposed on women alarming. And even more alarming was the euphoria with which hordes of women were throwing themselves into their new role.

* * *

They left just before midnight. It began to snow, the flakes whipped in frantic swirls in the gusty wind. Ella shivered and raised her collar. The talk this evening had depressed her and she felt weary.

Max's car was parked just opposite and as they crossed, she noticed a figure under a nearby tree. She recognised the large coat on the slim frame, and that fedora tilted forwards.

Jayden.

Watching.

Her heart jolted.

He stood a moment looking in their direction, then strode off down the road.

Ella was quiet as Max drove her home. What had Jayden been doing there? He couldn't have known she would be socialising in his former house. He must have just felt the need to look at his old home, wallow in childhood memories, maybe even find out who lived there now. And who had he seen? Her. The person who had helped his family was now entertaining herself in his stolen home. A bitter betrayal – he must hate her.

She suppressed a sob.

'Is everything all right?' asked Max. 'You are not yourself. You hardly said a word this evening. I really think you could make more effort when we mix with such influential people, especially Steiner. He is friends with Göring, Hitler's deputy. We may well be introduced to the Führer himself at some point.'

'Sorry. I'm rather tired from school.'

'How on earth can you be tired from a bit of embroidery?'

She clenched her teeth. 'It's much more than a bit of embroidery, Max.'

'Oh, come on Ella. Pull yourself together. What will you be like when you have to run our household and care for our children?'

She wanted to scream that she had no intention of running a household with him. And the thought of bearing his children made her shudder.

'You're right, Max. I'll make more of an effort in future.' Anything to keep him quiet.

He grunted and a few moments later, they pulled up outside her home. Ella was relieved at his perfunctory kiss on her cheek and their short goodbye. She wasn't in the mood for his tight lips on hers.

Later in her room, she pulled on her nightdress and stared through the thin layer of frost on the window. The ever-present basilica atop the Pöstlingberg was her anchor. Each night, as she gazed up at it, it was her quiet time, when she could think.

Sadness weighed down on her as she closed the curtains and climbed into bed and despair took hold. Jayden had seen her leaving his home, clearly after a social event with her fascist fiancé. He must hate her despite her attempts to help. She would feel the same in his position. She hoped one day she would be able to tell Jayden the truth of why she was with Max.

* * *

Sunday was *Kaffee und Kuchen* day and Max was very particular about this ritual of coffee and cake with his parents every weekend. When they arrived, Ella perched on the sofa next to Max. His father stood beside his usual armchair and frowned.

'Dagmar,' he called to his wife, who was putting the final touches to the table.

'Yes, dear,' she said, trotting over.

'What's this?' He pointed to a crimson, velvet cushion arranged in his armchair, a look of disgust on his face.

'It's a new cushion I bought. I found the colour rather attractive.'

'Well, I for one don't find it attractive, and I certainly don't want it, or any cushion for that matter, on my chair.'

He plucked up the offending article and shoved it hard against her chest. She flushed the colour of the cushion and took it from him.

'Cushions give such a homely feel to a room, I always think,' said Ella, brightly.

She received a withering look from Herr Giesler whilst his wife scuttled off to the kitchen.

After a few words of stilted conversation, they sat down at the table where an impressive gateau awaited them. As they ate, Ella remarked it was delicious and Herr Giesler complained the sponge was too dry. His wife made a humble apology at this, which made Ella wince.

As she had expected, Herr Giesler quizzed her on her progress at the Reich Bride School. She did her best to give the answers he wanted to hear, pretending to be enthusiastic. She surprised herself how good she was becoming at playing her role. Seemingly satisfied, he then turned to the others and changed the conversation.

'There is some exciting news for Linz's future,' said Herr Giesler as he shoved the last piece of uneaten cake to the edge of his plate. 'Reichsminister Hermann Göring is arriving in Linz tomorrow to oversee the founding of his huge steel works. It will bring jobs and prosperity to the town.'

Max looked impressed and nodded. 'It's a real honour to have Hitler's deputy visiting.'

'Indeed. He's also commander of the Luftwaffe and is building a massive air force.'

Ella paid close attention. Was this a sign of the impending war her father had spoken of?

'I've heard rumours that Göring has a brother who is not such a shining example for the Reich,' said Max.

'Ah, yes. Albert Göring. He opposes the NS Party: such an embarrassment to his family.'

'Is it true that he's in Vienna helping political opponents and Jews obtain exit visas to flee?' Max seemed eager to have this opportunity to engage with his father.

Herr Giesler frowned and glanced around the table. 'This is not a suitable topic of conversation in the present company, Maximilian.' His tone had turned terse.

'Apologies, Vater.' Max's shoulders sank and he stared into his empty coffee cup.

* * *

In the car on the way home, Ella asked Max what more he knew about Albert Göring in Vienna, but he had nothing to add. He remained sullen as he drove. It was his typical mood after visiting his father. Ella decided she would ask Tanja if she knew anything.

Her mind whirled; she could visit Freddie in Vienna and maybe he could help her locate Albert Göring. She could try to obtain visas for Jayden and his family, get them to safety. She smiled as she gave Max a kiss on the cheek goodnight. Visiting his parents that afternoon had provided some useful information. She left the car fired with a new surge of adrenaline and sense of purpose.

* * *

Hedy's father was a gentle bear of a man with a bushy beard and crinkly eyes. He spread his arms and hugged his younger daughter.

'Do as your big sister tells you and don't wander off and get lost in the crowds.'

'No, Papa.' Trudy looked up at Hedy and grinned.

Ella stood in the hallway with Hedy and Trudy, all three of them wrapped up in their winter coats saying goodbye to Hedy's father.

He rummaged in his trouser pocket and drew out a few coins. 'Buy yourself some *Lebkuchen*.' He placed a coin in Trudy's mittened hand and then gave a schilling to Hedy. 'You treat Ella and yourself too.'

Ella was very fond of Hedy's father, who had always treated her as family. She smiled at him. 'Don't worry, we'll take good care of Trudy.'

Soft, fat snowflakes fell as Ella, Hedy and Trudy crossed the Donaubrücke and headed for the *Christkindlmarkt*. Ella felt that rush of delight she always experienced when she saw the Christmas market for the first time each year. The grand baroque buildings of the Hauptplatz framed the fairy-tale scene of chalet-style huts draped with fairy lights. The snow drifted onto branches of fir trees that were dotted amongst the stalls.

The square was dominated by a huge Christmas tree that stood near the marble Trinity column. Hand-painted glass baubles hung from the tree's branches, their festive designs illuminated by twinkling lights.

Hedy held Trudy's hand as the three of them wound their way through the bustling crowd. Ella breathed in the familiar Christmas market smells: the savoury richness of grilled *Bratwurst* wrestling with the sweet aromas from bakery stands with their waft of cinnamon. The scent of rum and mulled wine spices emanated from the *Glühwein* kiosk.

Hedy and Trudy were drawn to the stand selling honey-roasted almonds, whilst Ella studied the adjacent kiosk. Large hearts made from gingerbread, *Lebkuchen*, hung from long colourful ribbons. Each heart was decorated with a message in piped icing sugar. One in particular caught her eye:

Beste Freundin

Without hesitation, she bought it and, holding it behind her back, joined the others who had just received their large paper cone of honey-roasted almonds.

Hedy held out her arm. 'Taste these,' she offered 'They're the best in the market.'

'First, I have something for you.' Ella presented Hedy with the heart. 'For my best friend.'

Hedy studied the *Lebkuchen* heart in her hands and gave Ella a fierce hug. She whispered in her ear, '*Ich habe dich lieb.*'

As was the custom, Hedy hung the heart around her neck.

'I'll never eat it,' she said. 'I'll keep it forever.'

The snow was falling faster now, cloaking the roofs of the chalet stalls, tipping the fir trees white, dusting powdered sugar on people's hats and scarves. Ella placed her hands on Trudy's narrow shoulders.

'Look straight upwards,' she said.

They both craned their necks to the sky. Above, a whirlwind of flakes flew down at them, circling them, enticing the girls to spin around until they too were white snow crystals swirling in the cold air. Ella became dizzy and stood still, momentarily blinded. Trudy was holding out her arms, still spinning, head tilted back, laughing. She swayed and Ella steadied her, breaking the spell. Trudy beamed, her face damp, snowflakes on her eyelashes.

'That was wonderful, like in a fairy tale where I was the snow princess.'

As they strolled through the market admiring the hand-carved nativity scenes, Ella's heart lifted with joy. She loved the sounds of the market: a children's choir singing carols, the ringing of bells and the excited chatter of children. She ignored the soldier uniforms that passed her by and whenever she saw military vehicles, she turned her head, determined to retain that special sense of Christmas.

They stopped at a *Glühwein* stand and drank hot mulled wine whilst Trudy had a fruit punch. Finally, they made their way home, the Danube thundering beneath the bridge. Away from the throngs of the market, the girls were freezing. The icy wind whipped at their faces and the snow had turned from soft flakes to a frenzy of stinging pinpricks. By the time they reached Hedy's house, a storm was gathering.

There were no lights on in the house and no smell of an evening meal being prepared. They stomped the snow off their boots outside the front door and deposited them on the shoe rack in the hallway.

'Mutti?' called Hedy.

The sitting room door opened and Hedy's neighbour, Maria, appeared. Her face was ashen. She looked from Trudy to Hedy, her eyes swollen and red.

'What's the matter?' asked Hedy, her voice full of panic. 'Where's Mutti?'

'She's lying on the sofa in the sitting room. The doctor gave her a sleeping draught. I'm afraid something terrible has happened.'

Ella reached out for Hedy's hand and clutched it tight. She held her breath, waiting for Maria to explain.

'There's been an accident,' Maria stammered. 'Your father decided to join you at the Christmas market. As he was crossing the road, he was hit by a military truck. I'm so sorry,' she choked. 'There was nothing that could be done.'

18

MARLENE

Excited chatter filled the cloakroom as the factory workers pulled on hats and coats. Marlene and her colleague, Verena, hurried out of the building for their hour-long lunch break. Just enough time to get to the site of Hermann Göring's new steel works and witness the arrival of the Reichsminister himself.

'He's very rich and cultured, apparently,' said Verena, her nose red from the cold. 'He loves expensive cars and even has a yacht! I've heard his villa is full of valuable paintings.'

'He does seem to be acquiring an impressive art collection,' agreed Marlene. 'One has to wonder where all these treasures come from.'

'What do you mean?'

Nazi loot and plunder – but she wasn't going to say as much to Verena.

Careful, Marlene. Verena is an ardent NS supporter.

'I just mean he must have some good connections, that's all.'

The air was cold and crisp. An insipid sun hung low in the winter sky. Marlene remained silent as Verena chatted on about Göring: how he changed his clothes six times a day and kept wild animals in his garden. And Marlene thought about how he'd initiated the Gestapo and ordered Jews to pay millions of Reichsmark for damage caused in the recent riots.

When they arrived at the site, a crowd had already gathered. Marlene heard eager talk of jobs, a better economy, industry coming to Linz. There was no mention of what exactly would be produced in the proposed factory. No mention of war. People were on a wave of elation that made them blind.

Marlene fought back a surge of despair.

As the motorcade arrived, the chants of '*Sieg Heil*' filled the air. Göring stepped out of the car and climbed up the few steps to a platform that had been assembled for his arrival. He was a heavy man, his military jacket stretched tightly across his chest. He smiled and joked with the crowd, but Marlene was not convinced by his jovial bluster. The man was, after all, Hitler's deputy, a position not attained by an amiable smile alone.

Göring was also commander of the German air force, so it was no surprise that the Luftwaffe appeared overhead to honour his visit to Linz. As the drone of the planes filled the air, Marlene looked up at the ominous sight, a chill running down her spine. How long before such planes began to unleash their bombs on neighbouring countries? Franz was right. They were heading for war.

When Marlene left work that day, she stopped at a road junction, pondering. Franz would be at his workshop later than usual, finishing a commode. She could turn right and head home where she would bake some Christmas biscuits. Or she could continue forwards, following the road straight to Otto's house. He had no wife to bake him biscuits any more; the fascists had wrenched her from his life.

Marlene walked straight ahead, memories of him as a young man coursing through her mind.

An hour later, Marlene was laughing at Otto, who had flour on his cheeks and dough stuck to his fingers. She had found various packets of baking ingredients in his kitchen and was showing him how to make *Vanillekipferl* and *Spritzgebäck*.

'My wife never allowed me in the kitchen,' he said, a gentle smile in his voice.

'I'm not surprised.'

Otto turned to her. 'Have you ever thought how things might have turned out differently?'

She brushed the flour from his cheek. 'Don't do this, Otto.'

'No, you're right,' he said, returning to brushing egg yolk on the dough. 'Don't get me wrong. We were happily married; we loved each other. But even so, I thought of you often. Sometimes in ways I shouldn't have.'

Marlene didn't reply, beginning to wash the mixing bowl instead. Otto continued, his tone wistful.

'We had some fun, didn't we? Queuing up for cheap tickets at the Landestheater with all those academics. We often saw *him* there.'

Marlene remained silent as she scrubbed dough from the biscuit cutters.

'It's hard to believe that intense, moody young man has risen to such terrifying power. He didn't have many friends, really; he was mostly with Kubizek.' Otto leaned against the worktop, a faraway look in his eyes as he reminisced.

The oven now hot, Marlene slid in the baking tray and turned the dial on the plastic timer: twelve minutes. She wished Otto would change the subject, but he carried on.

'I remember Kubizek saying our young Adolf got quite morose sometimes over an unrequited love. I've forgotten her name.'

Stefanie was her name. Marlene remembered it well, but she said nothing as her palms began to sweat. A hot flush soared up through her body, making her feel faint.

'I need to sit down,' she said, stumbling into the sitting room and falling into an armchair.

Concerned, Otto followed her, asking her what was wrong.

She fanned herself with her hand. 'I'm fine. It was hot in the kitchen, that's all.'

He brought her a glass of water, sat opposite and began to talk about his daughter who'd married and now lived in Innsbruck. Marlene was grateful for the change in conversation.

* * *

Later, they ate the freshly baked biscuits with a glass of *Eierlikör*. Marlene told him the sad news about Hedy's father; the funeral was to be in a few days. They then talked about the aftermath of the violence that terrible night in Linz.

'Everyone is afraid now,' Marlene said sadly. 'Of the police, the SS, the Gestapo. Afraid of their neighbours, their friends. We're living amongst collaborators and spies. Betrayal and death are always just a breath away.'

Otto looked at her with concern. 'I hope you're not involved in anything you shouldn't be. I know you, Marlene.'

'Don't worry. I'm involved only in what I should be.'

When she left, she kissed his cheek on the exact same spot where she had brushed away the flour. Had she let her kiss linger a fraction too long?

In bed that night, when Franz reached out for her, she sighed inwardly. It had been many months since they had made love, and that suited Marlene. She hadn't desired or missed sex; she always felt exhausted and down. Her body had become dry, brittle and unattractive; flesh sagged, and wrinkles deepened. She loved Franz, but physically? She didn't know any more. Best to get it over with and then she would have peace for a while.

She hoisted up her nightdress and waited for him to climb on top. But he didn't.

He stroked the side of her face and her neck slowly. Then he sat up and massaged her tense shoulders for a long time.

'That's nice,' she murmured, closing her eyes.

'Just relax,' he whispered.

He continued along her arms, alternating between firm massage and long tender strokes down to the palms of her hands. When he moved to her pelvis and upper thighs, she tensed. But he pulled the hem of her nightdress back down and stroked her thighs through the fabric. Her breathing slowed as her chest expanded. His fingers swept down her legs to her ankles. She began to drift on the edge of sleep. Her last conscious thought was the bliss of having the soles of her feet massaged.

She woke early after the best night's sleep she'd had for a long time. Turning on her side, she watched Franz sleeping and thought about how he'd caressed her last night. She dwelled on each moment until her body ached for his touch again. He stirred, turned on his back and opened his eyes. She kissed him on the cheek and started to stroke his chest. 'Good morning,' she said. 'I enjoyed my massage last night. I thought I'd return the favour.' Her hand travelled down his body. He moaned softly, responding to her touch.

She pulled off her nightdress and, with an urgency she had not felt for a long time, she straddled over him.

'This is a nice surprise,' he said, his voice thick with sleep.

'I want you,' she said, simply.

'You don't know how happy that makes me.'

* * *

On her way to work, Marlene was happily thinking about sex with Franz, pleased that they had grown close again, when she saw three boys building a snowman. She recognised the smaller boy; in the summer he had given her that note instructing her to meet her contact down by the docks. Her heart began to race. She'd been wondering when she would be contacted again.

She slowed her stride and looked at him expectantly. He ran up to her and held out his worn cap.

'Can you spare a pfennig, miss?'

There was a folded note in the cap. Marlene popped a couple of coins inside and, in the same movement, scooped up the note, the now familiar mix of excitement and fear coursing through her.

When she arrived at work, she went straight to a lavatory cubicle and bolted the door. She read the note; she was to meet her contact later that day at the train station. After tearing the note into tiny pieces, she threw it into the toilet bowl. After pulling the chain of the cistern above her, the water swirled. But some pieces remained floating on top.

Blast!

Water pipes groaned. She waited for the overhead cistern to fill with water, then yanked the chain again. Some of the pieces were sucked away, but still, a few floated to the surface. She began to sweat. It was silly to panic; she would try once more and if that didn't clear it all, she would just fish the remaining pieces out, put them in her pocket and dispose of them later.

The water cistern took ages to fill this time. Anxiety triggered one hot flush after another until Marlene felt quite sick. Finally, the noise of running water stopped and she pulled the chain for the third time. Holding her breath, she watched as the stubborn papers swirled around and sighed with relief when at last the remnants disappeared from sight.

When she opened the cubicle door, she looked straight into the puzzled face of Verena.

'What on earth were you doing in there? You were using enough water to empty the Danube!'

Marlene's face flushed with guilt. 'I'm not too well this morning.'

Verena raised her hands. 'Spare me the details. I'll use one of the other cubicles.'

* * *

Throughout the evening meal, Marlene worried what Franz's reaction would be. She waited until he'd poured himself a *Schnapps* and retired to his armchair.

'They made contact again,' she said, taking a seat opposite him on the sofa. 'Someone needs help.'

Franz frowned. 'When did this happen?'

'I received the message this morning and met the contact after work: the same woman as last time. A young man is in trouble. He had too much to drink and made some stupid remarks about some friends planning a coup against Hitler. What he said was all nonsense and it was at a private party, but someone reported him and he's wanted for treason.'

'Oh, God. He'll get the death penalty.'

'He's only nineteen.'

'Then we must help. But I'm worried, Marlene. The authorities are more vigilant now since the riots. The Gestapo seem to be on every street corner. Freddie and Ella will be home soon for Christmas, and we don't want to endanger them by association. When can we expect the boy and how long will he be staying?'

Marlene shook her head. 'I don't know yet. I'm to wait for further instructions.'

'All right,' he said, his eyes turning soft. 'You're an admirable woman, *Schatz*. I'm proud to have you as my wife.'

'Are you?' she asked. 'I'm just a tired, aged woman past her prime.'

'That's not the woman I found in my bed this morning.' He rose and took her by the hand. 'Let's have an early night.'

She smiled. 'Let's make it a late night.'

He chuckled, his eyes gleaming. It warmed her heart.

19

ELLA

The air in the house shivered with grief. Hedy's face was porcelain against her black dress; she sat on the sofa with her mother and Trudy. Ella took a cup of coffee from the sideboard and pulled up a chair to sit beside them. The mourners talked in hushed voices, shook their heads and shot sorrowful glances at the bereaved. It was unreal that they had just witnessed the coffin with Hedy's father being lowered into the frigid ground; cemetery workers had used jackhammers to hew the hole through the ice and snow.

Shock sat deep in Ella. Unable to think of anything to say, she held Hedy's fragile hand and choked back her own tears. Her parents stood across the room, and for the first time, she imagined what it would be like if she lost one of them. Pain speared her chest.

Snippets of conversation drifted around the room.

'...at least they are addressing the Jewish problem...'

Ella stiffened. Hedy's family friends didn't know about their heritage. What would happen if people found out? Especially now the family no longer had the protection of a Catholic husband or father. Memories flashed through Ella's head. Her and Hedy rummaging around the attic. The soft feel of the velvet cloth between her fingers; the gleam of the silver as they polished the menorah back to life; Hedy's mother's urgent confession and her trembling hands as she hid the precious candelabra.

Now, as Ella gazed up at the ceiling, she had a strange sensation: as if the menorah was whispering its secrets on waves of frosted air. She shuddered. It was vital she kept herself alert to any gossip: any possible threat to Hedy and her family. She would try to gauge any changing Nazi policy to mixed marriages. At first, they had been tolerated but things were changing day to day.

She squeezed Hedy's hand tighter. Her best friend turned to look at her with exhausted, glazed eyes. Ella felt the force of fierce love and the need to protect her at all costs.

* * *

Each day, the front room of the Villa Rosa grew colder. Ella could see her wisps of breath as she eyed the pinboard that had been erected on one side of the room. Today's lesson was racial hygiene and Frau Gruber taught this lesson herself. She stood in front of the empty fireplace, stock still, hands clasped before her, sharp grey eyes observing the girls who were mingling in front of the pinboard.

They had been asked to study various pictures. Ella winced as she looked at the drawings: grotesque caricatures, with labels such as *Jew*, *African*, *Gypsy*. Red lines highlighted various facial features, noted with a derogatory comment. In the centre of the board was a photograph with the title: *Aryan*. The picture depicted an athletic young man and woman. Both had blond hair and blue eyes. It seemed a sick irony that Hitler himself did not resemble this image.

The drawing of the so-called Jewish man bore no resemblance

to anyone that Ella knew. Not to Jayden, his father or his uncle. Nor to the man fleeing the burning synagogue with the holy parchments. If it hadn't been so evil, it would have been laughable. The depictions of the others with non-German ancestry were equally deplorable.

'Frightening, isn't it?' said Tanja as she sidled up, indicating the drawings.

'Terrifying,' said Ella, deliberately misinterpreting Tanja's words. The propaganda, the prejudice, all of it was terrifying.

'Jews are so malevolent looking.' Tanja gave an artificial shudder.

'You've shopped at what was previously the Pisinger store?' Ella asked, struggling to keep her tone even.

'Of course, who hasn't?'

'Did you find the family malevolent? Did they resemble these pictures in any way?' Tanja said nothing and gave a shrug.

'I always found them polite and friendly.' Ella faked a puzzled tone, her words a question. 'They greeted their customers with smiles and enquiries about their families.'

'They must be an exception then,' said Tanja curtly.

Ella knew she should let the matter drop. But somehow, she couldn't.

'Do you know any other Jewish families? Ones that should be feared?'

Tanja threw her a look of frustration and was just about to speak when Frau Gruber clapped her hands together, a sign for the girls to return to their seats.

Frau Gruber continued her sermon: the importance of pure Aryan blood to ensure the future of a German master race. The removal of deviant and inferior genes was crucial...

Ella switched off from listening; this hateful talk had been propagated for some time now. It sickened her. When, years ago, she had first heard the prejudice and saw the graffiti, she had felt a bit uncomfortable but not really touched by it. So much had been going on in her teenage years that fascist views had been peripheral to her. She'd never been very politically minded.

But now it was personal. Every hateful word was a punch in her gut. An attack on Jayden: someone she cared about. She was desperate to explain to him why he'd seen her leaving his family home. But what would she say? Was there something she could say or do to ease his pain?

* * *

There was only one thought on Ella's mind as she descended down the Pöstlingberg that Friday evening: to see Jayden. All the anti-Semitism that she had experienced during the week had resulted in a reverse effect: her feelings for him were heightened, and anger at the injustice was a fire in her soul. She harboured the hope that maybe he would be waiting for her again, hidden amongst the trees.

When she came to the spot where he'd appeared last week, she halted and looked around. He wasn't there. She stepped into the dark shadows of the fir trees, the scent of pine sharp in the clear, cold air. The soles of her boots crunched over the hard, frosted ground. Cones cracked beneath her feet. Tonight, the sky was clear and the nearly full moon was rising, so she was able to make out her surroundings. But she saw only spruce branches drooping from the weight of the snow. No sign of Jayden. She felt hollow with disappointment.

Her route took her along the river bank and from Urfahr, she could see the centre of Linz; snow cloaked church domes, emanating a deceptive peacefulness. She checked her watch. Mutti wouldn't be expecting her for another half an hour; there would be just enough time to walk into town before dinner.

As she hurried across the Donaubrücke, she had to stop herself from running. The last thing she wanted was to draw attention to herself. The Wehrmacht soldiers marched in twos back and forth across the bridge, always watching, always wary. Since the riots, the army and the police had increased their presence in the town. A checkpoint had been set up at the end of the bridge where spot checks were made on people entering the town centre. But it was a busy Friday evening, and Ella was waved through.

Snow softened the town, hiding remaining glass or rubble, blanketing ash-stained buildings. An artificial cleansing. Ella steered clear of the burnt remains of the synagogue and arrived in front of the door of Jayden's uncle's home. Or what remained of it. Planks of wood had been nailed together and an iron bolt ran across the front. The doorbell had been ripped from the wall so she banged on the makeshift door with her fist.

The window above opened. Jayden's uncle called out, his voice fearful.

'It's just me. Ella. I've come to see Jayden.'

'Oh, Ella. I'll send him down to open up.'

She watched the closed door, her pulse racing.

His light, quick footsteps; such a contrast to the sound of marching boots that had become the continuous accompaniment of everyday life. She heard him lift a bolt on the inside, and the door creaked open, then jammed. A lift and a jerk. Jayden pulled it open.

He greeted her without a smile and waited for her to speak.

'Can we talk? I must explain some things to you.'

'Like how much fun you have partying in my former home?'

'Please. It's not what it seems.' She glanced up and down the street. 'Can I come in? Just for five minutes.'

He stood back and she entered the hallway.

'Everyone is in the apartment,' he said. 'There's no privacy there.'

'Let's just sit here on the stairs.'

They sat side by side on the narrow, wooden staircase under a naked lightbulb that hung from the ceiling. The original glass shade had been shattered. Jayden looked tired in the sallow light.

He shook his head. 'I'm so confused about you, Ella. One moment, you're saving me from harm, the next you are gallivanting around my family home with your Nazi boyfriend. You're tearing me apart.'

The emotion and sadness in his voice brought tears to her eyes.

'I'm on your side,' she said, her throat tightening.

She took off a glove and put her hand over his on his knee. He looked at her, searching her face, trying to make sense of everything. They sat so close, legs, hips and shoulders touching. Tears trickled down her cheeks. His eyes widened and he gripped her hand.

'Tell me what's going on.'

'Are you two coming up then?' Jayden's father called from above.

'Just a moment,' he shouted back up. He took a handkerchief from his trouser pocket and dabbed away Ella's tears. 'It's a clean handkerchief. Freshly ironed too. My mother irons everything.'

Ella made a noise between a laugh and a sob. 'We can't speak now. Will you meet me tomorrow and I'll explain everything.'

'All right. But out of town away from prying eyes.'

They made some hasty plans and Ella headed for home, emotionally drained. Thank goodness she wasn't seeing Max that evening. There was some sort of meeting at Party headquarters he wanted to attend.

* * *

Snow had fallen again overnight and workers were out in the streets clearing the snow from the tramlines. The tram to the outskirts of town was slower than usual, but Ella was still on time to catch her bus connection. The bus took her out of Linz and into the countryside. After a fifteen-minute journey, Ella alighted in front of the snow-cloaked Gasthaus Waltraud. Behind the building, a hiking trail wound its way up the mountainside. She was so blinded by the sharp blue sky, the brilliance of the sun reflecting off the snow, that she couldn't see him at first. But then her eyes adjusted. Jayden was sitting on a snowy bench, waiting for her. They had arranged he would take the bus thirty minutes earlier to avoid them being seen together.

He stood and came to meet her, a bounce in his walk, a smile on his face: so different to yesterday. His black hair shone in the sunlight, his long wave of a fringe so different to Max's stark, cropped style.

They greeted each other with a simple hello. Ella had the impulse to give him a hug, but he remained a small distance from her, his hands in his pockets.

'Shall we walk?' He nodded up the snowy path that meandered along the edge of the forest.

They started off in silence, breathing in the crisp air, adjusting to the stillness away from the town. It was wonderful to be away from the confines of the Bride School. Away from the suffocating ideology that was pumped into her brain each day.

They took their time. In places, the snow was deep and the going more difficult. Ella wore her ski jacket and woollen trousers tucked into her robust boots. She was fit due to the daily gymnastics at the school, one of the few positives of being there.

They stopped to take in the view: pristine snow-clad forests clinging to steep mountain slopes and below, the shimmering Danube. An eagle soared overhead, circled and then disappeared on silent, powerful wings.

It occurred to her this was the first time they'd ever been truly alone together. Jayden's face was relaxed and he had colour in his cheeks: such a contrast to last night. Was this a good moment to explain everything?

'I'm pleased to see you happier today,' she said.

'I am. When I awoke this morning, the prospect of a day in the mountains, a day with you, lifted my spirits.' He glanced at her, a gold glint in his hazel eyes, a smile playing on his lips.

'But I thought you were so angry with me.'

'I was. Furious when I saw you leave my house. With *him*. It was a punch in my gut. I saw it as a betrayal, and I burned with anger.' He looked out into the distance. 'And hurt,' he added softly.

'I knew how much seeing me that night hurt you. I'm so sorry.'

Now, she must tell him.

'After you left yesterday evening,' he said, 'I thought about what you said about wanting to help. And you have already done so much. I can't blame you that we were forced from our home and it's not your fault that an SS officer now lives there.'

'But you can't understand why I'm engaged to a Nazi and attending a Reich Bride School?'

'No. But I know you want to explain, and I'm sure it's a long story. How about we have some lunch first at the *Gasthaus* further up? We can sit on the terrace, enjoy the view and then we can talk.'

Ella agreed, relieved. She wasn't ready yet to wade into her story.

They continued up the hill, walking closer together this time. When she stumbled slightly, Jayden held out a steadying hand. She righted herself easily, and his gesture wasn't required, but still it made her stomach flutter.

The *Gasthaus* had a prime position overlooking the Danube below. They sat outside and were given blankets for their laps by the cheerful landlord. His wife, a stout lady in a *Dirndl* and forest-green Tyrolean jacket, took their orders. It was not yet midday, and there were few customers at this time.

Ella adjusted her blanket.

'I feel like a grandma with this on my lap.'

'A very pretty grandma.'

She laughed at his obvious flirtation.

He laughed too. 'Sorry. That wasn't very subtle. I'm not very good at such things.'

'Oh, that's not true, Jayden. You have years of practice, charming your customers. It was me who was always tongue-tied when you spoke to me.'

'I thought you were rather monosyllabic but put that down to you not liking me much.'

'I don't believe that for one moment. You knew I was sweet on you.' Even she was surprised at her bold words. For the first time ever, she saw Jayden blush. 'I was just shy,' she added.

'You seem to have lost your shyness now. I like you better this way.' He grinned. 'I often think of how you pulled me down that alleyway.'

I kissed him, she thought, feeling warm in the sunshine.

She pushed the blanket aside.

The landlord brought two glasses of foaming *Bier*.

'*Prost*,' said Jayden, raising his glass.

'To friendship,' toasted Ella.

She wanted to ask about his forthcoming marriage to Ruth but their meals arrived: plates piled with huge helpings of *Gröstl*. The mountain air and the exercise had given her an appetite; the crisp, fried potatoes with onions and ham, sprinkled with herbs and topped with a fried egg, was just what she needed.

After the food and the beer, Ella felt drowsy and closed her eyes, tilting her face to the pristine, blue sky. The restaurant was busier now and chatter drifted on the breeze. Once they'd paid for their meal, Jayden pointed to a bench a little way off, set on the hillside overlooking Linz on the Danube. They sat there together. Close. Like yesterday on the narrow staircase. But this was nothing like yesterday. Now there was space and light, peace and openness. Now was the time.

She told him everything. How at first, she was in awe of Max: his good looks and enthusiasm for the future. She'd voted for the Anschluss, lured by promises of prosperity after years of hardship. Now she was ashamed and she wanted to help find out information. She also mentioned how she had a friend she was concerned about too. But she didn't reveal Hedy's name.

'You have a fiancé you despise, and you mix with the dangerous elite to help us?' His expression was full of concern. But something else too. Admiration.

Ella raised her chin.

'The opportunity was there. I took it,' she said. Looking at Jayden at that moment confirmed she had made the right choice.

He took her hand. 'Thank you.'

They continued along the path until it wound its way through the pine forest. A flash of movement caught Ella's eye: a young deer leaping between the trees, hooves pointed like a ballerina, and just as she spotted it, it was gone.

Jayden stopped to gaze up through the branches, a fringe of shadow and light falling across his face. The opportunity was too good to miss. Ella scooped up a handful of snow and flung it at him, hitting him in the chest.

He chuckled. 'Now you're for it!'

She tried to run, but the snow was deep in the shade, and she managed to trudge only a few steps before tumbling down. She turned on her back and stretched out her arms and legs, dragging them up and down, forming a snow angel. Pure childish joy.

Jayden trampled to her side, extending an arm. 'Very creative! Now get up before you're soaked through.'

She took his hand and tugged him firmly towards her. He dropped to one knee and grinned. 'You won't get me down in the snow.'

'Oh, really?'

She reached her arms around his neck and gave him a cheeky pout. He leaned down to kiss her.

Cold lips. Warm mouths.

A long, deep kiss.

A wild image entered her mind: the two of them entwined, naked in the snow.

She didn't feel the coldness beneath her, just the heat rising within. She could hardly breathe.

When their lips parted, she heard his fast breaths. She lay flat on her back, covered in snow, smiling. This time when he offered his hand, she took it, and clambered up. Her ski jacket had protected her from the damp conditions, but her woollen hat, hair and trousers were wet.

'Let's get back in the sun, so you can dry off,' Jayden said.

How could he be so sensible, when all she could think about was how her lips still tingled from his touch?

Back on the path, they stopped and kissed again, this time their bodies straining against their bulky clothes to touch each other.

'We shouldn't be doing this.' He sighed, playing with a strand of her wet hair protruding from her hat.

'I know. You're engaged.'

'Not any more.'

Her heart lifted.

'What happened?' she asked, trying to keep the delight out of her voice.

'It was a mutual decision; we realised we loved each other as lifelong friends. We weren't in love. Our families had always assumed we would wed one day, and we sort of drifted into it. Ruth will stay in Salzburg now.'

'Then us doing this, whatever this is, isn't a problem.'

'But my faith is. It—'

'I don't care about that. I—'

'Other people care.'

The magic of a few moments ago was melting as quickly as the snow on her mittens. She didn't want to talk about all this now; the pressure in her chest was returning. Images, unbidden, assaulted her. The flaming synagogue, Max beating the man on the bench, the bloom of blood on a camel coat.

'We can't be seen together,' Jayden said. 'You'd be arrested, or worse still, interrogated by the Gestapo.'

'Then we'll make sure we're not seen together.'

Jayden shook his head, his face sad. 'Even out here is risky. This is my fault for encouraging the situation: meeting you here. Alone. I... I think we should return now. Separately.' He checked his watch. 'If you're quick, you'll catch the next bus.'

She stood stubbornly, her hands on her hips.

'Go.' His voice had turned rough. 'This was a mistake. Go. Now.'

The glint in his hazel eyes was gone.

He frowned. 'I said: go!'

She stomped away from him, down the hill, determined not to cry. This was not the end.

* * *

As Ella entered the room with the other brides, there were murmurs of delight. A small fire had been lit in the fireplace. There was a rush for the chairs closest to the crackling warmth, Tanja acquiring a prime position.

'Looks like Frau Gruber finally caved in,' said Lisl, settling herself next to Ella. Lisl looked pretty today in a sky-blue pullover embroidered with tiny white flowers.

'Finally. It's well below freezing in here,' said Ella, glancing at the ice on the inside of the windows.

The room fell silent as Frau Gruber marched in, straight backed, stern faced: her usual stance for the racial science class. She stood next to a paper flip chart that had been placed on an easel at the front of the room. The lessons always repeated the same NS ideology on keeping the German race pure but with time, her classes were becoming more and more virulent. Ella would try to block out the hateful words, but like poison-tipped spears, they found their mark.

Images of her and Jayden kissing in the forest darted around her brain, and warmth spread in her chest.

'...in order to rid ourselves of the undesirables, it is the duty of every good German woman to choose a spouse who is genetically pure. This is one of the Ten Commandments for the German Woman.'

Frau Gruber swung her arm dramatically as she revealed the first page of the flip chart.

Ella stared at the list, the word *Commandments* jarring her brain. Nazis using biblical connotations was a startling development.

She must have gasped or swallowed loudly because the girl in front of her turned and gave her a sharp look.

Frau Gruber talked through the list, giving special emphasis to words like *duty*, *purity* and *loyalty*. The commandments pronounced women were the sustainers of the German race; their calling was to stay at home, produce many children, support and obey their husbands, keep a hygienic home, iron and polish their husbands' uniforms.

'But,' said Frau Gruber, pausing and stabbing the chart with her finger, 'the most important thing is this: to be culture bearers of the next generation. To educate the children in everything that our Führer stands for. To teach our boys loyalty to the Reich. To train our girls to be dutiful mothers and wives of the German *Volk.*'

Her voice had risen to a crescendo, and now she paused, breathless, and surveyed the young women before her. There was nodding of heads and murmurs of agreement. Ella glanced at Lisl; her face was a mixture of awe and fear.

Frau Gruber trembled. 'Your training is nearly complete, after which all of you will have the honour of pledging your loyalty to our Führer.' Her throat flushed crimson at the mention of her idol. 'The ceremony will take place after Christmas. After you have made your pledge, you will receive your official certificate, signed by the Führer himself, which will permit you to marry. You will be brides of the Reich.'

Ella felt sick at the thought of pledging her allegiance. How far would she go with this charade? Max was getting harder and harder to tolerate the more time he spent with his new Nazi friends. But she hadn't yet accomplished what she wanted to do: to get another look at the list in Heinrich's office, or any other papers that might be relevant. As Frau Gruber spoke on, her passion and devotion to the Nazi cause sent shivers down Ella's spine.

'...furthermore, we are honoured that a special guest will be attending the ceremony: you will receive your certificates from our Führer's deputy, Reichsminister Hermann Göring!' Eyes wide, she nodded, and then paused, encouraging cries of delight from the brides.

Frau Gruber clapped her hands and announced a ten-minute break, which would be taken outside in the fresh air. A few despondent faces turned to the frost-covered window. The naked branches of a silver birch tree whipped back and forth in the wind.

As the girls filed out, Lisl was stopped by Frau Gruber. 'The pullover you are wearing,' she said. 'Is it made in Germany?'

'I'm not sure,' Lisl stammered. 'It was a birthday present from an aunt.'

Tanja passed by and smirked.

'Turn around, please and lift your hair,' ordered Frau Gruber.

Lisl did as she was told, her face flushed.

Frau Gruber yanked the collar of the pullover and scrutinised the label through her metal-rimmed spectacles. She grunted with disgust and let it fall. Lisl turned to face her.

'As you are well aware, Fräulein the Reich Fashion Bureau has ordered every good German citizen to wear clothes exclusively made in Germany!'

'I'm sorry, Frau Gruber. I didn't think.'

'Go upstairs immediately and get changed.' She waved her hand, dismissively.

Lisl glanced at Ella before scurrying out of the room.

The girls all grabbed their coats and hats and pulled on boots. By the time they got outside, they only had a few minutes to snatch some air, trample footsteps in the snow and exchange a couple of words, before it was required that they return inside.

Ella sat beside Lisl, now wearing a grey cardigan over a white blouse. She looked distraught. Ella reached out and gave her arm a quick squeeze as Frau Gruber strode in once more. Ella noted the uplifted faces of the girls surrounding her, the admiration in their eyes. It scared her.

Frau Gruber's powerful voice filled the room.

'As women chosen to produce genetically pure children, your health is of the utmost importance. Therefore, before you receive permission to marry, you are required to undergo a thorough gynaecological examination.'

There were gasps amongst the brides. They shuffled in their chairs. Ella winced. No man had ever seen her naked. Not even the one who she'd had a one-night stand with in the back of the car after a dance: the only man she'd ever had sex with. She only knew of pregnant women who'd had such examinations. The thought of a Nazi doctor prodding around her most intimate part was alarming.

Evidently thinking the same thing, Lisl shot her a glance, her expression horrified.

'Now, now ladies,' said Frau Gruber, acknowledging their worried faces. 'There is nothing to worry about. I appreciate that a pure young woman may feel embarrassed...'

Ella felt the heat rise to her face. Pure? She was no longer a virgin. It had happened just once, but would the doctor be able to tell? Would she be scolded and refused the certificate? Did she even want to go through with the examination? Were all the other girls so innocent? Lisl for sure. But surely Tanja wasn't; she was always making innuendos about what she and Heinrich got up to. Or maybe sex with an SS officer was allowed – encouraged, even.

Her stomach churned. This whole situation was getting out of control. She was in over her head.

* * *

That evening, everyone sat next to the fire in the front room as late as possible to avoid retiring to their freezing bedrooms. Lisl, looking exhausted, had been the first to announce she was going upstairs and Ella decided to join her.

They'd hurriedly prepared for bed and jumped beneath their feather quilts, huddling down for warmth. Ella's nose felt like ice.

Now, she turned on her side to face Lisl in the opposite bed.

'Are you all right, Lisl? After the episode with your pullover?'

Lisl sighed. 'It was so humiliating, in front of everyone. I heard a couple of the girls snigger. To be honest, I don't fit in here.'

'You're not alone in that. I don't belong either, really. You've heard the comments made about Max not being an officer; I try to ignore it.' Ella was glad that she didn't belong to the Nazi circle.

'But I can't ignore it. The thing is, I want to belong to this community. It's important to Erwin that I'm accepted, that I make him proud.' Lisl sounded close to tears.

'I'm sure he's proud of you. He loves you.'

'I'm not so sure of either. He adored his first wife. She was the perfect bride. A wonderful hostess, beautiful and talented. She played piano and painted. I... I...' Her words choked on a sob and she began to cry.

Ella pushed back her covers and went to sit on Lisl's bed. Putting a hand on her shoulder, she said softly, 'Of course he loves you. He obviously sees your qualities: different to his first wife, but unique to you. Perfection can be tedious, you know.'

Lisl gave a wane smile and wiped away a tear from her cheek. 'I'll never be tedious then.'

They both laughed.

'Am I missing out on a joke?' Tanja swung through the door. Ella considered how the girl never seemed tired.

Ella shook her head and Tanja continued, shrugging off her

pullover. 'I'm so excited about receiving my certificate. From Göring himself, no less!'

Ella returned to the warmth of her bed. 'I'm not so excited about this examination, to be honest.'

'Oh, that. I'm not bothered. Heinrich is good friends with the doctor.'

Of course he is. Ella suppressed a smirk.

Tanja slipped out of her skirt and unrolled her wool stockings. 'I'm sure there won't be any problems.' She shivered and grabbed her nightdress from under her pillow. 'God, it's freezing in here. At least there's always a roaring fire at Heinrich's.'

At Jayden's.

Ella bit her lip.

Tanja pulled the feather quilt up to her chin. She shot Ella a sly look. 'Do you and Max, you know, do things. Do *it*?'

Ella was taken aback for a moment at Tanja's directness. She paused before answering. 'We're waiting till we get married.'

Tanja snorted. 'How sweetly old-fashioned. Risky, though. He might be lousy between the sheets.'

Ella had no intention of getting anywhere near a bed with Max. She was grateful he'd been satisfied with a quick fumble in the car.

Tanja turned to Lisl, who looked stricken by the conversation. 'And you,' she demanded. 'Erwin will be expecting a battalion of children from an eighteen-year-old. Although you are rather small,' Tanja said in a derogatory tone. 'It must be daunting following in the footsteps of a woman of experience, who knew how to please her husband. Or have you managed to satisfy him yet?'

Lisl's lip trembled.

'I think Lisl's personal relationship is exactly that. Personal,' said Ella sharply.

'Okay, okay. Keep your hair on. It doesn't interest me anyway.'
She turned her back on them and flicked off her bedside light.

Lisl threw Ella a thankful look.

Ella couldn't fall asleep that night. She imagined the scorn in the doctor's eyes when he discovered she was no longer a virgin. What if he said it was his duty to inform Max? Or worse still, Heinrich, who would then joke about it to Max's father over a glass of whisky? It was so unfair; men could have as many women as they wanted before marriage. In fact, it was seen as a positive quality. But who made all these rules? Men, of course. The Nazi's had defined a woman's role. Explicitly.

20

MARLENE

The potato goulash started to bubble. Marlene turned the gas down and gave it a stir. She was forgoing meat at the moment in order to save money for the roast goose at Christmas. It was more traditional to serve fried carp, but Franz had never been very fond of fine fish bones getting stuck between his teeth. This year, she would surprise him with a different meal. She smiled to herself. Things had improved between them recently; their slow, delicious lovemaking igniting her desire once more.

The red, plastic timer next to the stove let out a high-pitched ring and clicked to a stop. She pulled on her oven gloves, opened the oven door and took out the cake, placing it on a wire rack to cool. It was a *Gugelhupf*, a round, marbled sponge cake, high with a hole in the centre. Both Franz and Ella enjoyed a slice with a mug of coffee in the afternoon. It was a large cake for just the three of them. She would cut off a wedge and take it to Otto.

A sliver of guilt passed through her. She hadn't mentioned that she'd been seeing Otto. Franz had heard the news of the death of his wife and had been shocked, of course. But he didn't know Otto personally and Marlene had never told Franz about her previous involvement with him. By the time she'd met Franz, she'd just wanted to put the whole incident behind her.

When the cake had cooled, she sprinkled powdered sugar over it and cut out a wedge which she wrapped in tinfoil. She glanced at her watch. There was still enough time to take the cake to Otto and be back for when Franz returned from the workshop. It was Friday and Ella would also be home for the weekend. Marlene couldn't wait to see her daughter; she always missed her during the week.

* * *

That evening, as they ate their potato goulash, Marlene asked Ella about her week. Her daughter was always evasive about news from the school and Marlene had the distinct impression that she was hiding something. She moved onto the topic of Max.

'Do you want to ask Max for lunch on Sunday? It's the last Advent before Christmas and we haven't seen much of him lately.' Marlene was actually pleased about this, but felt she should at least offer. Bride School would soon be finished and she harboured the hope that Ella would decide against becoming a Nazi bride. At first, Marlene had thought the union with Max might keep Ella safe, but the fanaticism of the regime had become so repulsive that she now wished Ella had nothing to do with it.

'That would be nice,' said Ella, her voice flat.

Marlene looked at her daughter's strained face. It was obvious that Ella had become disillusioned with Max. Then why was she still with him? What was she up to? As Marlene collected the empty bowls, it came to her in a flash: Ella was at the school for more nefarious reasons than she was admitting and could be putting herself in danger. She would try to coax some information from her.

After Marlene had cleared the table, Franz looked around the kitchen. 'Did you manage to bake a cake this afternoon? I know I shouldn't, but I fancy a slice.'

He patted his rounded stomach and grinned.

Marlene fetched the *Gugelhupf* and placed it on the table.

'I see you've been nibbling already, *Schatz*. More than a nibble. Surely you didn't eat such a huge piece yourself?'

The base of Marlene's throat grew warm. She pulled at the neck of her blouse.

'Oh, I took some downstairs for Frau Bauer and her three girls.'

She stumbled over her lie. Did he notice? She didn't have anything to hide so why didn't she just tell the truth?

'Have you had any orders for furniture for the new year, *Liebling*?' she said, slicing into the soft, moist sponge and depositing a large slab on a plate.

If her husband noticed the swift change of subject, he didn't show it. He eyed the cake approvingly and picked up a fork.

'Unfortunately, no. I'm worried about the lack of business. Money is tight and people are nervous.'

'I know someone who wants a piece of furniture,' Ella said.

Marlene heard the caution in her voice.

'But I'm not sure you'd want a contract from him.' Ella paused. 'SS Officer Heinrich Steiner mentioned a cocktail cabinet.'

Marlene stiffened. 'The officer living in the Pisinger house?'

'Yes. It's a stupid idea. I wish I hadn't mentioned it now. Of course we don't want business from people like that.'

An uneasy silence fell on the table.

Marlene cleared her throat and in a quiet voice said, 'No, we don't want Nazi business. But if they are the only ones requesting furniture, sooner or later, we may have no choice.'

The irony was not lost on her. There she was considering Franz might work for them at the same time as planning her next act of resistance. It was a stark conflict but, in the end, she had to be pragmatic. They needed money, so why not take it from the damn Nazis?

* * *

Two days later, Marlene lit the fourth and final candle of the *Adventskranz*. She'd made the wreath herself with sprigs of fir, red ribbons and tiny pine cones. Each Advent Sunday, she'd lit the next candle and now all four were burning brightly. She glanced around the table, admiring her china plates decorated with sprigs of holly around the rim. Christmas was at the door. Freddie had arrived yesterday evening, dusted in snow and bearing gifts from Vienna. His cheery smile and easy laugh warmed her heart. She was excited to have the family back together again.

They all took their places at the table, including Max, who'd accepted Marlene's invitation to lunch. As she passed him the potatoes, Marlene couldn't help noticing how his handsome looks resembled his father when he was young. She brushed aside the unwanted memory. Max wore a light-blue shirt and navy tie: the swastika tie pin glinted in the midday sun that streamed through the window. This was the first time he'd come into their home wearing a fascist emblem. Franz's face had blanched when Max had taken off his jacket.

They tucked into the baked *Kassler*. Marlene served meat on this occasion because Max was their guest.

'Delicious,' commented Max. 'Thank you for inviting me, Marlene.' He spoke in that formal, polite tone of his. Slightly aloof.

'You're always welcome,' said Marlene, disliking herself for replying with the same stiffness.

Why couldn't they all just relax when Max was there?

It was no surprise when the conversation turned to the Göring steel works.

Max grew animated. 'The factory will make a huge impact on the prosperity of Linz. It will create hundreds, if not thousands of jobs. Not to mention the prestige of having the Führer's deputy as its patron!'

Marlene recalled how Göring had stood at the factory site: large and jovial, bathing in the crowd's adulation whilst German planes had flown above. She didn't trust him for a moment.

Max was still talking.

'...and even more jobs will be created with the building of a vast prison not far from town.' He beamed at everyone around the table. 'Nothing but good news.'

He pierced a piece of pink meat with his fork triumphantly.

'A prison?' Marlene frowned.

'Yes. A prison or work camp, or whatever you want to call it.'

Everyone except Max stopped eating.

'Why do we need another prison?' asked Freddie. His tone was even but Marlene saw the tension in his jaw.

Max peered at him as if he'd said something stupid.

'Because unfortunately, there are those who are trying to thwart the Reich. Communists, socialists and such. They must be dealt with severely. And of course, our land must be cleansed of undesirables.'

Marlene watched Ella blanch. In contrast, Marlene's face burned.

'What do you mean by undesirables?' Freddie's voice turned cool.

Marlene gave him a warning look, but he narrowed his eyes and gave Max a confrontational stare. The whole family seemed to hold its breath.

Max put down his cutlery.

'We all know the threat of the Jews: exploiting us, taking our money, weakening our genes.'

'They have committed no crime. You can't lock people away for their religion.' Freddie's face reddened. Marlene knew some of his student friends were Jewish.

She interjected, trying to defuse the situation. 'Freddie, please.'

'We can lock them up,' Max retorted, 'if they refuse to leave. They are being given the chance to sell their homes and businesses and leave our land.'

'But it's their land too,' Freddie shouted.

Marlene's stomach plummeted. This was not the family lunch she had hoped for and the conversation was becoming dangerous.

'It's not their land. They don't belong here.' Max pushed his plate away. 'Vermin,' he uttered.

The word hung in the room. Ugly. Evil.

Stunned silence.

Marlene bit her lip to control her fury. She and Franz exchanged shocked looks. She fixed her eyes on Freddie, who looked on the edge of exploding.

'Let us please all calm down. I'm sure none of us want to spoil a family Sunday lunch with a heated exchange we might regret. Max is a guest in our home.' *An abhorrent guest that we must tolerate for the moment.*

Freddie swallowed hard, every muscle in his face taut as he tried to contain his anger. Finally, he gave a brisk nod of acknowledgement.

Max ground his jaw, his eyes flashing as he looked around the table, waiting for opposition from another member of the family. There was none.

He pulled at the cuffs of his sleeves. 'Very well. Let us drop this conversation.'

Marlene stood and announced, 'Dessert?'

* * *

Max left promptly after dessert whilst the family were still sitting at the table. As Ella walked him to the door, Freddie sighed and shook his head. 'I don't understand how she can want to marry that man. I've kept quiet till now, but today was too much.'

'We need to handle this carefully,' said Marlene. 'You were out of control today, Freddie. You can't talk like that to a Nazi. It endangers us all. We need to be very clever here.'

She felt suddenly tired. Her plan to keep Ella safe by tolerating her fiancé was unravelling. Max was becoming too extreme. Too dangerous.

'I'm ashamed that my sister is to become a Nazi bride,' Freddie blurted out. 'There. I've said it.'

There was a loud sob from the doorway. Ella stood there, her lips trembling.

'There's a reason I'm with Max,' she said. Her face was tight, ashen.

Marlene swallowed, eagerly anticipating her next words. Ella took a deep breath and opened her mouth to speak, but before she could, the doorbell rang.

Franz got up to answer it. Marlene heard the voice of Frau Bauer saying she didn't want to disturb on a Sunday. She wouldn't come in but just wanted to offer some freshly baked *Plätzchen* she'd made. Franz's laugh drifted from the hallway.

'Are these biscuits in exchange for the cake Marlene brought you on Friday?'

A pause.

Marlene froze.

She strained to hear the mumbled reply. The front door shut and Frau Bauer's footsteps faded down the stairs. Franz returned, his brow furrowed. He looked at Marlene with questioning eyes. She'd told him a lie and now she'd been caught out.

What on earth could she say now?

21

ELLA

It wasn't till they were drinking coffee and enjoying the biscuits that Frau Bauer had brought that Ella returned to the subject of Max. The tension had been building as her family waited to hear what she would say. Ella put her half-eaten iced angel down on the plate.

'I know you're all wondering why I've chosen to marry Max. I admit that in the beginning, I found him attractive and charming, but that all changed when I heard things he was saying. When I saw him doing things...'

Her words came out like a torrent and she told them about Max beating the man on the park bench, how his new friends were fascists, how he'd insulted Jayden on the beach; that she'd become appalled at the way he behaved. Appalled at what the Nazis were doing: their persecution. She'd decided to act: to gather information at the Bride School and look for a way to help. That's how she had heard about the impending riots in November and how she'd had access to other information. She stopped short of revealing her rummaging around Heinrich's office, knowing that would alarm her parents too much.

When she finished, she gulped a huge breath, wiping tears from her hot face. Her family looked at her, stunned. She looked to her mother, instinctively. She saw a mixture of emotions in her eyes: fear, but also pride. The latter filled her heart and her tears subsided.

'My goodness, Ella. That's quite a story,' said Freddie.

'I'm speechless,' said Vati. He shot Mutti a look.

'My brave girl,' her mother said, her eyes bright. 'I suspected you had ulterior motives. Your actions are admirable, sweetheart, but put you in terrible danger. I want you to stop this charade. Break off your engagement.' She paused, swallowing hard. 'I'm scared for you.'

Ella's mind was whirring. She had thought about the consequences of breaking up with Max many times.

'I think there is a greater danger of angering Max and his parents,' she replied.

'But you'll have to tell him at some point,' Mutti said. 'And the nearer to the wedding, the worse it will be.'

'But not yet. I've made valuable contacts at the Bride School. Even though it's finishing next week, I'm in the middle of the Nazi circle now and I'm finding out things all the time. Look at how we were able to help Jayden's family the night of the riots.'

Her voice caught at the mention of Jayden's name. Did anyone notice?

'There's something else I want to do,' she continued. 'I'm going to Vienna to try to find a contact to get visas.'

'I know people.' Freddie's voice was filled with excitement, his tone having changed from one of disapproval of his sister to admiration. 'You can stay with me at the university.'

'Wait, wait. This is all getting out of hand.' Mutti shook her head. 'I'm not having the two of you risking your lives.'

Again, a look passed between her parents. Something secretive.

Ella rose from the table, stood behind her mother's chair and wrapped her arms around her. 'I'll be careful. But I have to do this. I can't just watch what's going on.'

Mutti stood and faced her daughter, taking both her hands. She gave Vati a meaningful look before she spoke. 'Ella, I'm extremely proud of you and you have the support of your father and me. We too are helping in our own way.'

Ella's heart skipped a beat. 'What—'

But Mutti raised her hand. 'No questions. It's safer that way. Just suffice to say we have contacts and are doing what we can.'

Ella burned to know more. 'Let me join you,' she said.

Mutti shook her head, her expression adamant. 'No, Ella. But I will support your endeavours anyway I can.'

* * *

Max was waiting for her at the other side of the Donaubrücke, hands in the pockets of his coat. His whole body posture exuded hostility. The argument with Freddie at lunch was worrying. If Max started telling people about Freddie's anti-Nazi views, the whole family could be in danger. And now that she knew her parents were involved in some sort of resistance activities, she feared the consequences could be terrifying. Ella took a deep breath as she approached him. She gave him her brightest smile, but it was met with a face of stone.

'Let's get ourselves a *Glühwein* and then we need to talk,' he said.

It being three days before Christmas Eve, the Christmas market was busy. They drank their *Glühwein* in silence. Ella had ordered hers with *Schuss*, the extra shot of rum warming her in the crisp night air and calming her nerves The two of them stood at a high, round table, the crowd bustling around them with chatter and bursts of laughter, the pre-Christmas merriment a veneer over the evil infecting the town: a thin layer of ice over the surge of the Danube.

Ella had the urge to flee. To never have to speak to Max again. But that would solve nothing. In fact, it would make everything worse. She must be clever now. Like Mutti.

A gulp of *Glühwein*. A wide smile.

'I love being here. With you.'

His expression didn't thaw. He cast a glance around them and leaned towards her.

'Ella, you know how I feel about you. But that episode with your family has me worried. I'm concerned about their political orientation and to be honest, I'm not so sure about your loyalties.'

'To the Führer, naturally.' She forced the words out.

'But it's clear that isn't your brother's stance. I felt extremely uncomfortable at lunch last Sunday. You must understand that as a Party member, I have certain responsibilities.'

She fought back her fear and linked his arm in his. 'They were only careless words. He didn't mean it.'

'Careless words are a dangerous thing.'

'I'll speak to him. Honestly, my whole family are very loyal to the Reich. And very fond of you.'

He gave her a sceptical look.

'As I am too.' She pressed against him and spoke into his ear. 'I love you and can't wait to be your wife.'

She was outside of herself as she spoke the words. She amazed herself at her ability to lie. At this moment, she had to say anything to pacify Max and keep her family safe. She pushed the thought of how she would get out of the marriage to the back of her mind. It was something she would deal with later.

'I'll take these back,' Max said and picked up the empty *Glüh-wein* mugs. He returned to the kiosk to claim his deposit on the mugs. As Ella waited for him, a few snowflakes fell. A band struck up nearby and people began to sing along.

'Let's go somewhere quiet,' Max said when he was back, taking her hand.

She was relieved at the gesture. Was he softening?

They stood on the river bank a little distance from the Donaubrücke. Whilst Max smoked a cigarette, Ella watched his face, trying to read his mind. He was deep in thought, probably weighing things up. Should he stay with her? Report her brother for speaking against the regime? A few words to his father and they could all be arrested. Guilty by association. Interrogated by the Gestapo.

He took a last puff and flicked the glowing butt into the snow, his expression grim.

She held her breath. What could she do to appease him? His ego was his flaw.

'I'm sorry, Ella, but—'

'Admirable,' she blurted.

'What's admirable?'

'You are. In every way. Your strength, looks and vision have a powerful effect on me. I'd do anything for you.' She took a step towards him, parting her lips.

His expression faltered. 'Anything?'

'Anything,' she breathed, mimicking Marlene Dietrich from a recent film she'd seen.

She closed her eyes for the kiss and thought of Jayden.

He kissed her, hard, aggressively.

They pulled apart. Max held her chin with his leather-gloved hand.

He squeezed. Hard.

'Things need to change if we're to stay together. I want more vocal support from you for the Party. And from your family too.'

'Leave them to me.' She struggled to talk in his grip.

'One chance, Ella. Just one last chance.'

She gave a slight nod before he released her. And as she rubbed the pain in her jaw, she knew he meant every word.

22

MARLENE

Christmas eve, *Heiligabend*, was heralded in with a fresh fall of snow. Late afternoon, the family exchanged presents and then sat down to their Christmas meal. Franz sliced the roast goose and Marlene served up the traditional red cabbage. She'd made it two days in advance so that it could marinate in the red wine, cloves, star anise and allspice berries.

The house smelt of Christmas: a mixture of savoury food tempered with the freshness of pine from the tree that stood in the corner. Marlene took a moment to look at her family, the warmth of love spreading within her. The perfect moment. If only she could capture it and hold on to that feeling for ever.

After their meal, Franz put out the candles on the tree with the small brass snuffer and then the four of them donned their warmest coats to set out for the local church in Urfahr.

The falling snow had a way of slowing the world, softening its edges, dulling the noise. Inside, the church was freezing, but as the congregation put passion into their carol singing, Marlene began to warm up. The sound of the organ music brought tears to her eyes.

Her thoughts drifted to Otto. He was spending Christmas with his sister in Gmunden. She was glad he would not be alone this first Christmas without his wife. She pictured his face when she'd arrived unexpectedly with the cake. There'd been something in his eyes that pleased and disturbed her simultaneously.

She'd blurted out a lame excuse to Franz about why she'd lied about taking cake to Frau Bauer: something about her hormones and sudden food binges. She'd been ashamed about how much she'd eaten. Franz had given her a puzzled look. He'd known she was lying and that had made her feel guilty.

The service finished with 'Stille Nacht.' A powerful elation filled the faces of the singers as the voices rose to a climax. Marlene noticed some of the few Germans present enthusiastically joining in. They probably didn't even know that 'Stille Nacht' had Austrian roots – that an Austrian priest wrote the words inspired by the calm of a snowy night.

It was not the Germans' anthem.

As the last notes echoed up to the rafters, thoughts of what the coming year would bring whirled in her head. Her family had come to a monumental decision: to resist fascism, to fight back, to help the persecuted. It made her both proud and terrified. To defy the Nazis was to be prepared to die.

23

ELLA

January 1939

Ella sat with her mother in the narrow waiting room directly opposite the portrait of Hitler. He was staring directly at them. Irritated, she picked up a newspaper from the coffee table, where again, Hitler glared at her from the front page. She threw the paper down.

Mutti took her hand and gave a light squeeze. 'Are you nervous?'

It was the day of her examination at the gynaecologist. Her first ever. She'd been prepared to attend on her own, but Mutti had insisted on accompanying her. Ella was pleased to have her by her side for reassurance.

'A little,' she said. She felt sick with nerves.

The door opened and a stern nurse in a starched, white uniform called her name.

As Ella rose, Mutti asked, 'Are you sure you don't want me to come in with you, *Liebling*?'

Ella shook her head. The thought of her mother watching a

strange man rummage around between her legs was too awful to bear.

Unlike the nurse, the short, portly doctor was all smiles. He jumped up to greet Ella with a hearty handshake.

'Ah, another of our wonderful Reich brides. Please take a seat whilst I complete some formalities.'

After she'd provided some basic details, he indicated a screen in the corner of the room.

'If you would please remove your undergarments.'

Ella hung her coat on the hook and hoisted up her dress so she could remove her underpants. She was unsure about her stockings. In theory, they could remain on, but that seemed even more embarrassing. She removed her garters and peeled off her precious nylons, rolling them neatly. She placed the garments on top of a stool and was overcome with an inexplicable sadness.

Finally, she dragged herself from behind the screen.

The doctor was waiting by the examination bed.

'Make yourself comfortable.' He spoke simply as if he was offering her coffee and cake. The nurse stood stiffly by his side, straightening various implements on a steel trolley.

Gingerly, Ella lay on the bed.

'If you could lift your dress, please,' said the doctor.

She did.

'A little higher?'

God, this was excruciating. She took a deep breath and hoisted up her dress.

'If you could bend your knees and open your legs. Try to relax.'

She wanted to cry from shame. How could Mutti have had two children and gone through all of this?

From between her legs the doctor chatted away about how he'd spent Christmas skiing in Innsbruck, and how gifted his daughter was at playing the violin. The examination was uncomfortable but not painful. And then it was over. She could get dressed.

Relief washed over her as she hurried to the screen, grateful it was behind her. She had to admit, the doctor had been kinder than she'd expected.

When she was dressed, he asked her to sit a moment.

'So, I'm delighted to say everything looks in perfect working order.' He beamed at her. 'I anticipate many children ahead, and no doubt you will be honoured with the Führer's *Mutterkreuz*.'

He had that gleam of adulation in his grey eyes that Nazis so often had.

'Just one question. Are you and your fiancé having relations?'

'Sorry?'

'Sexual intercourse. With your future husband?'

She caught her breath. He knew. The memory of her one-night stand in the back of the car sprang up. Maybe the doctor was guessing that she wasn't a virgin. What should she say? What did this doctor want to hear? This Nazi doctor. That she was pure?

Her cheeks burned and she averted his gaze.

He gave a hearty chuckle. 'No need for embarrassment, young lady. A bit of pre-nuptial practice with your intended is actually a good idea. Helps speed things along once you are married.'

'Yes,' she stuttered. And because she felt obliged to add an explanation, she added, 'We're very much in love.'

'Of course you are. Max is a fine young man. A perfect gentleman.'

'Oh, you know Max?'

'Since he was a boy. His father and I go back a long way. But you mustn't worry. Yours and Max's little secret is safe between the three of us.'

* * *

The Villa Rosa had turned crimson. The Nazi flags were draped on every wall. Additional portraits of the Führer hung over the entrance and in the hallways. The portrait over the fireplace was decorated in evergreen foliage. And in the long-abandoned fireplace, flames danced and wood crackled. The nervous brides straightened the chairs, smoothed their clothes and touched their hair. Today was the day: the Reich bride graduation ceremony. They would receive their certificates for successfully completing the course.

Ella studied the girls around her. All, although wearing their own clothes, wore the uniform of the perfect German wife: neat, modest, practical outfits in muted colours. Freshly laundered and ironed. Hair was tightly braided or swept back in a bun. Each face brightly scrubbed, devoid of makeup; they were wholesome, dutiful women ready to breed for their Führer.

The scene depressed Ella. Did these women really love their future husbands? Or were they in awe of their status and power? She suspected many were motivated by the prestige of the elite community. They were something to be envied: blessed by the Führer. These girls had escaped what they thought of as tedious, meaningless lives and were now driven by a new purpose and ambition.

The girls then filed into the hallway and waited in two rows on each side of the entrance. Frau Gruber opened the door and stood to attention. The grandfather clock struck eleven.

When the first parents began to arrive, Frau Gruber greeted them with a firm handshake, and then they were led by their daughters to the sitting room. Mutti and Vati appeared with wary eyes and pinned-on smiles. Ella gave them a nervous look and showed them to their seats. Mutti's face tightened as she eyed the Nazi paraphernalia adorning the walls. Ella winced but her mother collected herself quickly and gave her a reassuring nod;

they were all in this together. Ella had come this far and now she just had to play out the last scene of the Bride School drama.

A commotion sounded in the hallway and Frau Fink flew into the room. She announced the arrival of the Reichsminister. Hermann Göring swept in, a huge, flamboyant fur coat draped over his shoulders. Underneath, he wore the light-blue uniform of commander of the Luftwaffe. Everyone snapped to their feet and shouted the Hitler salute. Göring clicked his heels as he pumped up his arm. Frau Fink offered to take his coat but he declined, preferring to display his emperor look to its full advantage.

Ella looked at the awed faces around her, the adulation as they gazed at this powerful man. After keeping their arms raised for what seemed like an eternity, Göring gave the nod and they were permitted to take their seats. A long speech followed with the usual propaganda, but Göring had a way of speaking that made you sit up and listen; he was a theatrical man who enjoyed having an audience.

He presented the brides one by one with their certificates. Flushed cheeks and shaking hands acknowledged the honour. The event finished with the girls chanting in unison their pledge to the Führer. They were now officially permitted to wed their Nazi fiancés. The enormity of the moment made Ella feel nauseous. How and when was she going to break up with Max? She grappled with the panic, taking deep breaths.

Afterwards, everyone was served flutes of champagne and Göring toasted the new approved Reich brides. Polite conversation and mingling followed. As Frau Gruber talked to Göring, Ella noticed that they kept throwing glances her way. Had they found out about her and her family? Would they be exposed here and now in front of everyone?

Frau Gruber began to lead Göring towards her and her parents.

She glanced at Mutti, whose expression remained calm, but her eyes were alert.

'Allow me, Herr Reichsminister Göring, to introduce you to Fraülein Mayer and her parents.'

'I've been hearing all about you,' said Göring, studying Ella.

The room went strangely quiet, as if everyone was watching this moment.

Ella tried to swallow but her mouth was too dry. He studied her, waiting for a response. She opened her mouth but was unable to speak.

'Only good things, I'm sure,' chirped her mother in a voice that didn't sound like her at all.

'But of course,' Göring said jovially. 'I understand your daughter has recently completed secretarial college with excellent grades. As you know, I am building a steel works here in Linz and the planning department urgently needs secretarial support.' He adjusted the coat on his shoulders and fixed his look on Ella. 'If you are interested, of course.'

'It would be an honour,' she managed to say.

'Excellent. Well, I must leave now. The competent Frau Gruber will give you my office contact details if you decide to apply for the position.'

With that, he did a dramatic turn, fanning his fur coat, and strode off.

* * *

The blue Danube was white; a myriad of diamonds sparkled along its iced surface. The mighty river was frozen, its pulse suspended. Ella was always filled with awe when the Danube froze over.

She had learned to skate when she was three years old at her mother's side. Now she glided away leaving Max behind, who, although athletic, lacked Ella's agility on the ice. Many couples were holding hands, skating alongside each other, but she broke away, her body finding its natural rhythm. Her spirits lifted as she skated with ease and grace through the crisp, cold air, further from the crowds.

A spin. The swish of her skates.

Blue above. White below. Freedom and light.

Soaring. Soaring away from fear and guilt. Soaring away from an ugly world. Here the air was sharp and pure. Here her mind could wander and dream...

The blow took her breath away. Her skates skid from under her. She hit the ground with force, the side of her head bouncing on the hard ice. Her head swam as she tried to focus on the face peering down on her.

'Are you all right?' asked the young man. 'Sorry. I didn't see you.'

'Hey! You should watch where you're going.' A voice from the distance.

That voice. The one that made her heart flutter.

'I said sorry, didn't I?'

'You were far too fast and out of control.' That voice again. Was it really him? She struggled to open her eyes.

'I don't want any trouble,' the young man said and then skated away.

Ella squinted against the sun. Finally, she could see him.

Jayden stood over her a moment before kneeling down and holding out his arm.

'Are you hurt? Can you sit up?' His voice was full of concern.

'I... what happened?'

'That oaf skated right into you. Here, let me help you up.'

He put his arms under her shoulders and lifted her to a sitting position.

Her head spun.

'You're bleeding.'

He gently pushed her hair to the side of her forehead. Something warm and sticky dribbled down the side of her face. Her stomach heaved. Jayden held her hands. The gesture made the back of her eyes sting.

His breath puffed out in white whisps and melted against her cheek. A wave of dizziness made her fall against his shoulder and his arm wrapped around her.

'What's going on here?' Max called as he skated up. His expression was more of distaste than concern for Ella's wellbeing.

She reluctantly disentangled herself from Jayden.

'Someone knocked me over,' she said, hating the apologetic tone in her voice.

'Well, you were asking for it the way you sped off.'

'She's hurt.' Jayden hoisted her onto her feet and held her arm whilst she found her bearings. 'You could show some concern.'

'Looks like she's receiving more than enough concern,' growled Max. 'I'll take over now.'

'Are you all right standing?' Jayden asked.

'I said: I'll take over. Get your hands off her.'

Ella flinched at Max's tone. 'He was just trying to help me.'

Max stepped forward, his face crimson. 'Get your filthy hands off my fiancée.'

Jayden let go of her. She swayed slightly. 'You don't deserve her.'

'And I suppose you do? Filth like you.'

Max's right arm shot out, landing a punch on Jayden's jaw. Ella cried out as Jayden staggered back, nearly falling, but he managed to steady himself and then skated into Max at full force, grabbing him by the torso. They fell to the ice, tumbling over each other, striking vicious blows.

'Stop,' screamed Ella over their grunts and the dull thuds of their fists. She slid over to them and grabbed at Max, but he shook her off.

A crowd had gathered to watch, but Ella was too dizzy to focus on anything but the scene unfurling before her.

The ice ran red.

The crowd jeered; Ella was horrified at their enjoyment as the two boys continued to fight. Two police officers appeared, brushing aside the spectators, and hauled Jayden and Max apart. Both were bleeding: Max from his nose, Jayden from his mouth and forehead.

'This Jew attacked me.' Max stabbed a finger at Jayden, his voice nasal. He clasped his fingers round his nose.

'Lock him up,' a man yelled.

'It's a disgrace.' An elderly woman shook her fist.

Jayden's arms were twisted behind his back and he was marched off the ice.

* * *

It was still dark when she left the apartment the next morning. Fog, billowed along by blasts of wind, enveloped the town in ominous silence. She hurried over the Donaubrücke, head tucked down. As she approached the police station, she fought back the doubts about the consequences of what she was about to do: taking sides against Max would end this whole charade. Their engagement would be off but the truth must be spoken: Max had been the aggressor.

She marched up the three stone steps, indignant with anger, and pushed open the door. The police captain sat at a desk, a pistol at his waist. He looked up from a newspaper and on seeing Ella, shuffled some files together and adjusted his glasses.

'*Guten Morgen.* How can I help, Fräulein?'

'I would like to make a statement.'

He raised his eyebrows and indicated the chair opposite.

She sat down, pressing her knees together to prevent her legs from shaking.

He reached for an official form and tested his pen on the top corner. He threw it down with a huff and scrambled around in his drawer for another. With each second, Ella's resolve withered. She couldn't wait another moment.

'It's about Jayden Pisinger and his arrest yesterday. And I would like to see him. Please.'

The officer gave a strange smirk.

'I would be delighted to accommodate your polite request but unfortunately, I'm unable to do so.'

'Why is that?' she asked, her voice thin.

'Because Fräulein, Herr Pisinger is no longer with us.'

She started. Her worst fears had become reality. Jayden would now languish in some concentration camp. Or maybe he wasn't even alive—

'He was released about an hour ago.'

Ella stared at him.

'Would you still like to make a statement?' He grinned, revealing nicotine-stained teeth.

'That won't be necessary,' she said, rising.

He gave a knowing nod and pushed the form away from him. A glint from his wrist caught her eye. A memory of something familiar sprang up. She recognised that watch. It had belonged to Jayden's father. This time, it had been an advantage that a corrupt police captain took bribes; Jayden's father had exchanged his watch for his son's release.

She left the building, her body limp with relief. Jayden was safe. For the moment.

* * *

The next afternoon, Ella sat alone with Max in his parents' sitting room. He'd telephoned and demanded to talk to her.

'Why did you have your head on his shoulder?' Max's voice was ice calm. He crossed his leg and cupped his knee with his hands.

Ella had known this conversation would come and had prepared for it. 'I was shocked after my fall.'

'And you sought comfort from *him*?' His tone was full of disgust.

'He helped me. That's all.'

'I don't think that was all. I saw the expression on his face. On your face.'

'I really don't know what you're talking about, Max.'

'Oh, I think you do.' He rose from his father's armchair and crossed to sit next to her. She could smell the sugary sweetness of his generously applied hair cream. Gripping her shoulders, he said, 'I've been neglecting you,' and placed his mouth roughly on hers.

She tried to respond, but there was no tenderness in his kiss. It was more like an assault.

Pushing him away, she turned her head. 'No, Max.'

'No? This is not the first time we've kissed.'

'This doesn't feel right.'

'Maybe it would feel right with him?' he sneered.

She pulled away. 'It's best I go home now.'

Ella went into the hallway to collect her coat. Max stormed after her. As she raised her arm to the coat stand, he pounced on her, grabbing her shoulders, his face red with anger. 'How dare you walk away from me!' Spittle shot from his mouth and landed above her eye.

'Let go of me,' she shouted.

'I know what you need,' he hissed at her.

He spun her round away from him and shoved her face up against the wall, pinning her there with the full weight of his body. 'And I'm going to give it to you.' His breath was hot and wet in her ear.

His hand shot up the back of her dress and he squeezed the flesh above the top of her stocking. Then his fingers groped their way under the leg of her underpants and pinched her buttock hard.

She gasped, her face pressed against the wall.

He gave a triumphant laugh. 'All young girls want the same. Well, you're mine and I'm going to give it to you. No one else, you hear me? No one else!' He screamed the words at the back of her head.

His surge of uncontrolled power terrified her.

He tore at her underpants, scratching her skin, and yanked them down, exposing her.

'No. No!' She screamed at the brown-striped wallpaper. 'Let go of me!'

She felt him grappling behind her.

The sound of a zip.

His knee shoved between her legs, forcing them apart.

His grunts as cruel fingers tore at her skin and invaded her.

She screamed again. Louder this time. Desperate.

He clapped a hand hard across her mouth. She sunk her teeth into the palm of his hand, clenching her jaw with all her might.

The metallic taste of his blood. She bit harder.

He yelled, wrenching his hand from her mouth, and sprang away from her. Immediately, she whirled round to face him, panting hard and rearranging her clothes.

'How dare you attack me!'

Clutching his injured hand, he scoffed, 'It wasn't an attack. I thought it was what you wanted.'

'Liar. You wanted to humiliate me.'

'Oh, come on, Ella. Don't make an issue about it. You got me a bit excited. No big deal.'

Outrage pumped through her veins. 'Don't ever treat me like that again. Ever. People call you a gentleman. You're anything but that.'

He raised his hands in mock surrender, one palm bruised and bloodied.

'Calm down, for God's sake. Let's forget about it.'

'This is something I won't forget.' She grabbed her coat and threw open the front door. Max called after her as she ran down the pathway but she didn't look back.

24

ELLA

Vienna glistened in its snow-white brilliance. Ella linked her arm through Freddie's as he showed her the sights. She gazed in awe at the magnificent buildings from a bygone age: the Austro-Hungarian Empire. They strolled down wide, frosted avenues and ambled down narrow cobbled streets where sweepers were clearing the snow. They passed numerous coffee houses: some narrow and long, others tucked away in half-hidden niches, and those that were imposing, with grand façades.

It was one of these that Freddie stopped in front of.

'Here is one of the most famous coffee houses in the city. The Viennese come here to see and be seen. It's obligatory that we sample their renowned Viennese torte.' He pulled open one of the heavy glass doors. 'And tomorrow, I'll take you to my favourite hideaway coffee house, only known to insiders.'

They were greeted by a maître d' in a black suit who wove them through the tables. Ella craned her neck at the high ceilings where chandeliers sparkled. The walls were clad with rows of huge gold mirrors, alternating with brass wall lamps. They were seated at a table draped in a white embroidered tablecloth.

As Ella sank into the red upholstered chair with gilded arms, Freddie leaned across and laughed. 'Not my normal dive.'

After they'd ordered, Freddie asked, 'So what made you decide to visit so spur of the moment?'

'I have time now whilst I'm looking for a job.'

This was partly true. But the real impetus had been Max. She needed to create distance and time to think.

He'd turned up at their apartment with a contrite expression and a box wrapped in a red ribbon, containing chocolates from the finest *Chocolaterie* in Linz.

'Can I come in?' he'd asked as she stood in the doorway, looking at the proffered box.

'Actually, no.'

He'd had the audacity to look irritated at her reply.

'Look, it was a misunderstanding. Let's not make a big deal about it,' he'd said.

'Tell me, Max. How far would you have gone?'

'Nowhere, it was just a game, for heaven's sake.'

'Really?' Her tone was incredulous. 'Well, it didn't feel like a game to me.'

'You're being ridiculous, Ella. Let's move on.'

'I need some time to think things over. Please don't contact me for a few days.'

He had looked astounded as she'd closed the door – without taking the chocolates.

'There are the other reasons I'm here,' she said as the waiter approached, nimbly holding a tray on one uplifted palm. They fell silent until after he'd placed the formidable Viennese torte before them as well as soup-sized coffee cups.

'I want to continue with the plans we made at Christmas.' Ella glanced at the next table: two elegantly dressed ladies, the feathers on their hats bobbing as they nodded their heads in chatter. 'We can talk later in your lodgings at the university. Although no one could hear us amidst the noise.'

'Hear, no. See, yes.'

She crinkled her brow.

'Surely, you don't mean someone could lip-read our conversation.'

'They are everywhere.' He hesitated, then gave half a smile. 'The horse-drawn carriages, I mean. We must take a ride whilst you're here.' He winked at her.

They ate the delicious cake and sipped their coffee, talking of only sightseeing and the unusually cold winter. As they sat there, Ella took surreptitious looks at the crowd, wondering who might be a Nazi collaborator: someone eager to betray a fellow citizen for special favours. Below the glittering veneer of Viennese society lurked a murky undercurrent of fear and betrayal. And prejudices long hidden had erupted to the surface. The Austrian fascists were zealous in their support of Hitler.

Later, after a bowl of goulash from a street vendor, Freddie took her to his lodgings. She was shocked; the tiny room with yellow nicotine-stained walls was only furnished with a narrow, sagging bed and a chipped one-door wardrobe. She grimaced at the threadbare carpet and said, 'How can you live here? You don't even have a table and a chair.'

He grinned. 'This is how the other half live in Vienna. Actually, I only sleep here. My student friends and I use tiny tucked-away coffee houses for our sitting rooms. They are where all the intellectuals gather, sitting there all day nursing a coffee. I'll show you tomorrow.'

Ella washed in the tiny bathroom in the hallway that Freddie shared with six other tenants. She slipped on a long flannel nightdress and returned to his cold room. He was already tucked up in his sleeping bag on the floor. 'You take the bed, Ella,' he said. 'Although, to be honest, the floor is probably more comfortable.'

She clambered in and fidgeted around, trying to settle amongst the wire springs that prodded through the mattress. Once she'd found the right position, she said, 'Freddie, I want to find Albert Göring and ask him if he can help with exit visas. At Christmas, you said you could help.'

'I've already been making enquiries. I'll organise for you to meet my contact from the university.'

'Thanks. There's something else I've been meaning to ask you: what do you think Mutti and Vati are up to? At Christmas, Mutti intimated they were involved in anti-Nazi activities.'

'I was hoping you would be able to tell me, little sister. You're more at home than I am and get on well with Mutti.'

'She hasn't told me anything and avoids any discussion about it.'

'They're protecting us.' He yawned. 'Let's get some sleep. We'll talk more tomorrow.'

Within minutes, Freddie was snoring softly but Ella was too restless to sleep. She could hardly believe she would be asking for help from Albert Göring, the brother of one of the most feared and powerful of Hitler's men. It occurred to her she only had it on hearsay that he opposed the Nazis. She shuddered to think what would happen if she had gotten the situation completely wrong.

* * *

The coffee house they visited the next day was a complete contrast: small, low ceilinged with fringed lampshades and wooden chairs. Freddie led Ella through the fog of smoke past groups playing cards, men seated at chess boards and people sitting alone, reading. He indicated a small, private alcove with two benches. They removed their coats, threw them over an already full coat stand and tucked themselves inside the alcove. Newspapers were spread across the table.

'So, this is where you spend all your time,' said Ella, feeling more comfortable in her surroundings than at the grand café from the previous day. She smiled now. 'I like your sitting room.' The tables were full, the air charged with animated discussion. 'Is it always so busy here?'

'Always. Nobody minds if you sit here all day with one coffee, keeping warm. It's a favourite haunt of writers and artists, musicians and philosophers. Freud is a regular here as well as—'

'Hiding, are we?' A slightly built young man with glasses and tousled hair appeared. Freddie jumped up and pumped his hand, then introduced him to Ella.

The man gave a playful bow and slid along the bench next to Freddie.

'Werner here is an unusual mix of a mathematician and a poet.'

'Not at all unusual. Quite logical, actually,' he said.

Ella took an instant liking to him.

They were each served their coffee with a squat glass of water.

'What wonderful, sociable places these coffee houses are,' said Ella.

'Indeed,' said Werner. 'Unfortunately, the Nazis are closing down those that are run by Jews, or have a clientele with opposing opinions to the Reich.'

'Like most of us here,' added Freddie. 'That's why it's safer to speak here. But if they close this place down, I don't know where we will gather. Free thinking and open discussion in coffee houses is fast becoming a past luxury.'

Ella shook her head. The Viennese coffee houses were part of

Austria's culture. How sad they were being rooted out and destroyed.

Werner leaned towards Ella, his dark eyes wide behind thick lenses. Lowering his voice, he said, 'Your brother tells me you are looking for Albert Göring?'

She nodded, suddenly nervous. 'I've heard rumours he's been helping people with visas and passports.' Even to her own ears, her words sounded naïve. Again, she wondered if the rumours were true.

But Werner nodded. 'I'll take you to him. He's a trustworthy friend.'

The city was cold and damp that evening; a freezing mist swirled around the dim streetlamps and down the alleyways. Ella and Freddie hurried after Werner as he drew them away from the crowds through a maze of streets into a rundown part of town. Finally, he halted. They stood outside a small clockmaker's shop huddled between two derelict buildings. The shop was in darkness but Ella could just make out the carriage clocks displayed in the front window. Iron bars had been bolted across the glass.

Werner rang the doorbell, the chime echoing on the other side of the door.

He stepped back and looked up, showing himself, raised a hand and walked back to the doorway. 'They're coming,' he said.

Ella's heart fluttered with anticipation.

The door opened a crack, then wider, and a woman beckoned them in.

'This way,' she whispered.

They followed her through the shop past shadows of display cabinets, and through another door at the back. The woman flicked on a switch and a naked lightbulb lit up the room. They stood in a clockmaker's workshop; tools and clocks in various stages of repair were strewn across a workbench. On the far wall hung a long gilt-edged mirror. Ella held her breath. Is it here where they would await Albert Göring?

The woman said nothing but went to the mirror and ran her hand along the edge of the ornate frame. There was a click and the mirror sprang away from the wall. Ella gasped as a narrow doorway was revealed.

They descended steep, concrete steps until Ella could feel the air cool and smell the distinct odour of a damp cellar. The room they entered appeared to be a type of artist's studio; a man and a woman were bent over their desks, working, and a small printing press stood in the corner. A tall, slim man approached them wearing a tweed waistcoat over a pinstriped shirt. He had a serious, handsome face. Werner's eyes lit up as he struck out his hand.

'Albert. So good of you to meet us. Let me introduce you to my friends.'

Ella stared. This man was the younger brother of Hermann Göring?

The two siblings could not have appeared more different. The trim, modestly dressed man with soft eyes was a sharp contrast to his bulky, extravagant brother who wore his arrogance like a badge of honour.

Ella shook his hand. 'Thank you for your time, Herr Göring.'

'Please, call me Albert.' He waved his hand. 'I'm not particularly proud of my family name. And to be honest, my family are not proud of me either. I'm somewhat the black sheep of the family.' He gave a wry smile. 'What can I do for you?'

Ella explained she had friends in Linz that desperately needed papers to leave the country and how she'd heard of Albert's activities. She hoped he might be able to help.

'Ah, so word has already spread. Till now, my connection to my rather influential brother has protected me. The worst thing he needs is a family scandal, so he tends to ignore my activities. For now, I'll keep going till my luck runs out.'

He pulled out some stools from beneath a table and invited them to sit.

'Let me explain. There are two choices for your friends: either they come here with their passports and we produce exit visas using their existing passport information. Or we take new photos and provide new identities. Both options carry risks. And travelling here from Linz, there is always the possibility they will be stopped and investigated.'

Ella didn't even know whether Jayden and his family would come to Vienna, whether they'd even reached a decision to leave. But she wanted to have some real options for them when the time came.

'Is there an alternative to them having to come here themselves?'

Albert stroked his thick moustache whilst he considered her question. 'I know a photographer in Linz who might be willing to help. If someone inconspicuous brought the photos here with the required passport details noted correctly, it could work.'

'I could bring everything. Hidden, of course. I always have the perfect reason for travelling to Vienna.' She smiled at Freddie.

'That's a very dangerous idea,' said Freddie. 'If you get caught with false documents...'

'I agree,' said Albert. 'And another problem is we're snowed under at the moment.' He glanced over at his colleagues bowed over their work. 'I can't promise when—'

'Please. I'll wait till you're ready. And I'll bring the photos and details. I can look very innocent when I want to.' The smile she gave belied the fear that roiled in her belly.

Albert nodded and wrote something on a piece of paper. He handed it to her, saying, 'Please memorise these details.'

She read the name and address of the photographer in Linz and handed the note back to him. He struck a match and, holding the slip of paper over an ashtray, set fire to it. It curled into ash within seconds.

'Your friends are lucky to have you. There are few prepared to risk their lives for others. Be extremely careful and never underestimate the enemy.'

Albert's grave face sent a chill through her and for a moment, doubt settled in. But then she thought of Jayden's arms pulling her from the ice and the doubt melted away.

* * *

The flame flickered as the cold draught from the door to the cathedral swept in, then steadied again. Ella threw the used match in the box provided and stood back, gazing at the candle; it was just one amongst many rows. She said a prayer for the unknown woman who had been shot in front of her eyes all those months ago, allowing the memory to settle. Then she prayed for Jayden and his family's safety, for Hedy and her mother, and then all the others facing persecution. Surely here in the magnificent St Stephen's Cathedral in Vienna, God must be listening? She must ask for forgiveness for voting yes to the annexation. Guilt coated her tongue in a bitter film. She chastised herself every day. She'd voted on a whim for a better future without looking past the façade. Like so many, she'd been blinded by promises of a great country and its prosperous people. She'd chosen to ignore the dark side of the regime, the stories coming out of Germany and the hateful racism in her own country. She'd been naïve and selfish. Despair threatened to envelop her, but she quashed it. She had things to do; she must stay resolute.

Exiting the giant door, she stepped into the grey-white afternoon. Workers lined the road, shovelling snow into steep piles along the kerb. A horse and carriage passed; the couple huddled inside it, a fur across their laps, staring up at the towering spire. Ella waited until they passed and then crossed to the other side. She'd had some time for sightseeing alone whilst Freddie was attending lectures, but checking her watch, she realised it was time to make her way to his favourite coffee house. He would meet her there after his lecture.

After two tram rides across the city, she found herself a short distance from their meeting point when she came upon a disturbance ahead. A crowd had formed. A couple moved away, shaking their heads, and Ella stepped into the space they'd left.

She gasped.

Two brownshirts wielding batons hovered over a young woman brushing at graffiti on the wall of a building. Around her neck hung a large placard declaring she was Jewish.

Ich bin Jüdin

Beside her, a baby in a pram cried.

'The bottom of the wall is filthy too. Get down on your knees,' one of the brownshirts growled.

The young mother hesitated. She looked at the pram. The baby cried harder.

'On. Your. Knees.' The man put an arm on her shoulder and pushed her into the snow. She started to scrub the wall.

Ella stared at the spectators, their eyes darting away from her gaze. Some people were smiling, others were grim-faced, clearly shocked. Nobody did anything.

The baby wailed.

The mother cried and scrubbed.

The brownshirts smirked.

The anger and frustration that had been clawing at Ella all day surged through her and she hurtled forwards. The brownshirts looked startled as she lifted the screaming baby out of the pram, cupping its tiny head, and held it tight against her chest.

'How could you?' she yelled at the stunned aggressors. 'Bullying a young mother and baby. And all of you.' She turned to the crowd. 'Watching. Compliant. You should be ashamed of yourselves.'

'Lock her up,' called an elderly man, shaking his fist.

'No,' a woman called, stepping forward. 'The girl is right. Are we a civilised nation or a bunch of barbarians?'

'Hear, hear! Let them go.' A man pushed his way to the front.

'It's a disgrace.'

'Leave them alone.'

One of the brownshirts grabbed Ella's arm. She clung to the child. The crowd shuffled forward.

The second brownshirt waved his baton at the crowd. 'You're all under arrest.'

From somewhere in the crowd, a stone flew at the man holding Ella, striking his forehead. He loosened his grip on her and she managed to spurt to the mother, who had scrambled to her feet, and she pressed the baby into her arms.

'Run,' she urged.

A tangle of people surrounded the brownshirts, jeering and waving their arms. Spectators turned on each other whilst others scrambled away from the scene.

Relieved, Ella watched the young mother plop the baby in the pram and scurry off.

A brownshirt fumbled for his pistol and a shout rose up. 'Let's scarper.' People dispersed and Ella bolted off, slipping down a passageway between the houses. She ran on, not knowing where she was; all that mattered was putting distance behind her.

Eventually, she halted outside a bookstore to catch her breath. She would go in and ask her way back to the coffee shop. As her pulse calmed, she enjoyed a moment of satisfaction. She'd intervened and encouraged some bystanders to come forward. And those that had – not many but a few – gave her hope that there were some good Austrians left.

That evening, she lay on her side in Freddie's bed, her head propped up on one elbow. She looked down at her brother stretched out in his sleeping bag on the floor.

'I feel a bit guilty taking up your bed. Do you want to swap places?'

'No way. It's more comfortable here than on that wiry mattress.'

'Probably. It's like sleeping on a cattle grid.' Ella shifted her hip to avoid a sharp, coiled spring. 'I keep thinking about Albert Göring. Do you think we can trust him?'

'A very good question. These days, I only trust my family. And Werner, who's like a brother, and he trusts Albert. My gut feeling is yes. But the risk is there.'

'It's ironic, don't you think, that Hermann Göring's office might offer me a job.'

'Are you going to apply?'

'I think I will, yes.'

'Into the lion's den. I worry about you.'

'I worry about you, Freddie. I have the suspicion you and Werner are involved in activities at the university. Dangerous activities.'

Freddie sat up, his face solemn. 'Some of my fellow students have been arrested for their left-wing views. Others banned from university because they are Jewish. Professors have been fired for the same reason. But we mustn't let fear paralyse us. I am careful. And I have very clever friends. I'm more concerned about you in the clutches of your Nazi boyfriend.'

'I have Max under control.' Her tone came out angrier than she wanted. She'd lost control when he'd attacked her, and she'd left Linz without resolving things. Had her rebuff pushed him over the edge? Would he feel dejected enough to report Freddie's remarks at Christmas? If Max remained angry, he might report her whole family as anti-Nazis. He'd threatened as much when, at the Christmas market, he'd grabbed her chin. 'Just one last chance,' he'd said.

'Is everything all right, Ella?' Freddie broke into her thoughts.

She was suddenly eager to get back to Linz and close the rift between her and Max. It galled her to have to make light of his behaviour, but she had to keep Max happy until she had found that list again in Heinrich's study, and had procured exit visas for Jayden's family. Also, she needed to keep Max on her side to protect her family. But would it ever be safe to break off with Max? Somehow, she would have to think of a way.

'Everything is fine. I just need to give Max some clear boundaries, that's all.'

* * *

The tram driver held up his hand, signalling the tram was full. There was a chorus of groans as people shuffled back to reform a queue. Ella would have to wait for the next tram. The doors hissed, unfolding until they shut, and the tram clattered away. She checked her wristwatch and set her suitcase on the ground. She had plenty of time before her train departed from Wien Hauptbahnhof.

Freddie had wanted to miss his lectures in order to see her off at the station but she wouldn't hear of it. They'd said their farewells at breakfast, Ella promising to hug their parents from him. She intended to return as soon as possible and bring Albert Göring what was required.

She wondered how Jayden would react when she told him she could provide his family with exit visas. Would he throw his arms around her, his eyes filled with tears? And love? Her heart lifted and sank; helping him meant losing him. If he left Austria, she might never see him again.

The rattle of the tramlines made her look up. Another tram bound for the main station was arriving. A man ran across the road. His face sparked an image in her brain: a brownshirt looming over a woman on her knees; her frantic look towards a nearby pram. Now he was in civilian clothes but she recognised the set of his jaw. He too caught Ella's gaze in recognition.

People behind her pressed forward, eager to board, sweeping her to the open tram doors. Looking over her shoulder, she saw him stride towards the queue. She clutched her suitcase, edging along, praying the people would move faster. A man with a walking stick struggled on the steps of the tram.

Please, someone help him.

Indignant voices behind her.

'Wait your turn, young man.'

A quick glance back. Her pursuer was trying to push through the crowd, but his way was blocked. Ahead, a woman linked her arm with the struggling passenger and hoisted him up the steps.

Come on, come on.

Clamped between a mass of wet winter coats, Ella was lifted up inside the tram. She paid the driver and fought for a place to stand. The air was stale with the smell of damp wool, unwashed skin and food from the market. Her heart raced as she glimpsed the man through the window, nearing the front of the queue, scanning the tram windows.

Retreating behind a large woman with a shopping basket, she tried to slow her breathing. Passengers tutted as the woman bumped against them with her basket.

Finally, there was the hiss of the doors, a further shuffling up of passengers, and the tram lurched forward. Had he managed to get aboard? She tried to rationalise her fear; she had done nothing wrong. Just comforted a crying baby and said a few words to the crowd. But those few words were against the regime, and she had undermined the brownshirt. Under Nazi law, she could be accused of treason, and at best, she would be interviewed and questions about her family would be asked.

The tram jolted to a stop. Passengers rearranged themselves to allow others to exit the central doors. Someone trod on Ella's foot. She eased herself further inside towards the seated area. A tired-looking man caught her gaze. Crutches were propped up beside his seat; only one leg extended from beneath his worn coat. She'd seen many amputees in Vienna, soldiers horribly wounded in the Great War. Now talk of another war was circulating – surely not again?

He leaned forward. 'Are you all right, miss? You look very pale.'

She jumped as he spoke and then reassured him all was well.

'I would offer you a seat but...' He waved his hand at the crutches.

She gave a weak smile and looked away, scanning the passengers. The tram slowed as they approached the station. Passengers readied themselves: clutched children by the hand, straightened hats and gripped their belongings, ready for the mass exit. When the doors opened, the crowd moved as one, and Ella was lifted out of the tram. The snow on the pavement had been shovelled aside and everyone was forced to walk between walls of dirty, hard-packed snow. Looking around, she took a deep breath, relieved there was no sign of her follower.

As she crossed the road, another tram pulled up and spurted out its load.

And him.

He was one of the first out and running through the stream of people. They locked eyes for an instant before she broke away from the crowd and sprinted through the giant arched entrance of the station.

A blast of noise hit her: voices boomed from loudspeakers, brakes screeching as trains arrived, the shouts of guards and the shrill of their whistles. For a moment, she was disorientated, trying to remember the platform number on her ticket. Number five was where the train left for Linz.

She pushed her way to the gate area. Police, pistols at their hips, stood in twos surveying the crowd. Armed soldiers were positioned around the concourse. She quelled her fear; she had no reason to be scared of them. Why would they stop her? Unless the brownshirt alerted them.

She dared a peek over her shoulder; he was closing in fast. She had to lose him before she went through the gate; he mustn't know which train she was on. To her left was a ladies' cloakroom. She dived in.

Standing at a sink, shaking, she lowered her head, trying to think.

A smart woman in a fur coat was washing her hands next to her. She gave Ella a sideways glance and pulled a paper towel from the dispenser. Ella remained motionless, her arms rigid, hands clutching the porcelain. He would be waiting for her outside the cloakroom; she was trapped. Could she fight him off? A commotion would attract the police.

Think Ella. Think!

A hand on her shoulder.

She gripped the sink tighter.

'Excuse me. Are you unwell? Can I be of assistance?'

The voice was upper-class Viennese. Ella turned to see the woman in the fur coat looking back at her, concerned.

'I'm... not unwell. I'm trying to avoid someone.'

'Ah, an unwanted admirer.' The woman smiled. Her makeup was immaculate and large gold earrings hung from her ears.

'No. Actually, he's a stranger who is following me. Menacing me.'

'Oh! That's quite a different matter. A man pestering a young girl. You should alert a policeman.'

Ella shook her head. 'I'll miss my train...'

'Leave it to me. My husband is waiting outside. Just point this menace out.'

They exited together and the woman motioned to her husband to join them. A porter followed him with a trolley of luggage.

Her pursuer was watching. He frowned when he saw Ella pointing him out. The woman exchanged whispers with her husband and then he planted some coins in the porter's hand. The porter nodded.

Then the woman told Ella to walk on ahead.

Ella lifted her head and marched forward. The brownshirt fell into step behind her. He was close. Too close. Any moment now, he would grab her arm or knock her to the floor, drawing a pistol and announcing she was an activist.

She hurried on, allowing herself a quick look over her shoulder. The woman in the fur coat and husband were standing in her follower's way. He tried to skirt round them but the porter was also blocking his path with the trolley. The man knocked a suitcase to the ground and the husband grabbed his shoulder, a scuffle ensuing.

Ella had no time to watch, though. She bolted, tearing her green hat from her head and mingling with the fast-moving crowd. She approached gate five and pulled the ticket from her pocket. Looking back, she saw a commotion. A policeman blew his whistle and people had circled around to watch. The brownshirt was hidden from view.

She handed the guard her ticket, who tore off the bottom half, and she rushed to board the train. Only when she was seated and the train had pulled out heading for home, she allowed herself to breathe. Thank goodness for the woman in the fur coat. Were she and her husband Nazis too? Friend or foe? It was increasingly difficult to know these days.

25

MARLENE

The last of her co-workers had left the building. Marlene could now walk home alone. As she stepped out into the freezing February evening, she knew it was unlikely that a contact would be waiting for her. On the other hand, the Nazi persecutions didn't stop for bad weather, and someone might need a refuge. She looked up and down the dimly lit street. No one. There hadn't been a contact since before Christmas and she was desperate to speak to someone from the resistance movement.

Ella had returned from Vienna, enthusing about obtaining passports and visas. But the thought of her daughter travelling with false documents all the way to the capital terrified her. Surely there must be someone in Linz who could produce the papers. As soon as she was contacted, she would ask the question. Or even suggest the idea.

A couple hurried past her, heads down to the oncoming wind. They took no interest in Marlene. There were no children around to hand her notes. Once, an older woman had handed her a book outside the library. 'A good read,' she'd said and disappeared.

Inside the back cover, she had found a note of where to meet her next contact.

But she knew no names or addresses of the other resistance workers and simply had to wait until she was needed.

She reached her apartment without incident. Disappointed and weary, she pulled off her boots and stepped into her felt slippers. She opened the larder and removed two plates of food leftover from yesterday's Sunday lunch: a large slice of stuffed turkey and a few potato dumplings. She pursed her lips and patted her stomach. It seemed the less she ate, the more her midriff bulged.

She stared at the food, her appetite now gone. Franz would not be home this evening; he was working late into the night to finish the cocktail cabinet Heinrich Steiner had ordered. Ella had reported that Steiner repeatedly asked whether Franz would craft the furniture and it would have seemed strange to refuse the work. Marlene had helped with the designs and Franz had presented them to Steiner. In the Pisinger family's house. The thought brought acid up her throat and she ran the tap for a glass of water.

She walked into the sitting room. Franz's empty chair gaped at her, the impression of his body pressed into the upholstery. His weekend newspaper, carefully re-folded, lay on the coffee table. Silence like static buzzed in her head. She turned back to the kitchen.

Yesterday's food still sat on the table. It might keep till tomorrow – the larder was cold – but...

She washed her face and looked in the mottled mirror. Her skin was dry and flaky. She ran a finger around the inside of a jar of cold cream and dabbed cream on her reddened skin. The fine lines around her mouth and eyes didn't bother her; it was the way her chin sagged. It would be her fiftieth birthday next week. Nothing to celebrate. Sometimes, on better days, she felt young inside, playful, but when she glanced in the mirror, she was shocked, the woman outside not reflecting the girl within. Now, a dab of lipstick and a brush of her hair, and she was ready. For what?

She packed up the food, switched off the lights and closed the door quietly behind her.

* * *

'I would've shaved if I'd known,' said Otto, rubbing his hand over the stubble on his chin.

'Nonsense,' said Marlene, placing two plates of her heated-up turkey and dumplings on the table.

Otto struck a match and lit the stub of a candle in the middle of the table. Marlene's stomach fluttered at this simple action. She smiled at him. The grey in his eyes shone silver in the candlelight. A sliver of guilt pricked her.

'So, eat up before it gets cold.'

'How is Ella?' he asked.

He'd never met her daughter but Marlene had told him a little about her. She paused, nodding as she chewed.

'Still with August's son, Max?' he continued.

The mention of Max's father made it hard to swallow. She pushed a long-ago memory of August from her mind.

'She's been in Vienna visiting Freddie.'

'With Max?' Otto persisted, his eyes narrowing.

Marlene put down her knife and fork. Her appetite had still not returned. 'No. She went alone.' She would have liked to explain the true reason her daughter was with a Nazi. It was obvious Otto had heard about Max's family's political views. Painful knowledge to a man whose wife had been murdered by fascists.

'She's finding her way, Otto.'

A courageous but dangerous way.

'Surely, you don't want her to marry him?'

Marlene stood and picked up the plates now he'd finished his food. 'I didn't come here to talk about my children.' She took the plates into the kitchen and put them in the sink.

'I'm sorry,' Otto said softly, coming in behind her. 'Leave the dishes. Come and sit down. I want to show you something.'

Otto indicated she sit on the sofa and he turned to a set of drawers. She sat and watched his back; he was a big, broad-shouldered man with large, gentle hands. An unbidden memory surfaced: those hands stroking her breasts through her flimsy summer dress as they lay on a picnic blanket beside the Danube. She'd fallen in love with him that day.

He retrieved a book from a lower draw and sat beside her.

'Poetry by Robert Hamerling?' she asked.

Was Otto going to read poetry to her?

He opened the book, slipped out a photograph and handed it to her.

She stared at it, her thoughts a jumble of confusion. Her young self stared back at her: a slight surprise in her eyes, a shy half smile. Standing in a theatre foyer. She wore a high-necked embroidered blouse, her mother's brooch at her throat.

Marlene looked at Otto and frowned.

'I've never seen this photograph.'

'I know. But I've kept it all these years.'

'We went to the concert at the Linz Landestheater. I remember now; your friend, the photographer from the local paper, was there. You asked him to take my picture.'

'And by the time it was developed, it was over between us.' The sadness in his voice was raw.

She fought back the claws of memory picking at an old wound she thought had healed.

'That was a lifetime ago now.' She dropped the photograph onto the open book and stood up. She should leave.

Now.

This didn't feel right.

'Otto. I... I shall make some coffee.'

She moved around the kitchen in a daze. It had been wonderful at the theatre that evening, holding hands with Otto the whole time as the orchestra had played beautiful music that seeped into her soul; the happiest of evenings until the moment that had changed everything. A moment that had begun a spiral of events with the most dreadful of consequences.

The noise in her own throat jolted her and now she carried the mugs into the sitting room.

Otto stood by the gramophone player. The long-playing record spun on the turntable. He removed a piece of fluff from the needle with a tender finger and lowered the needle. Lightheaded, Marlene placed the mugs on the coffee table. The record crackled and then strains of Strauss floated into the air. The room seemed to contract, pressing in; Otto's presence filled the space around her, sucking the breath from her lungs.

He took a step towards her, his arms spread wide. 'Dance with me.'

She went to him, letting him circle one arm around her. He took her hand and led her deftly around the sitting room, in between the furniture. As they glided to the slow waltz, she was transported back thirty years when they'd danced at the outdoor summer festival, the air sweet with the scent of jasmine. Now she let her eyes flutter closed. His breath warm, close to her lips, a hair's breadth between them. Too close.

Her eyes snapped open and she met his soft gaze. What was happening? This was all wrong.

'I shouldn't be here, Otto. I must go,' she said, pulling away from him.

'We're doing nothing wrong. It's just a dance.'

Marlene grabbed her handbag and made for the hallway, heat flushing through her. She fumbled with the buttons of her coat.

Otto's face became forlorn. 'I'm sorry. Please stay and at least drink your coffee.'

'I don't feel good about me being here. I'm a married woman with two children, who happens to love her husband.'

'Of course. And I respect that. I'm just so grateful for your friendship since...' His chest heaved.

She hesitated before pulling on her hat and diving out of the door.

* * *

At home, alone in her marriage bed, she tossed around in confusion and guilt. She was seeing Otto behind Franz's back. She had never told Franz about him. Why not? Because it was all so complicated and had happened a long time ago; it hadn't felt necessary to rake through the past again and have to answer Franz's questions. Anyway, her friendship with Otto was innocent. But if that was the case, then why was her pulse thundering in her ears?

* * *

It was another week before Marlene was contacted. A mother pushing a pram dropped a bag of groceries in front of her. As Marlene stooped to help, the mother pressed something into her hand, which she quickly pocketed. At home, she read the note, which contained one word:

Krimskrams

The word meant jumble. Or bits and bobs. What could the message mean? Usually, there would be a meeting point, an address. She sat at the table to think, turning the word over in her mind. There was a small second-hand shop on the other side of town; she could picture the dented metal sign, *Krimskrams* over the doorway. That must be the place of contact.

She struck a match and watched the note shrivel to ashes, then grabbed her coat and made her way across town.

The shop was located in a derelict part of town. Neglected houses and abandoned shops lined a narrow street covered in dirty snow. One house had no curtains and Marlene saw an old woman, a shawl over her head and shoulders, sitting in front of an empty fireplace. The unmistakable rants of the Führer blared from her wireless out into the street.

The shop window of *Krimskrams* was true to its name. Bits and pieces from all areas of life lay cluttered on display: odd pieces of cutlery, assorted boxes for pills, trinkets and cigarettes, gaudy costume jewellery, chipped plates, plugs on chains, brooches, pipes, a doll without eyes... Through the window, she could see that the tiny shop was crammed with personal and household items displayed on sagging shelves and open cabinets.

As Marlene pushed open the door, a bell clanged above her. A strong scent of lavender water mixed with an underlying musty smell. And she could hear a rhythmic creaking noise. She looked around, her eyes accustoming to the dim light.

A shape moved in the corner of her eye and she let out a yell. A woman in a rocking chair was staring at her.

'I didn't mean to startle you. Can I help you?' she asked. The chair creaked as she continued to rock.

'I'm not sure,' said Marlene, beginning to wonder if she had misunderstood the note. 'I met a mother with a pram who dropped her shopping.'

She paused. The woman continued to rock but said nothing. Suddenly, Marlene felt foolish. This elderly woman in her rocking chair was unlikely to be a contact of the resistance.

'I'm sorry, I've made a mistake.' She was eager to get out of the stifling lavender air.

'What was in the shopping bag that the mother dropped?'

Marlene frowned. 'Why? Just packets of dried beans.'

'Anything else?'

'No. Just beans.'

The woman laughed, her face crinkling, her eyes alight and mischievous.

'Welcome to the *Krimskrams Postamt*.'

The woman clambered out of the rocking chair, her movements cumbersome. Marlene offered a helping hand but was waved away.

'I've been managing my whole life. And to relieve you from wondering: contracted polio at the age of three.' She limped heavily to the sales counter and produced a pencil and slip of paper.

'I'm sorry, but I don't understand why I'm here.'

'Our members need to be able to contact each other and I always played post office as a child so I've agreed to play again.' She glanced around the packed shelves of the shop and snorted. 'The Nazis won't bother with an eccentric old woman selling jumble. They're busy monitoring the coffee houses for secret messengers.'

Marlene felt a rush of excitement. 'Can I leave a message for... for whoever is organising our group? I have a suggestion for him.'

'Him?' The woman tilted her head to the side. 'Let's call our leader Bertha for now. Write your message and I'll see it gets passed on.'

Marlene took the pencil and tapped it against her chin thoughtfully. 'Friendly, local printer required,' she wrote and folded the note. Handing it over, she asked, 'What may I call you?'

'Today, I feel like a Trautel.' Stuffing Marlene's note into a chipped, cream vase, she added, 'You should have your answer in two days. In the meantime, I have a message for you.'

Marlene read the note the woman handed her. A visitor would be arriving at their workshop the following Monday.

Two days later, back in the shop, Marlene received her answer: a printer had been found. Marlene was relieved. As soon as false documents were being produced locally, there would be no reason for Ella to use her Vienna contact. Furthermore, it would enable the resistance to save a greater number of people from the clutches of the Nazis.

The soft light of the oil lamp fell on the face of the young man as he sat at the workbench eating the bread and sausage Marlene had brought. She watched him chew. His chin was free of stubble, his skin smooth and soft; he was younger than Freddie. Barely an adult and already a fugitive.

'Why do they want you?' she asked.

'I'm that lethal combination of a Jew and a communist,' he said wryly.

'Where will you go?'

'To Budapest, on a steamer down the Danube. Your friends have organised a fake passport to be brought here tonight.'

Marlene's heart lifted at the news. The printer in Linz had started his work. She couldn't wait to tell Ella.

Whilst the young man dozed on a makeshift bed on the floor, Marlene picked up her knitting. She'd started to knit scarves and hats for the fugitives who arrived at the workshop insufficiently clad for cold weather. A basket on the floor next to her contained items of finished knitwear. She glanced at the young man on the floor; he would need a scarf and hat, maybe the navy set...

A knock at the door. An ordinary knock. Not the agreed series of three double knocks.

She shot a look at the young man, who was now wide awake. A pause. Marlene dared not breathe. The knock came again, more determined. She could ignore it. Although the small lamp was lit, she'd closed the shutters.

Two more thumps. Someone knew she was there.

She tiptoed across the room, leading the young man to the wardrobe. She lifted the opening in the floor and he scrambled into the cold, frozen earth. He lay on his back staring at her, his face terrified. She felt sick as she shut him in.

She opened the front door to see the man from the neighbouring hut frowning at her. 'What are you doing here so late?' he barked. 'I thought I saw you bolting down the shutters.'

She balked at his tone and fought the urge to say it was none of his business.

Be careful. Be clever.

He peered over her shoulder and his eye caught the bedding on the floor.

'As you see,' she said, thinking on the spot, 'I'll be staying the night here.'

'I would've thought you'd be more comfortable curled up at home with your husband.' He gave her an unpleasant smile.

'Unfortunately, that's the problem,' she said, her voice meek. 'We've had a small marital disagreement. But thank you so much for checking on me. I'm fine, thank you.'

Eyes cast down. Shy smile.

He grunted. 'Well, I'm off home now. You should sort it out, say your apologies.'

Arrogant oaf.

She nodded and closed the door before he could say anything else to annoy her. When she let the young man out of hiding, his lips were purple.

The knocks that came several hours later were in the expected sequence and Marlene bid him well before he slipped away into the night, a new navy hat on his head and a thick scarf wrapped around his neck.

A few days later, she heard the news. A young dissident from Linz had been caught heading for Budapest with a badly forged passport, and had been sentenced to Dachau prison. Marlene was sad for the boy, and also disappointed: her hopes of a local counterfeiter were dashed.

Ella's mouth tasted sour as she knocked on Max's door. On the train back from Vienna, she had fought to quench her anger at him, focusing on what she wanted to achieve: placate Max so she could continue her act of a perfect Nazi bride. She needed to stay within the elite circle if she wanted to gain access to information from Heinrich's office. If she could find the names of those in imminent danger of arrest, she could try to get them papers to help them escape. It was a tremendous undertaking but she refused to be daunted.

When footsteps echoed on the tiled floor on the other side of the door, she prayed that Max's father was not at home.

It was his mother who opened the door.

'Oh, Ella. We weren't expecting you,' she said, dusting off some flour from her apron.

'I'm sorry to disturb you. Is Max at home?'

'Yes, please come in. I'm in the middle of baking August's favourite—'

'Thank you, Mother. I'm here now.' Max appeared, imitating his father's dismissive tone. 'You can get back to your chores.'

Ella's throat tightened as she watched his mother scuttle back to the kitchen. This was a clear vision of what her own treatment would be if she ever became Max's wife.

He showed her to the sitting room where they sat opposite each other, he in his father's armchair. He crossed his legs, lit a cigarette and began to blow circles of smoke, which he studied with interest. He did not look at her. It was clear he wasn't going to make this easy. She swallowed hard.

'I'm sorry about our disagreement, Max.' The words stuck in her throat. Looking at his arrogant face, she realised how much she hated him.

'Me too.' He dragged his eyes to look at her, his voice hard. 'I've been thinking, Ella. About us. Your family. Particularly, that anti-fascist brother of yours.' His tone was threatening.

'I've just seen him in Vienna.' She tried to keep the desperation out of her voice. 'He's changed so much since Christmas. He's mixing with a different crowd now, one much more appreciative of our Führer. He's going to join the Party.'

Max tilted his head. 'Interesting.'

'And concerning what happened between us. Please under-stand, I've been brought up to be a Catholic girl. To wait until I'm married.'

'Really? I have a different impression.'

'I didn't mean to give you the wrong signals.'

'What about the signals you gave that Jew boy on the ice that day?'

Ella took a deep breath. A clutter of pans from the kitchen. The sound of running water.

'That was nothing. I was dazed from my fall and grateful for help. I didn't realise who he was, at first.'

'Could you not smell him?' Max sneered, his face ugly.

Repulsion spiralled into Ella's throat, making it hard for her to speak. She had to get the conversation back on track.

'Let's talk about us, Max. Your parents have already told people about the wedding. Your father is proud that your bride attended an elite school normally reserved for SS officers.'

Max's eyes flickered. A moment of doubt.

'Let's not disappoint him.' She had his attention now. His arrogance had slipped. She rose and knelt beside his chair, and taking his hand, she spoke softly. 'Remember when you proposed to me in the *Biergarten*? How happy we were? How in love? Surely that feeling is still there. It is for me.' Her voice was not her own; she was an actress on stage.

'My father is mixing in high circles now. We mustn't embarrass him in any way,' he said, thoughtfully.

'Of course. Let's put this behind us.'

'Very well.' He gave her a sly look. 'You can get off your knees now.'

* * *

Ella did not sleep that night. Her bedroom did not get dark, the full moon lighting her room in silver-grey shadows. For a long time, she gazed out of the window. The church towers shimmered on its Pöstlingberg throne under a crown of bright stars.

Humiliation rocked through her; she had *knelt* before him. It was meant as a gesture of conciliation and love. But he'd twisted her action into one of servitude. Surrender. It was hard to fathom that a year ago, she'd been attracted to his looks and charm. And enthusiasm for Austria's future as part of the Reich. There was no sign of that charm now. And the way he spoke of Jayden... Revulsion gripped her.

She needed to see Jayden and let his warm heart cleanse her from Max's touch, his poisonous soul.

* * *

The sombre light and dank coldness of the stairwell was not the romantic venue of their last meeting in the forest. Side by side on the narrow stairs, they talked in low voices.

'Your lips are turning blue,' said Jayden. 'Why don't you come and join the family upstairs?'

She hesitated.

He mistook her silence. 'Sorry, of course it's a risk that a neighbour might get wind of you being here.'

'It's not that. I need to speak to you alone.'

She told him of her trip to Vienna, about Albert Göring's forgery team and how she wanted to help him and his family get out of Austria. 'I also know of a photographer in Linz you could go to. I could take photographs to Vienna and obtain false passports.'

'That's far too dangerous for you, Ella. They'll interrogate you and send you to a prison camp if you get caught.'

'I'm clever. I won't get caught. Speak to your family.'

Jayden sighed. 'My parents are torn; on the one hand, they want to leave and on the other, they don't want to lose their homeland. They're hanging on to the hope that things will get better.'

'They can come back. People will soon see through Hitler and he won't be around for long.'

Even to her own ears, her voice lacked conviction. She looked at Jayden's beautiful face. How could she even think of sending him away? Her heart grew warm and her body soft; the answer was simple.

'Why would you risk everything to help us?' He leaned closer. 'To help me?'

Her coil of tense emotions unravelled and burst out, as she exclaimed, 'Because I love you!'

She flung her arms around his shoulders, pressing herself hard against him, and kissed him. Shaken by her own passion. Thrilled as he responded. Heat in her belly, her groin. She wanted to tear off her coat. Her clothes. Feel his skin on hers. As they kissed, she fumbled open the top buttons of her coat and took his hand, placing it on her breast. He moaned and stroked her over the material of her pullover. More. She wanted more; her hands clumsy, yanking up her clothes. She led his hand inside her brassiere.

But the movement broke the spell and Jayden drew his lips from hers.

'Stop,' he panted. 'Please stop.' His voice was a plea. 'We must be rational.'

'I don't want to be rational.' Her mind was fog. Her body demanding.

'Neither do I,' he said, his breath calming now. He held her face in his hands and passed tender thumbs over her cheek. 'Ella, please think. You have no future with me. I'm a refugee in my own land. I have nothing. I can give you nothing. And according to the regime, I am nothing.'

'That's not true. You are everything.' Hot tears ran down her cheeks. 'Everything to me.'

The reality as she spoke tore open her heart, filling it with the sweetest pain. She gasped. Tasted the salt of her tears on her lips.

He pressed his forehead against hers. 'I don't want to ruin your life.'

'You would only do that if you didn't let me help. Speak to your family. I'll come back on Sunday evening at the same time.' Filled with determination, she adjusted her clothes and left him sitting on the stairs, wonder and confusion in his eyes.

* * *

Tanja opened the doors of the cocktail cabinet with a flourish. 'Look, everyone, at what Ella's clever father made for us.'

The group of girls made the necessary noises of appreciation.

'Heinrich is so delighted with it, he wants to commission more furniture from him.' She picked up a cut-glass whisky glass and turned to Ella. 'Heinrich says you must show us your father's workshop.'

Ella suppressed a sigh. She'd hoped that there would be only one commission. She knew her parents were involved in some way with the resistance, but they had steadfastly refused to reveal to her how. But whatever it was, her father suddenly being thrown into the spotlight of an SS officer was worrying. Did he suspect something or was he genuinely interested in her father's craft? She gave a weak smile and sought to change the subject.

'What a fine drink selection you have. We're spoilt for choice.'

'Heinrich stocked up for a cocktail party he held last week. He is quite the connoisseur, you know...'

The other girls crowded around Tanja to study the collection of spirits.

Ella sat herself down next to Lisl, pleased to have a chance to catch up with her. She asked after Erwin. Lisl gave a modest smile.

'He's pleased that I have my Reich bride certificate and intends to hold a party at his house, with me as the hostess.' There was no mistaking the alarm in Lisl's voice, but still, she looked over at Tanja with admiration. 'Tanja is so good with guests. The thought of hosting an evening scares me to death.'

'Don't worry, Lisl. I think it's something one can learn. Our future husbands don't expect us all to be like Tanja.'

'Erwin does. His first wife was famous for her entertaining.'

Catching a snippet of their conversation, Tanja appeared and slid onto the sofa next to them. 'What are you two gossiping about?'

'Parties. Which reminds me. Have you booked the location for your wedding?' Ella said, bringing up Tanja's favourite topic.

'Our wedding venue has been picked,' she announced loudly, looking around to engage others in the conversation. 'Hold your breath, ladies. It's the magnificent Weinzinger Hotel!'

She gave a smug smile at the appropriate gasps.

Lisl looked at her in awe. 'The hotel where our Führer signed the Anschluss agreement?'

'Not only that. Heinrich says it will be designated a Führer Hotel.'

'What does that mean?' asked Ella.

Tanja shrugged. 'It's top secret.'

The girls all looked very impressed.

'How about the rest of you? Lisl, what are your plans?' asked Tanja.

Everyone turned to Lisl. She squirmed under the scrutiny.

'Erwin is still considering where. But he wants a large venue; he has a huge family and circle of friends. It's all rather daunting, to be honest.' Her voice caught. She was on the edge of tears.

'Don't worry, *Liebling*, I shall help you,' said Tanja, making a grand gesture with her arm.

Lisl looked at Tanja in awe. 'Really? Thank you. The first thing that worries me...'

This was the moment Ella had been waiting for. She excused herself, casually picking up her black, patent handbag and headed out to the hallway where the cloakroom was. Chatter and music from the gramophone player followed her as she passed the cloakroom and halted outside the library. The door was closed. The last time she'd stood here, alcohol had fuelled her courage. Now, stone sober, it was outrage at injustice and inhumanity that powered her.

A check left and right. This was the perfect opportunity. She took a breath and reached for the door-knob.

It didn't turn. Locked. Her heart sunk. He'd become more vigilant now his fiancée was entertaining friends. Where would one keep a key? At home, they had a small commode in the hallway where her family threw all their bits and pieces on top. It had always annoyed her mother to see the clutter of keys, pens and match books left there. Now, Ella considered the elegant bow-legged commode, the only furniture in the hallway. There was nothing but an empty vase on top. Beneath were two slim drawers with brass handles. She moved towards them, keeping her eye on the sitting room door.

She pulled out the left drawer and scanned the contents: coins, a lighter, a coat button, a Nazi pin... but no keys. Closing the drawer, she turned her attention to the right-hand one. It jammed slightly when she tried to open it. She pushed it back in, re-aligned it and eased it back out. Several sheaves of paper and some pens greeted her. But no keys.

Dejected, she went to the cloakroom and locked the door. As she sat on the toilet, her gaze fell on the large brass key stuck in the keyhole.

She jolted. At home, one type of key fitted all the doors except her parents' bedroom.

Within moments, she was back outside the library door.

She slid the cloakroom key into the library door lock, and it turned with a satisfying click. Her stomach flipped at her success.

She slipped inside and felt her way in the darkness to where she knew the desk to be, reached for the table lamp and flicked on the switch. The desk was tidy: just a black notebook. There were no files scattered across the desk like last time. The memory rose unbidden: Heinrich looming over her, talking of curiosity and a beautiful woman in a cell who was no longer beautiful. She pushed the thought aside. She must be quick before people started to wonder where she was.

First, she checked the black notebook – a few jottings of things to buy: ink, paperclips... nothing of interest. In a quick motion, she pulled out the drawers on both sides of the desk. Bills, envelopes, notepaper. Drawing pins, an ink date stamp, a grey folder.

Her hand hovered over the grey folder. She looked to the door and listened. Music from the gramophone in the sitting room; a male singer enthusing about the *Vaterland*.

She flipped open the grey folder and rifled through the papers: letters and memorandums on Nazi-headed notepaper...

The list. Her pulse thudded in her ears. This is what she'd come for.

Words popped out at her: *Jewish heritage, surveillance....* The list was longer this time, obviously updated; there were about twelve names. Like previously, some names had been circled.

She ran an eye down the page; some surnames were familiar but most were not. Except... Newald.

Ella froze as she saw Hedy's surname, followed by her and her mother's first names. Young Trudy was on the list too.

The Nazis had discovered them.

She must warn them. And the others on the list as well. She snapped open her handbag and pulled out a small notebook and pen. She had come prepared. Frantically, she scribbled down the names, starting with the encircled ones. There was no time to write addresses. She would use a telephone book for that. As she scrawled the names as fast as she could, her head told her to stop; it was taking too long. But she couldn't bear to leave someone out. After she had noted the last name, she threw her notebook into her bag and with hands shaking, replaced the file in the drawer.

She hurried back out into the hallway and locked the library door. Key in hand, she moved towards the cloakroom so she could replace the key. Her hand was on the door handle when a voice startled her.

'There you are. I thought you had fainted!' Tanja stood, swaying, glass in hand, studying her with Lisl a few steps behind.

'Sorry I took so long. I was feeling queasy, but I feel better now.'

Tanja's gaze fell to Ella's hand. She wrinkled her brow.

'Why are you holding the cloakroom key?' she slurred.

Ella opened her mouth to reply, but could find no words, like a child caught sneaking a biscuit.

'Goodness, Ella. How much have you had to drink? I thought I was bad.' Tanja giggled.

'I don't know what I'm doing any more.' A false laugh and a shrug of the shoulders and Ella slipped the key back in the cloakroom lock. Affecting a sway to match Tanja's, she headed back to the party.

Lisl gave her a sympathetic smile as she passed.

Ella struggled to concentrate on conversation. She noticed Tanja giving her strange looks but the main thing on her mind was the notebook in her handbag clutched by her side, and how quickly she could warn Hedy of the danger her family were in.

'How did they find out?' asked Hedy.

Ella had been greeted at the door by two freshly scrubbed faces ready for bed. Now, she sat opposite Hedy and her mother, their dressing gowns wrapped around them. Ella had excused herself from Tanja's party, saying she was unwell. It wasn't far from the truth; she was sick with worry.

'I'm not surprised,' said Hilde. 'The Germans are quite fanatical about their paperwork. I have been preparing myself for this.'

Hedy's eyes were wide with shock. 'But what shall we do, Mutti?'

'Nothing. We carry on being the good Austrian citizens that we are.'

Ella paused, considering how to phrase her next words. 'As things have become dangerous, there is an option. I have contacts that produce visas and passports that could get you safely out of the country.'

'Thank you, but no. I'm not having you risk your life, and I'm not fleeing from my home. The home I made with my dear late husband.' Hilde's voice was calm, her face resolute.

'But Mutti, what if we have no choice?' Hedy took her mother's hand.

'There is always a choice.'

Ella was scared; she didn't like the way the conversation was going.

'I know this is sudden and a shock, but please think about my option.'

'Thank you. Of course.' Hilde's voice had a faraway quality; her eyes were glazed.

It was past midnight when Ella said goodnight and left. She was exhausted but knew sleep would evade her that night.

* * *

The following Sunday, Ella knocked expectantly on the front door of Jayden's uncle's apartment. She was eager to help get the family their exit visas. But when Jayden came downstairs, he shook his head. He'd spoken to them about Ella's offer to obtain papers, but his family refused to put her at risk or flee their home, choosing instead to wait and see if things deteriorated.

Ella was in despair. Lives of people dearest to her were in danger and were refusing her help. And by the time they realised they had to act, it could be far too late.

ELLA

Ella's eyelids drooped as her body rocked with the motion of the train. She felt too warm in the stuffy carriage, her coat bulky. In normal circumstances, she would have shed it, placing it folded on the rack above her head. But these were not normal circumstances. Tucked in the lining of her burgundy winter coat were two sheets of paper with the heading *Durchlassschein*: exit permit. After she'd found the list in the library, she'd located three of the other named families in the phonebook and contacted them. One thanked her but intended to stay put, whilst the other two accepted her offer of help. Now, three weeks after she'd found the list she was on the way back from Vienna with fake papers. She was exhausted; having been offered the job at the Hermann Göring office, she'd started at the beginning of the week. Getting used to the new environment and then travelling to Vienna at the weekend had left her drained.

Closing her eyes and leaning on the window, she thought about the others on the list that she needed to find as soon as possible. It would be quicker if she had help. Should she ask Mutti? No. She would be horrified that she'd taken the risk of snooping around Heinrich's office? Mutti assumed her trip to Vienna was just to visit Freddie.

Ella's thoughts wandered to how it was just over a year ago she'd run down the Pöstlingberg on a cool March evening, excited to witness the arrival of Adolf Hitler in Linz. How naïve she'd been. She cringed inwardly at the euphoria she'd felt. Guilt cramped her stomach as she visualised her crossing the circle for the Anschluss. Now she was feverishly planning how many people she could help escape the—

'*Ausweis, bitte.*'

She jumped, opening her eyes to see the train guard. People around her shuffled, searching in pockets and bags for their papers. The well-dressed man opposite her presented his card with an arrogant flick of his wallet. He gave the guard a smug smile and then glanced at Ella. She retrieved her identity card, deliberately holding it together with her new pass from the town hall.

'You work for Hermann Göring?' said the guard, clearly impressed.

'Indeed, I do.' It was her turn to look smug as she caught the stylish man's eye.

Having been accepted for a secretarial job for Göring's new steel works had been a stroke of luck. Not only did it give her access to information at the town hall; it gave her an element of protection – like now.

The guard handed her papers back briskly and moved on.

She smiled at the irony: the two opposing Göring brothers – here she was, her coat stuffed with illegal passes from one and on Monday, she would be at work for the other. She felt a sliver of a thrill. But also fear. The word *spy* leaped around her head. She had always told herself she was just keeping her eyes and ears open, using every opportunity to glean information. But what was that if not spying? And everyone knew what happened to spies who were caught. She shivered, suddenly grateful for her coat.

As she left the station in Linz, the first signs of spring greeted her. Snowdrops had given way to the first daffodil shoots, and buds of white blossom, still closed, bobbed in the breeze. Her first priority was to deliver the exit visas to the expectant families. Then home for one of Mutti's delicious Sunday roasts.

The anticipated aroma welcomed Ella as she stepped through the door but it was not accompanied by the usual smiles. The anxious expression on her mother's face told her something was wrong.

'Hedy and her mother have been arrested,' she said. 'Trudy is with us.'

Trudy's grave face appeared as she stepped into the hallway. 'I was at a friend's when it happened,' she explained.

Over lunch, Ella could hardly swallow as she listened to events that had taken place. When Trudy had returned home from her friend's house, the neighbours reported how Hedy and her mother had been shunted into a police car and driven away.

Without finishing her meal, Ella left and took the tram to the main police station to make enquiries.

Yes, her friends were being held for questioning, they said. No, visitors were not permitted. When the officer began to pry into how well Ella knew the detained, she shook her head. The glint in his eye cautioned her: guilty by association. She mumbled something about acquaintances and sped back home.

Sleep was impossible that night and at her desk in the town hall the following day, the notes she had to type up swam before her eyes. What could she do? The unanswered question played a loop in her head.

It had been agreed that Mutti would enquire at the police station on her way home from the factory. Ella was home before her and began to prepare dinner, Trudy at her side. For the hundredth time, Ella told her everything would be fine: the arrest was all a mistake.

Trudy looked at her, the skin bruised purple under her eyes. 'I'm scared,' she said quietly.

Ella dropped the potato peeler she was holding and wrapped her arms around the girl's fragile frame, cupping her head to her breast. A rush of maternal emotion swept over her. This was what it would be like to have a child: the love and pain, and the need to protect. She made comforting noises as Trudy sobbed into her apron.

The key turned in the lock. Ella and Trudy jumped up and ran into the hallway, pausing as they saw Mutti's ashen face.

'They've been transferred to the Kolpinghaus.'

Her mother's words dangled in the air. A brief moment of disbelief. Then the full meaning struck Ella with a blow that made her knees buckle.

The Kolpinghaus.

Gestapo headquarters.

* * *

The darkness brought the monsters. Men with cruel eyes, and mouths that barked out questions. Ella tossed in her bed. She could see the long leather coats as they circled a frightened girl strapped to a chair.

Hedy.

Ella's stomach spasmed and she jolted out of bed, ran to the toilet and vomited. Still feeling nauseous, she slid her back down the wall and sat on the floor, dropping her head to her knees. She felt helpless. What could she do? Hedy had been her best friend since she'd offered her Pez sweets on their first day of school: two excited five-year-olds on a warm August morning. Ella hadn't thought about their school days together for a long time. Now as the memories came tumbling back, she relived the intense, complex emotions of a female friendship that spanned most of her life.

She sobbed.

She retched over the toilet bowl.

She sobbed again.

As she dragged herself back to her room, she heard voices from her parents' bedroom. The door was ajar, a lamp on.

She peered into the room to see Mutti stroking Trudy's hair as she cuddled her close in bed. Vati lay on his side, watching them.

Mutti looked up. 'Join us,' she said.

Ella clambered in and her mother circled her free arm around her shoulders. They remained like that the rest of the night.

The only sound in the kitchen the next morning was the clatter of crockery and the whistle of the kettle on the stove. No one spoke. They sat at the breakfast table in their nightwear gazing at each other's exhausted faces. How could any of them face work? Or Trudy face school?

'We can't go asking questions at Gestapo HQ,' said Ella.

'Absolutely not. Just by enquiring, they would think we're guilty of something,' said her mother.

'But guilty of what, for goodness' sake? Hedy and her mother are model citizens,' said Vati.

'I have no idea. It makes no sense.' Mutti shook her head.

Because they have Jewish ancestors, Ella said to herself. She had the urge to share the secret but would not break her promise of silence. She glanced at Trudy and wondered if she now knew of her heritage. Probably not, Ella decided.

The familiar, early-morning sounds of an apartment block coming to life began: footsteps, scraping of chairs, the running of water. Front doors banged shut. Ella went to her bedroom to get dressed. She was buttoning her blouse when she heard a soft knock on the front door. Probably a neighbour needing some milk or sugar for breakfast; Mutti's footsteps on the parquet, the click of the door latch. Her mother's cry. Ella rushed into the hallway. Hedy and her mother stood in the doorway like two apparitions.

* * *

On the river bank, women, bent at the waist, dragged the nets filled with washing through the water. Not for the first time, Ella was grateful for the washroom in the cellar of their apartment block. She and Hedy ambled in silence, breathing in the spring air, the fragrance of young grass and sweet hyacinths. Ella waited patiently for her friend to speak; this was the first time they'd been alone together since Hedy and her mother had been released by the Gestapo.

'It was the waiting that was the worst,' said Hedy, finally. 'The fear of what they might do to us.'

'But they didn't hurt you?' Ella tried to suppress the fear in her voice.

'No. Not physically.' Her voice went quiet.

'It's outrageous. They had no reason to arrest you.'

'They know my grandmother was Jewish; that's a reason. Plus, someone told them Vati had friends in the church who were active against the Party. Mutti and I have no idea what that's all about...'

They halted under an oak tree, its yellow catkins drooping above their heads, and watched the Danube, tumbling grey-blue past them. Pollen wafted. Ella's nose prickled.

'I want to tell you what happened when I was interrogated by the Gestapo,' said Hedy.

Ella's heart beat double time. She took Hedy's thin hand and waited.

'In the room was an SS officer and a female official. She told me to remove my clothes. All of them. I hesitated and the woman yelled at me to hurry. As I undressed, the SS officer watched and said nothing. It was so horrible, Ella. The woman said she was searching for hidden weapons, as if I could conceal one in the places she looked!' She gave an angry sob.

Tears filled Ella's eyes and she squeezed Hedy's hand tighter.

'When the woman announced I was unarmed, I reached for my clothes. Then the SS officer finally spoke. He said I was to remain naked during our "discussion", as he called it.'

'Oh, Hedy, no.'

'I was terrified. Naked, cold and trembling. And the woman had taken my clothes when she left the room. At every moment, I thought he would lunge at me, assault me in some terrible way. But that was not his plan. He made me stand in front of him whilst he took a seat and asked me question after question, his eyes roaming over my body, deliberately staring at my most intimate parts with his disgusting half smile.'

'My God, Hedy. How long did this go on for? What did he want to know?'

'I think I stood there for about two hours. My legs were so weak, I thought I'd topple over. He accused me of hiding my Jewish heritage, accused my father of being a Nazi opponent. He wanted names of my father's contacts, and Mutti's. I didn't know most of the answers, didn't know what he wanted.'

'And did the same happen to your Mutti?'

'I don't know. She refuses to talk about it. I spared her the details of my experience with this Herr Steiner.'

Ella went rigid. 'The SS officer. His name was Heinrich Steiner?'

'Yes. Why?'

'I know him. He's the fiancé of Tanja, one of the Reich brides.'

'Nice friends, you have.' She gave a wry smile.

Ella grabbed her friend's shoulders and stared into her eyes.

'I'm scared for you. Let me help get you to safety; I'll get fake exit visas.'

Hedy shook her head. 'It's too late for that now. They'll be watching us.'

'No! We mustn't give up. There must be something...'

'Mutti is talking about getting Trudy out. The authorities are allowing some children to leave the country with the Kindertransport programme. Trains are leaving from Vienna, but obtaining the paperwork is a nightmare, apparently.' Hedy's voice was hollow, exhausted.

'I'll ask Freddie to help.' Ella was sure he could obtain the papers through his contacts in Vienna, but the thought of wrenching Trudy from her family turned her stomach. 'Would Trudy agree to leave without you?'

'Mutti would insist; she'd tell her we'll join her soon.'

'But you can't make her that promise?'

'No.' Hedy's tone chilled her. It echoed the worst emotion of all. Resignation.

28

MARLENE

It was springtime so Marlene chose the headscarf with the bluebell print: a birthday gift from her boss a few years ago. He'd been a good employer: hard-working and fair. But like so many businesses, the factory had been Aryanised and her boss had fled with his family to somewhere in South America: a place she could not begin to visualise.

She tied the knot beneath her chin, snatched up her basket from the kitchen and left before Franz or Ella was awake.

Hurrying across the Donaubrücke, she mapped out her day in her head. First stop was the *Krimskrams* shop to check if there were any messages, then to the market to buy groceries for the weekend, followed by an afternoon of cleaning and cooking. Her mind whirled; if only her body would keep up.

There was something new in the *Krimskrams* shop window: a tarnished brass candlestick in the form of a cherub, its arm extended to hold a candle. She grimaced. Not to her taste, certainly.

The smell of lavender and damp hit her as she pushed open the door. The woman who called herself Trautel was rocking gently in her chair, a plaid blanket over her knees, a book in her hand. Her eyes lit up.

'It's good you came. I have something for you.'

As she climbed out of her chair, Marlene noticed the outline of leg braces against the woman's skirt. She hobbled up to a shelf behind the counter where an assortment of chipped, ceramic vases were displayed. She reached behind the vases and retrieved a carved wooden music box which she placed on the counter.

'Please lock the door and turn the sign around,' she said.

Marlene swivelled the sign to *closed* and bolted the door.

Trautel flipped open the lid of the box; the thin metallic clang of Strauss' 'Blue Danube' played as the tiny ballerina turned, gradually coming to a halt. Trautel's arthritic fingers prised aside the red lining at the base of the box and withdrew a folded slip of paper which she handed to Marlene to read. A flush of adrenaline swept away her tiredness. Trautel then pushed an ashtray and a match book towards her, arching her thin, grey eyebrows. Marlene nodded and set the note alight. The paper curled and turned to ash.

Next stop was the market. It was already crowded when she arrived and she joined the long queue at her favourite vegetable stand. Moments later, a tall, broad man and a slightly built woman approached. Marlene stiffened: Max's parents. She had seen them occasionally in town but always from a distance. Now there was no way to avoid a conversation.

'What a lovely surprise,' said August, his voice too loud, his smile too wide.

People turned to look. Marlene winced but managed a polite greeting.

'It's been an age since we've seen each other,' he continued to bellow. His wife looked uncomfortable. 'But of course, we'll be seeing a lot more of each other once our children are wed.'

'I expect we will.' Her mouth went dry at the thought.

'Funny how things turn out, Marlene.'

There was an uneasy silence at the emphasis of her first name; his wife glanced at him.

'Hard to believe how far back we go.' He scrutinised Marlene's face as if revelling in her every wrinkle. She could taste the dislike on her tongue.

'That was another life,' she said with a dismissive wave of her hand.

'Not at all.' His smile was gone.

The sun disappeared behind dark clouds and the bright scenes of the market turned grey and flat. Marlene suppressed a shiver; feelings from the distant past reared up: August then. August now.

'How's your husband?' he asked.

Where was this leading? Before she could reply, he'd started to speak again.

'My good friend, Heinrich Steiner, is a fan of his craftmanship. I'm looking forward to seeing the famous cocktail cabinet myself at his drinks party next week. I mustn't forget to mention I know you...' He trailed off as if bored and frowned at the long queue ahead. He turned to his wife and announced, 'I shall take a stroll whilst you wait.'

After he left, unable to face making small talk with his wife, Marlene said she would look for a grocery stand with a shorter queue.

As she walked away, she chided herself for letting August intimidate her. His mention of his friendship with Heinrich, a high-ranking SS officer, had been deliberate. Although she had no need to worry – he knew nothing of her family's activities – the incident had unnerved her. But surely, he didn't still hold a grudge after all this time?

Slow, fat raindrops began to fall, like that night long ago as she'd rushed from the theatre, the wind picking up and a storm threatening. She'd been so young, her heart vulnerable, August's cruel words running a circuit in her brain. She should have stayed at the theatre with Otto. If only she hadn't been so stubborn. Why had fate played its cruellest card? She'd lingered in town whilst people around her had rushed home. By the time she'd crossed the bridge, she was alone with the storm. Alone except for *him*.

* * *

It was with relief Marlene noted there was no sign of life from the nosy neighbour's hut. She and Franz checked over their shoulders before slipping inside the workshop. The note at the *Krimskrams* shop had said they would receive a delivery that night; there had been no indication if their guest would be a man or a woman.

The shutters outside were closed. Franz deemed it safe to light the small oil lamp whilst Marlene put a kettle on top of the wood-burning stove and placed the biscuits she'd baked on a plate.

They waited.

Franz brushed varnish onto a small commode and Marlene continued her knitting. The cuckoo clock ticked loudly. At midnight, the tiny bird behind the clock door protested, tapping against the shut door that Marlene had bolted closed. Outside, the forest shifted. An owl hooted.

The knock, although soft, made Marlene jump. She shot Franz a look and was at the door before he could put down his brush. She gasped when she opened the door.

Her surprise was twofold: the dark-haired woman who she suspected of being the leader of their resistance group, 'Bertha,' had brought the fugitive herself. And most surprising was that the fugitive was a young girl about four years old.

'She's been through a lot,' whispered Bertha. 'Someone will collect her in about three hours and take her to a safe house.'

She gave the child a gentle push over the doorstep and then sped away, melting into the darkness.

Marlene struggled to control her shock. A child fleeing the Nazis. She murmured to the child soothingly as she wrapped her in a blanket. She asked her name but the girl didn't answer.

Franz looked uncertainly at the kettle. 'She won't want coffee.'

'We have a small amount of milk. I'll mix it with hot water.'

When the kettle had boiled, Marlene prepared the drink, crumbling one of her biscuits into the cup to sweeten it.

Huddled in blankets and cushions on the floor, the girl silently sipped from her cup, her expression motionless. Her long, dishevelled hair had come loose from her plaits.

Marlene stroked a finger against her hair and said softly, 'Shall I do your hair?'

A tiny nod. There was so much Marlene wanted to know about the girl. Where were her parents? What had happened that she must flee? But the girl was too fragile to ask, and the exchange of information was discouraged by the resistance. Marlene fetched a comb from her handbag and gently detangled her hair.

'You have beautiful, hair,' she told her. 'Longer than mine when I was your age.'

The girl finished her drink and Marlene lay down with her.

'Marie,' a small voice said eventually.

Marlene smiled.

'Can I hold you, Marie?'

The girl's answer was to press her bony body against Marlene.

They waited. Franz went back to his varnishing and Marlene kept Marie in a close embrace.

At two o'clock in the morning, the cuckoo gave a frustrated tap on the inside of his shut door; the clock ticked on. Marlene heard Marie's steady breathing. She allowed her own eyelids to fall.

A short time later, the workshop shook as blows hammered on the door.

Marlene's eyes snapped open. The knocks were brutal and threatening: not the agreed coded taps. Franz stared at her, his face frozen, whilst Marlene jumped up, lifting the light child into her arms and rushing to the wardrobe.

Further blows pounded on the door. A harsh voice bellowed, '*Aufmachen. Polizei!*'

Marlene stepped inside the wardrobe with the girl.

Franz called out a sleepy reply. 'I'm coming, I'm coming. Let me get my trousers on!'

Marie's wide, startled eyes were fixed on Marlene as she put the child down.

'We're going to play hide and seek,' said Marlene as she dropped to her knees and scrambled to lift the floorboard. She peered into the hole in the ground.

The coffin.

Fear and nausea clutched at her throat.

Marie looked at her questioningly.

She heard Franz's footsteps clump towards the front door. She had split seconds to lower Marie into the hole and get back out.

Put the child in the ground, she told herself.

Alone. In the dark.

Damn it. No.

She pulled the wardrobe door closed and felt her way in the darkness, lowering herself into the hole, pulling Marie down on top of her stomach, her face to her breast.

'Quieter than mice,' she whispered, pulling the board into place over them.

Cold, black earth entombed them. The darkness sucked out the air.

Men's shouts. The trample of boots. Franz's plaintive tones.

The dank, musty smell of earth filled her nostrils.

Despite the potato sacks Franz had lined the hole with, the damp seeped into her back.

Her whole body trembled; she couldn't do this. She couldn't breathe.

Space. She needed space. Light. She wanted to scream, clamber out, but Marie... Oh, God.

A small whisper: 'Don't be scared. I've hidden in the dark loads of times.' Marie's voice was calm, her body still.

Marlene's eyes smarted at the brave words. She squeezed her eyes shut and clasped Marie tightly, in wonderment that this small, courageous child was the one soothing the adult.

There was the sound of a scraping chair, a clatter of things falling to the floor – Franz's work tools perhaps? Boots, voices, drawers opening.

Footsteps came closer.

They stopped.

She held her breath. Gripped Marie's cardigan, balling her hands.

The wardrobe door creaked open. A heavy foot stamped on the floorboard.

Silence.

Hold your breath. Don't make a sound. But her body was too loud: her pulse, her heart, her breathing.

He was standing inches above them. He would bend down, notice the floorboard and lift it in triumph. A pistol would point in their faces: at Marie, still and quiet, just her little heartbeat quickening against Marlene's breast...

The wardrobe door slammed shut.

'*Nichts*.' The grunt was followed by retreating footsteps.

After what seemed like an eternity, she heard Franz's voice.

'It's all right. It's safe now.'

The floorboard lifted; air and light rushed in. Franz lowered his arm and hauled them from their grave.

* * *

The next day, still recovering from her ordeal, Marlene made her way to the *Krimskrams* shop. She'd have to tell Trautel that she and Franz were being watched and that they would have to pause their activities. Why were the authorities suspicious about them? What had they been looking for? False documents? Anti-Nazi leaflets? They'd found nothing but they might return. Thank goodness Marie had been collected an hour after the *Polizei* had left and would now be at a safe house somewhere.

As she approached the shop, it was clear something was wrong. Shattered glass littered the pavement and wooden planks were nailed across the broken window. The front door was boarded up too.

Marlene stared, open-mouthed.

Dreading the news of what might have happened, she knocked on the door adjacent to the shop. A woman her own age in a dirt-smeared apron and a floral headscarf appeared.

'Oh, yes,' she said smugly. 'Gestapo have her now. They took her away yesterday. Carried her, actually, what with her twisted legs and everything...'

Something caught Marlene's eye: the glint of a freshly polished candlestick on the hallway table. A jolt of recognition. She'd seen it in Trautel's shop window. The brass cherub, an arm extended to hold a candle. Her eyes narrowed as she studied the bitter face of the woman in front of her.

'Weird old crow, she was,' said the woman. 'Did you know her?' She studied Marlene with interest.

Marlene shook her head, saying she'd heard about the shop and just stopped by to take a look.

She left, gripped by despair. It was all going wrong. She and Franz were under suspicion, their rescue attempts halted. And Trautel, her fragile body in the hands of the Gestapo. She had no doubt that this brave woman would pay the ultimate price.

The waitresses in their summer *Dirndls* dodged between the tables, expertly delivering fistfuls of beer tankards to thirsty guests. The warm spring weather had brought the crowds to the *Biergarten* at the top of the Pöstlingberg, its superb view and cheerful staff making it a popular venue.

'Thanks, Ella, for agreeing to meet me,' said Lisl before cautiously sipping her small beer.

'We never had that much opportunity to speak alone at Villa Rosa. It's nice to have a chat, just the two of us.' Ella tore off a piece of a soft freshly baked *Brezel*. 'How are you and Erwin getting on?'

'I'm not sure, really. I'd imagined our engagement to be romantic. Erwin seems to have very little time for me. He's always dashing off to some important event with other SS officers, mumbling about big things happening.'

Ella's ears pricked up. What big things were happening?

'Max is the same. There's a Party meeting almost every evening, which always seems to involve copious amounts of alcohol.'

Lisl averted her gaze, playing with a beer mat. 'Do you think they have women at these meetings? You know, for entertainment and such? Erwin spent time in Berlin...' Her thin voice trailed off.

'I have heard that things can get bawdy, but I'm sure Erwin is not involved. You have nothing to worry about; he loves you.'

A roar of laughter erupted from a nearby table as four Wehrmacht soldiers slammed their beer glasses together and shouted, '*Prost!*'

They love it here, thought Ella; they think we're quaint.

'Aren't you worried about what Max gets up to?'

She didn't care if he had other women; at least he'd left her alone since that awful incident.

'I think these stories of wild parties are exaggerated,' she said, giving Lisl a reassuring smile.

Lisl's fair skin was reddening in the sun and her fringe was damp against her forehead.

'Do you want to get out of the sun?' Ella asked. 'We can take a walk around the model town. It will be cool down there.'

The girls descended the circular stone steps into the underground cavern, emerging in the Linz of the past under a starlit sky. There was hardly anyone around, most people preferring to spend time in the sunshine above ground. Down the side alleys, the creatures from the Grimm brothers' fairy tales leered at them from shadowy corners. Ella was again drawn to the huge stuffed bear on his hind legs, his claws hovering above her head. But today, as she looked into his clouded, dead eyes, she felt sad for him.

They halted at Sleeping Beauty, the life-size figure of the prince with his white horse arriving in the background.

Lisl sighed. 'The thing is, I don't know how to make Erwin really notice me. I have to prove myself somehow. It's the story of my life.'

'What do you mean?'

'I have three brothers who've always gained the full attention of my parents. I was just an insignificant daughter that would hopefully get married and be off my father's hands; we never had much money. Then when by some miracle, I attracted the attention of Erwin, an esteemed SS officer, my father saw me in a new light. I was suddenly worthy, a respected member of the family.'

'So now you have a new chance in life.'

How ironic that Lisl's saviour was no honourable fairy-tale prince but an evil, bigoted Nazi.

'And I will prove myself to him. I shall be the perfect Reich bride.' Lisl's expression was resolute.

As they sat in a meadow dappled with purple and yellow wildflowers, Ella leaned her head on Jayden's shoulder. The air was filled with the clang of cowbells and the hum of bees. She fiddled with the bow on her *Dirndl*; that morning, she'd tied it firmly on the front left side of her waist, signalling she was single. For fun, she'd retied it on the right to see how it would look if she were married. As she'd gazed at her image in the full-length mirror, she'd imagined having a husband. Not Max, but someone she truly loved.

Not someone. Jayden. Impossible, of course.

She'd sighed and tied the bow back in the appropriate place.

Mutti had turned from the stove to look at her as she entered the kitchen. 'You look pretty today. Are you meeting Max?'

She hesitated. Mutti liked Jayden, but she would only worry if she knew Ella was seeing him: the dangers, the implications.

'No – Lisl. We're going to the lakes. Probably Mondsee.'

The lie had made her face flush and she'd turned away.

Now Jayden took her hand. 'You look lovely. Why so traditional today?'

'It's a *Dirndl* made by a local woman with colours of our region; I suppose I wanted to identify with that.' The *Dirndl* was deep blue with white flowers. 'The colours signify the Danube.'

'Maybe we should be sitting on the river bank rather than overlooking the Mondsee,' he said.

She'd been happily surprised when Jayden had agreed to meet her out of town.

'I don't get to the lakes often. I love it here.' She gazed down on the azure lake, the deep green forests reflected sharply in the crystal water. A small village on the opposite shore nestled around a church with an onion-shaped dome. Its bells chimed the hour. She let out a sigh; it was as if she was sitting in one of Gustav Klimt's paintings.

'Don't you go on trips with Max?' Jayden said, his tone suddenly stiff.

'He's very busy with his new friends from the Party. I don't see him very much at the moment. Luckily.'

'He's a dangerous man. How long do you plan to go on with this pretence?' Jayden frowned.

'I keep thinking I'll stop, but then something vital crops up, like finding that list of names in Heinrich's library. Then I know I have to carry on. There are still so many I need to warn: those that don't know their mixed heritage has been discovered and that they could be arrested at any moment.'

'I want to help. I may even know the people from my years working at the store.' He stroked her hair. 'I worry about you. You shouldn't be doing this alone.'

'I worry about *you*.'

He shook his head. 'I still don't understand why you're putting yourself in such danger.'

She cringed inwardly: because people like her had voted for the Anschluss, given her country over to the Nazis, perpetuated the hatred of the regime. In a moment of stupidity and warped ideology, she had sanctioned the persecution. And the guilt was eating her raw. She had sided against Jayden.

'Give me the names,' he said. 'I'll contact those remaining on the list. You've motivated me to start fighting back, instead of just waiting for the next blow to fall.' He took her face in his hands. 'But I don't want you involved any more. I couldn't bear it if anything happened to you.' His voice was thick with emotion.

Heat surged through her, and as tears threatened, she kissed him.

Unlike that day in the forest, his response was immediate.

Urgent.

He pushed her down amidst the flowers and ran his hands over her breasts.

She arched her back, aching for him, stroking his chest, feeling the hair beneath his shirt.

The memory of him in his swimming trunks last summer on the beach fired her with longing to see his body, touch him all over.

He dipped his head to her cleavage, which was exposed in her low-cut *Dirndl* blouse, his lips and tongue hot on her skin. Fingers slipping beneath and stroking her nipples.

She moaned.

He fumbled with the tiny buttons, struggling with the slippery pearls and tight buttonholes.

'Let me,' she said, sitting up.

She undid the buttons one by one, from the top down to her waist where her apron was tied.

He knelt beside her, watching. She adored how his Adam's apple moved each time he swallowed, how his desire shone in his eyes, his lips parted.

Prising the bodice apart, she revealed the swell of her breasts.

She waited for him to touch her again. Yearned for his hands. On her. All over her. She grabbed the bow on the front of her apron and tugged it open.

'Wait,' he said, his voice thick.

She saw confusion in his face.

'No. I shan't wait.' She pulled the apron off and began to pull on the side zip of her dress.

'Stop. Ella, please.'

But she couldn't. Wouldn't.

'I want this.'

The zip down, the dress released, she let the blouse and bodice slip from her shoulders, leaving her naked to the waist.

'Touch me,' she said, placing a hand on her own breast.

He let out a loud moan and turned from her.

Turned from her!

She sat there like a fool, half her body exposed in the blinding sunlight, her skin white hot, perspiration dripping between her breasts, her nipples hard. And he'd looked away.

Humiliation overcame her, dousing her desire. She bowed her head and with shaking fingers, redid those tiny damn buttons. One after the other. And the whole time, Jayden sat with his back to her. Anger replaced her passion. She had served herself up to him, and he'd rejected her, in the most clear terms.

* * *

Over the next three days, Ella relived the scene over and over. How she'd stomped down the hillside, Jayden running after her; he'd stammered about not wanting to put her in danger, not wanting to hurt her. But her pride had got the better of her, and she'd remained silent and angry the whole bus journey home. Jayden had alighted several stops outside of Linz to avoid them being seen together, walking the rest of the way home. On the back seat of the bus, she'd peered out of the window and watched his forlorn face disappear down the dusty road.

Now, at her bedroom window, staring at the Pöstlingberg as dusk fell, she chastised herself for her reaction. It was obvious that Jayden cared for her or why would he have agreed to an outing to the Mondsee? He'd said he couldn't bear it if anything happened to her. Clearly, he was trying to protect her by creating distance between them. She would go and see him and talk things through; she couldn't just leave it like this. And of course, she needed to give him the list of names.

Shortly after ten o'clock, her parents went to bed, both of them having to get up early the following day. Ella waited a while before slipping out of the apartment and made her way into town, checking over her shoulder constantly for familiar faces.

It was Jayden's father who opened the upper window when she knocked, a look of surprise on his face. Jayden appeared moments later and the two of them took their usual place in the stairwell. She gave him the list.

'I'll take care of this, Ella. You've done an amazing job but it's off your hands now.' He tucked the paper in his pocket. The air was hot and stale. She grappled for her carefully planned speech, but her brain went numb.

'I love you,' she blurted out. 'And I know you love me.'

'Ella, listen—'

'I don't want to hear about how our love is dangerous and how you want to protect me. We can keep it secret for now, but we can find ways to meet, to spend time together, to love one another. I have loads of ideas—'

'I'm back with Ruth. I'm sorry, Ella. I'm going to marry her.'

Ella's body caved at the blow. Breathless, confused, she shook her head.

'Please forgive me if I gave you the false impression. It was wrong of me.'

Fury and pain erupted. She slammed her hands into his chest.

'Liar!' she screamed. 'I don't believe that was a false impression. The emotions are real between us. You don't love her. You can't mean it.'

Jayden's face was frozen.

His words were strangled as he stood up. 'I'm sorry I misled you. Goodbye, Ella. And stay safe.'

He climbed back up the stairs, leaving her alone in the suffocating heat under the sallow light of the naked light bulb.

A teenage boy, cross-legged on the sand, played guitar. Several girls sat around him, singing along to the German folksong, whilst three boys stood listening, bottles of beer in hand. Ella, who was perched on a tree stump at the entrance to the beach, watched: the perfect Friday night on a warm June evening. Only nothing about it was perfect: the boys wore Hitler Youth uniforms, the girls, swastika pins on their pretty dresses. And Ella was waiting for her Nazi fiancé, dreading an evening of holding hands, watching the sunset.

Max arrived looking agitated, sweat on his brow. He gave Ella a perfunctory kiss as she stood to meet him.

'I'm sorry, Ella. Something important has come up and I have to cancel our date.'

She swallowed her delight and did her best to give a disgruntled pout. 'To do with the Party?'

'I'll make it up to you. How about we have a picnic here tomorrow? At noon. I'll bring drinks if you can rustle up some bread rolls.'

Ella agreed and watched him stride off.

Happy to remain sitting on the tree trunk, she watched the beach fill with revellers celebrating the start of the weekend. Young and old spread picnic blankets on the sand or wallowed out into the cool Danube.

A wave of loneliness came over her. She would have loved to be here with Jayden, snuggled against him, tempting him with deep kisses as the sky darkened. But in the real world, he was not welcome here on the beach, and besides, he'd finished with her. Rejected her advances. Pain speared her heart. Frustration and longing overwhelmed her, and she allowed the large, warm tears to drip down her face.

When she'd calmed down, she made her way to Hedy's house, hoping she would be at home. She was lucky to have such a special best friend and she needed to hear Hedy's comforting, wise words.

When Hedy opened the door, Ella fell into her arms, mumbling, 'I'm so grateful to have you.'

The girls sat on the garden bench facing the mountain peaks etched dark against the navy sky. The air had cooled and Hedy draped one of her cardigans across Ella's shoulders. Ella told her everything about Jayden, her words gushing out: how she had fallen in love with him and how hopeless the situation was.

Hedy had remained silent a few moments, mulling over everything she'd heard, before saying, 'I'm sorry your poor heart is in this terrible mess. Even if you weren't engaged to Max, you couldn't be with Jayden officially. Jews are no longer permitted to date non-Jews. You'd both be in trouble.'

'What sort of world are we living in?' Ella's question hung in the air. 'What about you, Hedy? Who does your heart beat for? Are you still interested in the boy at the clockmaker's shop?'

Hedy sighed. 'How can I date anyone with the threat of my

Jewish roots being exposed to the whole of Linz? A Catholic boy would drop me instantly if he found out. And dating a Jewish boy would be an open admission and put my family in danger. I have to stay solo.'

Ella wrapped her arm around Hedy's waist. 'Sorry for being selfish and pouring my heart out. You don't exactly have things easy either.'

'It's not a competition for who is suffering the worst. What's important is that we have each other, whatever comes our way.'

'I'm still waiting for further news from Freddie. It all seems to be taking so long.'

Ella had written to him about getting Trudy on the Kindertransport. He'd replied that he would make enquiries, but had warned that the authorities were demanding mountains of stipulations, and countries like Britain would only allow entry if a child had a sponsor.

'I'm sure Freddie is doing his best. We must try to be patient,' said Hedy.

As they huddled together, darkness shrouded them and the bats came out, swooping for their prey.

* * *

The following day when Ella arrived on the beach, Max was already there, blanket rolled out and sipping a beer. Just the sight of him made her heart sink. She was desperate to be rid of him. Once Trudy had a ticket for the Kindertransport and she was sure that all those on the list wanting visas had one, she would finish with Max. But how? She would have to be careful not to hurt his pride. Somehow, she must make the idea come from him.

He looked grim when she sat down next to him, his face grey, his eyes red and puffy. His usual immaculate hair was greasy and uncombed. She was grateful he didn't greet her with a kiss.

'Was it a late night?' she asked, not caring about the answer.

'You know how these things are.' He took a slug of beer, his hand shaking. Even for Max, it was early in the day for a drink.

'I've brought bread and sausage,' she said, matter-of-factly. It looked like he needed to line his stomach, but he waved his hand in refusal.

'I've been thinking things over. I'm sick of working at my father's vinegar factory and I'm going to join the Wehrmacht.' He took another gulp of beer and turned to face her. 'And I've been thinking about our wedding.'

'Me too.' Now was her chance to plant the seed. 'We haven't seen much of each other lately. Understandably, you have important priorities now you are increasingly active in the Party. Maybe we've drifted apart. Perhaps you've had a change of heart. I'd totally understand if—'

'We should marry immediately. This month. A July wedding.'

Ella stared at him with horror.

His laugh was more of a sneer. 'You could look a bit more enthusiastic!'

'Why the hurry all of a sudden? We said autumn.'

'Because I'm tired of this dating business, waiting for the big day. I want people to acknowledge us as a married couple. I want you in my bed. I want a normal family life. I want children.' He sounded like a spoilt child.

'I don't think I'm ready yet,' she said, fighting to keep the panic from her voice.

'I don't see why not. Unless you're still lusting after that Jew boy?'

A rush of rage and she lost control.

'Don't you dare speak to me in that disgusting way. I can't

imagine why you would want to marry someone you clearly have no respect for.'

She started to get up but he grabbed her wrist and pulled her back down beside him.

'You and I are getting married. By the end of the month.'

'Why, in God's name? You don't even like me.'

'Let's just say you have certain qualities: a Reich bride certificate, a job with Göring and a young, healthy body.' He squeezed her wrist harder. 'And you will do what I want to protect your brother. You don't want the Gestapo sniffing around Freddie and your family.'

She stared into his hateful eyes, the ones she had once thought so beautiful. It was a mistake to have ever got involved with him. He wanted to control her, exert his power over her. She shuddered to think what her future would look like if she stayed with him. But she was trapped, in over her head. How on earth was she going to be free of him without plunging her family into danger?

* * *

It was a week later when Ella approached Hedy's house, a heavy sorrow slowing her footsteps. Trudy was already standing on the doorstep, her glossy, dark hair parted in the middle, two neat plaits framing her porcelain skin. Her tired eyes were dry; she was cried out now.

There had been terrible scenes when Ella had told Hedy's family that Freddie had secured a place on the Kindertransport. They had all wept as Trudy clung to her mother, refusing to leave. Hilde had told a stunned Trudy about her Jewish roots. After two days of discussion, arguments and a string of promises that they would all be united at some point, Trudy now stood numbly beside her mother, ready.

Hedy emerged with a small brown suitcase. There were strict regulations on what children's luggage was permitted to contain: bare essentials but no jewellery, no money or any object of value that could be traded later on. One small toy, but no camera, valuable pens, or expensive clothing such as a hat trimmed with fur. Such items would be confiscated by customs.

Ella held out her hand to take it from Hedy. The Kindertransport organisers had advised against parents dropping off their own children to avoid emotional scenes, and requested one accompanying adult only. Ella had been the natural choice.

'I can carry my own suitcase,' said Trudy, stiffly.

'Of course,' said Ella.

There was hardly anything left that Trudy could control in her life, but at least she could carry her own luggage.

The final goodbyes had obviously been said before Ella had arrived. Now, Hedy gave Trudy a swift kiss on the cheek.

'Send us a postcard of the sea.'

Hilde hugged her daughter briefly. 'Be polite to your foster parents.'

She gave Trudy a gentle push forward and nodded at Ella. Holding Trudy's free hand, she guided her down the pathway.

'*Ich habe dich lieb.*' Hilde's thin voice declaring her love for her daughter drifted after them. But when Trudy looked round, her mother and sister were already retreating through the front door.

The train rattled through the countryside. Trudy had her face pressed against the window. Brown and white cows grazed lazily on upper meadows, deep green forests clung to steep hills, all against the backdrop of mountains and valleys that stretched along a cloudless skyline.

How bitter, thought Ella, was this juxtaposition of the beauty of their country against the ugliness of the evolving events.

Trudy had been silent during the journey and Ella could see by the set of her shoulders and her turned head that she was angry with her. After all, it was Ella who'd asked Freddie to organise the transportation that had wrenched her from her family. She had already lost her father and now she was being forced to leave her mother and sister behind. All the talk of it being for her own good had not convinced her.

'I've never seen the sea either,' said Ella, trying again to engage the girl in conversation. 'Only in books and on postcards. Your foster family live in a town called Hove, right on the seaside.'

'I know that already,' Trudy said, her voice dull. 'And I know it has lovely English houses and that it's near a very smart town called Brighton. But I still don't want to go. I only speak a few words of English and I'll be forced to go to some stupid school where the children will make fun of my accent.'

'Oh, Trudy, I'm sure—'

'How can you be sure of anything?' She finally faced Ella, her eyes welling up.

'You're right, I can't be sure.' She put her arm around Trudy's narrow shoulders. 'But I imagine that the type of people who offer their home to an unknown girl, to care for her and pay for her keep, must be kind people, surely. And it's a temporary measure. We will find a way for you to be reunited with your Mutti and Hedy.'

'How?' said Trudy, her anger gone, her voice now full of hopelessness.

'We must have faith. We mustn't give up hope.'

'I'll try,' Trudy said, her voice so small that Ella's stomach twisted as she fought back her own tears.

* * *

Freddie met them at the station, a brown envelope in his hand.

'These are the papers, Ella, you have to give the organisers.' He pulled something out and handed it to Trudy. 'It's best you put this on now.'

It was a tag on a ribbon stating Trudy's name and a reference number. She slipped it over her neck. Labelled.

They exited the crowded station and Freddie led them to an agreed meeting point opposite the Hotel Schneller. A group of children of all ages had gathered: some older children carrying babies, others holding each other's hands, some looking bewildered, others excited as if going on holiday. Women with clipboards flurried around, giving directions.

Freddie pointed at one of the women. 'That's Rosa Schwarz who's organising the whole thing. The other women helping here are Quakers and will travel with the children.'

'Do you know the route they will take?' said Ella as she tried to take in the emotional scene.

'The train will travel to Holland and then the children will be taken by boat to Harwich. Then onwards by train to London.' Freddie paused and gave Trudy a gentle smile. 'Your foster parents will meet you there – in London.'

A clipboard lady approached, and Ella clutched Trudy's hand tightly.

'I must leave,' said Freddie. 'Only one accompanying adult. I'll meet you at that café,' he added, pointing to a red and white awning further down the road. Then he gave Trudy a reassuring smile and hurried away.

In a daze, Ella handed the papers over and watched as the woman made a tick on her list then checked Trudy's name tag. Ella looked at Trudy, the tagged children around her, their small suitcases holding the sum of their belongings, a crying baby in the arms of a young boy. Each child had a parent who had made the ultimate, heart-wrenching decision. Was this what Ella had voted for that day just over a year ago, as she had resolutely planted her cross in the circle, *Ja*? She sickened herself. Here she was sending off her best friend's sister to an unknown future. It was people like her who were responsible.

'It's best if you say goodbye now,' the clipboard lady said. 'I'll take care of Trudy. We will shortly be taking the children to the platform from which the train departs.'

Ella had not prepared for this moment; she fought back her rising panic.

Stay strong.

She cupped Trudy's face in her hands and fixed her gaze on the girl's wide, desolate eyes.

'These are good people who will get you to London safely. Write when you arrive and—'

'Don't leave me.' Trudy threw her arms around Ella's waist. 'Don't make me go. Please!'

'You have to do this for your Mutti and for Hedy, so they have peace of mind knowing you're safe.' Ella's voice trembled and tears filled her eyes. She kissed Trudy's hot, wet cheek, then disentangled herself and stepped back.

'Will I ever see you again?' asked Trudy.

'Of course you will.'

What else could she say?

'Promise?' Her tone was insistent.

'Promise.' As soon as the word passed her lips, resolution swelled in Ella's chest. Somehow, no matter what lay ahead, she would keep her promise.

It was time. The clipboard lady put a hand on Trudy's back and led her to a queue of children. Ella crossed to the other side of the street, having to force each step away from her best friend's sister. In a shop doorway, she watched Trudy, wearing the yellow summer dress sewn by her mother; she wore white ankle socks and navy T-bar shoes. Ella wished she had a camera, but instead, she mentally captured the moment, letting it burn into her mind.

A few moments later, the children were led towards the station entrance. Ella saw Trudy turn her head as she looked for her. Ella raised her hand but at that moment, a horse and carriage full of tourists clattered by. When the carriage had passed, the children were gone.

30

MARLENE

Marlene laid the blanket across the kitchen table and covered it with an old sheet. She put two heavy pots on opposite corners to hold it in place and plugged in the smoothing iron. Ella entered with the basket of washing that had been hanging outside to dry. Picking up one of Franz's shirts, Marlene frowned.

'We should've brought them in still damp.'

She placed the shirt on the table, put a clean dishcloth under the tap, laid it over the shirt and ran the iron up and down. She was sweating within moments.

Ella poured them some elderberry juice. As she helped fold the clothes, she said, 'Mutti, I have a bit of a problem.'

Marlene's senses spiked; she had been on high alert since the police had raided the workshop. She had refrained from telling Ella, not wanting to worry or involve her. Besides, Ella didn't know her parents had been hiding refugees there; Marlene had steadfastly refused to tell Ella anything that could endanger her.

'Max wants us to marry this month.'

Marlene slammed the iron down on the table. 'No! This has gone far enough. You must call off the wedding.'

'I know. I've had enough of it all. But what if Max accuses Freddie of being an anti-Nazi? This whole plan of mine has brought nothing but trouble.' Her voice cracked and she slumped down on a chair.

'Not at all. Look at all you've achieved. You heard about the riots and we got Jayden's family to safety. You found out about Albert Göring and the forged exit visas.'

'It doesn't seem enough somehow.'

Marlene turned from the ironing and took her daughter's hands in hers.

'We do what we can. And if you rescue just one person, then you have achieved something tremendous. I'm incredibly proud of you. But I'm also your mother and concerned about your safety. This is my fault for allowing this to have continued for so long. I need to think about the best way we can part you from Max. You look tired, Ella. Go and rest now.'

Ella went into the sitting room and lay down on the sofa. As Marlene continued the ironing, she had the awful feeling things were closing in on them. She blamed herself for not intervening sooner, for even allowing Ella to get engaged and go to Bride School. What had she been thinking? Ella was right about the danger to Freddie if Max turned vindictive. But she couldn't let her family be held to ransom. And yet she couldn't let her own son fall into the hands of the Gestapo. Somehow, Max must be kept quiet. But the question was, how?

Marlene felt the familiar throb start in her right temple. How would Max's father, August react to the break up? Since she had seen August at the market, the memories of that fateful night would not leave her alone. She had always maintained that she hardly knew August when she was young. But she had and it was him who had started a chain of events that were to have terrible, lasting consequences. And she, Marlene, had been the lynchpin.

* * *

The apartment was hot and stuffy when Marlene returned from work. Listless, she opened all the windows and went to the small refrigerator to fetch a beer. Changing her mind, she shut the door. Since her work for the underground had abruptly come to a halt, she was feeling down, impotent. Her mind had been working feverishly day and night for other ways to contribute to the opposition. And of course, there was the problem with Max. Feeling overwhelmed, she decided she needed to do something. Get out of the apartment.

She brushed her hair, changed her blouse and headed for the workshop.

Franz was surprised to see her.

'How about taking your wife out for a drink at the Klosterhof Biergarten?'

Tools in hand, her husband looked back at her with a sad smile. 'Normally, I'd say of course. But I have to finish these chairs this evening.'

She went up behind him and wrapped her arms around him. His overalls were covered in wood shavings and his hair rumpled.

'Just an hour or so, then you could come back here and finish.' She pressed herself up against his back and rubbed her hands over his chest. 'Please. This lady needs a night out.'

He sighed and she knew she'd got her way.

* * *

After Franz had removed his overalls, washed his face and combed his hair, they walked over the Donaubrücke and into town. The Klosterhof Biergarten was a throng of people on this warm summer evening, the atmosphere light-hearted, the air buzzing with chatter punctuated by bursts of laughter. It was just what Marlene needed to lift her spirits, a short respite from the worries that weighed on her mind. There were no seats available, so they stood under the tree canopy.

The unlit fairy lights entwined in the branches of the chestnut trees reminded her of Ella's twenty-first birthday just over a year ago; Ella and Max had seemed so in love.

As if reading her thoughts, Franz said, 'She's not marrying him. Talk to her, tell her to call it off. Why hasn't she told him yet?'

Franz's face was bright red, either from frustration, the heat or his blood pressure. Or the beer.

Marlene put a reassuring hand on his arm. 'She's just waiting for the right moment. I'm helping her plan what to say.'

'This whole idea was folly in the first place. She's twenty-two years old and should be looking for a decent man. Someone she really loves.'

'She's still young enough to find someone, Franz.'

'We were already married at that age. We don't want her ending up an old maid.'

Marlene laughed. 'Goodness, you're so old fashioned. Times have changed.'

'Not according to our government's way of thinking. Out of the workplace and into the kitchen is the new motto.'

A man's voice joined their conversation.

Marlene started. The voice belonged to Otto, who was struggling with two overflowing tankards of beer.

'Sorry for butting in. I'm just trying to get over to join my friends.'

'We've met before, haven't we? At that party,' said Franz, smiling. 'We were just leaving as you arrived.'

'That's right. But Marlene and I have known each other a little longer.' He gazed at her a fraction too long. A fraction too deeply, his expression soft.

'Well, nice to see you again. We don't want to keep you from your friends,' she said curtly.

Otto accepted her dismissal and continued on his way.

'That was a bit unfriendly,' Franz said.

'I couldn't be bothered with chitchat. I want to spend my time with you.'

Franz grinned, looking pleased.

She studied her husband. He had aged of course, his face fuller, his hair thinner. But his kind, brown eyes and the amiable nod of his head as he spoke were the same. His large, broad hand clasped his beer tankard and it still amazed her that such large hands could be so skilled at his craftmanship, yet so gentle when he touched her. How she loved this man: always solid by her side, a devoted father to their two children. It had never interested him to go drinking with the local men, who liked to escape to the nearest *Kneipe*. He was a homely man.

As they finished their drinks, two seats became free.

'Let's sit and have one more drink,' she said.

They wiled away another hour, during which time, she noticed Otto leave the *Biergarten*. He glanced in her direction but she averted her gaze.

The lanterns and fairy lights flickered on as darkness fell. Finally, they decided to leave and they ambled down the Landstraße arm in arm.

Marlene leaned into Franz. 'Let's go home. I want to take you to bed.'

She wasn't sure why, but she'd been aching for him all evening.

'I'd love nothing more, but we agreed if we went to the Klosterhof, I'd return afterwards to the workshop to finish off.'

They crossed the Danube and parted ways: he to the workshop

and she reluctantly towards home. She stomped along, restless and agitated. Otto shouldn't have acted like that in front of Franz: those meaningful looks. The last thing she wanted was Franz to discover they had been seeing each other. Harmlessly, yes. But secretly. And the last time she'd seen Otto, they had danced alone in his house...

She had to sort this out: tell Otto that she still loved Franz deeply and that she regretted it if she'd given him the wrong impression. She had meant to comfort him after the death of his wife, nothing more.

A little poke of guilt. A memory of her young, broken heart.

As she took the street in the direction of Otto's house, her stride didn't falter. She'd let herself get swept up in emotions from the past as well as empathy for Otto's loss. But now she had to put the record straight: make clear to him there would only ever be friendship between them.

He opened the door with an expression of surprise and pleasure.

'I won't come in, Otto. I just need to make some things clear.'

'That's silly to stand on the doorstep. Come through to the garden.'

She followed him through the house and out the back door. The sound of chirping crickets filled the night. He'd lit an oil lamp and some candles. A bottle of cherry *Schnapps*, an ashtray and a packet of cigarettes lay on the table. 'I'll fetch a second glass,' he said.

'No, really—'

But he was already walking back into the house. She gazed across the garden and up at the dark outline of the distant mountains. She must stay resolute and tell him at once what she had come to say. When he returned with a glass, she shook her head.

'At least sit down,' he said, placing the glass on the table and sitting down himself.

She sighed and took a seat, hands in her lap, thumbs pressed together.

'I want to make clear I love my husband and will never do anything to hurt him or endanger our marriage.'

'And you feel things went too far the last time you were here. I fully understand and I apologise. It won't happen again.'

'We must stop seeing each other.'

Otto said nothing and poured himself a drink.

'I haven't even told Franz that we've been meeting.'

'Why the secret?'

There was a knowing look in his eyes. She shuffled in her seat and nodded at the bottle.

'I will have one please.'

He poured a full glass of the burgundy liquid and handed it to her, his fingers touching hers as he did so. She gulped it down and angrily slammed the glass back on the table.

'Right, let's be honest here. We both know how much I loved you and how you ripped apart my heart. I cried every night for weeks, months. It was only two years later – when Franz arrived in Linz and we started dating – that a blossom of happiness reappeared in my life.'

Otto hung his head. 'I know. But I loved you too. I didn't plan it—'

'It doesn't matter any more! It's old news. Unfortunately, that night had consequences that I have to live with, daily.' She grabbed the bottle and poured herself another glass.

He frowned. 'What consequences?'

She shook her head and drank.

'There's something I must know,' he said, his voice soft. 'Do you still have feelings for me?'

Outraged, she jumped up. 'You have no right to ask me that!'

She threw the *Schnapps* down her throat and stormed out.

Her heart was still pounding when she arrived home and put her key in the door. To her surprise, Franz was already home, a newspaper folded and unread on his lap. Surely he hadn't finished his work? How long had she been gone?

Before she'd even sat down, he said, 'Where were you? It's nearly midnight.'

She opened her mouth but no words came out. Whatever she said would give the wrong impression. Why on earth had she not told Franz from the start? And a small teenage voice whispered: *because deep, deep, down, the wound was still there.*

'You were with him. I knew it. That's why I came back early. I saw the way he looked at you at the Klosterhof. And how uncomfortable you acted. Are you and he...'

His voice broke, and his eyes welled with tears.

'No, no!' She rushed to him, wrapping her arms around him, repeating again and again how much she loved him: that she had merely been trying to support Otto after the terrible shooting of his wife. And yes, they dated a very long time ago, but she had been little more than a child.

But when he asked why the secrecy, the deception, she stumbled over her words. Franz looked at her with distrust in his eyes.

That night, for the first time in their marriage, he slept on the sofa, and Marlene lay alone in their bed, wondering what on earth she had done.

* * *

The delicious smell of fresh bread and sweet pastry wafted out from the small bakery on the corner. Marlene occasionally shopped here and was acquainted with the owner – Herr Bäcker –

whose name couldn't have been more appropriate. She joined the
queue, nervously fiddling with the clasp of her handbag.

She had been at the market the previous Saturday when a
grey-haired woman with a large basket had bumped into her.
She'd apologised immediately and added in a low voice, 'Herr
Bäcker in Hamerlingstraße has the best *Himbeerschnecken* in Linz.
Try one and say Vilma sends greetings.'

And she'd gone before Marlene could utter a reply.

Now she waited in anticipation. The bakery had obviously
been chosen as the new point of contact since the *Krimskrams* shop
had been raided. Marlene admired the way the resistance refused
to be defeated, always springing back into action.

When it was her turn, she gave her order for the *Himbeerschnecken* and *Grüße* from Vilma. Herr Bäcker, a jovial man with a
bushy moustache, popped the pastry in a paper bag and bent
under the counter for a few moments before pulling out a folded
serviette and adding it to her items.

A short distance from the bakery, Marlene paused at a fountain. She perched on the stone edge and pulled out the serviette:
one word in pencil was scrawled across the paper:

Montags

Mondays were to be the day she should stop by the bakery to
collect messages.

She put the serviette in her pocket to dispose of later. Then,
sitting by the fountain in the sunshine, she happily ate her rasp-
berry pastry. It was as Vilma had promised: delicious.

* * *

It wasn't yet eight o'clock in the morning and Marlene was already sweating as she walked to work. She looked forward to the thunderstorm that was predicted later in the day. It would be lovely to dance in the rain, she thought, her hair and clothes streaming with cooling water.

What a ridiculous notion: women her age didn't behave like that.

As she neared the Danube, she slowed her step. Ahead, women who intended to wash their clothes in the river were being waved away by a row of policemen. A woman was weeping as she spoke to an officer who was taking notes, and behind her, a photographer sidled around a heap of something on the ground, clicking his camera.

'What's going on?' Marlene asked a woman who was heaving her basket up the grass verge.

'A body was washed up on the river bank. My friend back there found it. She nearly passed out from shock. I tried not to peek... but you know how it is.' Her large double chin wobbled. 'Not a pretty sight.'

'Do they know who it is?'

'A soldier. From the Wehrmacht. There's going to be trouble, that's for sure,' she said, breathing heavily from excitement.

An officer glanced their way and Marlene decided to move on. She didn't need any more trouble with the authorities.

By lunch time, the scarf factory was buzzing with the news. As Marlene walked down the line carrying out quality inspections, every worker had a theory as to how the soldier had met his fate: everything from falling drunk into the Danube to being brutally murdered by an anti-Nazi. The event certainly livened up the atmosphere, the workers gossiping happily till the end of the day.

The predicted thunderstorm did not materialise. It was too hot to eat inside that evening, so Marlene, Franz and Ella took their cucumber, dill salad and sliced ham out to the picnic benches in front of the apartment block. All their neighbours were outside too, the younger ones spread out on the grass. Franz chose to sit apart from Marlene.

It had been a week since their row over Otto. Franz had at least returned to their bed, albeit he did so lying on the edge with his back to her. He'd shrugged her off when she reached for him and their conversation was now reduced to the bare minimum. Marlene was at a loss about how to repair the rift between them.

Now she sat with Frau Bauer, the woman whose husband had been sent to Dachau. She leaned into Marlene. 'They're saying that soldier was dead before he hit the water. Murdered.'

'There'll be a huge investigation,' said Marlene. 'The Gestapo will be involved and they won't let up till they have the culprit.'

She shuddered to think what punishment the notorious secret police would dole out.

31

ELLA

It should have been the perfect summer day, but Ella had been dreading it. She and Max rowed along the mellow Danube, waving back to people sunning themselves on the grassy banks. Swans, regal and serene, glided past. Ella was grateful for the shade of her floppy straw hat and her airy sundress. They rowed at a leisurely pace, allowing themselves to drift on the gentle current. Max was in a good mood, complimenting her on her rowing skills and her tanned, toned arms. And when they stopped on the shore to eat their picnic, he picked her a bunch of wildflowers.

This was the Max that had first attracted her before she'd seen his ugliness. His changeable behaviour was totally frustrating. It would have been easier to break up with him if he were behaving as his normal vile self.

As they watched a steamer packed with day-trippers chug past, the conversation turned, as expected, to their upcoming wedding.

'My parents wish to invite your parents to *Kaffee und Kuchen* on Sunday to discuss arrangements.'

Ella swallowed hard. Now was the time.

Before she could speak, he laughed.

'My father made an innuendo about why there was a hurry for us to wed. But don't worry. I assured him about your virtue.' He gave her a sly look.

This was just the provocation she needed.

'Actually, Max. I have to be honest with you. I'm afraid I think we should break off our engagement.'

His blue-grey eyes turned to ice. She saw danger.

Tread softly, don't destroy his pride.

'It's not you. It's me. I wouldn't be an adequate wife for you.' Mutti had helped her to prepare her speech so as to protect his ego. 'I'm not good enough for you.'

'I arranged for you to attend the Reich Bride School for the purpose of you being adequate. Being good enough! Pull yourself together and stop this nonsense.'

The pleasantries from moments ago had vanished. She felt stronger. But she must be clever; her family's safety was at stake.

'Maybe I need a little more time to prepare for my duties. Maybe we could take a break. Consider.'

He glared at her. 'You don't love me, do you, Ella?'

His use of the word *love* took her by surprise. It had been a long time since she'd heard him use it.

It was out there now. The truth.

'And do you love me?' she challenged.

'I thought I did. When we first met, you were so passionate about the new future for Austria, so passionate for us. I loved the way you fawned over me. But you've changed. You voted for the Anschluss, but you're not vocal in your support of it. You even sympathise with the undesirables, that Jew boy for one.'

This was getting dangerous now.

'How could you even think that of me? I would never sympathise with the Jews.' Her words tasted sour in her mouth. 'I'm offended that's how you perceive me. Maybe it's for the best we part.' She hated that her words betrayed Jayden, but at this moment she had to protect Freddie and her family.

He jumped up and kicked at the ground. 'You think you can humiliate me like this and not pay the price? You are one very stupid, naïve girl.'

He sprang into the boat and rowed off, leaving her alone, sitting on the shore wondering how the conversation had not gone at all how she planned and at what point it had all gone wrong.

It took her one and a half hours to walk home. Too long to have his final words spinning through her head.

It was three days later when Ella was wrenched from her dreams by a thunderous banging that shook the whole apartment. Gentle daylight seeped through her curtains but a quick glance at her clock told her it was only five-thirty in the morning.

Grappled by fear, she stumbled in her flimsy nightdress into the hallway. Mutti and Vati were already there and looked at her, alarm in their eyes.

'*Aufmachen!*' bellowed a voice.

Mutti adjusted her nightdress, lifted her chin and opened the door.

'Good morning officer. How can I— Max?'

Standing in the doorway was a heavy-set policeman, and beside him, proudly displaying his swastika armband, was Max, white-faced and grim. Ella gasped. Mutti staggered a few steps back and the two men strode in.

Ella stared at Max in confusion. There was a hint of victory in his hard glare.

Cold dread wrapped around her heart.

'We have orders to search this apartment,' said the police officer, flashing a piece of paper and pocketing it before anyone could set eyes on it. A second police officer stepped inside behind them.

'Whatever for?' stammered Vati, looking suddenly frail and old.

'There is a warrant out for the arrest of Herr Jayden Pisinger. We are investigating anyone who may have had dealings with him. Or may be harbouring him.' He drew his pistol, pushed past the stunned family and stormed through the rooms.

To Ella's horror, Max explained to the second policeman the layout of their apartment.

'Why is he wanted by the police?' Ella met Max's gaze.

'He is charged with the murder of a soldier of the Reich.'

'The young man found on the river bank?' asked Mutti incredulously.

'Correct,' said Max as he stomped on down the hallway and into the sitting room: the same room where he'd eaten countless meals with her family, praised Mutti's cooking, drank Vati's wine and declared his admiration for her. Now he stood by as the policemen opened cupboards and drawers, searched under tables and pulled the upholstery from the sofa.

Mutti's fearful expression turned to anger and she demanded, 'What makes you think the young Herr Pisinger would be here?'

Ella's pulse throbbed in her ears.

A snide glance from Max.

Mutti's questioning look. First at Max. Then at Ella.

'Because there is evidence that there are relations between members of your family and the Pisinger family,' said one of the policemen, throwing a cushion across the room.

'Nonsense,' said Mutti. 'We know them only from shopping at their store. Who is making these accusations?'

Heartbeats of silence. Long enough for Ella to pray the next words would not be uttered. But Max's lips twisted.

'I am making these accusations. I have seen my now ex-fiancée fraternising with an enemy of the Reich: the very reason I have broken off our betrothal.'

Ella opened her mouth to challenge him, but her legs went weak. She leaned against the wall, confusion and despair whipping through her brain. What was Max's part in all of this?

As if reading her thoughts, he said, 'I reported Pisinger to the police. I saw him that evening on the river bank, arguing with that soldier. It was the last time the poor man was seen alive.'

'Liar!' screamed Ella.

Max gave a mirthless smile.

'What a passionate response for someone you hardly know.'

The two policemen approached, shaking their heads. 'No sign that he's been here.'

As the three men left, Max turned to Ella.

'He's not at his uncle's and he's not here. But we will find him. I'll make sure of it.'

* * *

After the police left, Ella went to work. The office was stifling hot. All the windows were open but the air was still. Expectant. Outside, the sky was darkening; thunderstorms had been forecast.

Ella stared at the blank paper on her typewriter roll, her mind in turmoil. Where was Jayden at that very moment? In hiding? But where? Or had they already found him and he was locked up in a cell? Or worse, being interrogated...

'That letter won't type itself, you know,' a loud, cheerful voice said.

Ella looked at her colleague who sat opposite, her fingers flying over the keys even whilst she spoke.

'Cheer up. Things can't be that bad.'

Things were that bad.

Ella began to type. It was Friday and people were chatting about their plans for the weekend. All Ella could think about was finding Jayden and helping him escape arrest. But how she would do that she did not know.

Once home after work, she ran up the stairs to the apartment. Her plan was to have a quick evening meal with her parents and then hurry over to Jayden's uncle's for any news. When she arrived home, the front door was open. Her father was welcoming someone in the hallway: his friend Ingo, the janitor at the Pöstling-berg grotto. Ella's heart sank. She wasn't in the mood for guests.

Mutti emerged from the kitchen, her face a sheen of sweat, greeted Ingo and gave Ella a sympathetic glance.

'Nice that you're home already, *Schatz*. Let's all go into the sitting room and have a drink.'

'How are things, Ingo?' Vati said as everyone sat themselves down.

Ingo sighed as he pulled out a large bunch of keys from a trouser pocket and placed them on the coffee table. Ella chewed the inside of her cheek; she just wanted Ingo to leave so she could talk to her parents about Jayden.

'Things are disastrous,' said Ingo. 'Problems on the Pöstling-berg tramline. It's the weekend and things won't be sorted out till Monday, so there'll be no trams till then. The boss has ordered me to close everything up.'

Ella sat up. This was the first time she could remember the Pöstlingberg being closed.

'But surely there are people who walk up to the top?' Vati said.

'They won't this weekend. Severe thunderstorms are forecast and the pathways will be rivers of mud.' Ingo wiped his forehead. This talk of storms worried Ella. Had Jayden found shelter? 'I for one am looking forward to some rain,' Ingo rattled on. 'The heat has been unbearable. Anyway, I'm taking advantage of this unexpected break and am taking the train later to visit my sister in Salzburg...'

Ella's mind drifted as her father showed Ingo an article in the newspaper.

She felt a gentle hand on her shoulder. 'Would you help me in the kitchen, dear?'

Ella jumped up with relief and followed Mutti out. Their movements were slow in the oppressive, humid heat.

'Have you heard any news about Jayden?' Ella asked.

'Nothing, I'm afraid. I feared Max would turn nasty when you broke up with him. He's shown his true colours.' Mutti began to fillet the fish. 'I've left a message at the bakery for help and I'll check back tomorrow if my contacts know anything. I hope Jayden doesn't fall into the hands of people smugglers. They demand a lot of money and can't be trusted.'

'I don't think he will. He's too sharp for that and doesn't have that sort of money.' Ella began to wash the green beans under the cold-water tap. 'Oh, this whole situation is appalling. Jayden is innocent and I don't understand why Max is accusing him. It can't be because of jealousy. Max doesn't love me.' Ella realised her mistake the moment the words escaped her lips. Her mother turned to her.

'Why would Max have reason to be jealous?'

Ella shrugged. 'He's a possessive type.' She didn't meet her mother's eye.

'Oh, Ella...' Her mother sighed. 'You and Jayden?'

'We're just friends, Mutti. I'll visit Jayden's family after dinner and find out what's going on.'

'I advise against that, Ella. The police will be watching us.'

The beans now washed, Ella attacked them with a knife, topping and tailing them ferociously.

'I have to go. It's people like me who have caused this situation.'

'What do you mean?'

She threw the knife into the sink. 'I hate myself, Mutti. I voted yes at the referendum.'

A painful sob stuck in her throat but she refused to cry out of self-pity.

'You're not the only one, *Liebling*. I did too.'

Her mother had spoken so softly, Ella thought she'd misheard. They looked at each other, and then Mutti gave a sad nod.

'I never told your father. We share the same guilt.'

Ella let the tears come and her mother wrapped her arms around her. When the emotion of their secret bond had settled and they wiped away their tears, Mutti said again that it was unwise for her to visit Jayden's uncle.

'I'm going anyway,' said Ella.

* * *

After they had finished eating, Ingo thanked Ella's parents for their hospitality.

'Please excuse me, but I must dash if I'm to catch my train to Salzburg.'

The family accompanied him to the door.

'When are you returning?' asked Vati.

'I'll take the first train on Monday morning and will be back in Linz by 7 a.m. Enjoy your weekend,' he called as he descended the stairs.

Ella breathed a sigh of relief. He was a nice man but there was so much going on right now. As she and her parents washed and dried the pans and dishes, thunder rumbled over the mountains in the distance. It was only eight o'clock, yet unusually dark for a July evening.

As soon as her chores were finished, she could hurry to Jayden's family at his uncle's apartment. She was desperate for news, sick with fear.

Just a quick plump of the pillows in the sitting room, and she'd fold the newspaper that lay spread out on the coffee table. But as she picked it up, underneath lay a bunch of keys.

'Ingo forgot his keys,' Ella said, taking them to her father in the kitchen.

'He'll be halfway to Salzburg by now. The grotto is closed over the weekend anyway. Pop them in the commode in the hallway and I'll get them to him early Monday morning.'

'All right. I'm off now.' She heard her own decisive, no-nonsense tone. Avoiding her mother's look, she headed for the front door, dropping Ingo's keys in the top drawer of the commode.

'Ella!' Mutti called.

She turned, ready to defend her decision to go.

'Take an umbrella. It looks like rain.'

* * *

The first huge raindrop plopped on her head as she crossed the Donaubrücke. Clouds the colour of granite hovered over the church towers. Within moments, the summer rain was falling fast. Ella smiled inwardly as she put up her umbrella. Mothers.

By the time Jayden's father opened the door to her, she was terrified of the news she might hear.

He beckoned her in and quickly shut the door.

'They haven't found him yet,' he said, his voice weak with exhaustion. Ella exhaled, a sweet moment of relief. 'The Gestapo have been here twice and the police are searching house to house.'

'Do you know where he is?'

'He has no money or papers. I'm trying to sort things out. Only then has he a chance of getting away.'

'I can help. Where is he?'

He looked at her, his skin sagging from his thin face. She hardly recognised the smart, genial shop owner who had always taken time to chat to his customers. His eyes were filled with pain.

'It's too dangerous. You should go home. You've already done so much for us.'

'Please, Herr Pisinger. I must go to him.'

He shook his head.

'Please, trust me. Jayden means a lot to me.'

Why was she struggling with words? Just say it, she thought.

'I love your son. And I will do everything I can to help him.' Her heart swelled as she heard herself say it aloud.

Tears filled the old man's eyes.

They must have checked over their shoulders a thousand times. Ella kept her umbrella tilted low over their faces as they huddled together beneath the teeming rain. Herr Pisinger led them out of town and turned up a track into the forest. Rivulets of water ran down the track, the way becoming slick with mud. Ella closed her umbrella as the trees became denser. Her summer shoes sank into the soft earth, mud slipping inside and oozing between her toes.

Herr Pisinger flicked on a small torch he'd brought, the light dimmed with paper held in place with an elastic band. They had come to a spot where two pines had become uprooted and had fallen across each other.

'Up there,' he said and then called out, 'It's all right, son, it's me. Ella is here too.'

A circle of torchlight appeared from beneath the trees and Jayden scrambled out, his curly hair plastered to his head, his shirt dripping. He looked as if he'd been swimming in the Danube fully dressed. All three of them did.

She sloshed towards him, nearly slipping in her eagerness to throw her arms around him.

'Ella, you shouldn't have come,' he said, holding her so fiercely that his actions belied his own words.

The three of them huddled under the fallen trees which gave a small amount of shelter and Herr Pisinger thrust a plastic bag into his son's hands.

'There is a thermos of coffee and bread. Also some money. I sold a couple of things. I brought your passport too. But I can't find anyone to get an exit visa.'

'I'll get one in Vienna,' said Ella. 'I'll take the first train out tomorrow.'

A roar of thunder crashed above them and seconds later, the sky blazed with lightning.

'You can't stay out in this all night,' she said, shivering.

'I have nowhere to go.'

She thought a moment. Maybe Ingo's visit that evening had been a blessing in disguise. 'I have an idea,' she said.

* * *

Her parents' bedroom door flew open as Ella entered, a pool of water circling her feet.

'Thank God, you're back home. You're drenched!' Her mother rushed to get a towel and started to rub her face and hair.

'It's just water, Mutti,' Ella said, taking the towel from her.

'Any news on Jayden?'

'He hasn't been arrested yet.'

Mutti would want to help too, Ella was sure. But would she agree to Ella's plan? Probably not.

'He's in hiding somewhere.'

'We could've hidden him in the workshop if we weren't being watched. Do you know where he is?'

'His father knows. I'm going to try to get papers in Vienna. I'll get the early train tomorrow.' It was best not to let on that she knew where Jayden was.

'All right,' Mutti agreed. 'You can give them to his father.'

Ella would give them to Jayden herself.

'I'm hoping to get news of help tomorrow from the bakery,' Mutti said, her face drained with exhaustion.

'Get some sleep, Mutti. I'll get out of these wet things.'

Mutti kissed her on the cheek and clicked the bedroom door shut.

As Ella went to the bathroom to strip off her wet clothes, she could hear Mutti and Vati talking. Hopefully, they would fall asleep soon.

In her bedroom, instead of putting on her nightdress, she slipped on trousers and a blouse and dug out a pair of hiking boots. Rain slashed at her window and a fierce wind picked up.

She looked at her watch. Waited. Looked again.

Tiptoeing into the hallway, her boots in her hand, she could now hear her father's snores. But was Mutti still awake? She always complained she found it so hard to fall asleep.

But Ella couldn't wait any longer. She eased the commode drawer open and gently lifted out Ingo's keys, hoping the noise of the storm would drown out any sound she made. Grabbing a rain jacket and torch, she slipped out of the front door and sat on the stairs to tie her boots.

* * *

Ella had climbed the Pöstlingberg thousands of times, but never at night in a raging thunderstorm. The narrow path that ran along the side of the tramlines had been a dry, stony track all summer, but now it was a seething mass of mud and churning water that tumbled downhill towards her. She tightened the hood on her rain jacket and waded upwards, the rain whipping against her face.

The occasional lights from the houses helped her see the way, but sometimes, she was plunged into darkness. She restrained herself from using her torch as much as possible; citizens were nervous and on high alert, and were likely to report anything suspicious. Her leg muscles strained as she tramped upwards against the oncoming sludge.

The sky flashed. Ella looked up as sheet lightning illuminated the Pöstlingberg church, startling white against the cloudy night sky. Not far now: she was three-quarters of the way up. It was not such a crazy idea after all; it would work—

Her right foot slipped from under her.

Lurching sideways, she grabbed at what she thought was a branch. But it was not a branch at all, just mere twigs that snapped between her fingers. She plummeted to the ground, striking her hip against a rock, and slid downwards until her feet found purchase. She flipped over on all fours, panting, all the while berating herself.

Get up, Ella. Don't be so weak.

Jayden. He was depending on her. His life depended on her. And she was kneeling in the mud with shaking legs, tears pressing at the back of her eyes.

For goodness' sake, girl.

Gritting her teeth, she pushed herself up and stamped onwards, leaning forwards into the wind.

She. Would. Do. This.

Lightning blazed the sky; the twin towers of the church towered above her, luminous.

A few more strides. A tree branch snapped loose and struck her shins. She stumbled and fell on one knee, her hands sinking into a mire of grit and sand. She pushed herself up.

Finally, she reached the tram stop at the top. The wind was brutal up here. Thunder so loud, her bones shook. She hurried past the church towards the entrance of the Pöstlingberg grotto. A barrier had been placed in front of the main door. Panic gripped her; she couldn't see him. She crouched down, slipped under the barrier and stood by the door, her fingers gripping the bunch of keys in her pocket.

Where was he? Had he been caught? He'd planned to climb up the Pöstlingberg, avoiding the path. Had he fallen?

A figure stepped out.

Jayden. Soaked and covered in mud.

Here.

'You made it!' she said.

A quick hug and she pulled out the keys. It was an arched, wooden door with a large brass keyhole. Discarding the smaller keys, she tried one of the bigger ones. It didn't fit. Wet, fumbling fingers. The next key didn't turn either. Heart racing, she slipped the remaining large key into the lock. It ground open.

As they entered the pitch-black cavern, Ella swayed her torch. To their right, the stone stairway spiralled down to the model town of Linz and the fairy-tale grotto. To the left were two doorways. The smaller one looked to be a storeroom, the other, an office. She tried the smaller keys and opened the office door. Inside, a desk stood before a panel of switches.

Shining her torch on the labels, she whispered, 'These control the lights in the grotto. Look: shop fronts, fairy-tale alleys, night sky—'

'I like the sound of night sky,' he said.

'So do I.' She flipped the switch. 'That will give us enough light downstairs.' She picked up paper and a pen from the desk. 'Show me your passport so I can note the details.'

She scribbled the information on the paper and stowed it in the pocket of her rain jacket.

The two of them descended the spiral stone stairway and walked through the town, past the darkened shops under the starlit ceiling.

'This feels so weird,' whispered Ella. 'Unreal down here. Alone.'

'You're not alone.' He took her hand.

She led him down a fairy-tale alley. 'Let's find somewhere to tuck you away.'

The exhibits were unlit; shapes and forms loomed.

'Not here,' she said as they passed the witch's gingerbread house of Hansel and Gretel. When they came to a model of a white castle surrounded by trees, a girl asleep by a spinning wheel, a prince and a white horse, she stopped. 'Here. I like this one.'

Jayden smiled at her. 'So do I. But in our story the prince is being saved by the princess.'

'He's more than worth saving.'

Despite being filthy, soaked and afraid, desire flared within her. They kissed. Pressing against him, she could feel every contour of his body through his wet clothes.

'I must get back before my parents miss me,' she said, breaking the kiss. 'And return the keys to the commode.'

'There's a storm outside. Maybe it's safer to stay here with me.' His eyes glinted.

She smiled. 'I need to get the early train to Vienna. Don't worry about me; going down the Pöstlingberg will be easier than coming up.'

'I'll bed down there and wait then.' He nodded at the straw-covered ground under the fake conifers.

'I hope I can persuade Albert Göring to forge me a visa quickly. I should be back by tomorrow evening.'

'Ella, be careful. I'd never forgive myself if anything happened to you.'

'I'll be fine. I promise I'll return tomorrow.'

'It might be best if you lock me in here,' he said.

Ella swallowed. 'But suppose you want to get out?'

'Suppose someone wants to come in?'

Her stomach clenched. She didn't know what was best.

'Lock the door, Ella. It will be safer for me. Go now and take care of yourself.'

Moments later, she stepped out into the night and locked the heavy door behind her. This didn't feel good, but there was no other way.

The storm had passed over and the rain had stopped. She slipped and skidded her way down the Pöstlingberg, returning home. As she tiptoed into the bathroom of her apartment, she prayed her parents wouldn't catch her in the state she was in.

For the second time that evening, she stripped off her wet clothes and dried herself in the bathroom. It was only when she saw the bruises forming across her shins and her hip that she noticed the pain from her fall for the first time.

As she put on her nightdress, she realised she only had a few hours to rest before catching the early train. In bed, she pictured Jayden alone beneath the ground in the fairy-tale grotto. It had been a wrench to leave him. She had been scared and thrilled being in that strange underworld. She imagined what would have happened if she'd stayed with him, and let a fantasy of them making love play out in her mind.

Please God, let him stay safe.

32

ELLA

The sun dazzled her as she exited Linz station late Saturday afternoon, the storms having vanished as quickly as they had come.

Ella was satisfied with her day so far: having arrived in Vienna at 8 a.m., she'd gone straight to Freddie's lodgings and woken him up. He'd dressed quickly on hearing about Jayden's plight and the two of them had paid Albert Göring a visit.

At first, he'd shaken his head. They couldn't produce the papers so quickly; they had a huge backlog.

She couldn't prevent the tears or the shrillness in her voice.

'He's stuck in an underground cavern charged with murdering a member of the Wehrmacht. He'll be executed if he's caught. We must do something.'

Albert rubbed his hand across his face. 'We could produce a fake exit visa, but it's impossible to get an entry visa for another country. There are queues outside every consulate and it can take months even if an application is accepted.'

'What are the options?' asked Freddie.

'If he gets stopped in the Reich, he might get away with just having his exit visa. So long as his name is not cross-checked with a list of arrest warrants. Germany is determined to expel Jews out of the country and is not so worried where they go. He could make up some story about waiting for entry papers to another country. But that means crossing a border illegally.'

'You mean climbing the Alps?'

'Yes, or sailing down the Danube as a castaway. Or driving or walking.'

'I suppose travelling by train is too risky,' said Freddie.

'Absolutely. Papers are vigilantly checked. And if there's an arrest warrant out for him...'

Now, just a few hours later, Ella had the exit visa tucked in the back of her brassiere strap. It would of course be better if Jayden wouldn't be forced to show it.

The whole journey back from Vienna, her tired brain had run through the escape options; each one was a momentous undertaking and fraught with danger. She stopped at a stall and bought bread and dried sausage for Jayden – he would be starving – then she headed for the Hauptplatz.

She could hear the jeers and shouts before she turned the corner. A huge crowd had gathered, angry men waving fists, but there was something else she saw in their faces: a grim pleasure. Women too, shouted and jabbed their fingers, working themselves into a frenzy.

She pushed her way forwards, trying to see.

'What's happening?' she asked a tall man who appeared to have a good view of the proceedings.

'Another example being made. A Jewess,' he sneered.

Her heart plummeted. Things were getting worse. The hatred had taken on a life of its own, feeding on fear and misinformation, morphing into some heinous monster. There was nothing she could do to help in the midst of this huge mob and she was inclined to turn away, unable to bear the scene. But turning away was the reaction of a coward. She continued to edge forward, ignoring the people who tutted at her and fought to keep their place.

Finally, a few rows from the front, she managed to peer over the shoulder of a short woman. And what she saw made Ella's breath catch in her throat.

The noise around her faded away and a buzzing sound filled her ears. Everything around her, the buildings, the people, the baroque marble column, dimmed. She only saw one thing.

Hedy on her knees, leaning over a placard. Four brownshirts, their legs astride, loomed over her.

'*Schreib es!*'

Hedy held a pen in her shaking hand. She gave the slightest shake of her head. An older, bald-headed brownshirt kicked her in the buttocks.

'You heard. Write what you are, Jew.'

Every part of Ella had shut down as she looked at the scene, numb, unable to believe what was happening. This girl, her best friend, was being forced to write on the sign. She was then hauled to her feet, the sign roped around her neck.

Ich bin Jüdin

The crowd roared. Some stones flew through the air.

Suddenly, everything burst into sharp focus. Ella's head cleared, and screaming Hedy's name, she drove herself to the front.

'My God, stop. It's Hedy. Don't you see? It's Hedy.'

The brownshirts looked at her aghast as if she were a mad woman.

Ella locked eyes with her friend, seeing her surprise, a flicker of love and then the total despair.

She shook her head. 'No, Ella, don't do this. Run.'

A brownshirt was already grabbing Ella's arm. She fought with him, shouting at him. She could hear her own hysteria.

'You're making a mistake! It's just Hedy!'

People rushed forward.

'Let them go. They're just girls.'

A man's voice.

'Traitor!' The yell of another voice.

A smattering of, 'Heil Hitler.'

Fighting broke out. The brownshirt threw Ella to the ground, her knees and the palms of her hands sliding along the concrete, her skin flaying. She scrambled back up and rushed towards Hedy. Just one man held her friend's arm now, the others engaged in an attempt to calm the mob. She snatched up one of the stones that had been thrown in Hedy's direction and flung it with all her might at the man's face. It cracked against his forehead and he whipped his arms up reflexively, blood oozing through his fingers.

Police sirens sounded.

Hedy, free from his grasp, swayed.

Ella reached out her hands and Hedy, dazed and ghost-like, stepped towards her, her arms straight out in front of her. They were so close. Their fingertips grazed against each other, their tear-filled eyes locked. She would grasp Hedy to safety. Their fingers curled with each other's. Nearly there—

Hedy's body catapulted backwards, and her fingers wrenched away. A policeman coiled an arm around Hedy's waist and lifted her into the air, the placard in her own handwriting swinging from her neck, blazing her crime. People were running and screaming, police waving batons. Ella watched as Hedy was bundled into a police van, before she herself was swept along with the crowds fleeing the square.

Ella managed to tear herself away and stumbled down a quiet side street, dropping down on the front doorstep of a house. Her head fell to her trembling knees.

How could people behave like that, to Hedy, one of their own? The picture of her friend, paraded in front of a cruel crowd, tormented and humiliated, burned in her mind's eye.

The front door opened and a stout woman with a broom in her hand looked at her in surprise.

'Well, I wanted to sweep my doorstep, but looks like I'll need a bigger broom.'

'Sorry,' said Ella wiping her sleeve across her tear-stained face. 'I'm leaving.' She began to rise, but the woman put a hand on her shoulder.

'Stay where you are. You look like you need a drink. And a handkerchief.' She glanced at Ella's running nose.

A few moments later, the woman returned with a glass of lemonade and a handkerchief. Ella blew her nose, and gulped down the cold, sweet drink.

'Thank you.' She handed the glass back.

'You're as white as a ghost. Perhaps you should come in and rest a while. I've just baked some biscuits.'

'That's very kind, but I have something urgent to do.' She held out the sodden handkerchief with an apologetic look.

'Keep it, dear. I hope your day gets better.'

Fuelled by the sugared water and adrenaline, Ella ran over the Donaubrücke. She longed to get back to Jayden but first she had to tell Hedy's mother what had happened. Maybe Hilde herself would now be in danger. But when she saw a group of neighbours outside the house, she knew she was too late. The front door had been barricaded and a placard with a swastika had been nailed to the door.

Hedy's neighbour, Maria, whom Ella had known for years, looked at her with tears in her eyes.

'The Gestapo took her,' she said, her voice cracking. 'When the police came a short while later and barricaded the door, I asked what was happening. They said the house was being requisitioned for the Reich.'

Ella left the small group that was discussing the terrible things that had befallen the family. She could hardly believe it herself; the death of Hedy's father, the interrogations by the Gestapo, Trudy having to be wrenched from her family and sent away to live with strangers, and finally today.

Her despair was so heavy, Ella had the urge to crawl into a ball and lie in the forest amongst the spruce trees, hidden from the world. But no, she wasn't finished yet; there was so much still to fight for and the thought of Jayden alone underground, waiting for her, drove her on.

First, she must get Ingo's keys to the grotto back out from the commode in the hallway. She prayed that her parents would both be at the workshop as they'd planned to be that Saturday afternoon.

A small piece of luck amidst the terrible events that were unfolding around her: when she arrived back, no one was home.

With the keys weighing down her dress pocket, she rushed to the tram station at the bottom of the Pöstlingberg. It was still closed, the barriers down across the track. A family was struggling up the path with their groceries. Not wanting to be seen, Ella avoided the main uphill path and picked her way through the trees and high-grassed meadows. Under the hot sun, the ground, although muddy in places, was passable now.

At the top, she stopped in front of the twin-towered basilica, which was gleaming in the sunshine, and looked around. There were much fewer people up here than when the trams ran, but still enough to make her cautious. She would have to wait till everyone was gone before she entered the grotto. She passed through the tall wooden doors and stepped into the cool, hushed silence one experienced when entering a church.

She chose a pew near the altar, and bowing her head, she closed her eyes and clasped her hands. She couldn't remember the last time she had sat here to pray. Sometimes, during a normal day, a fleeting thought of a prayer might wander through her mind, but today was different. Here in the pilgrimage church that crowned the Pöstlingberg, her prayers were passionate, spoken half aloud: a desperate plea for the safe return of Hedy and her mother, and the skill and courage to get Jayden to safety. The horrendous picture of Hedy with the sign around her neck emblazed itself on her closed eyelids. How could people be so vile and full of hatred?

She sat there, impatient to get back to Jayden. The few people that came in went about their business, lighting their candles at the altar before leaving. The light through the stained-glass windows blazed orange before it started to dim and still she waited, wishing that the summer days were not so long and darkness would fall. Finally, she rose, resolute in her task. If she only ever achieved one thing in this time of misery, it would be to save the man she loved.

Dusk was falling. The only person around now was the old church caretaker who disappeared behind the altar. Ella left the church and sneaked along the old stone fortification wall until she came to the barrier at the entrance of the grotto. She checked over her shoulder, left and right. Then checked again before slipping under the barrier. She had to step around a shovel and a pile of work tools before she could unlock the door.

She entered the darkness, waiting a moment for her eyes to

adjust, and then locked the door on the inside, before putting the key back in her pocket. Jayden must have left the lights of the stars on down below; there was enough of a dim sliver for her to see the spiral stone stairway.

As she descended, she ran her hand along the cold stone to guide her.

She emerged into the cavern and walked through the model town, resisting the urge to call out his name. She wasn't sure why. No one could have entered; she'd locked the door. Might someone else have a key? But why would they come here? Best to be careful. Just in case.

Soft footsteps past the bakery, the pharmacy and the watchmaker's shop. All dimly lit under the artificial starlit sky with a scythe of a moon. The eerie surroundings fired her imagination. What if he wasn't here? What if he'd been taken? Like Hedy. Or injured? Or worse? Her heart thumped so loud, she was sure he'd hear her coming. That was fine so long as he was alone.

She tiptoed down the alleyway; she didn't want to give him a shock, but she didn't want to alert an enemy. If only she had some type of weapon: one of the work tools left lying around up by the entrance. But that would mean going all the way back up the stairs.

She passed one fairy-tale scene after the other, peering at the figures frozen in time – Snow White, Rumpelstiltskin – half expecting a real-life figure in a Nazi uniform to jump out at her. Next came Hansel and Gretel. She halted in front of the gingerbread house, the old witch in the doorway, a cat on her shoulder, her curled forefinger beckoning. All around her, stuffed woodland animals lurked in the shadows. Was there a shuffling sound? A wolf baring its teeth loomed out at her. She shivered and hurried on.

When she came to Sleeping Beauty, there was no sign of

Jayden. He'd agreed to wait here, but he'd been alone for hours. Maybe he'd become restless and had wandered around the cavern.

Ella stepped past the trees.

A scuffle.

A swift movement. Arms gripped her.

She screamed.

'Ella, it's you!' Jayden released her, his expression pure relief.

'You scared me to death, Jayden.'

'And you me. When you didn't call out you were here, I thought your footsteps were someone else's.'

'I wanted to be cautious. I'm so afraid right now.' She fell into his arms. 'Thank God, at least you are safe.'

Her throat ached with pain as she buried her head into his shoulder.

'What's happened, *Schatz*?' He stroked the back of her head. Her legs felt weak. 'Let's sit a moment.' She handed him the sausage and bread she had brought and they sat down on the straw-covered ground between the fir trees. Ella told him all that had happened, from the first moment she heard the hostile crowd to the terrible moment Hedy was ripped from her grasp, her last words barely audible through her tears. Her whole body shook.

Jayden held her tight. 'Maybe they will free her again like last time. We mustn't give up hope.' But his tone lacked conviction and it made Ella cry even harder.

After that, they remained silent, Ella finding comfort in the sound of his heartbeat, his warm, musky smell, his gentle hands stroking the back of her neck, massaging her shoulder.

Eventually, she'd recovered enough to speak again. 'I have your papers with me. We should wait till later in the night before we make a move.'

'I don't know how I can ever thank you.'

'It's the least I can do when my ex-fiancé is accusing you of murder. He's so full of hate and cruelty, I'm ashamed that I was ever with him. How can he lie that he saw you that night?'

Jayden let out a deep breath. There was a pause. 'He did see me. We saw each other down by the Danube.'

Ella jolted and turned her face to him, frowning. 'I don't understand.'

'It was just getting dark and I was on my way home along the river. I heard raised voices and saw two men: Max and a young soldier. When Max noticed me, I hurried away to avoid a confrontation.'

'Then what happened?'

'Nothing. That's it. But there was something off about the situation...'

'In what way?' She could hear the exhaustion in her voice.

Jayden shook his head. 'It's not important right now. You've been through so much today. Rest a while.'

He lay back on the straw and she nestled against his shoulder. The situation was so bizarre; she felt as if they were players on a stage, surrounded by theatre props: a figure of a maiden asleep beside a spinning wheel, a halo of red and white roses above her head, a slumbering baker slumped over his mixing bowl, and all around, forest animals and dwarves. She had been spirited into a world of fairy tales, yet the reality of life was a hair's breadth away. Her eyes felt heavy, her limbs exhausted.

Finally, she let her eyelids close but she could still feel Jayden's fingertips running up and down her arm. His lips grazed her forehead. His voice, soft and low.

'I lied about being back with Ruth. I wanted to keep you away from me. To protect you. I'm sorry, I know I hurt you.'

She gave a gentle laugh. 'I didn't believe you. Not really.'

He chuckled softly and brushed tiny kisses along the side of her face, over her throat. She lay perfectly still, luxuriating in being passive; last time, she had ripped her own clothes from her body, only to be rejected. Now, in her stillness, every thrilling sensation was amplified. He shifted and she half opened her eyes to see him kneeling and unbuttoning her dress. She watched his dark curls as he worked his way down. The idea of him opening her like a gift made her shiver with pleasure.

When the last button was undone, he flipped the two halves of her dress apart and paused to gaze at her. She raised her arms to him.

'My God, I love you,' he murmured. 'My heart is torn knowing to love you is to hurt you.'

'Not loving me would hurt me more.'

She pulled him down to her. Kisses so deep, she existed inside of him. Hasty hands, trembling fingers, clothes pulled aside, taste, smell, skin against skin, soul touching soul. Dissolving together, becoming one. Complete. Safe. Untouchable in their cocoon of pure love.

Afterwards, dressing hastily, they laughed at their surroundings.

'I'd imagined something more romantic for the first time we made love,' said Jayden.

'You'd imagined us together?'

'Of course! Some days, as I unloaded crates at the market, I thought of nothing else. But I fantasised about you lying naked on a bed of flowers on the bank beside a blue Danube, or on the deep mattress of a four-poster bed in a beautiful hotel overlooking the Wolfgangsee.'

Ella stroked his cheek and ran a thumb over his lips. 'We still have time to do all those things.'

'Do you think so? Really?' His voice had grown solemn.

'Definitely,' she said, jumping up. 'But one step at a time. Right now, we have to get out of here.'

'I'm afraid that won't be possible.'

Ella's heart turned to ice. Her mind went blank as she stared at the man who stood in front of them, aiming a pistol.

Max.

She tried to gather her thoughts but fear and incomprehension fogged her brain.

'It's me you want. Let Ella go,' said Jayden, rising slowly, his hands up.

Max's pistol followed his movements. 'Stand still, both of you, hands on your heads.'

They did as he asked.

'You thought you were safe locked up in here?' Max scoffed. 'That old caretaker at the church couldn't give me the spare key fast enough – well, not when I put a gun to his head. Didn't help him much, unfortunately.'

Bile rose in Ella's throat.

'How did you know we were here?' she murmured.

'I've been watching you for a while, Ella. Ever since your Bride School friend told her husband she caught you snooping around Steiner's house.'

'Tanja!'

Max laughed. 'Lisl, actually. Your so-called friend. She couldn't wait to impress her husband. He told the police to keep an eye on your father's workshop too.'

Ella's heart sank. Lisl had betrayed her.

Max's eyes cast down to her half-opened dress and lingered there. He curled his upper lip.

'You're a disgrace to the women of the Reich, contaminating our pure blood with the unclean. You disgust me.' His words were venom puncturing her veins. She saw her own hate reflected in his eyes. 'And you gave yourself to a murderer too.'

'Jayden is innocent. This is some terrible misunderstanding,' she said, finding her voice. But she could see the amusement in Max's eyes; there was no misunderstanding. Max knew Jayden wasn't the culprit. 'Are you after Jayden because of me? Because you think—'

'Don't flatter yourself, Ella. I harbour no feelings for you other than distaste.' Max aimed his gun directly at Jayden's head. 'Your journey ends here, Pisinger. A Jew who murdered a German soldier can expect only one outcome.'

'You know I had nothing to do with his death. I know what I saw: the two of you shouting at each other. He was distressed and threatening you. The last person to see him alive was you.' Jayden's voice rose in anger. 'Let Ella leave. She isn't involved in any of this.'

'Isn't she? No doubt you've told her what you heard.'

'I haven't told her anything. I heard nothing, just the two of you yelling at each other.'

Random thoughts sparked in Ella's mind.

'Who was the soldier, Max? A good friend of yours? One of the boys you were out with every night?'

'Let it be, Ella,' hissed Jayden.

'It doesn't matter what she knows. Neither of you will ever speak of me again.'

His words were clipped and hard as he wavered the pistol between them. Ella looked into his wild eyes and knew. He would shoot them both.

Fear clawed at her throat, making her words come out raw. 'I don't understand, Max. Think of what we had. You loved me once.'

He gave a hollow laugh. 'Are you still so naïve? You were a means to an end. A bride at my side to complete my respectable façade. A wife to bear a family for the Reich. The perfect cover.'

'Stop,' said Jayden. 'Say no more and you can still let her go.'

'I don't trust you, Pisinger. I'm sure you've told her my secret – the secret I've worked so painstakingly to protect.'

Ella glanced from one man to the other, confusion jostling with clarity in her mind. She should say nothing. Stay silent. Her life depended on it.

But she could not.

'What secret?'

As she blurted out the words, the coldness of death slid through her bones. If this was to be the end, she wanted to understand everything that had led to this moment.

Silence. Dense and threatening. Her arms ached from holding them above her head.

Conflicting emotions flickered across Max's face. Sweat beaded on his forehead. He levelled the pistol at Jayden's chest, his finger on the trigger.

'No.' Her voice was a moan.

Please, not Jayden first.

If they were to die, then let it be her first. She couldn't bear to watch her love die before her eyes.

She let out an uncontrollable sob, tears falling down her cheeks and her arms flopping down to her side.

Max turned the gun on her.

'Yes, weep for the man responsible for your death, snooping around down by the river. Eavesdropping on a lovers' quarrel.'

Ella gasped.

'You heard correctly. Lover. You see, my dearest ex-bride, I like men. And marrying you as quickly as possible was how I was to keep my cover, keep me safe. Sure, I kissed and touched you, but it brought me no pleasure. I hoped with a bit of fantasy that I could do my duty and become a father. We were to be the perfect SS family.'

Her sobs halted. Hot, powerful anger shook her body.

'You manipulative hypocrite! You persecute Jews as undesirables, yet in the eyes of the Nazis, you are one yourself. No different to a Jew.'

Max's face flashed scarlet. 'How dare you compare me like that!'

Her fear had flown and she screamed, 'How dare you use me like that!'

'Enough,' Max said, cutting her off. He pointed the pistol at Jayden once more, his arm firm, steady.

'You killed him,' said Jayden. 'Your own lover. He was threatening to expose both of you because you wanted to break things off with him. He was drunk and furious.'

'It was so easy,' Max snarled. 'I put my arms around his pathetic neck as if to give him a forgiving kiss. He whimpered as I strangled him. I only had to drag his body a few steps to the Danube.'

'That night, when you cancelled our date on the beach,' said Ella, realisation dawning. 'Did it happen then? The next day, you were so frantic and wanted a hasty wedding.'

Max narrowed his eyes. 'How astute of you. But now I'm not frantic. I'm totally calm.'

Ella knew he would shoot; he was ready. She turned to Jayden. They searched each other's eyes, and in a split second, it was all there: the pain, the sadness, the passion, the love. And their goodbye.

Now, throw yourself in front of him. Take the bullet. It would give Jayden a chance.

She gulped a breath but before she could move, there was a flash of movement from the corner of her eye. A glint behind Max's shoulder, a flash at the side of his head. A sickening thud. His body jerked forward and the sound of his gun going off ricocheted around the cavern. Jayden collapsed to the ground, clutching himself. Ella screamed and flung herself to his side. She glanced up to see Max sprawled out, bloody and motionless, and standing over him, a metal spade in her hand, eyes flashing, was her mother.

33

MARLENE

He lay at her feet, blood trickling down the side of his face. He didn't move but she raised the spade again, hovering over him, the flame of fury still burning. This crazed young man had been about to murder her daughter.

Her daughter.

She would kill to save her daughter.

'Mutti,' cried Ella.

She could hear Ella's voice far away, but she remained standing, stock still, the spade ready to strike again. If he lived, Max would hunt Ella down; she would never be safe.

Her pulse thundered in her head as she gripped the handle and—

'No, Mutti.' Ella's hands clasped around her arm. 'You are not a murderer. Leave, quick. I think he's still alive but he didn't see you. Go home. I'll tend to Jayden and get us out of here.'

Marlene lowered the spade, her mind clearing from the red mist. She picked up the pistol that had fallen from Max's hand and removed the leather ammunition pouch from his belt. Then she hurried over to help Ella, who was kneeling at Jayden's side, desperately trying to staunch the flow of blood, her hands on top of his hands, as he groaned in pain.

'There's so much blood...' Ella's face was panic-stricken.

'Let me see,' said Marlene, clarity returning.

Hopefully not a stomach wound; that could be fatal. But the blood was coming from his upper thigh. She had seen injuries at the factory and was not affected by the sight of blood, but Ella looked ready to faint. Jayden had a large hole in his thigh and in which she suspected the bullet was still embedded. She tore off her cardigan and tied it tight around the wound.

'There's bound to be a first aid kit in the main office. I'll go and search. Give me the keys, Ella. I know you have them.' She had noticed them missing from the drawer, and she knew her daughter; thank goodness her intuition had led her here. She'd offered a prayer of thanks that the entrance to the grotto had been unlocked. She imagined Max had not thought to lock it behind him as he'd stormed below intent on killing Ella and Jayden.

Ella now handed her Ingo's keys.

Placing the pistol in her daughter's hand, she said, 'You stay here and keep the gun on Max. I don't think you'll have a problem though; he's out for the count.'

Ella nodded.

'Leave without me,' said Jayden suppressing a moan. 'Ella, you must flee. Leave me and go.'

Marlene watched as Ella tenderly stroked his face, her tears falling on his cheek. 'You and I are staying together from now on. I'll never leave you.'

Seeing the love in her daughter's face, a hard lump formed in Marlene's throat.

'The trams will be fixed early on Monday and the workers will return here. We don't want them to find you with a shot Nazi and a pistol in your hand,' said Marlene. 'We're going to get you out of here.'

She left them and ran through the model town.

Once in the main office, it didn't take long to find the first aid kit. A toolbox also caught her eye, inside which was a Swiss army penknife. She scooped it up and looked around. A bottle of high-percentage *Schnapps* stood on a shelf. Perfect.

Within a few minutes, she was back again, Max still lay on the ground in the same position, Jayden was paler and sweating. She knelt by his side and set to work whilst Ella cradled Jayden's head in her lap. First, Marlene poured some of the alcohol over the blade of the knife.

She paused and looked at Jayden. He grimaced and nodded.

Best to do this quickly. She removed the cardigan she'd bound around his thigh.

As she poured alcohol over his wound, he roared.

'Ella, hold his leg as tight and still as possible. And keep watching Max.'

She prised open the hole in Jayden's thigh with her fingers. The bullet was there. She bit her lip and went in with the knife. Swift movements. Blood and tissue. Screams from Jayden. She had no medical experience but she had a steady hand from her craft work. And the objective was simple. Get this damn bullet out.

Jayden twisted his leg away from her.

'Hold him tighter!'

So much blood oozing, she could hardly see what she was doing: slick crimson coating her hands. The knife gouged into his flesh. And then it plopped out: the bullet falling into her hand. Relief swept through her. And a moment of pride.

Another slosh of alcohol. Another scream from Jayden.

'Enough.' He sounded angry now. But that was fine. The adrenaline would give him strength.

She picked out a needle and thread from the first aid kit. Visualising she was sewing together a seam on a dress, she swiftly closed the wound and then bandaged it firmly. With two children who used to climb fruit trees or stumble down mountain paths, binding a wound came easy to her.

'What are we going to do, Mutti?' Ella's voice was strangled with panic.

'First, you and I have to get Jayden down the Pöstlingberg. I already made contact at the bakery. We have help to get him out of Austria.'

'I'm going with him.'

'No,' said Jayden.

'You're wounded and need help. Besides, the police will be after me too,' she said.

Marlene struggled with the truth of Ella's words but she knew there was no other choice. She had to let her daughter go. There was no time to dwell on it, so she turned her attention to Max. He lay on his side, unconscious, but for how long would that be the case? She grabbed bandages from the first aid kit and glanced at Ella.

'Help me.'

They rolled Max onto his front and bound his hands behind his back and his ankles together. She took the spare keys from Max's jacket pocket.

'That should keep him till staff arrive on Monday,' Marlene said.

'What if he dies before then?'

Marlene didn't reply. All she said was, 'Let's get out of here.'

They hoisted Jayden to his feet, supporting him under his arms, and half dragged him up the stairs and out of the grotto. Marlene locked the door behind them. It was a clear night with a half-moon and they were able to see their way down the Pöstlingberg path. Marlene prayed no nosy neighbours would be prying out of windows to witness three shadowy figures stumbling down the Pöstlingberg. Jayden stifled his pain, allowing only the occasional soft groan.

'Mutti,' Ella whispered. 'Hedy and Hilde have been arrested. It was awful...' Her voice faded away in breathlessness as they struggled on.

Marlene fought hard not to let this terrible news overwhelm her.

Stay focused. Get to the first safe house.

Earlier that afternoon, she'd checked the address that had been scribbled on the serviette from the bakery: just outside of Urfahr. But could Jayden make it?

Once they reached the tram station, Marlene led them behind the sweet-scented jasmine bushes that lined the narrow street leading out of town. There were few houses here and at this time of night, there was no one around.

Now the ground was flat, Jayden managed to hobble along with grim determination, and after about twenty minutes, they came to a one-storey wooden house.

They walked through the small front garden, cluttered with garden tools, crates, a wheelbarrow, flowerpots and a chicken coop. Marlene gave Ella a look of reassurance – more reassurance than she actually felt.

She gave the series of coded knocks on the door. How many times had she been on the other side of a door like this? Waiting in the workshop to provide a brief safe haven. Now she was experiencing the desperation of a fugitive, the hope and fear of placing your life in the hands of another.

Footsteps.

The turn of a key.

The door opened, a light shone, and a rifle pointed straight at them.

Marlene shot her hands above her head. 'I recommend the *Himbeerschnecken* from Herr Bäcker.'

The rifle lowered, and behind stood a short woman with waist-long, grey hair in a full-length nightdress.

'I've been expecting you. Come on in.'

* * *

Marlene's adrenaline had faded by the time she climbed the steps to their apartment; a strange calm had settled over her.

Franz ran to the front door as she entered. 'Where have you been? It's one o'clock in the morning! You didn't leave a note.'

'It all happened so fast. Pour me a *Schnapps* and I'll tell you all about it.'

As she told him, she watched his eyes widen with horror.

'I wanted to kill him,' she said. 'And in that moment, I would have. Ella stopped me.'

'You would have been wanted for murder.'

'No one saw me except Ella and Jayden. But if Max survives, he will report them.'

'It would be better for everyone if he was dead,' Franz whispered. He put his head in his hands and groaned. 'And now our daughter is on the run with a Jewish boy accused of murder. If they catch her...'

Fear-laden silence filled the space between them.

Marlene had a strange numb sensation. Her heart had turned to ice. She stood. 'I'm going back up there, to finish it.'

Franz's head jerked up.

'No! You don't have a weapon.'

'Neither does he. I gave his pistol to Jayden. I wiped my fingerprints off the shovel and threw it in a bush outside.'

She was already in the hallway picking up the keys when Franz ran after her.

'I'm coming with you. I'll bring the hammer and screwdriver from under the sink.'

Halfway up the Pöstlingberg, Franz was panting hard. Marlene shouldn't have let him come; she was fitter than him. She could have handled Max alone.

Or could she? Only if he was still unconscious, or weak. He was a fit, physically trained young man, and she was a fifty-year-old woman. She was deluding herself. It would take the two of them. The rift between them over Otto had closed in an instant; they were united; mother and father committing the ultimate act to protect their daughter.

'She shouldn't have fled with him. You should have stopped her, Marlene,' he said, whilst pausing to catch his breath.

'Nothing I said would have made a difference. You didn't see them together like I did.' She placed a hand on his arm. 'She loves him.'

'Then we better save them both,' Franz said, his voice full of determination, and he strode on, picking up his pace.

At the top, Marlene scrambled about in the bush and retrieved the spade whilst Franz hovered over her with the torch. The light flashed over the blood-streaked blade.

She saw Franz flinch.

At the entrance, she tried to turn the key softly but it still clanked, and the door creaked as she pushed it open.

'I'll go first,' whispered Franz, gripping the hammer.

'Let me. I know where I left him,' she said, stepping forwards, wielding the spade like a sword.

The night-sky lights were still illuminated above the model town and they tiptoed close to the darkened façades of the buildings. At the junction to the fairy-tale alley, Marlene held up her hand to stop. She peeked around the corner.

No one there.

Soft footsteps. Hushed breaths.

A prince and a white horse came into view. A sleeping princess. a forest—

Max wasn't there. Just stains of blood on the ground. Strips of bandages. And the penknife she'd used to remove the bullet from Jayden's leg. She had thrown it to the ground in haste. Max had seen it and had managed to inch his way over to it.

Marlene's heart plummeted. She turned to Franz, putting a finger to her lips. His face was ghostly white, his forehead covered in a sheen of sweat. They followed a trail of blood: streaks and drops. She knelt down and dabbed a stain with the tip of her forefinger.

It was dry. She frowned.

The trail led them in a curve as they followed the wall inside of the turret.

A gush of cool air. An open door.

'Of course,' she groaned. 'An emergency exit. I'm so stupid not to think of it.'

* * *

The Monday-morning air was cool, the humidity swept away by the weekend storm. As Marlene walked to work, the events of the weekend pounded through her brain, making her head throb. Had Ella and Jayden been caught or was everything going to plan? She would have to somehow get through a day at the factory acting as if everything was normal.

Heading down a narrow street, she saw some of her friends from the factory ahead of her. Normally, she would have called out and hurried to join them. But she wasn't in the mood to chat, her mind tormented with worry. Behind her came the sound of an automobile, moving fast. She stopped and turned. A black car screeched up beside her and two men grabbed her and thrust her into the back seat.

Although she had half expected this, she was still terrified. The man in the suit next to her was cleanly shaven. She could smell his breakfast on him: coffee and cigarettes.

'Am I under arrest?' she said, feigning puzzlement.

His thin, angular face turned to her. 'Not at all. We would just like to ask you some questions.'

She didn't need to ask who *we* were and what they wanted to know. She looked out the window as they crossed the Donaubrücke, passing the spot where it had all happened thirty-two years ago. The river was a calm soft blue, a sharp contrast to the tempest that had churned beneath them that night. If she had acted differently then she would not have been in the situation she now found herself in. How every action, no matter how brief, shapes destiny, and not just for oneself. One moment in time.

The rest of the journey followed in silence. She worried about Franz. Had they picked him up too? He'd left early to return the grotto keys to Ingo, intending to remain silent about what had taken place in his absence. His plan was to then go to the work-shop and nail shut the floor in the wardrobe, closing off the hidden space. Had he got there in time to hide the damning evidence against them? Her chest squeezed.

The car drew up outside the now infamous building.

The Kolpinghaus: Gestapo headquarters.

She climbed the stairs with a mix of dread and resignation. Somehow, she'd always known she would end up here. She passed under the huge swastika flag and was led under a portrait of the Führer, down a narrow hallway. At the end, two soldiers stood guard outside a closed door. The Gestapo man with the thin face knocked first before opening it.

'Frau Mayer, Herr Officer Steiner,' he announced.

She flinched at the sound of the name.

Steiner stood up from his desk, tall, thinning fair hair precisely parted on the left.

'I believe we have met, Frau Mayer, at the Reich bride ceremony.' Marlene recognised the man as Tanja's husband. Who lived in Jayden's family's house. 'Your daughter is acquainted with my wife. Please, take a seat.'

His words were polite, but his tone was devoid of emotion.

She sat, pressing her nails into the palms of her hands. Forcing herself to meet his eyes, she gave him an enquiring look.

He gazed at her without speaking.

She waited. A fly buzzed around the window behind him. It settled. Silence again. Was he waiting for her to speak first? He was unnerving her. But of course that was his intention.

The fly began to buzz again. Steiner whipped a file from his desk, spun round and swatted it with startling ferocity. It fell lifeless to the floor. He slapped the file back on his desk and spoke.

'I am sure you know why you are here, Frau Mayer.'

'I must apologise but I don't, Herr Steiner.'

'Let's not play games. Where is your daughter?'

'I'm afraid I have no idea.'

He sighed and leaned forward on his elbows, chin on his hands.

'When did you last see her?'

She thought for a moment. 'Friday evening. She said good-night before she went to bed.'

The first lie. She had gone to bed before Ella, but she wanted to convey the impression her daughter had been tucked up safely in bed for the night.

'And the next morning?'

'I slept later than usual. When I awoke, she had gone out.'

'Where to?'

'I don't know.'

Don't mention Vienna; that would raise all sorts of questions and drag Freddie into the conversation.

'She didn't mention what her plans were the previous evening? She left no note on Saturday morning?'

'No, she didn't.'

'Is that not strange?'

'Not really. She is a grown woman with a life of her own.'

'And you have not heard of her since?'

'No.'

He narrowed his eyes. 'Very well. I shall give you some time to reflect on your answers.'

Marlene was led by a soldier and a warden down a flight of stairs into the basement. The warden unlocked a door and told her to step inside. It was a narrow cell without a window. A single naked light bulb hung from the ceiling. The only furniture was a metal bed without a pillow or bedding.

The warden was a huge man, with a belly that indicated he enjoyed his beer. He looked her up and down with beady eyes. Her stomach turned. Would he order her to strip? She'd been horrified when Ella had told her how Hedy had been treated.

The warden stepped up close so she could smell the stale sweat and unwashed skin. She almost gagged.

'Take it off.'

'Sorry?'

'Your watch. Give me your watch.'

She was so relieved, she didn't think to ask why. It was only when she was alone in her locked cell that she realised she had no idea what time it was. There was no window or clock. The only light was from the electric bulb. Perching on the hard bed, she thought it through: they had picked her up before work, so now it must be around mid-morning.

Did they have Franz here? In the same building? She had stopped herself from asking Steiner about her husband. She didn't want to implicate him.

Without a sense of time, she began to feel disorientated. She was also thirsty and needed the toilet. She paced the room.

Where was Ella at this very moment? How far had they got? Jayden was wounded and no doubt this would hinder their progress. If they were caught...

Her stomach went into a spasm of fear. Images of terror assaulted her: Ella manhandled by German soldiers, or running through a meadow, guns firing behind her, falling, bleeding...

Marlene collapsed onto the metal bed. Everything was falling apart: her precious daughter on the run for her life, her dear husband perhaps in the hands of the Gestapo. If they searched his workshop and found the hiding place, she couldn't bear to think what would happen to him.

Her family...

Time passed and still she was left alone with her thoughts.

It seemed like hours later when the key turned and the heavy metal door opened. It was the warden.

'Come. You're wanted upstairs.'

He took her arm in his tight grip and marched her to Heinrich Steiner's office, giving her an unnecessary shove in the back as they entered the room. Again, Steiner offered her a seat. He looked bored.

'Where is your daughter?'

'I told you. I don't know.'

'When did you see her last?'

Steiner fired one question after the other. All the same as the ones previously. Marlene gave the same answers, her mouth parched. She eyed the water carafe on Steiner's desk and finally plucked up the courage to ask for a drink. He nodded and poured her a glass. She drank thirstily. When she had finished, Steiner drummed his fingers on the desk; she noticed he wore a heavy silver ring with the SS symbol of a skull.

'Where is your daughter?'

The questions continued as did her automatic answers. A clock on the wall told her it was three in the afternoon. Above Steiner's head, Adolf Hitler glowered at her. If she looked hard enough, she could see the slightly built nineteen-year-old she remembered him as, often seen at the Landestheater with his friend Kubizek. A memory swooped in of Otto chatting to her about them in the—

'You are deliberately being unhelpful. I urge you to reconsider your answers. We will talk again later.'

The warden led her back to the cell. A tray had been placed on the bed with food, and a chamber pot in the corner: signs that did not bode well for her imminent release.

'Remove your shoes,' the warden ordered.

She looked down at her navy peep-toe shoes.

'Why?'

'Do it,' he growled, holding out his hand.

She slipped out of her shoes. The concrete floor was cold under her bare feet; she didn't wear stockings in summer. He took her shoes, a smirk on his face, and left, the door clunking shut behind him, the key clattering in the lock.

Sitting down on the bed, Marlene stared at her feet. What would happen next?

She ate the plate of dark bread and ham, and drank the warm water. She waited an hour or maybe two.

Footsteps outside.

The door swung open. Heinrich Steiner stepped in, followed by the warden whose body odour filled the room. The warden closed the door and stood with his back against it, his tiny eyes shining. Marlene wondered why she had not been called to Steiner's office.

She stood up and faced him.

'Where is your daughter?' he asked.

'Again, the answer is the same. I don't know.'

His arm flew from his side and the back of his hand whipped across her face. The force of the blow knocked her to the floor, her ears ringing. The distinct taste of blood filled her mouth.

She propped herself up on one elbow and put her fingers to her burning lips.

'Get up,' Steiner said.

She looked up at him, stunned. The room swam before her eyes.

'Get up,' he shouted.

She scrambled up and stood before him, hating the way her body shook.

He fiddled with the SS ring on his finger. He'd split her lip; blood was running down her chin.

'You're an attractive woman, Marlene. May I call you Marlene? It would be regretful if I was forced to maim you.'

'I... I don't know what you want from me,' she stammered.

'Where is your daughter? It's a simple enough question. We

know she is aiding a murdering Jew.' The muscle in his jaw twitched violently. He turned his ring.

She shook her head.

His hand balled into a fist and he punched her in the face, flinging her against the wall. She slid to the floor.

He stood over her. 'We will talk again.'

* * *

The naked light bulb blazed through her closed eyelids. Her face was an odd sensation of throbbing pain and numbness. She ran a finger over the swellings, dried blood and ruptured flesh. Thank goodness there was no mirror in the cell.

She lay on the bed, her head pounding, listening. Footsteps outside. She flinched, holding her breath. He was back – to beat her again. Shivering, she opened her eyes and stared at the door. But the footsteps receded.

A long time passed. It was probably nighttime. But the hanging bulb continued to blast the room with its harsh, unforgiving light. She laid an arm across her eyes and tried to collect her thoughts, assess the situation.

It was dire.

She needed a plan, but pain and exhaustion fogged her brain. Fear clawed at her insides, not so much for herself but for Franz and Ella. Her helplessness was sucking her down into an abyss of despair. She grappled against the pull: fight, damn it. Use your brain. But despite her best efforts, a solution would not come.

The footsteps came again and her whole body tensed. The key turned, the door opened and Heinrich Steiner strode in looking fresh and relaxed. As he approached her, she could smell soap and a sharp lemon cologne.

She struggled to sit up, her whole body aching.

'Good morning, Marlene. I trust you had a comfortable night.'

'Most pleasant, thank you,' she slurred through swollen lips. The sarcasm gave her a thrust of adrenaline. She glanced at the new warden on duty: young and earnest. Too young to witness a woman being beaten.

She stood slowly to face Steiner, her hate making her strong.

'Are you going to hit me again?' she asked. Her face felt lopsided, and one eye was half shut.

'No. Not today. I find it more effective to wait a couple of days till the flesh is just beginning to heal. Then I start again.' He smiled.

A couple of days? How long were they going to keep her here?

'Hold out your hand, Marlene.'

'So you can break my fingers?'

'An interesting proposition. But no, I have a gift for you.'

Confusion silenced her and like an automaton, she did his bidding.

He retrieved something from inside the breast pocket of his uniform and pressed it into her open palm: light, hard, metal.

Her breath caught in her throat.

A gold band.

A wedding ring. The one she had slipped on Franz's finger twenty-nine years ago. Everything around her faded and slowed. Her breath. Her heart.

She closed her fingers around the ring. With dread, she stared into Steiner's cruel eyes. Some words fumbled their way from her swollen mouth.

'Is he – is he?'

'Dead, do you mean? Not yet.'

Marlene's body slumped. She fought to keep upright.

'I shall return later. Hopefully, you will feel more talkative then.'

He marched out of the cell, giving the warden a swift nod. The door clanged shut.

Marlene fell onto the bed, cold with fear, terrible images raging through her mind. Screaming, she pounded her head with her fists, trying to drive away the thoughts. When she had calmed, she allowed herself to cry slow, quiet tears. There was a grim justice in all of this, of course. She had voted for this, put her cross in the circle, *Ja*. Yes to the regime that now ruled Austria. Yes to the Nazi doctrine of persecution. Yes to the oppression of alternative views and free choice. She was as guilty as every self-declared Nazi. Hitler promised to make Germany a great nation again. But at what human cost? Would she or Franz now pay the ultimate price? These thoughts tormented and jeered at her, ripping at her heart and darkening her soul.

And all the while the cruel bulb lit the room with its harsh glare.

At some point, the young warden brought a tray of food. A second stood guard at the door, watching.

Marlene spoke to the warden. 'Is he coming again soon? Herr Steiner?'

She hated the frailty in her voice.

'He might not,' he replied. Did she see some pity in his eyes? 'Herr Steiner is very occupied preparing things for the Führer's visit tomorrow.'

'Herr Hitler is coming to Linz?' She leaned up on one elbow.

'Indeed. I understand he will be paying our headquarters here a visit.'

The young warden said no more and retreated from the room.

So, Hitler would be in the same building as her. Memories of him thirty-two years ago overwhelmed her. How ironic if she were to be killed whilst he was in the same building as her.

Destiny was closing the circle.

34

ELLA

Her name was Beatrice and she had been widowed in the Great War. She was a potter and made her living from selling her hand-painted jugs and plates. She did not tell Ella more than this, other than that she would continue to offer a safe house to refugees until she was caught. She wasn't afraid of the Gestapo; she had her cyanide pill.

Beatrice opened a lid on a large pot on the stove and served them both a bowl of *Sauerkraut* with chopped *Kassler*. They ate on the sofa, Jayden's legs supported on Ella's lap.

'I don't know how to thank you,' said Ella. 'Why do you do it? Risk your life.'

'Because the alternative is to be a bystander. Something I can't bear to live with. I have no family to protect or nourish, nothing to sacrifice other than myself.' She stood, taking their empty bowls. 'Let me tell you what's going to happen. The next contact should arrive at dawn. I have no idea about the following part of your journey, but you should rest now.'

Jayden groaned and put his hand to his leg.

'And you, young man, need aspirin.' Beatrice fetched him the tablets and then the three of them settled down to sleep. Ella made Jayden comfortable on the sofa and lay down on the floor beside him. She remained awake for some time, listening to the soft snores from Beatrice as she dozed in an armchair. Jayden shuffled around for a while and then fell silent, the aspirin obviously taking effect.

It was hard for Ella to grasp the reality of the situation. She had said goodbye to her mother with a hurried embrace and had no idea when they would see each other again. Or her father, brother or home. This was how it was to be a fugitive: your whole life left behind with no idea what the future would bring, the next days, the next hours. A void of the unknown. Your life in the hands of strangers.

But one thing was for sure. She would face whatever came with Jayden at her side. Amidst the sterile world of hate and persecution, something magical had happened. A seed of love had planted itself in her heart and had seeped into every fibre of her being. And as she lay on the floor of this kind woman's house, dwelling on her love for Jayden, the power of that love made her strong and resolute.

It felt that Ella had closed her eyes for mere moments when a rap on the door made her start. Beatrice rose from her armchair, wide awake and alert within seconds. She nodded at Ella and went to open the door. A woman mumbled something and Beatrice replied. Code words exchanged, the woman entered the room. She was young and pretty and not what Ella had expected as the next contact. She eyed Jayden's ripped trouser leg and bandages and shook her head.

'I wasn't informed that one of you were wounded. It's too dangerous.'

'I'll be fine,' said Jayden. 'Just a slight flesh wound.'

'Can you run if you have to? I doubt you can even walk. You will be a burden.'

Jayden pushed himself up and holding his thigh, swung his legs to the floor. He clenched his jaw as he moved, his face grey.

Ella winced, feeling his pain. She put an arm through his and helped him to stand.

'I can do this alone.' He gave Ella a small smile. She watched him grit his teeth as he took shaky steps across the room. As he walked, his gait improved slightly.

The young woman looked dubious.

'I'll help him,' Ella said. 'We can manage. Please, we won't burden you.'

'I'm not convinced. But I can't leave you two here. We'll have to make the best of it. Right, this is how it works. You can call me Anna. Outside is a small truck with boxes of textiles: tablecloths, curtains, pillowcases, etc. which I am delivering to Hohenems on the Old Rhine. The goods are for the Sonne Inn. Both of you are included in this delivery. Your next contact will be at the inn. Any questions?'

Her tone was not unfriendly, but matter of fact; she had a job to do.

'We can't thank you enough,' Ella said.

'Your mother has thanked us many times over in the past.' Anna's expression softened.

'How long will it take to reach Hohenems?' asked Jayden.

'It's nearly five hundred kilometres, so all day. We should reach the inn by nightfall.'

'What about petrol?'

'It's all planned. We make two stops at friendly petrol stations.' Anna gave a sharp nod. 'We've done this before, you know.'

Ella was in awe of the confidence and bravery of this young woman who was probably no older than she was. Ella had imagined their transport would be in the back of a wagon filled with vegetables, driven by a burly farmer. Anna was a complete surprise. She wore a yellow summer dress and her long red hair was braided around her head: an unlikely looking activist.

They said goodbye to Beatrice, who handed them food parcels and then went outside to the truck. Dawn was breaking and the air already warm. Birds chirped and darted, alighting on a heavily laden redcurrant bush in the front garden.

The back of the truck had an open cargo area that was stacked with boxes. Some of the flaps were open, revealing embroidered textiles neatly folded. Ella and Anna helped Jayden clamber on board and then Anna showed them where to sit: their backs against a long vertically placed cardboard box at the back of the truck behind the cab. Anna flipped open the side of the box. It was empty.

'You can hide in here in an emergency,' she said, 'but otherwise, if you sit here amongst the boxes, heads down, it's unlikely you will be seen from the road. If there is danger, I'll bang on the back window and give you the thumbs-down sign. Then you must both lie inside the cardboard box and use the inside string to close the flap.'

They huddled down. There was just enough room for Jayden to stretch out his wounded leg. His face was flushed.

Ella placed a tender hand on his forehead.

'I'm fine.' He smiled.

She kissed his warm cheek. 'Of course you are.'

They set off, Anna driving at a steady pace, handling the curves of the country roads with ease.

By mid-morning, the sun was scorching down on them from a cloudless sky. There was no shade in the back of the truck so both were drenched in sweat and the water bottles from Beatrice were nearly empty. Huddled down, they were unable to see much but the road they travelled on was quiet. Jayden looked exhausted.

'Close your eyes, and lean on my shoulder,' Ella said.

He did so and held her hand.

At one point, Anna pulled up at the side of the road and ran round the back, a pink straw sun hat in her hand.

'I found this in the glove compartment.' She gave it to Ella and climbed back in the cab. Ella perched it softly on Jayden's head as he dozed. Meanwhile the skin on her face tightened and stung.

Eventually, the road led through a forest of tall pines and the shade was a balm for the skin. The truck halted and Anna's face appeared.

'We can make a quick toilet stop here. There is a stream so you can refill your water bottles. Our next stops will be the petrol stations, but you won't get out till we reach Hohenems. Two minutes.'

They clambered out, their bodies stiff and slow. When they reached the stream, Ella knelt down and, cupping her hands, soothed her face and tongue with the cool, sweet water. The scent of pine and the touch of the spring water revived her.

She glanced up at Jayden, who was standing awkwardly; he couldn't kneel.

'Close your eyes.' She smiled. 'Here comes a shower.'

She filled a water bottle, and poured the water over his head.

'Heaven,' he murmured.

Limping back to the truck, Jayden grumbled, 'I'm just a burden to you now. If we run into trouble, I won't be able to protect you.' His face crumpled. 'I'm useless.'

'You're far from useless and we won't run into trouble.'

She prayed it was true.

* * *

Some hours later, a sharp rap on the cab window made them jump. Anna gave the thumbs-down sign. Jayden scrambled inside the empty cardboard box, on his side, bending his knees to fit in, then Ella, her back tucked against his chest. She pulled the string on the inside of the flap and closed them in.

The truck came to a stop. Men's voices approaching. Ella strained to hear over her heartbeat.

'Good morning, officer. How can I help?' Anna's breezy voice did not sound like Anna at all.

A man's chuckle. 'I'm not an officer. Just an ordinary Wehrmacht soldier.'

'Maybe not yet...' A girlish flirt.

Another chuckle. 'Just a routine check. May I ask what you're transporting?'

'Do you think I'm carrying contraband?' A tinkle of a laugh. 'Actually, my family has a small textile business and we deliver to hotels. We hand-embroider the linens ourselves.'

'May I take a look?'

'Of course,' Anna replied, light, relaxed.

Ella tensed, rigid with fear, Jayden's hot breath coming faster on the back of her neck.

The tailgate clanged open.

The sound of rustling.

Then Anna's voice. 'Let me show you the tablecloth I did myself.'

The snap of linen being thrown open.

'Very impressive. And what's in the boxes behind?'

'Just more of the same, really. Curtains and such.'

'I'd like to take a look.'

'Ah, I've impressed you with my handiwork.'

The shuffle of boxes moving. The truck bed shook and a boot stamped on metal. Jayden's arm gripped tighter around Ella's waist. She tried to fight back the panic, suppressing the thought of a rifle pointed at them as they lay there trapped and helpless. The end of their journey.

A rip of cardboard.

'What are these?'

'Oh, they are my favourite. Cushion covers. Let me unpack them and show you, they are so beautiful—'

'That won't be necessary. You may carry on now.'

Boxes shifting. A boot step. The clunk of the tailgate closing.

'Thank you. I often do this route. Maybe I'll see you again...' The trill of Anna's voice retreated as she climbed back into the cab.

They drove off. Ella exhaled.

A few moments later, a non-urgent knock on the glass. The coast was clear.

As they shuffled out of the box, Ella looked up at the window to see Anna glance back over her shoulder, smiling, her thumb held proudly aloft.

* * *

They reached the small town of Hohenems at nine o'clock in the evening. As they climbed out of the truck, the first drops of rain began to fall. Thunder growled over the mountains.

Anna took them to the Sonne Inn, a small traditional guest house with wooden balconies and window boxes bursting with red geraniums. She stopped at the entrance.

'This is where we part,' said Anna. 'You will be contacted later this evening. A room has been arranged here for you to spend the night.'

'And what happens next?' asked Ella.

'We get you over the border. To Switzerland.'

Fear and excitement pulsed through her and she wrapped her arms around a surprised-looking Anna. 'Thank you for everything. I think you're amazing.'

Obviously, Anna was not used to compliments. For what seemed like the first time, she was speechless.

'Where will you stay tonight?' Ella asked.

'I have a friend here in town. Good luck.' She shook their hands. 'You'll be getting out just in time; with the latest movement of the German troops, I fear war is unavoidable now.'

'War,' murmured Ella. 'I can't believe we've reached this point.'

Anna left and Ella was sad to see her go.

Once inside, the receptionist gave them the key and they walked past the bar where two older men sat on stools drinking beer from ceramic tankards. One glanced at Jayden as he limped past. What a state we must look, she thought. She couldn't wait to freshen up.

The first thing she did when they entered the room was throw open the window. It was raining heavily now and the air had cooled. Ella didn't like the glassy look in Jayden's eyes or his flushed cheeks. He obviously had a temperature.

'I think I should check that your wound isn't infected, *Liebling*.'

Jayden shook his head. 'Best to leave it bandaged up. We haven't a change of dressing anyway.'

'I'll ask at reception for aspirin to keep your temperature down.'

'I'm fine—'

But she was already out the door.

Downstairs, the same two men were still drinking at the bar.

She felt them watch her as she passed... and asked for aspirin at reception. Back in the room, they'd just finished the last of their food from Beatrice when there was a knock at the door: their contact.

The young man shook their hands, pulled up a stool and grinned.

'I'm Edmund and I'm going to get you two away from the Nazi bastards.' He opened the rucksack he'd brought with him and pulled out three bottles of beer. 'Let's drink to that. *Prost.*'

Edmund was friendly and relaxed, but Ella preferred Anna's cool efficiency. As they sipped their beers, Edmund told them the plan: they would leave just before dawn and walk down to the river, the Old Rhine, which was on the border with Switzerland. He smiled at Ella's alarmed expression. Normally, it was no more than a stream, he explained, waist deep, and he had helped many refugees wade over to safety.

He looked out of the window. 'But let's hope it stops raining.'

'But we don't have entry visas for Switzerland,' said Jayden. 'They'll send us back.'

'We have Swiss contacts. A friendly patrol guard will meet you on the other side of the river and take you into St Gallen. A police officer there will help with false papers.'

It astounded Ella that there were so many people illicitly aiding refugees at great risk to themselves. She looked at Edmund and her heart swelled at the human kindness of the escape helpers. And these ones were not asking for money.

'Why are you helping us?' she asked.

'Because I don't want to close my eyes and pretend bad things aren't happening. And if I were to die tomorrow, at least I've given some people a chance of survival. I've made a difference.'

'If we make it over the border tomorrow, I want to help too. From the Swiss side.'

Jayden nodded in agreement. 'Me too.'

Edmund left a short while later, saying he would collect them early the next day.

'The aspirin worked,' said Jayden as they lay back on the bed. 'I'm feeling better now.'

She touched his forehead; it was cooler. He took her hand and kissed her palm.

'We will make it tomorrow,' he said. 'And we'll be free from Nazi Germany.'

'And we can be together,' she said. 'Every day.'

'And every night,' he mumbled, kissing the inside of her wrist.

Goosebumps ran up her arm.

'Undress me, Ella.' His voice was thick.

'But your leg. Maybe we shouldn't.'

'Be gentle with me.' A smile in his voice.

They made love with slow, tender caresses, absorbing each precious touch, prolonging the moment, allowing their desire to intensify as if this was their last night together. And as this thought flitted across Ella's mind, the rain pelted down and thunder rolled over them.

35

MARLENE

Marlene paced her cell, rubbing her bare arms in an effort to warm up. It was summer outside and she was wearing a short-sleeved blouse and cotton skirt but here below in this windowless room, the air was chilled. She then sat on the bed and rubbed her naked feet; they were blue. Her face throbbed and her back ached from when Steiner's fist had flung her against the wall. Every sound on the other side of the locked door made her jump. But no one came.

There was nothing to do but be alone with her thoughts, and that was exhausting; long-ago memories battled with present reality. Fear for Franz tore at her insides. She tried to reason that if he'd managed to secure the hiding place at the workshop, there was no evidence of any wrongdoing on their part. But had they picked him up beforehand? Or maybe the only reason they were being held was because they wanted to know where Ella was. But the truth was that neither she nor Franz had any idea.

When the key sounded in the lock, she sat up on the bed. It was the young warden, bringing in a paper plate of dark bread and a small chunk of cheese, and a paper cup of water. No chance to use crockery as a weapon to get her out of here.

'Any news from Herr Steiner?' she asked, to which he shook his head and left.

The longer she waited, the more her fears grew into demons. She lay down and closed her eyes against the glare of the light bulb; that light was driving her crazy. She turned on her side to face the wall.

Heavy footsteps. Boots. A voice. His voice.

The door opened and Heinrich Steiner stomped up to the side of the bed. She sat up.

'So, Frau Mayer. Do you have anything to tell me before I visit your husband?' He sounded different: irritated rather than coldly calm.

'Please don't hurt him. He's done nothing wrong. We don't know where our daughter is. You must believe me.'

Steiner's face contorted in rage. He leaned down and grabbed her hair, pulling her off the bed and across the floor. Her scalp burned and her eyes watered. She curled up, shrinking against the wall as he towered above her.

'You are lying. I'm asking for the last time. Where is she?' He drew back his boot and she instinctively held her arms across her face. Furious kicks came, one after another: at her chest, her stomach and her pelvis. She heard a crack and felt white-hot pain. She screamed, then came another crack. Fire seared through her chest.

'Sir, I believe you are required upstairs. Immediately,' came the young warden's voice, bold. 'Preparations are being made for the Führer's arrival.'

Steiner halted, panting, his face red. Marlene looked up at him, black clouds framing her vision, nausea rolling through her. He exhaled, straightened his jacket and smoothed his hair.

'I have no time for this now,' he hissed.

He left and the cell door slammed shut. Marlene's stomach heaved and she vomited on the floor.

The room swayed. The floor tilted. She was falling, falling through black, swirling clouds. And then there was nothing.

* * *

A young man's face came into view. His voice was soft, concerned. Freddie. Her son. He was with her. Something cold and soothing on her forehead. Water lifted to her swollen lips. Drops dribbled down her chin. She focused and frowned. It wasn't Freddie, but the young warden, a cold compress in one hand and a paper cup in the other. She was sprawled on the floor.

'Can you sit up?' he asked.

As she tried, her whole torso locked with pain. She gasped. The pain was familiar; she'd fallen out of a tree once picking apples and broke her ribs. Damn Steiner. Damn him!

'Let's try to get you to the bed,' he said.

One tiny, excruciating moment at a time, with the warden's help, she got to the bed and tried to find a position that was the least agony, settling on her side.

'I'll bring you painkillers from my grandma,' he said in a low voice. 'I have a lunch break later.'

'Please – find out about my husband. What's happened to him?' The exertion of each word left her breathless with pain.

'I'll do what I can,' he said and left.

Marlene lay completely still, taking slow, shallow breaths.

Time passed in a daze of pain and anxiety. She could not remember a time she had felt so totally helpless. She closed her eyes against the bright light bulb but still, black lines leaped across her eyelids.

The cell door opened, its metal hinges squeaking. She turned her head, terrified that it was Steiner back to beat her again, but it was the earnest young warden. He pulled two tablets out of his pocket and handed her a drink of water. She took them, not caring to ask what they were. 'Thank you,' she whispered. Glancing down at Franz's wedding ring that she'd placed above hers on her ring finger, she said, 'Have you heard anything about my husband?'

The young warden shook his head. 'Only that he is here. Helping with enquiries.'

Before he turned to leave, he said, 'Try to sleep.'

'Please. The light.'

He shook his head. 'Orders, I'm afraid.'

He left. Moments later, the room was plunged into merciful darkness. The medicine began to take effect; drowsiness overcame her. She slept.

* * *

Heinrich Steiner appeared mid-afternoon the following day. Marlene had a rough idea of the time because the kind young warden had told her it was noon when he'd brought her some lunch.

Clutching her ribs, she struggled to sit up. There was not a part of her body that did not hurt. She felt as if she had been trampled beneath a stampede of horses. It was terrifying how much damage one man could do with a minimum of effort. She shuddered to think what Franz had been through.

She tried to read the expression on Herr Steiner's face. He was calmer than yesterday; obviously, things were going well with the Führer's visit. He tilted his head to one side, a sly look in his eyes.

'I acknowledge that you don't know where your daughter is. Keeping you here brings us no advantage. You can be of more use back home. Sooner or later, she will contact you. And rest assured, we'll be watching and listening for that moment.' Steiner stiffened. 'You are free to leave.'

Marlene blinked. The words she had been praying to hear astounded her. She'd thought she would never leave this place alive. Obviously, they hadn't found the hiding place under the floorboards. Franz must have nailed it shut, so there was no evidence against them. Relief flooded through her.

Shuffling onto her feet, she asked, 'And my husband?'

'It's being arranged for him to leave.'

'I shall wait for him.'

'Go home, Frau Mayer. He will join you there.'

The young warden appeared with her shoes, watch and handbag. She took her belongings, hobbled out of the cell and dragged her broken body up the stairs. On the front steps of the Kolpinghaus, she squinted into the hard, blue sky.

She crossed over to the other side of the street and lowered herself onto a bench. The noise of everyday life surrounded her: people chatting as their shoes clicked past on cobbled stones, motor-car engines, horse hooves, the cry of a newspaper seller.

She was free. Alive. Soon, Franz would join her. She tried not to think what his injuries might be, but they would be together again, and she would nurse him back to health.

She didn't want to go home without him. Should she wait here on this bench, watching the entrance of the Gestapo headquarters? Or go back inside and ask when he was due to be released?

As she considered what to do, a black car flanked with a motorcade of police pulled up outside the Kolpinghaus, followed by a military truck. Wehrmacht soldiers jumped out and lined the entrance, standing to attention.

Moments later, SS officers exited the building, followed by the man himself. There he was, his fine hair parted on the right, his famous moustache perched over his lip.

Adolf Hitler.

The bench on which Marlene sat was so close, she could just make out the ice blue of his eyes. He glanced across at her. She froze, unable to take her eyes off him.

He wouldn't recognise her of course; she was over thirty years older and her face was disfigured by her injuries. But maybe it was her damaged face that made him look twice; was there a flicker of acknowledgement in his expression before he climbed into the car?

A hard look acknowledging how the briefest action had changed destiny? Did he remember how she had called out to him that night?

Hitler climbed into the car and the motorcade drove away.

She sat on the bench, her eyes fixed on the entrance of the Kolpinghaus. Any moment, Franz would appear.

She waited. The sun moved round and she no longer sat in the shade. She was vaguely aware that she was thirsty and in pain, but every ounce of her being focused on the moment Franz would walk to freedom. At one point, the Luftwaffe flew overhead, the ominous drone of the engines reverberating across the sky. Were they on the brink of war as so many feared?

Two smartly dressed women left the building, chatting: maybe typists.

What time was it?

Marlene struggled up and shuffled across the road, her arms wrapped around her ribs as she entered the Kolpinghaus.

'I'm waiting for my husband, Franz Mayer,' she told the woman at reception. The woman picked up a phone receiver, spoke a few words and then led Marlene down the corridor. To Heinrich Steiner's office.

Marlene's hands began to tremble. Could she bear to face this monster of a man again?

For Franz. Yes.

Heinrich was smoking. He glanced up at her and then stubbed out his cigarette with slow, deliberate movements, continuing long after it had been extinguished. He studied the ashtray for what seemed an inordinate amount of time.

'Take a seat, Frau Mayer,' he said, finally.

'I'm more comfortable when I stand. Please can I see my husband now?'

He fixed his gaze on her: flint-grey eyes that didn't blink.

He remained silent.

Fear coiled in her stomach.

'I'm afraid that's not possible. He is no longer here.'

Where had they sent him? Dachau?

Steiner stood up and squared his shoulders. His upper lip curled.

'Unfortunately, your husband became unwell during questioning. He collapsed quite suddenly. We did what we could.'

The room swam before her eyes. She teetered, struggling to keep her balance. She tried to speak, but gasping for breath, her throat constricted and only rasping sounds came from her mouth. Claws of terror encircled her heart.

'Your husband is dead, Frau Mayer.'

The claws pounced then, shredding her heart. Jagged blades of white-hot pain tore through her.

A visceral scream.

Falling. Falling off the precipice and into a void of terror. A last moment of realisation that all of the suffering was her fault. This was her punishment. She plummeted into an eternal blackness from which she knew she would never return.

36

ELLA

The waist-high Old Rhine, the stream Edmund had talked about, which one could wade across, had vanished. Instead, they were greeted by a black, churning torrent of a river swollen by the rain. The three of them, hidden amongst the rushes on the river bank, stood knee-deep in the cold mud. In the early dawn light, they could see the opposite side of the river. Switzerland.

'How well can you swim?' Edmund's earnest tone held none of his friendly optimism from yesterday.

'I'm used to swimming in the Danube, but only in good weather,' said Ella. She looked at Jayden, who was leaning on her heavily. He'd woken up with a fever and was clutching his thigh.

'You know the truth, Ella,' he said. 'I'm too weak to swim. But you can make it.'

'Not without you.' Her voice rose in panic.

'You must go. The police will find you and the penalty for aiding a Jewish murderer—'

'We're going together. There must be a way.' She turned to Edmund, her mind racing. 'How about a float, something Jayden can hold on to?' She waved her arms around her. 'There are enough broken branches after the storm.'

'It could work,' he said.

They retraced a few steps through the rushes and back amongst the woods. They came upon an uprooted tree, too large for them to manoeuvre but a perfect place for Jayden to rest. Ella and Edmund scrambled around the wreckage from the previous night's storm, quickly discarding branches that were unsuitable. With each passing second, the sky became lighter, and the moment of them crossing in the dimness of dawn was past.

'Here,' called Edmund in a low voice.

They dragged the branch he'd found back into the rushes.

'We need a rope or something,' he continued. A moment of blank looks. Then Ella pointed to the elastic braces that held up Edmund's trousers. He chuckled, unclipped them and adjusted them to the fullest length. 'You're brilliant,' he said.

Both she and Jayden would be secured around the waist with the trouser brace, then tied to the branch and she would swim them both across. Jayden draped an arm around her shoulder. '*Liebling*, are you sure about this?'

Before she could reply, a noise came from behind.

The sound of squelching mud and rustle of reeds. A scurrying animal?

Ella looked back. All three of them froze.

Max in a Wehrmacht uniform, legs astride in knee-high boots, grasping his pistol with outstretched arms. Down one side of his purple, bruised face ran a bloody scar. He shook his head and gave a grim smile.

Ella stared at him in disbelief. Max was here? How had he tracked them down? She and Jayden had come so far, on the verge of escape. No! This can't be...

'Oh, Ella, why the surprise? Surely, you didn't think I'd give up so easily.' He spoke with derision in his voice.

She gave Jayden a frantic look and saw the shock in his face. Her knees weakened as Max continued to speak.

'The police chief in Linz was alerted to your presence at the Sonne Inn. I had already persuaded him to inform only me if he heard of your whereabouts.'

Ella thought about Jayden's father's watch on the police chief's wrist. Max had bribed him. And those men at the hotel bar yesterday with watchful eyes; they'd informed the police.

She looked at Max's disfigured face, and in his hate-filled eyes, she saw the blackness of his soul.

'Max, please...' She knew her plea was useless. There would be no mercy; this was the end.

Max pulled the trigger, the gunshot punctuating the quietness of dawn.

Edmund screamed, his body jerking backwards. He fell to the ground.

Max then turned the gun on Ella. Her heart stopped, her body turning to ice as she faced death.

Jayden lurched forward and catapulted himself at Max's legs.

'Go, Ella. Go,' Jayden yelled as the two men fell on top of each other and into the rushes.

Ella was inches from the river. All she had to do was spring into the water. Swim to freedom.

She glanced at Edmund's lifeless body with horror; he had died trying to save them. Then she shot a look at Jayden, wrestling for his life. How could she leave him, the man she loved more than her own life, to the mercy of Max?

Within a heartbeat, she'd thrown herself towards the grappling men. Max was now on top of Jayden, his pistol inching towards Jayden's head, Jayden gripping Max's wrist, but his strength was weakening, his eyes closing. Ella grabbed a fallen branch and whacked it against Max's arm. And again. And again.

The gun dropped from his hands.

Max roared and turned on Ella, grabbing her ankles, wrenching her to the ground. She tried to scrabble for the gun, her fingers sliding through mud, and eventually, they found the cold steel. Grabbing it, she flipped on her back, but Max was on top of her, wrestling the gun from her grasp. He screamed, his spittle spraying her, his angry animal smell in her nostrils. His strong fingers tearing at hers, pulling the gun from her grasp.

Bang! The gun between them exploded.

Her body shook, vibrations shuddering through her core. A heavy, crushing weight. Pressure on her chest. She couldn't breathe. She couldn't breathe.

She closed her eyes.

'Ella, my God, Ella.' Jayden's voice.

The weight lifted slowly. She opened her eyes, trying to focus.

She could see Jayden grunting as he rolled Max off her. She was splattered with blood. But she felt no pain.

'Ella, are you hurt? Show me, my God.'

She sat up. Max lay lifeless on his back, a huge, gaping hole in his stomach, blood gushing, running rivulets in the mud.

Jayden pulled her into his shaking arms.

'All you ever do is save me,' he whispered. 'When the gun went off, I thought...' He began to cry. 'I love you. You've fought so hard for me, the least I can do is get across this damn river...'

* * *

Ella swam with a power she didn't know she possessed. Her goal was a muddy river bank, an isolated, unspectacular spot. Safety and freedom were now in sight.

Before attempting the swim, she'd strung the elastic trouser brace around Jayden's waist and helped him hoist his upper body over the branch and secured him there. He was barely conscious. After knotting the other end of the brace around herself, she'd slid them out of the rushes and into the water.

Now, they were over halfway across but the current was pulling them further down river. All that mattered was that they crossed the border, but still, the friendly border guard Edmund had spoken of would be waiting directly opposite where Edmund had told him they'd be. But swimming against the current was an impossible task and despite her best efforts, they veered off course.

Every few moments, she glanced back at Jayden to check his head was above water. She could see the fight in his eyes, the fight to stay conscious, the fight to make it for her. She could see his love for her and this knowledge pumped her heart, pumped her arms, pumped her legs. She swam and swam.

On reaching the river bank, she hauled Jayden and the branch from the river, untied herself and rolled Jayden onto his side. He coughed and spluttered up water. Then, when she knew he was safe, she let herself collapse onto her back, where she lay trembling with exhaustion, gasping for breath. Her eyelids closed against the warm morning sun.

A voice speaking German called out, though the accent was unfamiliar. 'Hello there! I thought you would drift down this way.'

Ella opened her eyes to see a man in uniform with the words *Border Control* on his jacket.

Relief flooded through her.

The guard was a broad, strong man and he hauled Jayden along the path easily. Ella's legs barely kept her up. They made it to his patrol car and after a five-minute journey, stopped outside the border patrol office.

As they entered the office in their dripping clothes, Ella had a moment of doubt. What if they were sent back to Austria? Back to the German Reich?

But a tall, athletic man jumped up to greet them.

'My name is Paul Grüninger. I'm the police captain of this canton, St Gallen. Welcome to Switzerland. You are in safe hands, now.'

37

MARLENE

Linz, 1907

As the horse and carriage pulled up outside the grand entrance to the *Linzer* Landestheater, Marlene strained her neck to get a better view of the arriving guests. From her position in the queue, she could see a doorman open the carriage door and a glamourous woman clad in a fur-trimmed cape descended.

'It's so exciting watching everyone arrive!' Marlene exclaimed, clasping Otto's hand.

'It's a very special atmosphere,' he replied. 'I hope we're not queuing in vain; standing tickets are limited.'

'Maybe trying our chances on *Die Fledermaus* is a bit optimistic since it is one of the most popular operettas by Strauss.'

'Well, we've arrived early and are near the front. They should start to let us in soon.' Otto looked towards the red rope across the side door.

Marlene glanced up at his handsome profile and his neatly trimmed, full moustache. She could hardly believe how happy she was. Blessed. That's how she felt. Blessed that he'd seen her beside

the Danube, peeling off her stockings. It made her blush to think
of it yet the memory thrilled her every time. And the last fourteen
weeks and three days had been the happiest in her life. Life was
wonderful; she enjoyed her embroidery work at the small textile
company, and on the evenings Otto didn't have business in Salzburg, he would escort her to the coffee houses of Linz.

He caught her look of adulation and smiled, his eyes soft with
love.

'You look beautiful this evening, Marlene. I'm proud to have
you by my side.'

At that moment she knew; he loved her as much as she loved
him. Her first love. And only love because he would soon propose
marriage. She was nineteen years old and knew what she wanted.
And that was to be Otto's wife.

The queue began to shuffle forwards. Otto stood on his toes,
looking over shoulders.

'Not too many ahead of us – oh, there's an acquaintance of
mine, Kubizek. He's with a friend I'm not so keen on: a rather
intense young man named Hitler.'

'Oh, Adolf. I know him, slightly. I don't like him, to be honest.
He's often at the Klosterhof Biergarten in summer.' She had sometimes noticed him glance at her with a look of disdain when she
and August had been flirting with each other. The thought of
August made her wince. At first, she'd been attracted by August's
good looks, but he'd become too forward in his advances and
when she'd rebuffed him, he'd turned nasty. But that was before
she'd met Otto, who behaved like a perfect gentleman.

Another horse and carriage pulled away from the theatre and
moments later, a chauffeur-driven automobile arrived. The crowd
turned their heads to stare. A beautiful young woman emerged,
draped in a forest-green, velvet cape. She had flawless porcelain

skin and wore her thick fair hair rolled up under a net-brimmed hat.

'That's Stefanie Isak,' whispered Marlene. 'Mutti used to work as a maid at her house.'

A striking young man then alighted from the automobile and took Stefanie by the arm, giving her a tender look.

'That won't please Hitler,' said Otto. 'According to Kubizek, he's besotted with Stefanie.'

'Hitler knows Stefanie?'

'He doesn't actually know her but sees her strolling with her mother along the Landstraße. Kubizek told me she doesn't even know Hitler exists. But he writes poetry for her, insists she's the ideal woman and intends to marry her. The man's obsessed.'

Otto's words gave her an uneasy sensation. There was something about Adolf that she found unpleasant; the few times they had exchanged words, he'd looked at her as if he was judging her. But mostly, she had little to do with him; he seemed more comfortable in the company of his small circle of male friends. The thought of being the subject of his obsession sent a shiver down her spine.

Marlene and Otto crossed the threshold into the imposing foyer, decorated with gilt chandeliers, plush, red carpets, and walls hung with photographs of stage stars and famous musicians. The audience divested themselves of their coats at the cloakroom counter, the women taking slow, elegant steps in stunning, full-length ball gowns. For a moment, Marlene thought her dress too plain, but then she remembered how Otto had said how beautiful she looked and that was all that mattered.

A photographer was taking pictures of people standing on the grand stairway.

'He's a friend of mine who works for the *Linzer Volksblatt*,' Otto said, gesturing to the man as he led Marlene through the crowds. 'I'll ask him to take a photograph. Just for us.'

They waited their turn until they stood where the elite of Linz had just posed and blinked into the flash. Then Otto insisted she should pose alone. After they'd had their photographs taken, Otto thanked his friend and said, 'I'll come by your office and collect the pictures in a few days. Just for me, of course, not for publishing.'

He winked and they moved on.

They took their standing places at the back of the theatre, Marlene revelling in that expectant thrill before a performance began.

'One day, I'll bring you here and we'll have the best seats in the house.'

One day! He envisaged a future for them. Her heart soared as the orchestra started to tune their instruments.

The experience was overwhelming: the music, the singing, the stage and costumes. All the while, they held hands, Marlene feeling as if she and Otto were the only ones encompassed in this whirl of emotion. This was truly the best moment of her life.

After the performance, people piled into the foyer, commenting on the turn in the weather. Rain fell heavily, and gusts of wind blew through the open theatre doors.

'Looks like the first autumn storm is heading our way,' said Otto. 'Let's get you back home quickly.'

Whilst Otto queued for their coats, Marlene headed to the ladies' cloakroom. As she approached, Adolf and his friend Kubizek caught her eye, deep in conversation. Adolf appeared to be distressed and Kubizek placed a reassuring hand on his shoulder.

He's upset about Stefanie, she thought as she joined the queue of women.

Thunder rumbled in the distance and the rhythmic sound of heavy rain could be heard from inside the theatre. In the cloakroom, she patted her rolled-up hair in front of a mirror and rearranged a hairpin.

As she left to return to Otto, a familiar figure crossed her path. Her heart fell.

August halted abruptly. 'Ah, Marlene. It seems half of Linz is here tonight. I noticed you earlier with your latest admirer in tow.'

'I don't have admirers and Otto is not "in tow". We are dating. Excuse me, but—'

'Dating? That's strange.' August feigned a puzzled expression.

She didn't like the smugness in his voice.

Ignore him and walk on, she told herself. But she couldn't help but comment. 'I can't see why that is strange,' she replied.

'I have a friend in Salzburg and I visited him recently,' he continued. August always had the ability to annoy her. 'I saw Otto there.'

'Well, he has business in Salzburg.' She tried to turn away but August was intent on talking.

'Actually, he attended the same theatre the night I did.' At that, his eyes flashed danger.

Don't listen to his gossip. Get your coat.

But Otto had never mentioned a theatre visit...

'Yes, I know,' she said, feigning indifference. 'There are some wonderful performances in Salzburg.'

'I must say, you are a very liberal young woman. Dating a man who has a fiancée.'

Her heart stopped.

Snide lips. Ugly words. Lies.

'I did a bit of research,' he continued. 'They've been engaged for six months, apparently. She comes from a well-off—'

Marlene turned away from the glee in his eyes. None of this was true. She would clear it up with Otto immediately.

He looked startled as she ran to him, her chest so tight, she could hardly breathe.

'Whatever is the matter, *Liebling*?' He had buttoned up his coat and held hers over his arm.

'You don't have a fiancée, do you, Otto?' she panted. 'Of course you don't. How ridiculous!'

His face turned to stone.

'Otto?' She tried to keep the panic from her voice. Why was he silent? 'In Salzburg. A fiancée? Is it true?'

She looked into his guilt-filled eyes. He bowed his head.

Her stomach lurched. God, no!

'Yes, it's true. But let me explain. It was before I met you—'

She sprang from his outstretched hand. 'How could you?' Her voice shook.

'Please. We need to talk. Let's go to the coffee house next door and—'

She turned from him, unable to listen to another word, and fled through the foyer. People stared at her as she ran outside, without her coat. Otto chased after her, calling her name, but she didn't turn around, sprinting to the tram stop where the tram's doors were folding shut. She slipped through at the last moment.

His face at the window. Distraught. The tram pitched forward and he was gone.

She stood crammed between wet coats and dripping umbrellas. The air smelt of damp wool, smoky breath and sweet perfume. She gagged. Her head began to ache.

Why? The word pounded through her head. Why would he do such a thing?

Why? Why? Why?

The tram emptied as it made its way through town. When a

seat became free, she sank onto it and gazed out of the window, but all she could see was her own miserable reflection staring back at her. He'd kissed her goodnight so many times. And had then left town to kiss another woman, to tell her how beautiful *she* was, to tell her how he loved *her*.

She put her hand to her mouth, forcing herself not to retch.

The wind lashed the rain against the windows. Persistent gusts of wind rocked the tram from side to side. Twice, her head butted against the glass.

Her mind went through every moment they'd spent together, searching for clues or reasons. Had she been so blind? Had she fantasised a romance where none had existed? Pain at his betrayal tore at her heart and bored deep inside her soul.

Finally, the tram had run full circle and arrived back at the theatre. And still she had no answer to her question: why?

She stepped from the empty tram, her leaden legs splashing through deep puddles. The doors to the theatre were now shut, the lights off. The coffee house next door had closed. For a moment, she wondered if she should have gone with him there to listen to his explanation. But what possible reason could he have given for deceiving her so cruelly?

The streets were deserted; people had rushed home out of the storm. Within seconds, she was drenched, her carefully rolled hair from earlier now plastered to her skull. Autumn leaves lay in sodden piles along the pavements.

She shivered in her soaked dress that clung to her body as she headed to the Donaubrücke. There were no trams running, no people crossing.

As she stepped onto the bridge, the wind picked up on the river and a ferocious gust threw her against the side of the railings. She clung her fingers into the iron latticework and began to edge her way across. Beneath her, the water roared. The sky crackled with white-hot lightning. A few seconds later, thunder bellowed.

She was terrified.

Her eyes smarted from the wind. She could barely see; most of the lanterns that usually lit the bridge had gone out. The dark, rolling clouds hung low over the broiling river. Clinging to the railing, she made her way across. One step at a time.

A figure appeared out of the gloom. Someone else was on the bridge, grasping the railing.

No, not *grasping* the railing – *climbing* the railing! What on earth were they doing?

She called out but her words were whipped away.

She hurried closer, and called again, 'Hello there. Hello!' This time, the person heard her call and stopped climbing, turning to look at her. It was a man, his overcoat flapping wildly in the wind. His face was familiar; she realised she had seen him just a few hours ago at the theatre. Her heart sank.

Adolf Hitler.

The last thing she wanted to do was stop and speak to him but the situation demanded she say something. She frowned up at him and shouted, 'What are you doing up there?' He stared at her for a long moment, gripping the iron latticework, rain streaming down his face, his coat billowing around him. Lightning flashed and his face was illuminated: skin the colour of wax, an expression as fixed as stone. And below, the furious Danube crashed under the bridge, a surging torrent of unrelenting power. He clambered down and once he had both feet on the ground, he snarled at her, 'It's not what you think I'm doing.' Thunder boomed. He put his face up to hers, his expression taut and hard. 'And if you start spreading rumours...' He didn't finish his sentence but as lightning struck again, she saw the steel glint in his glare, his hard blue eyes fixed on hers. She stepped back, then he turned and strode in the opposite direction.

She stared after him, stunned for a moment, then hurried over the bridge, head down against the driving rain, wondering what she had just witnessed. Had Adolf been so distraught over his unrequited love for Stefanie that he'd intended to throw himself from the Donaubrücke? Her call had distracted him. He'd looked almost embarrassed at first, as if he'd been caught out. But then he'd become angry, threatening. As she finally reached her apartment block, drenched and freezing, she put the incident out of her mind. It was no concern of hers; the only thing that now occupied her thoughts was Otto and how he had taken her young heart and ripped it to shreds.

* * *

It was only years later, long after Hitler had left Linz, and she became aware of his rise to power, that the repercussions of that night began to haunt her. Time and again she berated herself for running from the theatre. What would have happened if she had not been so stubborn and had gone to the coffee house with Otto? If she had not walked onto the bridge and distracted the young Hitler from his intended action? Would he have jumped? She could never know. In her deepest moments of despair, she blamed herself for being in the wrong place at the wrong time; for changing the course of history into one of horror. At other times, she told herself that even if she had not interrupted him that night, he may have changed his mind and climbed back down; that history would have taken the same course.

She could never know. She could never have peace. She would for ever carry the burden of her fate.

38

ELLA

Linz, Austria, August 1945

Ella, Mutti and Freddie sat on picnic blankets beside the blue Danube, looking at the town of Linz on the other side, the American zone. Here in Urfahr, with the Pöstlingberg behind them, they were in the Russian zone. The war was now over. It had started on 1 September 1939 when Germany invaded Poland, two weeks after Ella and Jayden had arrived in Switzerland. They had reached safety, but for the rest of the world, the horrors of war had just begun.

The Swiss police captain, Paul Grüninger, had provided them with falsified documents that had allowed them to remain in Switzerland. He did the same for countless other refugees, saving them from certain death. He was eventually caught out and arrested. She owed him her life. And in turn, she and Jayden had themselves become involved in a network that enabled those persecuted to cross into Switzerland.

This was the first time she'd seen her family in nearly six years, having been allowed by the Russian forces to visit. Jayden had not accompanied her, unable to face his home country that had been involved in the persecution and murder of the Jewish community.

She sighed as she looked across at Mutti and Freddie unpacking the picnic basket. Of course, there was someone missing. Vati.

The familiar ache swelled inside her, the pain of loss still raw. Ella had written to her parents with her address in Switzerland. It took seven months for her mother's letter with the terrible news to reach her. She and Jayden had married in Switzerland and two years ago had become parents. Her father would never see his grandson, Hannes. Now, she turned to him where he lay in his pushchair and brushed his dark, wavy hair out of his eyes. Although he looked very much like Jayden, there was a hint of her father in his smile.

* * *

When she first saw the worn, battered house, it evoked such a flood of emotion in Ella, she nearly turned and ran away. But she'd set herself a task and she was going to see it through. She walked up the steps of what was once Hedy's home and knocked on the door.

A young woman with a baby on her hip answered. At first, the woman was wary of Ella's story but when Ella was unable to stop her tears, the woman allowed her to enter.

Up in the attic, she stepped carefully past unfamiliar items. The possessions of Hedy's family had been disposed of long ago, but there was one she hoped may still be up here. She came to the spot where Hilde had hidden the small silver menorah all those years ago and prised the wooden board away. Putting her hand in the space, her fingers trembled as they touched velvet.

The silver candelabra was tarnished black like it had been

when she and Hedy had first found it. The memories engulfed her, the weight of sorrow crushing down on her. She would polish the menorah till it sparkled and then she and Jayden would take it to England to where Trudy lived in Hove. Ella had acquired Trudy's address from the authorities in England and had written to her regularly. The planned trip to see Trudy after all these years, however, would be a sad one; they would have to confirm to sixteen-year-old Trudy what they had all already feared: Hedy and Hilde had not survived the concentration camps, like the millions of other Jews.

Jayden's family had managed to escape on a steamer down the Danube to Budapest and had then travelled on to Palestine. Jayden hoped that somehow, they would be reunited one day.

* * *

The time in Linz was treasured by all. Ella also met Otto, who was a regular visitor. His devotion to her mother was obvious but Mutti had told her no one could replace Vati and friendship was all she could offer him. Ella was pleased Mutti had Otto.

The days flew by, and soon it was time for Ella to pack up her suitcase and return to Geneva where she now lived with Jayden. He'd found work at a clothes store and had been promoted to manager, whilst she worked at a kindergarten and so was able to be with little Hannes.

She packed the menorah carefully between her clothes.

In the sitting room, Mutti was playing with Hannes. She had been shocked when she'd first seen how her mother had aged, but the smile now on her face as she played with her grandson seemed to soften her lines and her pain. The spark of how her mother had been before the war lit for a brief moment. And that brief spark was enough to give Ella hope for the future for all of them.

39

MARLENE

Marlene waved as the train pulled out of the station. Ella's and Hannes's heads poked out of the window. They waved till they were out of sight. Seeing Ella again and meeting her grandson had filled her with a joy she had no longer felt possible.

She walked through the battered town of Linz. It had been heavily bombed the last two years of the war; the Göring steel works had been building tanks and weapons and as such, Linz had become a prime target. The allies had promised to help rebuild the town, and people would have to learn to rebuild their lives. Somehow. The Austrian's early optimism for the Nazi regime had soon faded as sons, brothers, fathers and loved ones lost their lives far from home. And even as the outcome for the German army was hopeless, Hitler had demanded every man fight to the death.

Marlene showed her pass to the American on patrol and walked over the Donaubrücke towards the Russian sector, stopping briefly at the point where that night, in 1907, she had met Hitler on the bridge. How many millions of times had she asked herself why God or fate had led her there? She had never told anyone about what had happened. She would take that secret to her grave. And how many times had she hated herself for voting for the annexation of Austria because she'd been scared?

She had lost her husband for her sins and had never found out the truth of what really happened to him. The Gestapo did not allow her to see his body, but had merely presented her with a box of his ashes weeks later.

For a while, she'd been unable to continue with her resistance work because she was under scrutiny from the Gestapo. But once the war was in full swing, they had turned their attention to other matters. She then was able to aid the resistance once more. But despite that, she'd felt no redemption. All the horrors of war and her own guilt had left her hollowed out. But in these last few days with Ella and Hannes, something had shifted. She had felt a warmth in her soul that surprised her. A glimmer of hope.

When she arrived at Otto's house, he had laid out a cold supper in the garden. They ate and talked about Ella and Hannes. They drank some local Austrian wine and, sitting on the bench together, gazed at the Pöstlingberg until it grew dark. They sat in silence, and she thought about how Otto had deceived her all those years ago: how he'd let her fall in love with him when he'd promised himself to another. He'd explained how his forthcoming marriage into an upper-class family had been encouraged by his parents. How he'd thought that his fondness for his fiancée could turn to love. But then he'd met Marlene on the bank of the Danube and found true love. He'd been planning to break off his engagement, just waiting for the right moment. August's spiteful gossip that night at the theatre had destroyed everything. Afterwards, Marlene had refused to see Otto or to read the letters he'd sent her. All these years, she had been too proud and hurt to allow the wound to heal completely. Or to forgive.

Now she reached for Otto's hand.

40

ELLA

Geneva, Switzerland, August 1945

Hannes had his faced pressed up against the window as the train slowed, passing under the steel, arched ceiling of Geneva station. Ella stroked the back of his head. 'Let's see who can spot Papa first.'

Ella scanned the crowded platform as the train came to a stop.

'Papa, Papa,' cried Hannes, his little hand banging on the glass.

She saw him then. Jayden's eyes were searching the carriage windows and his whole face lit up as he caught sight of them. Ella lifted the suitcase down from overhead, clutched Hannes in one arm and retrieved his pushchair from the end of the carriage. As she struggled down the steps, a young woman came to her aid, helping to set up the pushchair. But as Ella set Hannes down, he toddled off on plump, shaky legs towards his father. Jayden fell on one knee and scooped him up in his arms.

Ella watched Jayden swing their son onto his shoulders, where he perched, his hands buried in Jayden's curls. The sight of her small family made her heart swell with love, and something else too. Thankfulness.

Jayden came to her and kissed her softly on the lips, Hannes teetering above them.

'I missed you,' he said. 'Very much. It's been years since we've been parted.'

'I know.' She stroked his cheek. 'I'm glad to be home.'

As they left the platform, she thought about what she'd just said. Was Geneva her home? She and Jayden hadn't yet decided if they would stay in Switzerland. They'd talked about living in England if they could get the required papers, and they would look into the possibilities when visiting Trudy.

They walked out of the station into a warm summer's afternoon, the sky as blue as when she'd left Linz a few hours ago. Reminiscing, she thought of the myriad of times she had swum in the Danube, climbed the Pöstlingberg and crossed the Donaubrücke. A part of her would always remain an Austrian girl, but now it was time to look to the future. She glanced up at Hannes giggling as Jayden bobbed him up and down on his shoulders. Slipping her arm through Jayden's, sweet contentment enveloped her. She was with the man she loved and their wonderful son. Her heart was with them, her family, and they would forever be her home.

AUTHOR'S NOTE

The inspiration for this story came from my mother's childhood. She was born in Linz and grew up during the war years. I spent many happy summer holidays there, visiting the lakes and mountains, as well as beautiful towns such as Salzburg and Vienna. No one spoke of the war. It was only much later that I discovered Hitler's connection to Linz. During my research, I came across a memoir written by Hitler's close friend, August Kubizek which told of an event that got me thinking...

The main characters in the book are fictitious. However, many of the supporting cast were real: the painter who created the miniature town of Linz, Ludwig Haase, the Swiss border guard, Paul Grüninger who saved the lives of countless refugees, and of course the Göring brothers. I was so fascinated to learn that Albert strongly opposed the Nazi regime, even procuring false papers, that I had to include this in the story. The Villa Rosa, although fictional, is based on the numerous Bride Schools that operated across Nazi Germany. The Pöstlingberg with its beautiful church, grotto and Linz exhibit remains a top tourist attraction today.

The people's vote for the annexation of Austria into the Reich is a controversial point. To this day it is unclear how much of the result was manipulated and how much was fuelled by fear. There was however a sizable part of the population that was pro-Nazi and actively persecuted the Jewish community.

ACKNOWLEDGEMENTS

I'd heard much about second-book syndrome and how producing a work that is a worthy follow-up to a debut, can be a daunting task. Luckily, I have a clever agent, Clare, and an astute editor, Emily, who were both brilliant in helping shape this book. A huge thank you to both of you, and to the fantastic team at Boldwood. I am extremely fortunate to have the support and enthusiasm from wonderful friends and family, particularly my husband, Sigi and daughter, Claire. Thank you from the bottom of my heart. Finally, my warmest thanks to you the reader. I hope you enjoyed the story.

ABOUT THE AUTHOR

Helen Parusel is a debut historical novelist, having been a teacher and a clothes buyer for M&S. She lives in Hamburg, and her first book is based on the Nazi invasion of Norway in 1940; while her second is inspired by war stories from her mother's homeland of Austria, where she spent her early holidays.

Sign up to Helen Parusel's mailing list for news, competitions and updates on future books.

Follow Helen on social media:

instagram.com/helenparusel
x.com/HelenParusel

ALSO BY HELEN PARUSEL

A Mother's War

The Austrian Bride

Letters from
the past

Discover page-turning
historical novels from
your favourite authors
and be transported
back in time

*Join our book club
Facebook group*

https://bit.ly/SixpenceGroup

*Sign up to our
newsletter*

https://bit.ly/LettersFrom
PastNews

Boldwood

Boldwood Books is an award-winning fiction publishing company seeking out the best stories from around the world.

Find out more at www.boldwoodbooks.com

Join our reader community for brilliant books, competitions and offers!

Follow us
@BoldwoodBooks
@TheBoldBookClub

Sign up to our weekly deals newsletter

https://bit.ly/BoldwoodBNewsletter

Made in United States
North Haven, CT
30 June 2024

54252053R00205